"EVERYTHING ABOUT YOU EXCITES ME, YOU KNOW...."

The velvety note of desire in Gil's voice sent shivers down Selina's spine.

"I want to touch you and kiss you and make love to you. Do you want me to, Selina?"

Even as he spoke, he brought his mouth to hers. His kiss was penetrating—his tongue licked sensuously along her lower lip, coaxing her mouth to open. In one powerful movement he brought his body over hers, the hard masculine length of him resting intimately against her.

"I don't know what I want anymore," she gasped, unable to force her brain to think.

"Fight it all you want, Selina," Gil whispered hotly, "but sooner or later you'll come to my bed."

While a voice inside her head desperately denied it, yet another stronger voice suspected he might be right....

WELCOME TO...

SUPERROMANCES

A sensational series of modern love stories
from Worldwide Library.

Written by masters of the genre, these longer,
sensual and dramatic novels are truly in keeping
with today's changing life-styles. Full of intriguing
conflicts, the heartaches and delights of true love,
SUPERROMANCES are absorbing stories —
satisfying and sophisticated reading that lovers
of romance fiction have long been waiting for.

SUPERROMANCES
Contemporary love stories for the woman of today!

LEIGH ROBERTS

MOONLIGHT SPLENDOR

A SUPERROMANCE FROM
WORLDWIDE

TORONTO · NEW YORK · LONDON

To Carolyn, Kathy, Carol and the gang —
I couldn't have done it without them.

Published September 1983

First printing July 1983

ISBN 0-373-70081-4

Printed in Canada

CHAPTER ONE

SELINA MONTGOMERY STOOD QUIETLY in the production kitchen at the California Culinary Academy. Her head, with its tall paper chef's hat, was cocked attentively. In front of her at the scrubbed-wood worktable was Hans Meirsinger, the head chef.

He handed her her notebook and a typed menu. "I went through your notes carefully," he said, his heavily accented English reverberating among the stainless-steel fixtures. "For your final exam we must really challenge you. The menu is difficult, but I am confident you can produce it in the required three and a half hours."

She looked down at the slip of paper in her hand: leek soup with chive-and-basil butter, scallop mousse, champagne *sorbet*, medallions of lamb with prune sauce, julienned vegetables, *salade verte* and white-chocolate soufflé.

Hans watched her with a smile lurking in his stolid brown eyes. "Your notebook was excellent," he added. "I hope you really have tried all the dishes?"

She met his bland gaze with a smile of her own. "If I haven't, I will have after this exam is over." The menu was challenging, and she actually hadn't tried the white-chocolate soufflé. But she felt confident of making a good showing.

Hans waved her away peremptorily. "You have thirty minutes to study the recipes and make your plans. As you know, you must put the notebook away before you begin to cook. Next—Andrew Corbett."

Selina joined the other two students who were taking the final that afternoon. They sat at a table in the dining room and studied their notebooks with intense concentration. She soon lost herself in the recipes, making out a swift timetable and coordinating in her mind where all the supplies were and how best to secure the equipment she would need. She barely noticed when Andy Corbett joined them with his test menu.

But when the thirty minutes were up, and they scurried into the kitchen, she spared a moment's thought for Andy. Being charming, amusing and insouciant wouldn't help him much in a final exam, she thought. But Andy was approaching his tasks with an unaccustomed air of proficiency. She smiled a little grimly to herself as she cleaned the leeks. At least this time it looked as if she wouldn't have to bail him out of a botched project.

She worked swiftly until she had to wait for the ice machine to produce enough cubes to cool the melted white chocolate and butter for her soufflé. She let her eyes wander around the room. She would miss this kitchen, a marvel of stainless-steel efficiency, with its big ranges and walk-in refrigerators, its scrubbed-wood work surfaces and glass window wall open to the dining room. She glanced out and saw the judges just finishing their soups. Desperately she scrabbled all the ice there was into her big stainless-steel bowl. She would have to hustle to be done on time.

As she whipped egg whites, she saw Andy arranging his entrée, *osso bucco milanese*. With surprise she noted it looked perfect.

"Pretty good, huh?" He placed the garnishes carefully and regarded the finished product with a smug smile.

"It looks wonderful, Andy." She smiled back, unable to disguise her incredulity at his success. "You must have spent the whole night reading your notebook."

A momentary look of uneasiness crossed his mobile face. "Yeah, well—your meal will be great. Of course, you'll come out at the head of the class—you always do." The faint resentment in his voice stung her, but she dismissed it. Right now the important thing was to do her best on the final exam and graduate as a full-fledged chef. She could think about the intricacies of her relationship with Andy later.

While her soufflé baked, she watched the judges through the glass window of the kitchen. Looking dwarfed by the big empty dining room, they sat at one table, solemnly eating and making notes. Andy's entrée, she noticed, made a favorable impression. She felt a faint stirring of disquiet. Feckless Andy, who never had his notebooks up-to-date, who depended on her to discreetly rescue him from his many mistakes—how had he managed to complete his menu without once sidling over and asking for help?

The judges finished their salads. She glanced at the clock and opened the oven, inhaling the rich aroma of chocolate that rushed out to meet her. The soufflé stood up proudly from its pristine white dish. She set the dish on a serving tray, smoothed back the disordered curls of her red gold hair, straightened her hat and proudly carried the tray out.

She heard spontaneous murmurs of delight from the judges as she plunged two spoons into the shiny crust. The soufflé practically floated onto the serving plates. She offered a dusky bittersweet chocolate sauce and watched complacently while the judges, exclaiming about the mixtures of chocolate, helped themselves to seconds.

She received their enthusiastic comments with a smile that sparkled in her gray green eyes. Although the final scores wouldn't be posted until the next day, she knew that hers would be more than passable.

THAT EVENING, celebrating with Andy and her roommate, Molly Hutton, in a small pub much frequented by the students and staff of the academy, she lifted her glass of beer with satisfaction. "Here's to tall white hats and the talented women who wear them," she proclaimed with a teasing smile at Andy.

Instead of laughing, he frowned petulantly. "Really, Selina. You could at least hand out a little praise for my achievement today. It isn't as easy to come from behind as it is to stay at the top of the heap."

Molly snorted. She worked in the placement office

of the academy. Her delicate features and petite figure were in decided contrast to her earthy approach to life. "You wouldn't have needed to come from behind if you'd tried keeping ahead," she said forthrightly. "You've got through school by the seat of your pants. Aren't you afraid you'll wear them out if you use them anymore?"

"I need another beer," Andy muttered sulkily. He moved over to the bar, his blond head obscured in the murky light.

Selina stared after him, a thoughtful frown furrowing her brow. "Wasn't that a little harsh? He did do an excellent job today."

Molly shrugged. "It just irritates me the way he always expects you to get him out of trouble and cover up his mistakes, and then thinks he's really clever when he does something right." She glanced curiously at Selina. "Are you really going to start a catering business with him?"

Selina looked into the frothy amber depths of her beer without really seeing it. There it was, the question she didn't want to confront. Andy assumed it was all settled—first their business and eventually their personal life. She knew if she worked with him, it would be even harder to put aside his suggestion that they live together, become lovers. A few months ago it had seemed possible, even desirable; now she felt she was being backed into a corner when Andy urged his plans on her.

"I don't know," she mumbled, aware that Molly was still waiting for an answer. "He can use his uncle's professional kitchen, and he's got some capital...."

"And you've got the know-how," Molly nodded sagely. "He'll laze around the kitchen being charming, and you'll work your fingers to the bone. Sounds great."

Selina pushed small square hands through her curls impatiently. "What do you expect? It's getting pretty late now to be looking for another job. I've got to do something—woman doesn't live on air alone."

Molly's expression grew thoughtful, and Selina knew she was mentally reviewing the placement files. "There aren't any good openings now," she agreed, draining her glass. She looked around for a waiter. The pub was crowded with a cross section of San Franciscans: other students from the academy; dock workers from the nearby wharves; surrealistic-looking people of both sexes with spiky purple hair and leather clothes; a sprinkling of men and women in three-piece suits earnestly discussing the economy. But waiters were in short supply, and Molly stood, preparing to trek to the bar. "Unless you want to slave for someone else as *sous-chef* at five dollars an hour," she said over her shoulder, "or unless something turns up in the next couple of days, I guess you're stuck with—"

"Andy? Have you seen Andy?" Peering over Molly's shoulder was Marybeth Williams, clerk-typist and general dogsbody at the Culinary Academy. If it had been possible to look out of place in the weird assortment of people filling the pub, Selina reflected, Marybeth would have achieved it. In spite of working in a chef's school, she was as thin as a wraith. Everything about her was thin—her dull blond hair, her wrists extruding from the heavy wool coat she clutched, her ankles in sensible flat shoes. Even her nose was a miracle of boniness.

"He's over by the bar, Marybeth. Want me to fetch him for you?" Molly eyed her office mate speculatively, and Selina felt the same expression on her own face. It was hard to imagine what Marybeth wanted with Andy.

Marybeth collapsed into Molly's vacated chair as if her strings had been suddenly cut. "No—oh, no. I thought he said—I must have misunderstood...." She looked a trifle wildly at Selina. "Please don't think—I know he's your boyfriend, but—oh, dear! What should I do?"

With quick sympathy Selina leaned forward and patted Marybeth's hand. "Just take a few deep breaths," she advised. "Molly will get you something to drink." She sent a swift look toward her roommate. Molly nodded and vanished. "What's the matter?" Selina asked Marybeth. "Is there any way I can help?"

To her consternation Marybeth burst into tears. "I didn't realize—I didn't mean—oh, dear, how awkward it all is. You see, I thought there would be nothing really wrong with it—just to let him have a glimpse of his test menu. But now—well, I feel just awful. It was wrong, I know it was wrong. But he said..." she sniffed woefully, groping for words.

Selina froze in her seat. Now she knew why Andy was so touchy about his success in the final. "You showed Andy his final exam yesterday," she said flatly.

Marybeth nodded forlornly. "Chef Meirsinger brought them to me to be typed up, and when Andy—I know I shouldn't have." She sniffed again mightily. "But he was so—well, I was just—swept away." For a moment her expression softened. Then, as she caught a glimpse of Selina's face, she quailed. "What should I do? How can I—"

"Why, Marybeth." It was Andy, his voice warmly caressing with an undertone of laughter, as if he were sharing a delightful secret with the typist. "Here, let me buy you a drink." He leaned toward her, charmingly confidential. "You'll be glad to know that I *think* I passed my final."

Hiccuping loudly, Marybeth jumped up, her chair crashing to the floor behind her. "I don't—you shouldn't—oh, dear!" Hugging her coat closely to her, she turned, stumbled over the chair leg and was gone.

Andy looked after her, a crease between his well-shaped brows. "What's got her goat?" His voice was faintly aggrieved.

Selina pushed her beer away, unfinished. Suddenly she knew she could never work with Andy, never let him share her life in any way. "You're really something," she said with disgust. The shocked expression on Andy's face just made her angrier. She tilted her chin defiantly as she met his indignant stare. "I don't respect you, so I don't really like you, either. And that means I couldn't work with you. Goodbye, Andy."

She pushed past him, past Molly returning with two brimming glasses, out into the cool moist San

Francisco air. For a moment she stood, her eyes automatically searching the fog-shrouded sky for any pinpoints of starlight. Instead of the pain of heartache, the anxiety of uncertainty, she felt relieved. With a sense of freedom she realized she had no job, no prospects and very little money, but it didn't matter. If necessary, she would be someone's slave for five dollars an hour. But at least she wouldn't be charmingly browbeaten by Andy.

Her exultation welled up from somewhere deep inside, spreading her lips in a broad grin. She ran down the sidewalk toward her little car, her arms outstretched as she drank in the salty mist. "Free at last," she sang off-key. For two years, school and Andy had filled all her thoughts. Now she was ready for a change. "Come on life!" she shouted, oblivious to stares from tourists. "Throw me a curve. I can handle it!"

A SOLITARY RAY OF SUNLIGHT found its way through the heavy damask curtains and moved timidly around the stately room, touching the gilded frame of the portrait hanging on one wall with sudden glory, illuminating the aquiline nose, fierce hawk-like eyes and tight-lipped determined mouth of the old man painted there. Then the light spilled down, haloing the dark hair of the man standing below the portrait, highlighting the same high-bridged nose and piercing eyes. Only the mouth was different: full lipped and sensuous. He stood, isolated in the sun's glow, before a wide expanse of polished mahogany table, around which were seated other men whom the sunlight did not deign to touch.

One of these men cleared his throat—a harsh, aggressive sound. "So what's it going to be, Duchenay?" he demanded, his voice falling heavily into the silence of the room. The man who was standing looked at him, his face carefully expressionless. One hand tucked negligently into the pocket of his well-cut gray suit, he surveyed the other six men in silence. A couple of them shifted uneasily under his gaze.

When he spoke, his voice was even, somehow fitting the somber elegance of the boardroom. "May I remind you that you are not chairman of the board yet, Mr. Warner, in spite of Jock Hartfield's illness. Do you have his support for this—suggestion?"

Fred Warner stiffened, an angry flush splotching his face. "I have the support of a majority of the board members, Duchenay. As vice-chairman, I consider it my responsibility to keep Purity Corporation in tip-top shape, whether the chairman is able to preside or not." The threat was implicit in his voice.

Gilmartin Duchenay did not raise his voice. "Then it doesn't look as if I have much choice, Mr. Warner." One of the older men began to speak in protest, but Gilmartin held up his hand for silence. "I don't agree with you that Purity Corporation is stagnating. I don't think my grandfather would have agreed, either." The assembly's collective gaze traveled up to the portrait that hung behind him, noticing Gilmartin Duchenay's resemblance to the features captured on canvas there. "But when you back up your statements with threats to have me displaced as president unless I increase Purity's market share, my only alternative is to do just that.''

Fred Warner opened his mouth to reply, but the older man who had begun to speak before was on his feet. "We're not all convinced by what Warner says, Gilmartin," he roared, his face rapidly purpling. "Damn it, you've done a fine job since you took over four years ago." He glared at Warner, who returned his look impassively. "I say let the boy have his head as we've been doing. Certainly none of you can deny you've benefited from his administration."

"Thanks, Henry." Gil smiled affectionately at his old champion. "But Mr. Warner and his— cohorts—" his eyes grew cold again as they swept the four men clustered on one side of the table—"don't seem to feel they've benefited sufficiently since their tenure on the board began. So, gentlemen, if you want us to branch out, we will. And we will be successful, as we always have been."

"Success has very little to do with it," Warner insisted, his gravelly voice sounding implacable. "This corporation is run more like a mom-and-pop store than the multibillion-dollar operation it is. It needs shaking up—action! Diversification! I'm not trying to threaten you, Duchenay. I realize your family feels sentimental about a business started by your grandfather. But for your own good you'd better go after some virgin territory! There are food-production people out there who probably don't know how Purity could streamline their operations. I'm simply suggesting that if you can't get us a bigger market share somehow, a different chief executive officer can."

Duchenay regarded Fred Wartner coldly. "Is there any further business? No? I suggest we adjourn."

He watched as the men filed out. Henry Farnham and Squire Phillips, the last of the older board members, stayed for a moment to indulge in low-voiced indignation over the newcomers' perfidy. But eventually they wound down and took their leave. Except for Gilmartin, the room was empty.

Wearily he slumped in his chair at the head of the table and ran his hands through his thick dark hair. He had maintained an imperturbable front before Fred Warner and the others, but the effort left him feeling drained of energy. Their demands should have have been forseen, he admitted wryly to himself. When Warner had acquired enough Purity stock to force a seat on the board and to nominate his own people to replace several retiring members, Gil should have realized a power play was in progress. But he'd been immersed in upgrading the portion-control operation and so had been taken by surprise.

Well, now he would have to make good his boast. Find a new product market or service and bring it into the Purity fold. He knew he would do it, just as he had realized four years ago that his father's brief illness would be fatal; just as he had known that the board, then composed of his father's and grand-father's associates, would tap him for the presidency. Some part of him always knew. Prescient, that's what his mother, Magda, called it. He smiled briefly, thinking of her. She claimed his gift came from her mother, remotely descended from gypsy ancestors. Whatever it was, it was sometimes uncomfortable but always reliable. Since it prophesied success ahead, he wasn't too worried. But a finger of uneasiness touched him just the same. That all-knowing part of him also told him there was something else ahead—something that could hurt him in ways he'd never experienced during his entire business-dominated life.

He shrugged, dismissing such thoughts. At least this new corporate crisis would mean he could get out of attending the party tomorrow night. There had been some mention of a girl who was visiting the people giving the party, but he hadn't allowed himself to be firmly committed. Society in St. Louis, Missouri, could be very stratified, with old French families like his considering themselves the cream. But he found the debutantes too young, too frivolous; they stirred no chord within him. And he would be very busy for the next few months—too busy, he hoped, to be subjected to the parties designed to display young feminine charms to eligible bachelors like himself.

His eyes roamed around the boardroom as he recalled Warner's contemptuous remarks about a "mom-and-pop" operation. Certainly the elegant room belied that accusation. From the richly glowing colors of the huge Bukhara rug to the restrained folds of the damask draperies, the room conveyed the impression of wealth and taste. His grandfather had amassed the wealth; his father had had the taste for beautiful things, filling his office and home with precious acquisitions from trips to Europe and Asia. Having grown up with such things, Gil rarely took the time to stand back and admire them. But now, with Fred Warner's harsh voice still echoing in his ears, he ran his hand lovingly along the smooth mahogany of the long boardtable, made in the eighteenth century for some ducal mansion. He didn't feel sentimental about the business started by his grandfather; business and sentiment didn't readily mix, and Gil was a good businessman. But he was proud of it, as an American success story; proud of his grandfather's rise from produce vendor to millionaire corporation president; proud of his father's able management of that corporation.

Gil reached for the telephone that stood on a side table. Punching in a number with the familiarity of long usage, he leaned back in the leather armchair, turning slightly so he could see his grandfather's portrait hanging behind him. It amused him to trace the similarities in their faces—and the differences. His mouth, he knew, came from his mother's family— another bit of gypsy heritage, along with the deep dimple in his strong square chin.

His mother's voice on the telephone snapped him out of his reverie. He smiled unconsciously as he took in her absentminded hello. She had probably been in the garden and was still there in spirit.

"Mother? I won't be home tonight. Got to catch a flight for San Francisco to see MacMillan. Have Murphy pack me a bag, and get Pete to bring it down here, would you? I'll go directly to the airport after work."

"But Gil, dear." His mother's voice was fully alert now. "I did want to talk to you. It's about Rita. She's gone."

Gil looked blankly at the telephone receiver. "Rita?"

Magda answered patiently, "Rita is the cook, or was. She left a note saying she was going to marry a golf pro. We have a big dinner party coming up at the end of the week, you know."

Gil swore under his breath. "This is the third one in five months," he snapped. "Why can't we keep a cook?"

"I'm sure I don't know. We pay them enough." Magda sounded amused, and in spite of himself Gil smiled ruefully. She always managed to be untouched by any household crises, preferring to leave most things to her competent housekeeper, Mrs. Murphy.

"What we need is a chef," Gil decided. "Some man who'll feel more of a commitment to his position than those flighty women. I'm going to be implementing a new phase of operations soon that will call for us to do even more entertaining. I'll find a chef in San Francisco and bring him back."

"Won't that be expensive?" Magda made her remark perfunctorily. Gil knew she had already relinquished the problem of the cook to him.

"That's not important now. I'm relying on cinching some vital deals around the dinner table. Rita wasn't that great, anyway, as I recall. Hal MacMillan will know where to look for a competent chef, and if we pay enough, he'll stay at least until I'm over this bad patch."

"Is Hal McMillan coming back with you?" His Mother's voice regained its animation.

"I don't know what his plans are, but I do know he'll be at the dinner party on Friday."

"I'll tell Mrs. Murphy about packing for you, then. See you when you get back, dear."

"Tell Betsy goodbye for me." Gil hung up the telephone and sat for a moment, his brows creased in thought. One of the reasons he was sanguine about finding a new market was that, unknown to Fred Warner and the rest of the board, he was already sounding out some hotel owners about using Purity Corp. to cater the food served in their restaurants. Hal MacMillan owned several hotels in various cities, some of whose restaurant operations had never managed to be profitable. But MacMillan was proving hard to sell on Purity's food. Now Gil would have to step up his pressure, hoping to pull off a coup that would put him firmly back into the driver's seat of Purity. After a few minutes' thought he left the boardroom, striding down the thickly carpeted hall to his office, remembering to make a note of his promise to find a chef for Magda.

SELINA EMPTIED THE LAST DRAWER in her dresser and zipped her duffel bag shut with a sigh. She glanced wistfully around the high-ceilinged bedroom that had been home for the last four years. She would miss even the creaky old floorboards and the sagging mattress on the ancient brass bedstead.

Molly peeked around the door. "About finished? Want me to carry something down to the car?"

Selina indicated the bulging duffel bag. "If you feel up to tackling that, I could bring the rest of it."

She looked at her roommate's serene face with affection. Four young women shared the roomy flat, converted from the second floor of an old Victorian mansion, but Molly would always be the one she felt closest to. They had been roommates since graduating from high school eight years ago, when all they could afford was a little box on the fourth floor of an apartment building. They had both been secretaries then, and Molly still enjoyed clerical work. But Selina had always wanted to be a chef, and after six years of saving up tuition money, she'd quit to go to the California Culinary Academy. She'd even been able to steer her friend into a job in the personnel office there.

She staggered down the steep stairs and out into the bright sunlight, heaving her suitcase and backpack onto the sidewalk with relief. Molly was already admiring the rickety little Fiat with a proprietary air. Selina settled into the driver's seat to show her the intricacies of starting the car.

"Now remember, you have to kind of kick it into reverse." Selina regarded her friend dubiously. "You sure you want to buy this thing? It's not the easiest car in the world to drive."

Molly pushed wispy bangs out of her eyes and nodded confidently. "I'll get the hang of it. Nothing on wheels has ever stumped me yet." She patted the dashboard of the little Fiat affectionately. "Pretty soon she'll know her master's hand."

Selina slid out of the driver's seat of the car and walked around to the passenger side, pausing to cram her bags into the back seat. A random gust of wind straight off San Francisco Bay ruffled the burnished copper of her hair, and she paused for a moment before getting back in the car to take a last look at the city she was leaving.

Tall Victorians across Sacramento Street shut out the view of the bay, but to her left the street dipped sharply, and if she strained her eyes, she imagined she could see Lands' End and the blue breakers of the Pacific. To her right, after a roller-coaster series of hills, the Transamerica Pyramid thrust its angular finger into the blue sky.

Taking a deep breath, she got into the car. She had loved her life in this city. Now it was ending, but a new adventure was in store. Although she felt a few sentimental tears well up in her eyes, underneath was the excitement of traveling outside her native state, the challenge of a new job among strangers.

Molly spared a moment's attention from the surging San Francisco traffic to give her a knowing look. "It's a good thing that super job turned up," she said loudly over the noisy engine. "Otherwise you might have had to eat your words to Andy."

"No way." Selina shook her head vigorously. "The wool has been pulled from my eyes," she declared dramatically. "I have permanently parted company with Andrew Corbett."

"What did he do to make you so mad, anyway?" Molly's small face was alive with curiosity. "First thing I know, you're telling me to find you some job as a wage slave. Did he—as they say—assault your virtue?"

"In a manner of speaking." Selina chuckled. She

hadn't told Molly what Marybeth had revealed, realizing that her friend might feel obliged to take some official steps to nullify Andy's test results. Selina was disturbed he'd passed by cheating, but she shrank from telling tales.

"Really? What happened?" Molly steered the car onto the freeway. "I just figured he cooked the exam results or something. I didn't realize there was sex involved." She smacked her lips expectantly as she waited for Selina's story.

"You figured—what?" Selina asked weakly. Molly looked at her sharply, then swerved the car back into the proper lane.

"So that was it." She snorted. "Don't worry, I won't tell. That skunk deserves to have his diploma taken away, but it would involve too much heartburn—a terrible thing for a chef's school." She was silent for a moment, and Selina was grateful for the chance to pull together a convincing story that wouldn't implicate Marybeth should her roommate ask further questions.

But for the rest of the drive to the airport Molly talked of mutual friends and activities. They played "do-you-remember," and this time the tears Selina felt in her eyes were for old friends and good times. *Don't be silly*, she scolded herself. *You're not leaving for the rest of your life. It's time for a change. You've got your career to think of.*

And from a career point of view this move was much better than any position as *sous-chef* she could have got in San Francisco. The day after her climactic scene with Andy, Molly called from the academy's placement office. "A new listing has just come in," she'd told Selina with great excitement. "It's in Missouri—St. Louis, I believe. I don't know if you want to go that far. But everything else has been filled by now, although I'm sure we'll get some more openings in a month or so. Can you wait a month for work?"

Selina couldn't wait. The thought of traveling was tempting to someone who'd never even been on an airplane before. And the idea of being a private chef, able to experiment and develop her own distinctive recipes, was intoxicating. Besides, the salary being offered by the St. Louis job was so munificent that it was hard to turn down. By working there a couple of years, she could easily save enough money to go to Paris for advanced training at the famed Cordon Bleu. Then, work in restaurants until she had a reputation and some capital; then, open her own place.... Such dreams were commonplace among the seniors at the academy, but Selina was blithely confident that hers would come true.

So she packed, sold her rickety car to Molly and got ready to leave immediately. The opening must be filled right away—that was one of the conditions. Molly had no sooner mentioned to Selina's future employer that the academy's top graduate was available than he'd snapped, "Fine. I'll leave a ticket at the TWA desk in the airport. It's tomorrow morning's flight. Thank you very much, Miss Hutton."

Now Molly steered the little car into the airport entrance and swept up to the terminal section reserved for departing flights. Selina jumped out and pulled her suitcases from the back. "Thanks for giving me a ride," she said, poking her head into the car.

"Don't mention it," Molly replied. "Gave me a chance to get used to my new car." She regarded her friend soberly. "I'm going to miss you, honey. If things don't work out, just let me know. I'll hunt you up a better job, maybe one back home. And we'll all be thinking of you."

Selina blinked back tears again, reaching blindly to squeeze Molly's hand. Then she loaded up her bags and headed into the terminal.

CHAPTER TWO

SHE WAS THE FIRST in line to board the plane, excitement building in her again. A glance around the people waiting in the lounge to board hadn't revealed anyone who looked particularly wealthy and epicurean enough to have a private chef. By the time she was settled in the business section, she was agog with curiosity about her new boss. Realizing that she'd forgotten to ask Molly her employer's name, she reached into her carry-on bag for the envelope that held her ticket. On it was scrawled in strong angular handwriting, "The Château, Ladue, Missouri." Selina chided herself for her carelessness in forgetting to find out about the name. She knew Molly had checked him out, because she remembered her roommate talking about the prominent hotelier her new employer had quoted as a reference. But, engrossed in packing as fast as possible, she hadn't heard Molly mention any names, and the file folder containing the paperwork was packed neatly in her suitcase.

She buckled her seat belt carefully, glancing around, trying to act as if she flew every day. It was disappointing that she wasn't by a window, although heaven knew she shouldn't be complaining about a free plane ticket, window or not. So far there was no one sitting in the extra-comfortable seat next to hers. Flight attendants bustled up and down the aisle, skating dexterously around the milling passengers who were stowing away their carry on luggage and settling comfortably for the flight.

Leaning back, Selina closed her eyes for a moment to catch her breath. It had been a hectic few days since graduation, and even the thought of the tall white chef's hat she had so proudly packed in her suitcase paled beside the mixture of excitement and apprehension she felt. If only she didn't have the bad taste of Andy's behavior in her mouth! Without realizing it, she clenched her small hands around the arms of the seat.

"Don't worry, we're not taking off yet," said a deep voice at her side. Selina's eyes flew open, and she released her death grip on the chair arms. Standing in the aisle looking down at her with a hint of impatience on his face was the handsomest man she'd ever seen.

He was tall, slim but broad shouldered in his perfectly fitting gray tweed business suit. His hair was thick and dark, severely disciplined except for one lock that tumbled untidily over his high forehead. He pushed it back automatically. Dark faintly amused eyes glinted at her. She realized then that she'd been staring.

"I'm not worried," she snapped, annoyed with herself for appearing to gawk at him just because he happened to be—nice looking. *Nice looking!* said a voice inside her. *He's an Adonis!*

Shut up, she told the voice sternly. One look was

enough to tell her this man was poison. He was the kind who left you swooning helplessly as he walked away, his casual interest assuaged. She didn't need involvement with any man right now, certainly not one as handsome as this. With this man, she sensed, a woman would want to be the only one in his life. And she wasn't the type to fill that role.

She sat up a little straighter, trying to make herself seem taller than her five-foot-three-inch height.

"Do you mind if I get by," he requested in the same deep voice. Without looking at him, Selina twisted her knees sideways to make more room. He could have gone around to the other aisle, she thought, determined to find fault with him. As he moved past her to the seat next to hers, his body brushed her knees, sending faint alarms up and down her spine.

She sniffed to herself. Men! They couldn't help coming on to any woman they saw—even those who didn't really interest them. She hadn't really had much to do with men before Andy had swept into her life. She had been carried away by his own estimate of his good looks and charm, and it had been a while before she thought to look beneath the surface. What she saw there made her turn away from deeper examination uneasily, although it was enough to keep her from succumbing to Andy's passionate advances. His kisses had been pleasant, but she'd discouraged anything more intimate, in spite of the pleading in his handsome face. She glanced covertly at the handsome man next to her, comparing his face to Andy's.

Her former friend had lighter hair and blue eyes.

With such a charming smile, she thought, still staring absently at the stranger. Andy's smile could have melted bombe, let alone a poor vulnerable female heart. It was no wonder Marybeth had been taken in by him.

Selina had been hard put to understand what made Andy so determined in his pursuit of her. At first she'd thought it was just her undoubted ability to interpret a recipe with flair that led him to seek her out for tips and pointers. But he'd soon made it clear he was after more. His charm and easy manner made his kisses acceptable, but some inner caution had always made her leery of letting things get too passionate. And although he grumbled about her medieval attitude, Andy had accepted it.

But lately he'd let her know that he expected more. He'd even mentioned marriage, although she'd laughed and taken it for a joke. She hadn't known why she'd been so reluctant to commit herself to the only man who'd ever asked her to marry him. But now she realized that his basic instability had shown through the smooth veneer of good-humored charm, subconsciously alerting her to the foolishness of a long-term attachment.

After arriving at this analysis, which she rather smugly felt to be uncommonly penetrating, Selina came back to the present with a start. A new sound had been added to the high-pitched whine of the airplane—a rumbling thundery sound. The plane was moving, taxiing down the runway prior to lifting off.

Next to her the attractive man stirred restively. He looked at the empty seat across from him. "I guess he got cold feet," the man snorted. "Probably too temperamental for St. Louis."

"I beg your pardon?" In her bemused state Selina had thought for a moment the man was speaking to her. Then, as he turned to look at her, she realized he'd been speaking to himself. *He probably thinks I'm making a play for him,* she thought, angry with herself for catering to any man's vanity.

She lifted her fingers self-consciously and toyed with one of the bright tendrils that escaped the combs with which she confined her hair. But somehow she couldn't look away from his eyes. Held captive by their compelling gaze, she realized they weren't really dark. They were brown, but seemed somehow lighted from within, giving them an amber glow. A dark circle around the edge of the iris made her think of some keen-eyed creature—an eagle! His eyes had that same fierce, proud look.

"Shall we introduce ourselves?" His words held an undertone of amusement. Confused, Selina put her hand in his outstretched one. To her surprise he turned it palm up, cradling it in his warm hand while he lightly traced the lines with his index finger.

"A very definite lifeline," he said in a musing voice, his eyes fixed on Selina's bewildered face. "You are very strong willed, independent—even stubborn. I guess that goes with your hair." She found herself responding to his teasing smile with a reluctant grin of her own.

His finger continued moving across her palm, sending warm currents through her. "You'll have a long life and lots of children—but you must be careful to choose the right man to be their father. There is heart trouble in store for you if you don't watch out.''

Her lips twisted into a mocking grimace. She tried to pull her hand away, but his grip tightened. He appeared puzzled.

''You seem to be engaged in some kind of manual labor—there are so many calluses.'' He prodded a small spot near the base of her little finger, where the big handle of the chef's knife had hardened her skin. Then he lightly massaged the flesh below her thumb. ''But according to your Mount of Venus, you're a very sensuous person.''

He looked directly into her eyes again. The teasing smile slowly died as his eyes probed deeper into hers. She felt suddenly deprived of breath. There was something deep in those amber eyes that compelled her. She wrenched her own gaze away.

''It seems a bit anticlimactic to ask your name now that I know so much about you,'' he said. His lips quirked again into that attractive boyish smile.

''I'm Selina Montgomery,'' she said primly, shaking his hand quickly and drawing back before he could give her any more interesting revelations about herself. ''And you must be King of the Gypsies.''

He tossed his head back in a deep musical laugh, the errant lock of hair dropping over his forehead as he shook his head. Automatically he pushed it back.

''My name is Gilmartin Duchenay,'' he said, smiling. ''But my mother swears she's got gypsy blood in her. I really learned to read palms just as a joke. But sometimes it comes in handy. Confess, now—I was right about you, wasn't I? Or are you too stubborn to admit it?''

Selina had been hesitating, but his perceptive question caused her to chuckle. "I am stubborn sometimes—but only when I'm right," she admitted. "It does seem to go with the hair." She smoothed it back ruefully.

The flight attendant paused by their row, and Selina's new acquaintance handed her a glass of the white wine the man carried. "I still haven't got used to that," he said, sipping his own drink.

"Wine?" Selina paused in the act of tasting it.

"No—being served by a steward instead of a stewardess."

So, he was one of those! "I suppose you think he's demeaning himself, doing women's work," she said, curling her lip.

Gilmartin Duchenay looked at her in surprise. "Not at all," he said coolly. "I meant just what I said. I've been flying for ten years now, and I'm just not used to male flight attendants yet. I'm all for it, though."

"Oh." *That's put me in my place*, Selina thought. "You fly on business?"

He nodded curtly. To avoid seeming as if she were prying into his life, Selina absentmindedly began the procedure they followed at the academy for tasting wines. She held her glass to the light, looking critically at the color. She swirled it as well as she could in its plastic cup and sniffed the bouquet. Sipping cautiously, she rolled a small amount around on her tongue before swallowing it.

"Are you a wine expert at your tender age?" She looked up to find him regarding her with amusement.

"I'm not an expert, of course. That takes years of developing your palate," she said defensively. "I do enjoy tasting wines, though, Mr. Duchenay."

"Just call me Gil," he said casually. "I'd feel as if I was at a board meeting if you called me Mr. Duchenay. What does your undeveloped palate tell you about this wine?"

"Well..." she said hesitantly. "I *think* it's from one of the big vineyards—Moravi, perhaps. Chablis—probably 1978. Not, of course, a great wine, but perfectly drinkable."

His lips twitched. "You Californians," he said tolerantly. "You must have been tasting wine since you were a baby to be so precise." He signaled to the flight attendant. "May we see a bottle, please?"

Puzzled, the man brought one over. It was Moravi Chablis, but a jug wine, not vintage.

"You were very nearly right," Gil said, looking at her thoughtfully over his glass.

Selina was mortified. Jug wines should be easy to tell from vintage varietals. "I should have known it was nonvintage, though," she said, biting her lip.

"It's not a life-and-death matter," Gil finished his glass, refusing the attendant's offer of more.

But it is, Selina thought. Knowing wines was part of a chef's duties. She had been weak on wine tasting in school. And now she was leaving California for Missouri. How would she improve her knowledge in the wilds of the Midwest?

Gil had taken his attaché case out from beneath his

seat. "Excuse me," he said politely to Selina. "I have some paperwork that needs to be done."

His finely traced dark brows drew together in a frown of concentration as he immersed himself in work. Selina studied him on the sly for a few minutes. The aquiline nose and square chin added somehow to his eaglelike image. Remembering the thrill that had gone through her when he suggested she had a sensuous nature, she looked down at her hand. The mound of flesh below her thumb did swell voluptuously, contrasting with the square workmanlike appearance of the rest of her hand.

Her sensuous nature had never been awakened by Andy, she thought ruefully. At first she had enjoyed his kisses; such attentions hadn't often come her way in her busy work-filled life. But when his caresses intensified, calling on her for a deeper response, she'd been left—not cold, but definitely cool. Her aloofness had intrigued Andy, who was used, she supposed, to easier conquests. *I was probably just a challenge to him* she thought rather bleakly, suddenly struck by this aspect of their relationship that hadn't occurred to her before. "The unattainable and therefore desirable woman." It was disappointing to think it wasn't her personal attributes that had caused his flattering pursuit, but Selina was nothing if not realistic, and she knew that though she was reasonably attractive, she had none of the "come-hither" that seemed so necessary for sex appeal.

Draining her glass, she determined not to dwell on the past anymore. *With a little effort and some more wine,* she told herself, *I could get maudlin and weepy.* Although she was leaving all her friends behind, she would make more in the Midwest. She began speculating about the family she was to work for.

According to the envelope that had enclosed her ticket at the TWA counter, her new job was not actually in St. Louis, but in Ladue, which she supposed was a suburb. All she knew about St. Louis was that it was on the Mississippi River and had a baseball team called the Cardinals. But she didn't have the slightest idea about her employer or his reason for being in San Francisco. She looked around the business-class compartment, wondering if he was on this flight, and if he knew *her* name. There was a portly well-dressed man sitting across the aisle from her. He looked as if he knew the importance of eating well, she noted with a smile. Perhaps he was her new employer.

The flight attendants were bringing trays of food around now, and Selina realized that she was hungry. She had been too busy packing to stop for lunch today. She sniffed hungrily at the aroma of the food on the tray set in front of her. Gil, she noticed, had put away his briefcase and was eating his food in a businesslike fashion, chewing briskly and swallowing with dispatch.

Selina poked the entrée with her fork, trying to figure what it was. From the smell, it must be chicken, she thought, but she couldn't see anything recognizable. She took a bite, chewing gingerly and trying to determine what it was by texture.

"What is this?" she asked the flight attendant.

"Chicken à la king, miss." He hurried on to tend other passengers. She gazed at her plate in disbelief. This glutinous mass of tasteless sauce and evidently precooked meat was chicken à la king? She tried a bite of the broccoli that accompanied the dish, but it was limp and tasteless, too.

"What's the matter? Is your palate too immature for the food?" Gil was smiling as he looked at her, but something about his expression challenged her to complain. She ignored the warning.

"This is food?" She put her fork on her plate with quiet finality. "You couldn't tell by me."

"What's wrong with it? Tastes okay to me." His eyes were frosty. "Perhaps it's not 'vintage' enough for you."

"That's probably its trouble," she retorted. "I imagine that this is 1978 food that's been in the freezer too long. Or it could be current food but prepared by a chef whose frontal lobes were destroyed in a tragic accident. Or maybe it's—"

"There's no chef involved in this food," Gil said, his voice quietly dangerous. "I happen to know it's prepared using the latest automated techniques, according to the specifications found in popular cookbooks."

"Automated techniques!" Selina gulped her water. "We're talking about food here, not razor blades or milk cartoons! Food is for humans to eat! It should be fixed by humans!" She picked up a spear of broccoli and brandished it in front of him. "This broccoli is an outrage! It used to be alive, pushing toward the sun, full of vitamins and protein. Now it's about as nourishing as a piece of paper!''

Gil's face tightened. ''This meal,'' he said, pushing away the broccoli, ''contains one-third of the minimum daily requirement of vitamins and protein. It's completely nourishing, and I find it quite palatable!'' He shoved a bite of chicken into his mouth and chewed defiantly. Selina was pleased to note that he seemed to have trouble swallowing it.

''You're out of your mind, then,'' she told him. ''Whoever's responsible for foisting this stuff off on an unsuspecting public should be—'' she groped wildly for a suitably horrible punishment. ''Should be sentenced to eat it for the rest of his life!'' she finished triumphantly.

He looked at her with dislike. ''Well,'' he said sardonically, ''your wish will come true. My corporation supplies food to this airline—and many other places, too. So, I suppose I'll be eating it for quite a while.''

''*Your* corporation?'' Selina was stunned. ''You mean—the corporation you work for? Why don't you change jobs?''

''I mean Purity Corporation, which is owned by my family and operated by me. And I don't plan on selling it just because you don't like my food, Miss Montgomery. What makes you such an all-fired expert, anyway?'' His smile was scornful. ''I didn't have you pegged for the domestic kind of woman who plays around in the kitchen all day.''

Selina narrowed her eyes. She could feel herself losing her temper. ''I don't play around in the kitchen all day. I work, Mr. Duchenay," she replied crisply. "I'm a chef."

His mouth dropped open. He closed it quickly, but his face wore a thunderstruck expression. When he spoke, his voice was almost pleading. "Tell me something," he said quietly. "What are you doing on this airplane?"

Selina looked at him haughtily. "I don't know that it's any of your business," she said. "But I'm going to Ladue as a personal chef. For a *very* important person," she added impressively.

"Do you know this person's name?" His eyes were oddly intent.

"Well—not exactly," Selina admitted. "It was all settled so quickly. But I have his address here." She pulled out the envelope that had held her plane ticket, with the address in Ladue scrawled on the outside.

Gil looked at it for a long moment, then turned his head away. "Of all the rotten luck," he groaned.

Selina stared at him, a terrible presentiment filling her mind. "It's not—not *your* address, is it?"

It seemed like forever before he nodded slowly, his face still averted.

"Oh, gosh! Oh, how terrible!" Selina gaped at him, wondering if he was summoning up the courage to fire her. "I . . . I suppose you won't want me to work for you now," she said in a small voice.

He turned finally, directing his amber eyes in a critical survey of her, from the riotous tendrils of bright hair, down her softly rounded breasts and small waist, to her slim ankles and small sensibly shod feet. "You won't last very long," he said with a sigh.

"I don't understand you." Selina was taken aback.

"I wanted a man this time. All our cooks get married and leave. I thought a chef would be more dependable. When mother told me that Rita, our last cook, had eloped with a golf pro, I said I'd get someone who wouldn't be running off with some man." He repeated his assessment of her face and body. "You're far too pretty to last six months."

"Well thank you for nothing!" Selina drew herself up angrily. "What makes you think men have a monopoly on dependability? Not only am I an extremely well-qualified chef, I'm at least as dependable as any man you'll ever hire." She sniffed bitterly. "But go ahead and take the job back. I wouldn't dream of working for you now. Too bad we're already on the way to St. Louis; you'll have to buy me a return ticket."

He looked at her with exasperation. "See? I said you wouldn't last long, but I didn't realize it would only be two hours." His hand closed around her forearm, accidentally brushing against the side of her breast, and she moved uneasily in her seat. "I'm afraid," he said firmly, "there's no possibility of a return ticket for you just yet. I need a chef right away, and you're the one I hired. You don't get away so easily, Miss Montgomery."

She looked at him defiantly but was captured and held by the intensity of his gaze. Again she felt a strange powerlessness undermine her will as she stared deeply into the golden brown orbs. *How odd,* she found herself thinking, *there's no reflection of me in his eyes.* Then she blinked and pulled her gaze away, shrugging off his hand irritably.

"Fine words," she snapped, trying to ignore the way the pressure of his hand still lingered on her arm. "You got exactly what you wanted, Mr. Duchenay. A competent chef with no interest in playing around. So when you look for an excuse to get rid of me, you'll have to think of a better one than my sex."

"No interest in playing around?" With a skeptical look he picked up her hand again. "No one with your Mount of Venus is uninterested." He glanced into her palm again, and suddenly his expression changed. Like a man on the verge of an important discovery, he scanned the lines feverishly. His grasp on her hand stirred up disquieting sensations in Selina's bloodstream. She tried to pull away, but Gil tightened his grip, raising his eyes. The look in them shot an instant bolt of electricity through every cell in her body. For a moment it was as if all defenses were down between them. She felt as if the surprise and incredulity she could see on Gil's face were mirrored in her own features.

He pulled gently on her hand, and Selina leaned toward him like a magnet finding iron. She knew their lips would meet, knew the kiss would affect her more than anything she'd ever experienced.

"More wine, sir? Miss?" The flight attendant paused beside Gil's chair, bottle poised to pour. Gil blinked and dropped Selina's hand, gesturing the man away impatiently. For a moment Selina swayed toward him. Then, flooded with embarrassment at her eagerness to kiss a total stranger, she slumped back into her seat, trying to quiet her racing heart.

Gil's voice was slightly breathless when he spoke but otherwise showed no hint of the emotions Selina had found so overpowering. She had difficulty remembering what they had been talking about before Gil had looked into her eyes and changed her life. She shook her head angrily. Where had that unwelcome thought come from? With an effort she tried to concentrate on what he was saying.

"Actually I'm sure you'll do just fine." His glance at her was brief and, she felt, impersonal. "I certainly hope you find it agreeable at the Château. You'll really be working for my mother, you know. There's an important dinner party coming up at the end of this week. Mother will tell you everything else you need to know."

Selina straightened her shoulders and got a grip on her fading poise. "I look forward to it," she said, trying to keep her own voice as level as his. Then, as he bent his head once more over his briefcase, she took a deep breath and tried to put the last few minutes into perspective.

Why had he subjected her to that inexplicable scrutiny? And why had she responded like an adolescent? Her pulse was still racing from the brief encounter of their eyes. But Gil was evidently going to pretend it never happened. Remembering the eager— almost shameless—way she had responded, Selina was relieved that he was disinclined to take it further. *Just concentrate on your work*, she scolded herself.

Perhaps Gil had been trying her out to see how committed she was to the idea of not playing around. Well, he would see. If he wanted a businesslike employee, she would be that employee, even if she had to take a cold shower every day.

With an inward sigh she dug out the paperback she'd bought to read on the flight. It seemed a cruel twist of fate that the first man to stir her pulses, to give her a sense of what passion could be like, turned out to be her boss. *Otherwise,* she thought with a grim smile, *I could just drag him off to my lair and work my wiles upon him.* As it was, she would have to keep a tight check on her emotions to avoid revealing the effect he had on her. She stole a glance at him. He sat with his briefcase open, papers strewn about, but he was staring into space with a bemused expression that accorded ill with the image she had of Gilmartin Duchenay, efficient businessman. She found herself wistfully speculating about what it would be like to feel the touch of his lips. Enough of this, Selina decided and plunged ruthlessly into her book. But it was impossible to be unaware of him or the currents of electricity he could generate just by the presence of his warm body next to her.

By the time the plane approached Lambert Field in St. Louis, Selina was still on the first page of her book.

CHAPTER THREE

THEIR ARRIVAL IN ST. LOUIS was blurred for Selina by fatigue, and by the fact that Gil kept his hand on her arm as he helped her through the boarding lounge. She wanted to pull away but found it impossible not to give in to the warmth that ran through her whenever he touched her. *Don't get carried away,* she told herself soberly. He was far too handsome for her peace of mind. The most she could expect from him was a brief fling. She doubted he was the type to lose his heart over the chef. She reminded herself to think of her career path. This job was a stepping-stone to a future she intended to carve for herself. Just the idea of involvement with Gil was madness.

Selina shook her head, too confused by the state of her own emotions to make any sense of her thoughts. But she admitted with an inward chuckle that it was pretty cool of her to think about having an affair with a man she'd just met, and who was, moreover, her employer. She resolved to put business first and forget about romance.

Throughout the disembarkation process, while Gil whisked her through the lofty arched terminal to a hired limousine, throughout the wait until their bags were collected, she repeated to herself, *He's my boss.*

He doesn't even appreciate good food. He's just my boss.

They drove away from the airport, through the tender green foliage of May. The road humped over rolling hills, past office parks and apartment complexes and occasional patches of meadow. It was nothing like the drive from San Francisco International to town. Selina looked around in wonder.

"Where's the city?" she finally inquired.

Gil gave a start. "What? Oh, St. Louis proper is east of here, by the Mississippi. My place is in Ladue—not much farther now."

Even the quality of the air seemed different to Selina. It was softer, definitely hotter than the crisp breezes of the Bay Area. Although air conditioning in the limousine got rid of the heat, it couldn't really eliminate the moisture. Selina found it intriguing, although she knew the humidity would probably turn her hair into a mass of unmanageable corkscrews. She rolled down her window a little way. The smells of freshly mowed grass, flowering lilacs and hot asphalt permeated the limousine's pristine interior.

She glanced at Gil, but he was lost in frowning abstraction and didn't notice the car had been invaded by plain old outside air. She took a moment to study his profile, with its clean lines of nose and chin, and the determined-looking eyes. Even the deep cleft in his chin seemed to add strength, not softness, to his countenance. Before he could catch her scrutinizing him, she turned away.

The limousine moved onto a bustling highway, then turned off again. And suddenly they seemed to be in the country. The road was narrow, winding around trees and hills. On either side of them the ground sloped away, with occasional glimpses of a stone turret or a rosy brick wall to indicate the presence of palatial homes.

Selina was craning her neck for a longer look at a particularly intriguing Tudor-style home when Gil said, "Here we are." The limousine turned past stone gateposts and onto a smoothly paved road that curved through a sloping parklike space dotted with tall oak trees and evergreens. The effect was so artless and natural it took Selina a few minutes to realize the grounds had been carefully planned.

"How beautiful!" she exclaimed involuntarily. Gil looked pleased.

"That's mother's doing. She loves landscape gardening and redesigned the grounds soon after marrying my father."

The drive topped a rise and Selina gasped. Spread before her in a small valley was a building that might have come from an illustration of French châteaux. It wasn't the size that was impressive, although it rivaled some of the Nob Hill mansions she'd catered parties in. The gray stone of the building and its graceful outlines harmonized completely with the terraces and gardens that surround it.

Off to one side were the gaily striped umbrellas that denoted a pool area. Behind the château rose green slopes, crowned at the top with more magnificent oaks. At the front a small stream fell over some rocks to make a charming waterfall.

She realized that Gil was looking at her and turned

to meet his amber gaze. "I'm...totally flabber-
gasted," she admitted. "So much space! Where I
come from, very few people are fortunate enough to
have this kind of room."

For a moment his face relaxed into a grin. "I
thought the West was the home of wide open
spaces," he said teasingly. Then the gleam of amusement in his eyes vanished, replaced by an intent probing regard that reduced her to idiotic babbling.

"It looks very old," she said breathlessly. "I suppose it's very old?"

"Not really," he replied coolly. "Built in 1909."
His lips turned up knowingly as he made a slow
survey of her flushed, confused face. She turned to
look out the window, reeling transparent, as though
he could read her emotions more easily than any
business report. "It's supposed to be a copy of the
Château du Chenier in the Loire Valley," he told
her as she gazed out the window, apparently in rapt
contemplation of the Château. "According to my
grandfather, we were descendants of that family—
probably the black sheep."

Selina turned back to the approaching building.
The limousine stopped at great double doors, and the
driver pulled out their bags as Gil guided her up the
steps. With all the grandeur, Selina expected the door
to be opened by a uniformed butler. But Gil merely
unlocked it with a very modern-looking key and
ushered her inside.

The cool, lofty hall was a welcome relief from the
hot, moist air outside. She glanced around, en-
tranced. The walls were paneled with lovely gleaming

wood and hung with pictures; the vaulted ceiling was smoothly plastered. But the furnishings mingled antique and contemporary pieces, giving the rooms a homey lived-in feeling.

Gil looked around. "I wonder where mother is, and Betsy."

Betsy? Perhaps he was married. Selina was dismayed at the feeling of desolation that flooded her when the thought occurred to her. He hadn't acted married on the plane, she thought, feeling again the warm impression of his fingers on her palm. But then, no one seemed to act married anymore.

"Does—Mrs. Duchenay—run the household?" she asked, trying to assume a competent air.

"If you can call it running," Gil answered, smiling tolerantly. "As I told you, mother loves gardening. She'd spend one hundred percent of her free time on the grounds if she could. Even her clubs and charities involve gardens. We have a housekeeper who comes in every day—"

He was interrupted by a small whirlwind that swept down the curving oak staircase and latched onto his midsection. "Gil! You're back! Now we can get the colt!"

Gil gave the whirlwind a hug, then disengaged himself carefully. Selina saw a girl of about twelve with the same dark hair and amber eyes Gil had. She was in the gangly, awkward stage, although there was the promise of beauty in the wide planes of her face.

"Act your age, scamp!" Gil gave the dark head a loving tousle. "What's this about a horse?"

"It was such a darling little colt," the girl began

eagerly, "at the Clayton show, and mother said you'd have to approve before we could get it. I'd do the work, Gil, honest I would. I'd feed it and curry its silky coat. . . ." Her face grew dreamy.

Gil cast his eyes expressively toward the ceiling. "Just like you took care of the cocker spaniel, and the parrot, and the monkey, I suppose?" Before she could answer, he turned her to face Selina. "Mind your manners, Betsy. This is Miss—I mean, Chef Montgomery, who'll be cooking for us." He put an affectionate arm around the girl's shoulders. "My sister, Elizabeth Warrington Duchenay."

Betsy regarded her with the clear-eyed steady gaze of youth. "She's not a man," she observed.

"Do tell!" Gil's eyes were unreadable as they scanned the evidences of Selina's womanhood.

"I thought mother said we were getting a man this time, because of Rita running away and Martha getting pregnant—"

Gil's brows drew together. Before he could reprove the girl, Selina stepped forward, holding out her hand. "How do you do, Betsy," she said gravely. "I'll try to stay awhile, even if I'm not a man. What's your favorite food?"

Betsy's face lighted up. She slid an arm into Selina's. "I like brownies best," she confided, "although pizza's really good, too. Will you make pizza sometimes, Chef Montgomery?"

Gil snorted and Selina said quickly, "Of course I will, if your mother likes it, too. Pizza can be very good indeed. And please just call me Selina, right?"

"Okay, Selina." Betsy nodded approvingly. "I'll come and help you cook. I love making things in the kitchen."

"You can be my *sous-chef*," Selina said. Answering the question on Betsy's face, she added, "That's like assistant chef." She couldn't repress a chuckle at the realization that she might have been slaving away as a *sous-chef* at this very moment if Gil hadn't come to the rescue. Suddenly she was free of homesickness, though she had no doubt that it would come back from time to time.

"Where's mother?" Gil was asking, his glance sweeping once more around the lofty hall.

Betsy shrugged. "She's out grubbing around in that old vegetable garden," she said, disdain evident in her voice. She smiled up at Selina winsomely. "I don't like gardening," she confided, "although mother's so keen on it. But I do like eating the stuff—'specially corn on the cob. Can we have corn on the cob tonight, Chef Selina?"

"It's a little early in the season for that, isn't it?" Selina said diplomatically. Gil glanced impatiently at his watch.

"I have to go over to the office for a late meeting," he said. "Betsy, can you take Miss—Chef Montgomery out to mother and make sure she gets settled in all right?"

Betsy nodded, suddenly assuming a dignified air. "Of course I can. Will you come with me, Chef Montgomery?"

Selina smiled to herself as she inclined her head in a suitably solemn way. But the exuberant Betsy popped out as Gil went to the front door. "We'll go get the colt tomorrow, okay, Gil?"

They heard him laugh as the door closed. Betsy took Selina's hand.

"Come on," she said. "Just leave your bags here. Pete, the gardener, will take them to your suite later."

Selina allowed herself to be towed along by Betsy's eager hand. She caught glimpses of beautiful rooms on either side of the hall, but they ducked through a swinging door under the stairway and entered a more utilitarian setting. The floor was still tiled in black-and-white marble squares, but the walls were painted a cream color instead of being wainscoted.

"I like this part of the house best," Betsy said as they walked into the kitchen. "There's not so much to break back here."

Selina looked around approvingly. The kitchen was a mammoth room but had been redesigned in the last few years. The restaurant-size range was conveniently located near big stainless-steel refrigerators and a huge scrubbed-wood work island. Aluminum and copper pots and kettles hung from a rack above the island, and a very efficient-looking dishwasher occupied space next to the sinks.

Betsy caught her look at the dishwasher. "We all do the dishes when there's no company," she said, opening the refrigerator for a critical inspection of its contents. "It's lots of fun. Of course, there's usually company." Her eyes crinkled in a wide smile. "You should see Gil in his apron. It really makes him act silly."

Selina raised her eyebrows but forbore to comment. She moved to Betsy's side to help inventory the refrigerator.

"There's a freezer over there," Betsy volunteered, munching on a carrot. "Rita, the last cook, put a lot of stuff in there. She was always making bread and freezing it."

Selina nodded absently. The refrigerator was almost empty. "What have you been eating since she's been gone?"

Betsy shrugged. "Eating out mostly. I don't mind it for a couple of days, but I don't like having to get dressed up all the time. Mother's been going out of her mind trying to figure out what do do about the big party Friday."

"That is only too true." The words accompanied the creak of the back door opening. Selina whirled to see a tall tanned woman carrying a basket full of vegetables enter the kitchen. The woman plopped her basket on the worktable and fanned her face with the straw hat she'd been wearing.

"It is really getting hot out there," she observed. Her eyes were gray, not amber, but they held the same keen intelligence as Gil's. She came forward, taking off her gardening gloves and stretching her hand toward Selina in a gesture of goodwill.

"You must be our new chef, since Betsy's displaying the impoverished state of the refrigerator for you. Welcome to the Château."

Selina grasped her hand, noting that the grip was unusually strong for a woman. For a moment she met the keen eyes, feeling that she was being measured.

"And you are Mrs. Duchenay," she said, summoning all her poise.

"I'm Magda Duchenay," the older woman said. "You've met the youngest member of the family, I see." She pulled Betsy to her for a brief hug.

"Mother, Gil didn't say I couldn't have the colt. So can we go tomorrow and get him?" Betsy raised an imploring face, forgetting for a moment to finish her carrot.

"We'll talk about it later, dear. Aren't you supposed to be practicing your piano lesson?"

Betsy's shoulders slumped in exaggerated despair. "Oh, mother," she wailed. "It's really impossible. It's torture, it really is. I'm sure *madame* didn't mean for me to actually learn it!"

"Nevertheless," Magda said firmly, "you give it a good shot. Now scoot." She pushed the girl toward the front of the house, and after seizing another carrot, Betsy went with dragging feet.

Magda looked after her in fond exasperation. "I remember that part of growing up," she said, smiling at Selina. "It passes, and that's the best that can be said about it."

Selina nodded in agreement but found it hard to believe that the graceful woman in front of her ever had an awkward stage. Magda Duchenay must have been over fifty, she thought, but her dark hair showed no trace of gray, and her face was youthful and alive. *If Gil is thirty-four or thirty-five,* she mused to herself, *and his mother was eighteen or twenty when he was born...."*

"I can see you're doing sums in your head."

Magda's voice uncannily echoed her thoughts. "Betsy was born long after I had any thought of having another child. But I think she's kept me young; you have to be on your toes to keep up with her." She laughed, a warm comfortable sound, and Selina felt herself relaxing. This woman didn't seem nearly as formidable as her surroundings would indicate.

They went through the kitchen, Magda pointing out various pieces of equipment. "We do a lot of entertaining because of the business," she explained. "That's why we hire someone to cook exclusively. The only other live-in help on the place is Pete, the gardener, and he acts as watchman and lives over the garage."

She pushed open a door adjoining the kitchen to reveal a charming boudoir, decorated in fresh shades of green and yellow, with comfortable furniture, a nice stereo set and small TV built into a wall unit, and small-paned French doors opening onto a little terrace.

"This is your suite," she said, smiling at Selina's delighted expression. "The bedroom and bath are through there, and the terrace is your private one. You don't mind being off the kitchen, do you?"

"How could I mind?" Selina was looking through the French doors toward the swimming pool just visible beyond her terrace. "I've never had so much room to myself."

"Have you been training to be a chef very long?" Magda's expression was frankly curious. "I didn't think women could officially be chefs."

"They can these days, especially at the school I

went to," Selina said, laughing. Magda sat in one of the wingback chairs in front of the tiny fireplace, and Selina sank into the other one. "I was a secretary at first. The aunt and uncle who raised me felt a girl should have a marketable skill, and that was the one they chose. But I didn't enjoy it. And I've always liked cooking. My parents operated a little deli with a gourmet-food section before they were killed in a car wreck." She paused for a moment, remembering the time. Looking up, she saw the silent sympathy in Magda's eyes and smiled brightly. "So I saved until I had enough for the academy's tuition. It took six years to get the money to support myself while I took the course, and two more years of training, but I've finally achieved my goal."

"Well, I certainly hope you'll be happy here and stay with us a long time." Magda smoothed the slip-covered back of a small sofa, her brow contracted by a frown. "I don't know if Gil told you about Rita—"

"Don't worry," Selina interjected. "I don't plan to get married or anything. I'm strictly a career girl." Her laugh was breathless as she remembered the assault Gil had unleashed on her emotions. Magda's keen eyes seemed to pierce her defenses.

"That wasn't what I was about to say." The older woman dropped a hand lightly on Selina's shoulder. "Please feel free to have your own social life. As long as it doesn't interfere with your work, you are entitled to do whatever you chose. Although there's usually a dinner party on Saturday evening, we generally have a hefty brunch Sunday morning and then just snack the rest of the day. Rita was off from Sunday noon through Tuesday afternoon. Is that satisfactory?''

It was more than satisfactory, and Selina said so. Moving back to the kitchen, they discussed markets, supplies and help. "Mrs. Murphy hires additional help to wait table and clean up for the large parties. And of course, when you cook for just the family, we enjoy helping with the dishes and cleanup.''

By the time Magda left to change from her gardening clothes, Selina felt her confidence soaring. In spite of wealth and social position, the Duchenays seemed warm and unpretentious. Used to the capricious behavior of San Francisco socialites for whom she'd catered parties, Selina rejoiced at the welcome she'd been given. Magda Duchenay projected an aura of gracious ease. It was impossible not to feel that working for her would be made as pleasant as possible. And Betsy, although she might become a nuisance, certainly seemed cooperative, she reflected. Turning to the sink, Selina began scrubbing the baby beets and carrots that Magda had brought in from the garden and carefully washed tender leaves of lettuce. That left just Gil. She frowned to herself, remembering how easily she'd responded to him. She would have to guard her feelings carefully and do everything she could to quell any future responses. She sighed. He was so attractive and was obviously good at flirting, an art she'd never had much practice in. If he had tried to captivate her, she might have had trouble not losing her heart to him.

She found a well-stocked freezer full of cuts of meat, carefully packaged and dated by the errant

Rita. Quickly she thawed some chicken breasts in the microwave oven.

BY SEVEN O'CLOCK she'd prepared a simple but elegant *suprêmes de volaille à la meunière*. The chicken breasts with their coating of seasoned flour were ready for the final sautéing. Ingredients for peach shortcake were set out at one end of the worktable.

She stopped to change her stained apron for a fresh one. Pausing in front of the little mirror over the sink, she made an impatient sound at the sight of her hair escaping from its confining combs and rioting wildly around her flushed face.

"Don't slick your hair down." Turning as she pushed in a comb, she saw Gil lounging in the kitchen doorway, looking immaculate in well-fitting trousers and a V-neck velour pullover that showed the tanned outlines of his throat.

"Hello. I . . . I didn't expect to see you here," she stammered, groping for something to say. After all her fine reasoning an hour before, it was disconcerting to feel that jolting rush of excitement at the sight of him. He began his lazy survey of her, his eyes traveling warmly over her face and throat, down her apron-clad torso and faded Levi's. His look was almost as physical as a caress, and she turned back to the mirror to escape the feelings it aroused in her.

"I live here, remember?" In the mirror she saw him stroll closer, flicking his glance at the orderly preparations for dinner that were grouped on the worktable. "You didn't have to begin work so soon, Ms. Chef. Tomorrow would have been fine."

"Mrs. Duchenay suggested that, but I don't mind saving Betsy from restaurant food tonight." She made her voice light as she busied herself at the worktable. He watched her in silence for a moment. *Probably,* she thought, suddenly desolate, *he just came to check up on me, make sure I knew what I was doing.*

"Why aren't you wearing your white hat, Chef Selina?"

"I never wear it when I cook at home," she began, then paused in confusion. With a sudden change of mood Gil turned her to face him, his hands urgent on her shoulders.

"And this is your home for the time being, right?" His eyes probed hers with an intensity that left her breathless. "You don't have the feeling it could be your home for the rest of your life?"

Bewildered, Selina shook her head. "I know you want a chef to stay for a while, but be reasonable, Mr. Duchenay! Of course, I plan to honor my commitment to you, but it's not very likely I'd want to spend the rest of my life as a personal chef."

The intensity died out of Gil's eyes. He seemed to realize for the first time that he was gripping her shoulders and removed his hands, leaving her feeling oddly bereft. He wiped a hand over his face, and Selina noticed suddenly how tired he looked. "Sorry if I seemed a little—vehement," he muttered. "I've been working some long hours on a business reorganization, and that plus jet lag seem to have got to me."

Selina looked at him thoughtfully but said nothing. His demeanor had been more than vehement. There had been an uncanny look in his eyes, as if he heard more in her words than she knew she was saying. Stealing a glance at him, she saw him looking at her, his expression one of earnest interest. Then he smiled with a sudden flash of charm that left her weak in the knees.

"Well, why don't you let me carry in something to make amends for my overbearing ways?" His voice was light as he approached her. "Shall I take that tray?"

"Certainly." She almost stammered, pushing the tray of canapés along the worktable surface toward him. For some reason she couldn't face the thought of perhaps accidentally touching his hand. Though his manner was merely friendly, something in his eyes when he looked at her made her heart start racing.

He grasped the tray, but didn't lift it from the table. "You know," he said conversationally, "your eyes are just the color of San Francisco Bay when it's cloudy." He leaned a little closer, and Selina swallowed, willing herself not to tremble. *What is the matter with me,* she thought wildly.

"I think," said Gil with a teasing look, "that it's inappropriate for you to call me Mr. Duchenay when you want me to kiss you."

It was all she could do to force the words through her dry lips. "What—what makes you think I want you to kiss me?"

"Gil," he prompted, moving his face a little closer to hers but not touching her. He didn't need to. The air between them almost crackled with the tension of their words.

"Gil," she murmured hypnotically, wondering if it was just her imagination that made his face seem to loom nearer every moment. His lips, she noticed, were almost classical in their outline, firm but full. She tore her gaze away from them and found herself staring into his eyes, gleaming golden within their darker circle.

"I know you want me to kiss you," he breathed, sending shivers down her back as the little gust of air brushed past her cheek, "because I'm psychic." He moved back a little as if to gauge her reaction to his pronouncement.

Selina blinked several times. "Psychic?" she asked uncertainly.

Gil nodded, the teasing smile back on his lips. "So better watch your thoughts around me, Chef Selina. I'm liable to fill your order before you get around to asking for it."

He picked up the tray and left the room. Selina sank onto her stool, trying to assimilate what had just happened. *He was joking, of course. But he did know I wanted him to kiss me,* she argued with herself. *So what? Just because he can read me like a book, does that make him psychic?*

She was mopping her forehead when Betsy bounded in with a shining clean face. The girl sniffed the air ecstatically. "Boy, whatever it is smells great! When do we eat?"

"Is everyone ready?" Betsy nodded and Selina got up. "Well, it will only take me a few minutes to finish the dinner. But you'll have to show me where the dining room is if I'm to serve it."

Betsy gave her a puzzled look. "Didn't Gil explain? When it's just the family, we always eat buffet-style. I carry in the food, and he clears up afterward."

"Oh, of course." Selina moved to the stove to begin sautéing the chicken.

"You are going to eat with us, aren't you? Mother thought you should."

"I don't think so." Anything to avoid another encounter with Gil, Selina thought. "It's kind of your mother to ask me, but I'd rather stay here and keep an eye on things. I'll have my dinner later."

When Betsy had left, carrying a large tray very carefully, Selina stood for a long moment, gripping the edge of the sink. Gil's perceptiveness hadn't gone quite deep enough. She hadn't just wanted him to kiss her. She had wanted him to embrace her, to light the kind of fire in her body that no one had lighted before, that could only be put out with more fire.

But that idea is not smart, she told herself sternly. It simply wasn't like her to desire a man she'd only met that day. And of course, desire was all it was. There could be no thought of love between the owner of Purity Corporation and his private chef, or at least not the kind of love she had always imagined was necessary before indulging in any intimate relationship.

She resolved to try to avoid Gil. It shouldn't be too difficult since he evidently spent long hours on the job. She intended to do her job well, to perfect as many skills of her trade as she could, and when she felt the time was ripe, to move on. Involvement with Gil would only complicate her timetable.

I intend to be the best chef I can be, she vowed, tossing her head defiantly. *When I've achieved that, I'll let myself fall in love. But not before.*

CHAPTER FOUR

IT WAS FRIDAY, the day of the big dinner party. Glancing at the clock, Selina calculated she had three hours left to complete her menu before it would be time to assemble the food for serving. She went over to the worktable and perched on her stool while she marked some items off the schedule she'd prepared.

Profiteroles in oven. She drew a black line through that entry. Next on the list was preparing the celery hearts to go with the *filet de boeuf*. She got a bunch of celery out of the refrigerator, noticing with pride the evidences of her industry. The shelves bore a large bowl of artichoke bottoms, ready to be turned into *fonds d'artichauts farcis*. The mushroom *duxelles* were ready and waiting in a covered container, and the *filets* were marinating in another one.

Mrs. Murphy came bustling in as Selina began trimming the celery. The housekeeper was a large capable woman, who delighted in the organizational details of running a big household. She enjoyed the dinner parties, she had confided to Selina, because they offered "more scope."

"Have you a copy of the menu, Selina?" Mrs. Murphy consulted her own list, a frown puckering her forehead. "I like to put a copy of it in a little stand on the sideboard in case the guests are interested."

Selina wiped her hands on a towel and opened the drawer in the worktable. "I have the one I made for Mrs. Duchenay," she said pulling out the neat card on which she'd inscribed in her best calligraphy the dishes she had planned to serve at the first big dinner party of her career as private chef. "She didn't seem too interested."

Mrs. Murphy laughed at Selina's rueful expression. "The food isn't that important to her, although she knows it's the main feature of the party. Mrs. Duchenay concerns herself with the flowers and expects us to have everything else right." Mrs. Murphy glanced over the card and nodded approvingly. "Very nice, my dear. You seem to have everything under control. Are you sure you don't want some extra help?"

Selina shook her head. "I'm doing fine," she insisted. "For some reason it seems easier this first time to do it all myself. This is no occasion to break in an unfamiliar helper." A smile lighted her face. "Besides, Betsy's feelings would be hurt. She's appointed herself my chief assistant."

Mrs. Murphy sniffed. "And much better for her than her usual flibbertigibbet ways. She's certainly taken a fancy to you, Selina."

"It's mutual, I assure you." Selina laughed. "I never had a little sister, so it's fun to have Betsy around."

The housekeeper looked over Selina's timetable, bestowed a few words of praise for so much organization and hurried off to supervise table linens and crystal. Selina worked swiftly on the celery hearts, envisioning the beautiful appearance of the *filets* when they were surrounded by the celery, steamed baby carrots and cherry tomatoes.

She was wielding her big knife enthusiastically when a hand gripped her shoulder, almost causing her to hack off her finger instead of a celery frond. She turned to glare up at Gil, who stood behind her. She hadn't seen him since their disturbing encounter on her first day at the Château.

"Don't you ever do that again!" She narrowed her eyes dangerously at the bland look on his face. "This knife is *very* sharp," she said, enunciating carefully as if to a child. "You must never, never startle anyone using a very sharp knife."

He backed away a few steps, holding up the bottles of wine he carried as a shield. "Sorry, Chef Selina. I just wanted to consult you about the wine."

Her hands flew to her mouth. The wine! In the excitement of planning the menu, she'd forgotten all about wines to be served with each course.

"Don't tell me you forgot! No chef on her way up the ladder can ignore the palate!" But Gil dropped his teasing tone at the stricken expression on Selina's face.

She tried to dismiss it as a momentary lapse. But her perfectionist nature wouldn't allow her to. She already felt shaky about her knowledge of wine. Now she was forgetting about it altogether! How could she be first-rate if she ignored such an important part of her art?

"Everybody makes mistakes," Gil said in a reasonable tone, putting an arm lightly around her shoulders. "Don't take it so much to heart."

She shrugged his arm away, rejecting the comfort he offered. "You don't understand," she said, disturbed anew by letting Gil see feelings she would have been glad to conceal.

Gil's hands closed on her shoulders again, and he turned her to face him, his expression puzzled. "Look, forget it. It's really the host's responsibility to provide the wine, and I don't mind in the least parading my expertise before my guests."

For a moment she hesitated, wondering at the sparks of electricity that seemed to crackle in the air whenever he touched her. Looking into his eyes, she could see he was affected, too. His expression grew intent; his face came closer, and Selina knew he was going to kiss her. The thought made her panic. If he kissed her, it would mean there was something between them, and she couldn't handle it. What if it turned out badly? What if it complicated her plans for her career?

She wrenched away from the hands that were warm on her shoulders and lashed out, seeking any words that would bring more distance between herself and the man whose effect on her was so uncontrollable.

"I hope you know more about wine than about food." Her fear gave her voice a cutting edge that moved Gil an involuntary step back. "Otherwise, whatever you've selected will hardly go with the meal I've prepared."

He narrowed his eyes. She saw the glint of anger in them but was unable to stop herself.

"I hope you like the menu," she went on when he remained silent. "Of course, I can hardly expect you to know how good food tastes after eating what Purity Corporation puts out. Maybe if you had more appreciation for quality food preparation, you wouldn't be having trouble at work."

She stopped, aghast, hand pressed to her mouth. Gil's face was like an angry mask, white dents on either side of his nose showing how hard it was for him to control his temper. "How did you figure that out?" he asked, his voice hissing through clenched teeth. "By listening at doors?"

"I didn't—Betsy said," Selina stammered. It was true that she didn't really know Gil was in trouble with his board. But Magda had made a couple of vague comments about the reasons for their increase in entertaining, and Betsy, who'd picked up a garbled version the way youngsters often do, had dramatically informed Selina the previous afternoon that if Gil didn't do something drastic soon, they might be forced to beg their dinner in the streets. Selina had put no credence in Betsy's story, but somehow the implication that Gil's job was on the line had found its way into her unprovoked little speech.

Now that she needed it, her audacity deserted her. But she made herself face him unflinchingly. "I shouldn't have said that," she said stiffly.

"That's right," Gil agreed, his voice dangerously smooth. "You were hired to cook, not to pass judgment on business matters that are out of your ken.

Kindly remember that in the future, Chef Montgomery.''

Miserably Selina inclined her head. Now there would be enmity between them. It would keep him from using his dangerous charms on her, but it was a far cry from the cool businesslike relationship she had envisaged. She found that she craved his friendship and respect when it seemed she had thrown both away forever.

They were interrupted by Betsy, who bounded into the room carrying a basket full of silver serving dishes. She wore the apron Selina had given her with an important air.

''Mrs. Murphy asked me to bring these in and make sure they were ready to use,'' she said, plopping the basket down on the table and picking a strawberry out of the containers that sat there. ''Are we on schedule so far?''

''Everything's moving along just fine.'' Selina was surprised that her voice came out normally. She still felt shaky from the series of emotions she'd gone through since Gil entered the room.

Betsy subjected her brother to a critical stare. ''What are you doing standing around like a statue, Gil? Don't you know we have work to do in here?''

He slapped her hand lightly as she reached for another strawberry. ''Your work seems to be sampling the food—just try to leave some for our guests, all right?'' He looked at Selina expressionlessly. ''I'm working, too—acting the part of *sommelier* for the party.''

Picking up the wine bottles, he presented them to

Selina. "For the first course, I thought a Pouilly Fumé. Then to accompany the *filets*, a Cabernet Sauvignon—California wine, as a compliment to Hal MacMillan. For dessert, an old French Sauterne laid down by my grandfather. Does my lack of expertise show?"

His voice deliberately taunted her. Selina had to swallow before she could reply.

"Perfect choices." The Sauterne bottle was encrusted with dust, and she reached out absently to trace the crest engraved on the neck. "How do you come to know so much about wine?"

"My grandfather and father were both wine buffs. Between them they accumulated quite a cellar. I learned more or less by osmosis. Too bad you're not interested in wine, or I would be glad to show you the cellar someday."

Selina turned away with no heart for the hurting game they'd evidently initiated between each other. Betsy began clamoring for another errand, and Gil took his bottles and sauntered away. Pushing their encounter out of her mind with difficulty, Selina charged into the unfinished tasks that had to be done before dinner.

BY SEVEN O'CLOCK everything was finished that could be done ahead, and the preparations were completed for last-minute items. Selina sent Betsy off to dress, since the girl was expected to dine with the others.

"This will be more fun than usual, even if the relatives are coming," Betsy said, snitching one of the *profiteroles* she'd been helping fill with pastry cream.

"It's a family party?" Selina polished the base of a footed silver platter with a towel before beginning a construction of *profiteroles* and strawberries that would tower over the sideboard like an exotic pyramid.

"Oh, no, it's some kind of business, I think. Mr. MacMillan and the other people have something to do with hotels—I don't know what exactly. But mama went and invited Aunt Charlotte and Hailey and some other regular people, too."

Silently Selina applauded Magda Duchenay. Although she could be very vague about her household, she was a good hostess who took pains with arranging the table and keeping conversation rolling at parties, according to Mrs. Murphy. Evidently Magda thought a table full of hoteliers might be a little claustrophobic without the leaven of "regular people."

"I usually don't like dinner parties," Betsy went on when she'd swallowed the last bite of her pastry. "Everyone's so old and dull. But this time I helped cook the food, so it will be neat to see how people like it."

"Just don't jump down their throats if they don't." Selina grinned and pushed her young assistant out the door. "Scoot now."

She collapsed on her stool, tenderly massaging one aching instep. Magda came in, clipping on her earrings and glancing around.

"It smells wonderful," she said, smiling at Selina. "I'm sure you've done a great job, my dear. I just wanted to warn you that one of our guests is from

San Francisco—Mr. MacMillan. He fancies himself a noted gourmand and likes to come back and congratulate the chef after a meal he enjoys. So be ready for an invasion. Has Mrs. Murphy found you someone to clean up? I don't want you to have to wash dishes after all you've done.''

Selina felt exhilarated to know that a San Francisco epicure would pass judgment on her meal. Although the menu she had planned was very traditional, with few of the daring touches found in the Bay Area's most innovative restaurants, she was confident her work would win accolades from anyone interested in food.

Realizing that Magda's question went unanswered, she nodded. ''I understand I'll have two cleanup helpers, starting in half an hour or so. I was afraid they'd get in my way if they came any earlier.'' She smiled at Magda. ''Besides, Betsy's been helping. I hope you don't mind that she was playing scullery maid.''

''Heavens, no!'' Magda put one arm around Selina's slender shoulders and gave her a warm hug. ''I just hope she was really helping and not hindering you. It's good of you to let her be your 'shoes chef,' as she calls it. Rita didn't like youngsters in the kitchen.''

''She's a real help,'' Selina said firmly. ''And I enjoy her company.''

''Bless you, child.'' Magda gave one more look around, the keenness of her eyes belying her vague air. ''Everything looks fine. Wish us luck. The MacMillan deal could be very important to Gil, and so far Hal is holding out.''

The door swung shut behind her, leaving her scent hanging in the air. Selina clutched her curls, hoping desperately that everything would turn out. After her *faux pas* earlier, she would feel to blame if Hal MacMillan should have indigestion and decide not to do business with Purity Corporation.

Selina's helpers arrived, and things got hectic in the kitchen. Course after course was assembled, carried out by the two hired waiters and brought back demolished with reports of high praise. She found a moment to slip into her bathroom and bathe her overheated face, combing her hair back severely and donning a fresh tall white hat. But the heat and excitement in the kitchen brought little tendrils of red gold around her face in no time.

After the few remaining *profiteroles* were brought back to the kitchen, she heard the subdued murmur of people approaching through the hallway. Quickly she marshaled the waiters and helpers into a line, hiding the unwashed dessert plates, and took her place in front of them.

The swinging door flew open, and a portly form advanced across the kitchen floor. "Where is this magnificent chef of yours, Duchenay?" Mr. MacMillan's voice was as large as his girth. He stared in amazement at Selina, whose tall hat added enough inches to her height to bring her up to his chin. "Don't tell me all that wonderful food was cooked by this wisp of a girl."

"I do tell you that." Gil's voice was terse as he met Selina's eyes for a moment, his own holding a stern expression. Clinging to his arm was a buxom young girl, who looked barely out of her teens. She was pretty, with a small-featured face and curly brown hair.

"This is my cousin, Hailey Drumm," Gil said, introducing her to Selina. He added dryly, "She's been in raptures over the food all evening."

"Now don't make me sound stupid, Gil." Hailey giggled and held up a hand in warning. "And don't say I can do that without your help. It wouldn't be gallant!"

Their easy banter was interrupted by Mr. MacMillan, who surged over to Selina. "Where did you learn to cook like that, young lady?" He pumped Selina's hand up and down enthusiastically.

"At—at the California Culinary Academy in San Francisco," Selina stammered. She found Hal MacMillan overwhelming. He was a large handsome man in his late fifties, who exuded an air of ingenuous friendliness that was at odds with the shrewd expression in his eyes. Releasing Selina's hand after a tingling handshake, he draped an arm around Magda's shoulders, smiling down at her with fondness.

"Well, Magda, with cooking like that around, I may finally see you put on a pound or two to spare." His voice was gently teasing, and Selina noted the warmth in Magda's expression as she laughingly replied.

"We're lucky to get Selina on such short notice," she mentioned. "She was the top graduate in her class."

Hal MacMillan raised his eyebrows. "I've eaten at the academy's dining room several times—quite impressive. You're a very talented young lady." He turned to Gil with a broad smile. "If I thought Purity could serve up the kind of food your Chef Montgomery puts out, I'd sign on the dotted line tomorrow." He sighed, shaking his head. "Mass production just can't compete with the kind of labor-intensive preparation a chef does."

Inwardly Selina winced. It was more or less what she'd said to Gil earlier, but in his present mood this would probably only serve to make him angrier with her, since she'd unwittingly shown up the defects in Purity's product. She stole a quick look at him. For a moment she glimpsed an expression of sudden inspiration—she could almost see the wheels going around. Then Hailey spoke, and a social mask came down over his face, shutting out all signs of private cogitation.

"It sounds so exciting!" Hailey pushed closer to Selina. "I'd love to become a chef. As you can probably see, I enjoy good food without the proper moderation!"

"Nonsense." A new voice spoke from behind Hailey, and an older woman pushed her way through the crowd. Politely Gil introduced her.

"My aunt—actually stepaunt, if such a relationship exists. Mrs. Charlotte Drumm, Miss Montgomery, our new chef."

"My daughter exaggerates," Mrs. Drumm pronounced. She was taller than her daughter, but her figure showed none of Hailey's admitted indulgence. In fact, she held herself so stiffly that Selina wondered if a human body actually existed under the expensive clothes and immaculate hair. She gave the impression of being so rigidly groomed and manicured that nature had long since ceased to have anything to do with her. Her face, with its perfect mask of makeup, looked sharp and predatory beside her daughter's rosy laughing countenance.

"It was certainly good cooking," Mrs. Drumm continued in her perfectly modulated voice. "But one always expects perfection from dear Gilmartin." She laid one skinny hand on Gil's arm as she spoke, giving him a smile of saccharine intensity.

Selina felt her own smile grow stiff. In the few seconds that Mrs. Drumm had looked at her, it had been obvious that hostility was her only feeling toward the new chef. Magda's warmth and unpretentiousness had ill prepared Selina to encounter immediate dislike in other members of the family.

A slim laughing young man wiggled past Mrs. Drumm to bow low before Selina. He was goodlooking in a rakish way, with wavy brown hair and blue eyes. She was reminded of Andy and had difficulty keeping her face from mirroring her desire to flee this crowd of well-wishers.

"Chef Montgomery." The young man took her hand and pressed a reverent kiss on it. "I'm Ricky Carson, friend of the family, and I bow before your exquisite food. If you're not married, will you be mine? I will give you anything if you'll only cook an occasional feast for the gods like we had tonight."

"Really, Ricky!" Magda laughed along with everyone else but removed him firmly from his position before Selina. "You mustn't entice our new chef away before we've had time to experience all her specialties.''

Selina smiled politely, but her head began to throb. So many strange faces on top of an exhausting day gave her the sensation of being swept along uncontrollably into a situation she could not handle. She raised one hand to push the curls away from her face, and Magda spoke quickly.

"Well, let's not keep the kitchen crew chatting all evening. Would anyone care for more coffee? Charlotte?''

"Exquisite!'' Hal MacMillan's voice rose above the murmur of assent from the other guests, and he kissed his fingertips in Selina's direction. "I'm looking forward to the next occasion, dear lady.''

Selina murmured something, she couldn't tell what. The faces began to swim in front of her in a blur. Suddenly she felt she could sleep for a week.

The company filed out, talking quietly among themselves. Behind her, Selina heard the hired waiters begin to stack plates. She had turned back to the work of cleaning up when she noticed that Hailey was still there, peeping around the door with a conspiratorial look on her face.

"Psst! Selina!'' Hailey slid back into the kitchen and smiled confidingly. "I hope you don't mind if I snatch a few words with you. I just wanted to say—well, I've been thinking of starting a dessert-catering business—making desserts for some of the small restaurants. Do you think you could advise me about costs and things?''

Selina warmed to the younger girl's look of admiring confidence. "Certainly, if you like," she said. "I'm off Sunday afternoon. Why don't you come by, and we'll talk about it."

"Great!" Hailey bounced toward the door, then turned back. "But whatever you do, don't tell mother!" she warned. "I simply have to make some money to get out from under her thumb, but she'd squash this idea faster than she'd squash a slug! See you Sunday."

Hailey left before Selina could protest that if her mother didn't approve the plan, perhaps she'd better not get involved. *Oh, well,* she told herself, *I can talk about it with her Sunday.*

Mrs. Murphy entered with her usual brisk tread. "Well, that went off very nicely," she said, sending a comprehensive glance around the untidy kitchen. "Now, Selina, why don't you just leave the cleanup to us and relax for a bit. You've done your part very creditably."

Selina allowed herself to be guided toward her suite. She sank into one of the wing chairs by the little fireplace and stared at the empty hearth.

It had been a busy day and a hectic introduction to what lay ahead. But as she stretched her arms above her head, she reveled in the thought of work to come. Her treacherous mind brought up the unfortunate episode with Gil, and she winced again as she realized that her regrettable temper had got the better of her once more. It would be hard now to get back on a friendly footing with him, but perhaps it was for the best.

Hal MacMillan's praise had been stimulating. For

the next dinner, she thought sleepily, she would try something more unique—something that could make full use of the excellent produce Magda coaxed from her kitchen garden. And next time she would not forget to schedule wines. She really needed to tour the Château's wine cellar to find out what resources were available in-house, as it were. Somehow Gil's knowledge of wine seemed to add a different facet to his personality. She wouldn't expect a man who thought airplane food was good to have a distinguished palate. Perhaps she could find some way to interest him in food, too. Maybe by the time she was ready to go to France for advanced schooling. . . .

Lost in the agreeable picture of Gil on his knees, pleading with her not to desert him for the Cordon Bleu, she was startled to find she had dozed off in the comfortable chair. With a huge yawn she pulled herself up and headed for the bathroom. Tomorrow she would be busy replenishing her supplies and updating her journal on the success of the dinner. Time to get some sleep.

CHAPTER FIVE

BETSY BOUNCED INTO THE KITCHEN on Sunday morning just as Selina finished making a big pitcher of fresh orange juice.

"Aunt Charlotte and Hailey are coming to brunch today," she announced, inspecting a bowl of melon balls that sat on the worktable and popping one into her mouth. "We saw them at church," she continued with difficulty around the mouthful, "and they just invited themselves over."

Selina nodded absently, her mind checking through the menu to be sure she hadn't forgotten anything. "Eggs Benedict, chicken livers, melon and strawberries, pastries, juice, coffee and tea," she murmured, placing the pitcher of juice on a tray and adding two more glasses for the unexpected guests. "You can carry this out if you want, Betsy."

"Well, it ruins *everything*," Betsy declared dramatically. "You and I were going to go to the zoo this afternoon, and Aunt Charlotte will stick around forever, gabbling away about her stupid garden and boring everyone. It's simply horrible!"

Selina turned away from the refrigerator to frown at her young helper. "I am not interested in hearing you talk that way about your relatives, Betsy," she said firmly. "I doubt your aunt will notice if you leave after brunch. We can still go to the zoo after you've done your duty by your guests. Perhaps Hailey will want to go, too."

Betsy scowled, but before she could say anything, Hailey herself pushed open the kitchen's swinging door. "Yoo-hoo!" she called, smiling as she spied Selina at the worktable. "Something smells awfully yummy out here. Do you mind if I watch you finish up? Perhaps I can help."

Selina did mind, not wanting a distracting audience. But Hailey's questions and comments were generally keen and to the point. The girl had obviously read about food preparation and seemed well informed.

She turned from watching Selina sculpt a melon to greet Gil as he sauntered through the door. "Hope you don't mind if I hang around in your kitchen, Gil. Selina does everything so well, I know I can learn a lot from her."

Gil leaned against the worktable and gave Selina a slow considering look that made the hair prickle along the back of her neck. She stared back at him with a mutinous expression. She hadn't seen him since the dinner party, keeping herself out of the way in the kitchen or exploring the local markets. It was absurd, she had decided, to feel guilty about snapping at a man so obviously able to take care of himself as Gilmartin Duchenay. But nonetheless, she couldn't help regretting her temper and made new resolves to try to get it under control. The feeling that she ought to apologize more completely for her caustic remarks warred in her head with the feeling that he deserved what he'd got. The effect had been to keep him prominent in her thoughts. But she wasn't about to allow him to see her confused emotions—not if she could help it.

"So, Selina does everything well?" he murmured indifferently. She refused to meet his eyes, concentrating on her task. Gil reached out a lazy arm and took a melon ball, contriving somehow to brush her palm in the process. She felt his fingers pause on the soft swell of flesh he had called the Mount of Venus, and an involuntary shiver of delight flowed through her veins. Infuriated at her instant response, she turned abruptly away.

"There are too many spectators in the kitchen," she said clearing her throat. "Hailey, could you take in the melon? Perhaps one of you would take the coffee urn." She hesitated to name Gil, shying away from the intimacy of saying his name but unwilling to reduce him to a coldly formal "Mr. Duchenay."

The door swung shut behind Hailey and Betsy. Thinking Gil had gone with them, Selina collapsed against a counter, wiping her forehead with a towel and feeling suddenly exhausted.

"My sentiments exactly." She whirled as Gil's voice, lazy and mocking, sounded behind her. He lounged by the coffeepot, looking superficially relaxed in his tan cords and open-necked shirt. But she sensed the tension within him as he confronted her, and immediately her instincts drew her taut.

There was silence between them for a few minutes. She could feel him studying her, taking in the wide-spaced eyes, the short nose with its sprinkling of freckles, the generous vulnerable mouth. Then his gaze moved lower, lingering on the round fullness of her breasts as they strained against her severe white apron. "Why do you wear that thing, anyway?" he asked, his voice husky.

"So I can wipe my hands on it instead of my jeans," Selina said, her own breathing erratic despite her efforts to control it. She shook her head slightly, trying to bring him into focus. "I think they're waiting for the coffee in the dining room."

"Do you?" Although the words they spoke were idle, they dropped into the charged silence of the kitchen like atomic particles. Selina could hardly breathe; she grasped the counter edge behind her for support. Gil moved slowly toward her as if he moved through deep water. Numbly she waited for him to reach her, to hold her closely so that the weakness in her legs would no longer matter.

Then the swinging door hissed again, and Charlotte Drumm's decisive tones bit through the air.

"Well, Gilmartin. I didn't expect to find you here. Men don't really belong in a kitchen, do they?" Her small eyes, curiously alive in the mask of maquillage, darted from Gil to Selina. She wore an affable smile that seemed no more real than the silk gardenia pinned to the jacket of her elegant suit.

"What a chauvinistic statement, aunt." Gil picked up the coffee urn and placed it on a heavy silver tray. As he turned away, the tension lessened palpably. Selina drew a deep breath, uncertain whether to be relieved or disappointed that they had been interrupted. Their encounters were so electrifying that she was afraid to have one go any further for fear she would be plunged into a physical confrontation she was not prepared for.

Gil, however, seemed to suffer no lingering effects. The teasing smile returned as he glanced at Selina. "After all," he said smoothly, "everyone knows all the great chefs are men."

An undignified snort of laughter escaped her before she could hold it back. "So far," she retorted, then bit her lip. The playful banter had put them back on a friendly footing, but she wasn't sure that was a good idea. She felt somehow that with Gil, being friendly might not be enough. And any greater intimacy was just what she was trying to avoid. She picked up one of the large frying pans and used unnecessary vigor to turn the sautéed chicken livers it contained into the glass liner of a silver chafing dish. Some of the livers spilled onto the counter. She muttered an imprecation, pushing them hastily aside. Betsy came in as Gil passed through the door with the coffeepot, and Selina gestured peremptorily to her helper to carry out the chicken livers, but Charlotte Drumm showed no signs of leaving. Realizing she was a relative, Selina stopped short of ordering her out of the kitchen.

She was conscious of the older woman's eyes on her as she assembled ingredients for hollandaise sauce. The silence began to grow heavy, as portentous as it was with Gil, but with none of the exciting overtones.

As she lifted a pan of poached eggs, Mrs. Drumm

spoke, startling her so that she almost dropped it. "My daughter tells me you are quite a chef." There was a condescending note in her voice that caused Selina to stiffen, but she made her voice noncommittal.

"Kind of her." She took up a slotted spoon and carefully fished out an egg, blotting it with paper towels and depositing it on top of an English muffin-ham combination.

"Of course, good cooks run in my family," Mrs. Drumm said, a touch of complacency in her voice. "But if it doesn't come naturally, I suppose you could learn how to cook at school."

Selina nodded, her mind on the poached eggs. Mrs. Drumm talked on, rambling, as far as Selina could tell, about the Duchenay family. Selina's attention didn't sharpen until the older woman mentioned gypsies. "Not a really good family, the Gilmartins, if the story is true," she was saying with disapproval. "I never really thought James should marry her, although, of course, one doesn't believe that nonsense about the gypsy blood."

"Umm," Selina said absently. Then she looked up from the last of the poached eggs. "Gypsy blood?"

"Probably just one of Magda's stories." Mrs. Drumm sniffed. "But of course, the Gilmartins are an old St. Louis family. Almost as old as the Duchenays." She smoothed her smart sculptured gray hair and regarded Selina fixedly.

Selina pretended to be unaware of the older woman's gimlet stare, but it made her uncomfortable. She wished she could get rid of Mrs. Drumm as easily as she had Betsy. But the soigné figure perched incongruously on her work stool would obviously not take kindly to being asked to carry something into the dining room.

Whisking egg yokes and clarified butter together, Selina managed to tune out Mrs. Drumm's voice. But as she poured sauce over the assembled eggs Benedict, the meaning of her visitor's chatter became clear.

"...and it would be so suitable," Mrs. Drumm was saying. "His money, her family connections, you know. The Drumms are related to everybody who's anybody in St. Louis, and of course, my own mother was married to Gil's father's brother after my father died. He was a Congressman, you know." She paused with a self-approving sniff. "And naturally Hailey's simply crazy about him—and he's quite fond of her, too. We're all expecting an announcement any day now."

"Announcement of what?" Selina tried to sort out the bewildering pronouns.

"Of Gilmartin's engagement to Hailey, of course." Mrs. Drumm looked at her sharply. "Perhaps you'll get to cater the reception—making food for all the first people of the area. What a boost for your career!"

Selina returned the other woman's look, her eyes growing greener. "All that is in the future," she said levelly. "Right now, I need to serve these eggs to some hungry people. I don't really have time to chat."

"You're certainly touchy." Mrs. Drumm moved

stiffly off the stool. "I simply thought it would be a kindness to drop a little hint into your ear—nothing personal, of course—"

"Little hint? I'm afraid I don't understand." Gripping the saucepan of hollandaise, Selina turned to face Mrs. Drumm. All this talk about forthcoming weddings was getting on her nerves.

"I suppose all redheads lose their tempers easily." Mrs. Drumm's voice was disapproving. "I could see that you were playing up to dear Gilmartin, and heaven knows he's popular with all kinds of women—so handsome and so very *wealthy*—" she eyed Selina with meaning. "So I thought it my duty to tell you—"

The swinging door whooshed open, and Gil strode in, followed by Betsy. "When do we eat?" Betsy asked plaintively. "I'm starved! What are you doing here, Aunt Charlotte?"

Gil looked from Selina's flushed face and stormy eyes to Charlotte Drumm's smug countenance.

"You all seem to find the kitchen so attractive," she said. "I see no reason why I should not, as well. So nice chatting with you, Miss—I mean Chef Montgomery." Gathering up her gloves and handbag, Mrs. Drumm sailed from the room.

Selina finished pouring the hollandaise with steady hands despite the angry beating of her pulse. So Gil's stepaunt thought she was nothing more than a gold digger? She banged the empty saucepan viciously into the sink.

"You don't seem very amused by Aunt Charlotte's 'chat,'" Gil said, standing by to take the dish of eggs. "The family name for her is Auntie Duty because she's always coming up and telling you some grim thing she thinks it's her duty to let you know. You should feel flattered if she's taken you under her wing."

"Huh!" Betsy snorted inelegantly, diving for a tray set out with Selina's carefully made Danish pastries. "I remember the time you got so mad when she wanted you to take Hailey to that debutante ball, and you told her to go to hell, and she had one of her spasms—"

"Enough, scamp!" Gil opened the door and gestured Betsy to take the tray and go. "No use letting all the skeletons out of the closet at once." He picked up the dish of eggs and regarded Selina soberly. "If she said anything to hurt you, please just ignore it. Nobody comes out unscathed from an encounter with Aunt Charlotte, but I wouldn't want it to upset you."

"Gracious!" Selina laughed, hoping it didn't sound too threadbare. "What a song and dance because your aunt wants to have a chat with the cook! Is that so unheard of?" Knowing from Gil's expression what the answer to that was, she made hurried shooing motions with her hands. "Now get those eggs out of here while they're still warm."

But after he left, she sank onto a stool, depression overcoming her. It was degrading to have anyone accuse her of scheming to snare a man. Mrs. Drumm obviously figured that Gil's money and social position would be attractive to someone who had to—heaven forbid—cook for a living.

Selina didn't set much store by the outmoded notion of social stratifications. Gil's wealth and prestige were burdens and not advantages in her mind. Having been raised in the belief that work is important, she couldn't imagine wanting to live a life of idle luxury.

But Gil himself—that was something different. For a moment she allowed herself to see him as a possible lover. The thought was electrifying. He was certainly handsome enough for anyone, she thought wryly. She knew he had a sense of humor, one that matched her own ready appreciation of the ridiculous. But more important was his steadiness, his dependability, the aura he projected of hard work and success. Selina admitted she admired Gil for managing his business so well, for meeting his responsibilities to his family.

In fact, she realized suddenly, if it weren't for his uncomfortable ability to know what she was thinking before she knew herself, he would be too perfect. She shivered, thinking of the way he had aroused her by just brushing his fingers over her hand. She had never felt such intensity of emotion from Andy's touch.

Mrs. Drumm had deliberately implied that Gil had known many women. And Selina had no doubt that he was as successful in love as in business. That he was still unmarried seemed to indicate that he was discerning in his choice of a lifelong mate. She put little credence in Mrs. Drumm's gossip about Hailey and Gil. There had been no sign of more than family feeling between them.

Even so, there can be no question of marriage for us, she sighed, her shoulders drooping. What Charlotte Drumm had said was partially true. Gil had a position to maintain. He would doubtless wish his wife to be more at home in the drawing room than in the kitchen. And she had no desire to give up her absorbing, rewarding work for a meaningless social round.

But he certainly seemed to want something from her. The question was, she admitted with painful honesty, how much would she surrender when it eventually came to the crunch. The electricity that happened between them whenever they met might easily explode into mutual passion. But she didn't want to be left as a badly burned victim of the explosion.

Her head dropped to her arms, which rested on the worktable. The longing that filled her was not just for the release of passion. *You're fooling yourself,* she thought harshly. Such comfort could be dearly bought at the expense of her independence, her need to wrest a good living with nothing but her own two hands. She shook her head in determination. Gil could not be allowed to disrupt her careful long-term plans. But an affair—surely that wouldn't be too dangerous?

A temporary affair would have seemed distasteful before. But now she was horrified to realize that even the briefest liaison was too tempting to resist.

At least when it ends, I'll have something truly wonderful to remember, she reflected wryly. Then she had to laugh—worrying over the end of an affair that hadn't even started yet! *And it won't start if I can help it,* she resolved suddenly. There was no percentage in even thinking of falling in love with Gilmartin Duchenay. All it would earn her was heartache, and that was something she could do without.

She sat up briskly and walked purposefully to the sink. With a renewed energy she began to scrub dirty pots and pans. Mrs. Murphy had promised her a part-time assistant for cleanup, but so far no one had materialized. The sound of running water masked the kitchen door opening. But Hailey's voice made her turn from the sink.

"You shouldn't have to wash dishes after that kind of cooking," Hailey exclaimed. She set down the stack of plates she carried and pushed Selina gently away. "Let me do it—better yet, let Gil do it! The great food exec needs to learn how the humble people live."

"I'll have you know, Miss Drumm, that I have my own apron here." Gil, entering behind Hailey, took an apron off the hook in the broom closet and solemnly tied it around his waist. "Not only that, but I have achieved so much skill with the pot scrubber that I've been voted number-one dishwasher in the family." He dipped a big sponge in the soapy water and waved it threateningly. "Scoot, ladies. My assistant, Miss Betsy, and I will make these dirty dishes vanish before your very eyes."

Betsy, who had innocently followed Gil into the kitchen, donned her own apron with reluctant hands. "I don't want to wash dishes! Selina and I are going to the zoo."

Gil paid no attention to this poor-spirited talk. Before she quite realized it, Selina was relaxing on her terrace while the faint swish of the dishwasher blended into the song of the tree leaves in the wind.

Sun poured down on the lemon-colored canvas of the sling chairs and the lemon-and-white-striped umbrella over the little iron table. The moist shimmering heat seemed laden with the scents of freshly cut grass and sweet spicy honeysuckle.

"Selina," Hailey said, sounding eager. "Do you mind if we talk? About starting my own business, I mean."

Selina opened her eyes and squinted against the sun. Hailey was perched on the edge of a sling chair, her hands clasped tightly in her lap. "I'll be glad to listen," Selina told her, "but I'm not sure how much help I can be."

"Well," Hailey began. "I desperately need to get started on a career. But mother is so gothic! She exists in the old days, when girls were debutantes and sat around waiting for Mr. White Knight."

This didn't sound as though Hailey planned to marry Gil. Selina sat up and listened with more interest.

"I love food," Hailey said with a deprecating glance down at her plump figure, "as I guess you can tell by looking. I know I could make a go of some limited catering—desserts to start with, for the smaller restaurants that want terrific desserts but don't really have the resources to turn them out. I love to bake," she added with pride. "And I have some wonderful family recipes for cakes and things."

Selina nodded. "It sounds reasonable," she admitted. "Why aren't you doing it? Lack of capital?"

"Actually, no." Hailey looked away for a moment. "I've managed to save just enough money to get me started. The problem is mother! If she knew I even contemplated doing this, she'd find some way to stop me." Her face darkened with resentment. "And I'm tired of her always telling me what to do! I'm old enough to manage my own life now!"

"That's understandable." Selina frowned. "Can't you just be—firm with her? Explain to her as you did to me what you want to do and why?"

Hailey shook her head with finality. "You don't know mother," she said glumly. "Really, it has to be this way. Can I count on you?"

"I don't know quite what you want from me," Selina told her. "My work here is full-time, and if I were going to work on the side, I'd have to consult Mrs. Duchenay. She hired me, so she'd have to know."

"Oh, I don't want you to work with me." Hailey leaned forward earnestly. "But I know I'll need advice—help with transposing my recipes into larger amounts, finding suppliers and figuring out how much of everything to order—technical things like that. I just want to know that I can come to you, not interrupting or anything, and ask questions."

Selina hesitated and Hailey pressed on. "It would be all right with Magda and Gil, I know it would," she said, clasping her hands again. "But mother absolutely mustn't know. Will you do it?"

If Hailey had asked before Mrs. Drumm's performance in the kitchen, Selina might have said no. It wasn't right to help someone deceive a parent. But Mrs. Drumm deserved no special consideration. Hailey was to be commended for her desire to start a business, not deterred.

"I'll give you all the help I can as long as it doesn't conflict with my main responsibility," she promised. "Where are you going to work?"

"Thank you, thank you!" Hailey jumped up from her chair and gave Selina an impulsive hug. "I knew you were swell when I first saw you!" Then she seemed to recall that she was now a sober business-woman. "I've rented a little hole in the wall in Maplewood," she said, referring to a nearby suburb. "It has one of those metal-sink units, and I'm dicker-ing with a restaurant that's going out of business for a stove. I still have to get some equipment, but I won't need much to start with. When I make some money, I'll get a big mixer and all those other trap-pings of success."

Selina responded to the younger girl's friendly grin. Hailey was as cuddly and roly-poly as a cute lit-tle puppy, but she had a level head on her shoulders. "If you don't mind explaining to Magda," Selina suggested diffidently, "I know there are a few boxes of pots and pans and dishes stored over the garage that no one seems to know what to do with. Perhaps she'll give them to you."

"Sell them to me, you mean," Hailey corrected. "Everything's strictly business. I can't wait to get started!"

Betsy came running onto the terrace, her face

eager, her mind intent on the zoo. "Gil's coming, too," she shouted. "Let's go, Selina!"

Mrs. Drumm, followed by Magda, emerged in time to hear Betsy's words. "A family outing," she said smoothly, giving Selina a hostile glare. "How nice. Hailey and I would love to come."

Selina was too relaxed to respond to such basic maneuvering. "I doubt if there'll be room for me in the car," she mumbled sleepily. "I'll just stay here and soak up some sun, maybe swim a bit." She caught a flicker of annoyance on Gil's face, but the expression was gone before she could be sure it had been there.

She smiled and waved as the Duchenays and their guests piled into the car and eventually departed. Turning back to the house, she experienced a welcome feeling of freedom and privacy. The family was nice—for the most part, she thought, remembering Aunt Charlotte—but she wasn't used to being around people so intensively. In San Francisco she could shut the door of her room or go for a walk in Huntington Park and be sure no one would disturb her. Here, Betsy was always popping in and out, or Mrs. Murphy, or Magda with a basket of vegetables.

She was determined that she would take advantage of her two days off until Tuesday and not just hang around cooking meals. Perhaps she should do a little recipe research and check out some suppliers. Magda had mentioned that she was welcome to use one of the family cars when she wanted. And in the evenings the hill in back of the Château would make an ideal place to get in some stargazing. She would miss the monthly meetings of her astronomy club back home.

The return to the house led her past the swimming pool. The water looked cool and refreshing, and for one wild moment Selina was tempted to strip off her clothes and skinny dip. There were no neighboring houses in sight, but she resisted the idea, making her way to her bedroom where she slipped into her suit. Looking critically at herself in the mirror, she decided that perhaps she should get a new swim suit. Hers was old, since there wasn't much opportunity to swim in San Francisco, where the ocean was cold all year around. The straps were a little frayed, and the color had faded from its original sea green to a paler shade that wasn't particularly becoming. The plunging neckline had no bra, and her nipples pushed gently against the elastic fabric. It might be a good idea to get a suit that was less—provocative, she mused, noticing the way this one molded her softly rounded hips and buttocks. After slathering her sensitive skin with sun block, she picked up a towel and headed for the pool.

She swam lazily for a while, back and forth in the silky water, then climbed out and after another application of lotion, stretched out on a lounge chair. She didn't want to fry her skin, and if she was careful, she would get enough protective tan to keep from turning red at the slightest exposure. Eyes closed against the sun's glare, she drowsed, listening to the hum of bees in the nearby herb garden. She was almost asleep when she heard footsteps crunching on the gravel path from the house.

Squinting, she sat up and swiveled around. A

young man who looked vaguely familiar was walking toward her with a jaunty step. Where had she seen him?

"Hello!" he called, rapidly closing the distance between them. "Remember me? Ricky Carson, Gil's friend. I stopped by to see him, but no one seems to be home at the house."

"They've gone to the zoo," Selina told him, feeling slightly at a disadvantage with her hair in wet spirals around her face and her swimsuit still damp.

Ricky raised his eyebrows. "Leaving you here all alone? Good thing I came along to entertain you." His grin was impudent, and she stiffened, not being in the mood for raillery.

"Don't feel obligated to do that, Mr. Carson," she replied, her voice level. "I'm not in need of entertainment. I was really thinking about taking a nap."

"Don't let me stop you," he replied promptly with a devilish grin. "In fact, I could join you. Who knows what we might cook up together, Chef Selina?"

His sheer effrontery took her breath away for a moment. Then she threw back her head and laughed. "Do you always proposition women you barely know?" she asked when she could find the breath to speak.

Her laughter didn't seem to discompose Ricky at all. "Usually," he admitted, smiling. "And I usually strike out, as I'm evidently going to do with you. But nothing ventured, nothing gained, I always say."

Selina shook her head in wonder. "You are indeed going to strike out," she said firmly. "I'm definitely not interested in your offer. Thanks, anyway."

"All right." He looked wistful. "I did want to captivate you with my carefree charm. I thought perhaps you might try to find the way to my heart through my stomach. Perhaps you could throw a few scraps my way even if you're not interested in my excellent body."

Selina dissolved into helpless laughter. "Certainly," she sputtered. "Just lurk around the kitchen door some night, and I'll toss something out to you."

"Thanks!" Ricky looked down at her with a smile, then suddenly leaned down and gave her a light kiss on the lips. "Let me know when you want to get more serious. I'm always willing!"

Selina pushed him away with a smiling rebuke. "Don't bother holding your breath. I'm not in the market for any romance. Better luck with the next woman you see."

The kitchen door banged before Ricky could reply. Gil appeared on the gravel path that led from the house. His face was tight with some emotion Selina couldn't identify. "What are you doing here, Ricardo?"

Ricky looked surprised. "You told me to drop by this afternoon, and we'd discuss the coaching schedule." He glanced at Selina. "Gil and I have a baseball team of kids from the city, and the season starts next week."

Gil passed a hand over his forehead. "You're right," he muttered. "Well, I'll call you tomorrow." His tone was clearly dismissive. Ricky shrugged and turned away.

"Okay. Talk to you later. Nice speaking to you, Selina. Don't forget about those scraps."

Selina smiled and watched him walk toward the drive. When she reclined again in her chair, she was startled to find Gil standing right next to it, more or less looming over her. "Back from the zoo already?" For some reason her voice didn't sound like hers—it was breathy, and she had a hard time forcing the words through her throat.

"I dropped everyone else off and came back for a while." Gil's eyes bored into her until she wanted to squirm in her chair. Only an effort of will held her still. "Why did Carson kiss you?" he demanded suddenly.

"Did he?" Selina blinked, trying to remember. Ricky's kiss had been so lighthearted it had made no impression on her at all. "He was just being silly, I guess," she added, infuriated with herself because she was starting to stammer. "He seems to think flattery will get him anywhere."

"And did it?" There was an implacable note in Gil's voice that unnerved Selina.

"Of course not!" She stared up at him, puzzled. "Why would I be interested in him?"

Gil relaxed a little and sat down on the end of her lounge chair. "Lots of women are." He offered no other explanation for his inquisition. Selina felt her hackles rise at his high-handed manner.

"You sound like a dorm mother," she grumbled. He watched her without replying, capturing her eyes for a moment with his compelling gaze. Immediately her heart began to step up its rhythm. *Help,* she thought, starting to swing her feet to the ground and escape into her suite. But Gil put his hand on her knee, and she froze, unable to shake off the disturbing contact.

"Aren't you going to ask me why I came back?" His voice was husky, his eyes seeming to hypnotize her. Mutely she shook her head.

"I left them all there so no one can interrupt us. I came back because I wanted to talk to you alone."

Selina's mouth went dry. The note of intimacy in his voice sent sensuous shivers through her. Waves of delicious weakness spread from her knee, where his hand still rested, up through her loins, giving her a feeling of voluptuous pleasure. Gil's eyes dropped to the top of her swimsuit in a look as caressing as a touch. Under his gaze her nipples grew taut. His hand on her knee shifted until it was softly stroking the flesh of her inner thigh.

"You excite me, you know." Except for that velvety note of desire, his voice was even, almost conversational. "Everything about you makes me want you—your eyes, your mouth, your hair—I want to touch you and kiss you and make love to you. I want to hear that you love me." The hand that was stroking her thigh moved along the curve of her hip and briefly cupped one breast. Selina shuddered and collapsed limply against the back of the lounge chair. She opened her eyes again as Gil's finger touched her lips, tracing their outline.

"What do you think about that, Selina?" His voice was warmly coaxing. "Would you like me to kiss you? When I kiss you, you'll remember it. And you'll want more—just as I want more of you. Do you want to take that chance?''

She looked at him, confused by the passion that clouded her mind. "I don't—take chances..." she gasped, unable to force her brain to think.

He moved nearer. "Don't bother trying to fight it," he murmured, his words reaching her through a desirous haze. "It's predestined, you know. I knew when I looked at your palm on the airplane that we were going to be—close. Very close.''

Selina licked lips that had suddenly gone dry. "How—close?" she whispered, unable to tear her gaze from the mesmeric force of his eyes.

In reply his lips came down on hers, tasting gently, their softness disarming to her wildly throbbing heart. His hand stroked her neck slowly, coming to rest on the pulse point. He moved his lips against hers with infinite care, causing her heartbeat to skip. She heard his low chuckle, and then he pulled back, bringing both hands up to cup her face.

"Well?" he said challengingly. "I've told you how I feel. What do you say, my sweet Selina?" This time when he brought his mouth to hers, the kiss was more insistent, as his tongue licked gently along her lower lip, coaxing her mouth to open. Lost in the sweet melting sensations he created, she let her lips part. In one swift movement he brought his body over hers, the hard masculine length of him lying half on top of her in the sturdy lawn chair. One hand ran along her bare shoulder, making her aware as she had never been before of the smooth feminine softness of her flesh. His teeth nibbled seductively on her full lower lip, then his tongue flicked into her mouth, sending a flash of heat coursing through her.

His hand moved down her arm, bringing her own hand up to his chest. "I don't want to play alone," he growled softly into her ear. "I've got more clothes on than you. Do you think that's fair?"

Without volition Selina began undoing the buttons of his shirt. She slipped her hand inside, probing delicately across his firmly muscled chest, feeling the smooth planes and the tracery of rough hair around the flat nipples. He made a noise deep in his throat as she touched one nipple hesitantly. She had never realized that she could caress a man like this....

The thought sent a shock wave through her. What was she doing? Hadn't she resolved to maintain a cool business relationship with the man whose lips were right now brushing fire across her cheekbones? She sat up suddenly, sending Gil sprawling on the lawn beside the lounge chair.

"No!" she cried, straightening the bathing suit straps that had been pushed off her shoulders. "It won't work!" She looked wildly down at Gil, his shirt unbuttoned to the waist by her own hands. His molten eyes were narrowed as they fastened on her face. "I don't—you can't make me do this!" Selina cried. "Can you?" Her eyes wavered and dropped before the consuming flame that burned in his.

Gil's voice was ragged when he spoke. "I won't have to," he said, pushing dark hair off his forehead with an unsteady hand. "You'll see. I'll be here when you're ready."

He got to his feet, brushed off the elegant slacks he

wore, took a deep breath and seemed prepared to
stroll casually back to the house. Selina gaped at him.
A moment ago he'd been all fire and heat. Now he
was cool as one of Magda's cucumbers.

"I don't understand you!" she cried to his retreating back. He stopped and turned to look at her.
"You—first you say—you tell me—and then you just
walk away! What—how—"

A smile twisted his lips at her incoherent utter-
ances. His voice was understanding. "Fight it all you
want to, Ms. Chef," he said gently. "But what I say
is true." He reached out and pinched her chin lightly.
"I am psychic, you know," he told her, his eyes teasing. "I may have to take a cold shower now, but
sooner or later you'll come to my bed."

He strode toward the house, leaving her gaping
after him. She shook her head in bewilderment.
"He's wrong," she said forcefully to the vacant air.
"He'll find out that I don't come crawling to any
man's bed." She watched Gil as he disappeared into
the kitchen without a backward look. With some desperation she insisted to herself, *He's got to be wrong!*

CHAPTER SIX

SELINA FLED. She took one of the bicycles she found parked in the spacious garage after checking with Pete, the gardener, that it would be all right. And she pedaled grimly about the woodsy roads and bridle paths until she was sure everyone was back from the zoo.

The exercise did nothing to clear her mind. She could think only of Gil's hands on her skin, his mouth on hers; such thoughts made her feel all over again that sweet flood of desire he'd produced so effortlessly. When she realized she was wishing he hadn't taken no for an answer, she stopped pedaling and flung herself on the grassy side of the road.

Staring up at the limitless blue of the sky, absently tracking the path of several portly clouds, she gave up chasing the problem around and emptied her mind, relaxing. When the sun began to edge toward the horizon, she sat up, suddenly feeling better. She had panicked for a good reason. It wasn't too intelligent to get involved romantically with an employer, especially when he was as rich and handsome as Gilmarten Duchenay. Mounting the bike and moving as fast as her tired legs would let her, Selina started back. She sighed as she turned into the

Château's drive. It really was a good thing she was too much of a professional to get involved with Gil. Otherwise she might find herself administering to his vanity by fulfilling his prediction that she would soon come to him....

She parked her bicycle back in the garage, took a quick shower and consulted Pete again.

"Let's see," he drawled, squinting at the row of automobiles that filled the front half of the building. He was a short wiry man of middle age, his skin weathered by the elements, his movements deliberate. "The missus needs the Mercedes tonight, and Mr. Gil don't let nobody else drive his 'Vette. Will that Audi do you?" He pointed to the medium-sized sedan, its metallic green paint gleaming in the twilight.

Selina nodded impatiently. "Anything that has an engine," she said, glancing over her shoulder in spite of herself. "I—have some errands to do."

"On Sunday night?" Pete's skepticism was mild. "I think there's some maps in the glove compartment," he added, handing her a set of keys. "She's all filled up and ready to go. Have a good time, now." This was said with a broad grin and a wink. Puzzled for a moment, Selina realized he thought she was going to meet a man. She grinned back at him before backing carefully out of the garage.

She drove aimlessly for a while, then pulled over and got out a map of St. Louis County, peering at it in the car's dome light. She noticed a planetarium listed among the notable spots of the area and located it on the map. It wasn't too far away; she could drive there in ten minutes. Surely in the summer a planetarium would be open in the evening. She needed the soothing company of the stars. Their predictable behavior provided such a contrast to their human counterparts.

MONDAY EVENING HAILEY CAME BY with her recipes, apologizing profusely for encroaching on Selina's time off. Selina welcomed her appearance. She had spent the day driving around, locating suppliers, talking to bakers, meat packers and so forth. She was tired but restless, and Hailey's task just suited her mood.

"It's been a long time since I did this sort of thing," she murmured, taking the list of ingredients and wrinkling her brow as she studied them. "Let me get my calculator."

They were sitting at the worktable, heads together over Selina's notebook, when the door swung open and Gil came in.

Not expecting him, Selina didn't look up at first. But something electric in the atmosphere warned her that the person at the door wasn't Betsy in search of an after-dinner snack. She raised her head slowly, her gray green eyes widening as she met the passionate intensity of Gil's gaze.

He held her eyes for a moment, then smiled slowly, his expression full of sensuous promise. Selina swallowed nervously. She knew Gil realized the effect he was having on her, and that irritating thought steadied her a little.

Hailey's effusive greeting filled the tension-charged silence. "Selina and I are working on my project—you know," she bubbled to Gil. "I didn't realize cooking involved so many calculations."

Gil raised unbelieving eyebrows as he strolled closer to the table. He was still dressed in his well-tailored tan business suit, the jacket slung over his shoulder, tie loosened and shirt unbuttoned. The fit of the satin-backed vest accented his slim waist and broad shoulders, hinting at the supple strength of his body. Reluctantly Selina tore her eyes away from a survey of his torso and saw an amused gleam in his eyes that indicated he knew just what she'd been looking at. Blushing fiercely, she shoved her stool back from the worktable and jumped up. "I'll get the scales and some flour," she mumbled, fleeing to the pantry. She took a few deep breaths before bringing the big jar of pastry flour to the worktable.

Gil was studying their calculations. "Looks like a chemistry experiment," he said as Selina set up the scales on the table.

She slanted a glance at him. He looked tired, she realized suddenly. He must have just come from work. "Cooking is just chemistry on a more domestic level," she agreed.

He moved closer, till she could feel the heat from his body. "I'm all for chemistry," he murmured, his words for her ears only. She froze for a moment, feeling the now familiar waves of desire spread through her body. He put his hand casually on the small of her back as he leaned over the table to study her notebook. With effort she kept her breathing steady, although she knew she was betrayed by the trembling she couldn't suppress.

Hailey didn't notice the byplay. She was busy measuring a pound of flour, writing down the number of cups it contained and knitting her brows over the result. "So if one cake has half a pound of flour—let's see—"

Selina shook off the torpor of her body. "I think you should change your recipe a little, Hailey," she commented. "The cakes with the finest texture use very little flour. Ground hazelnuts or walnuts bind the mixture without adding weight."

Gil moved away to rummage in the refrigerator. "Hope you don't mind if I eat," he said over his shoulder. "I'm starved—didn't get time for much lunch today."

Selina looked up from her figures. "Would you—shall I make you some dinner?"

He flapped a dismissive hand toward her, his head deep in the refrigerator. "Nonsense." His voice was muffled. "You're off tonight, in case you didn't remember. I'm capable of fixing myself a meal, even if you have a low opinion of my abilities."

Selina began an indignant protest but was distracted by a question from Hailey. She bent her attention to figuring out proportions of all the ingredients in Hailey's recipe for chocolate-velvet cake, which she said came from her grandmother. "There," she announced after a few minutes. "Now all we have to do is multiply. How many cake pans will your oven hold at one time?"

She glanced up to see Gil adding the final layer to a

Dagwood sandwich of incredible size. Fascinated, she couldn't tear her eyes away as he mashed down the top slice of homemade bread and managed to cram the unsteady structure into his mouth. He caught her gaze as he chewed lustily and winked.

"Ten," Hailey said.

"Huh?" Selina brought her mind back to the problem at hand. There was something so endearing, so "little boy," about Gil sometimes, she could almost forgive his lamentable taste in food. "Ten cake pans? Five cakes, in other words. So we'll just get the proportions for five. You shouldn't mix it in too large a batch, anyway."

In another half hour they'd hammered out the final recipe, with Selina giving Hailey tips on mixing, buying ingredients in bulk and other minutiae of professional baking. "And be sure to try the recipe with just one cake the first time," she cautioned.

"Of course." Hailey leaned back and stretched, massaging her hand and shaking it out to relieve the writer's cramp from copying the recipe over. "If I do the same thing to my other recipes, will they come out right?"

Selina stretched, too, noticing that Gil was listening intently to their conversation. "It's really a process of experimentation," she told Hailey, wondering why Gil was feigning such interest in a subject like food. "You just have to try until you get it right. I'll be glad to help you—on my days off, of course." She glanced at Gil.

He made an impatient gesture. "As far as I'm concerned, you can help Hailey anytime you want. I'm sure you'll discharge your obligation to mother faithfully. If you have spare time in the evenings and want to squander it on my silly little cousin—'' he sent a ferocious glare toward Hailey, which reduced her to helpless giggles ''—you're welcome to.''

''In that case, let's try out the chocolate-velvet recipe now. Next time you come over, we can pick a different recipe, and meanwhile at least you'll have the chocolate recipe to work from.'' Selina jumped up and moved briskly around the kitchen, turning on the oven, rummaging in the refrigerator for ingredients. Gil made no move to leave, merely stretching his legs out in front of him and looking on with a sardonic smile as he finished his sandwich. She tried to pay no attention to him, but it was hard to concentrate knowing he watched her with those lambent amber eyes.

Hailey mixed the cake, and it was duly deposited in the oven. Selina set the timer, and they regrouped around the worktable. Gil regarded her curiously.

''It really is a complicated business, isn't it?'' he murmured, more to himself than to her. ''I always figured cooking was cut-and-dried—so much of this, so much of that. But it's almost—intuitive, the way you do it.''

Selina burst out laughing. ''You don't need to say 'intuitive' as if it's a dirty word,'' she teased. ''Cooking really is cut-and-dried in the final analysis, but getting there is where the intuition—and training—comes from. The best recipe in the world can taste flat and boring if made from indifferent ingredients. And the best ingredients can be spoiled by improper technique.''

Gil's face was thoughtful. Hailey laughingly challenged him to tell them what caused his brown study. He flashed his crooked teasing smile at Selina and said, "I'm afraid to tell. Ms. Chef will jump down my throat."

"I promise." Selina held up her hand solemnly. "I swear on Julia Child's apron, I'll be as sweet as pie."

"Well..." Gil hesitated for a moment. "I wondered if you could let me lick the bowl," he said at last. She knew it wasn't what he wanted to say, but she didn't press him. They were getting along so well this evening, almost as if he'd been a good friend— like the men she'd studied with at the Culinary Academy. Then his knee found hers under the table, and she realized with a stab of excitement it was nothing like her former friendships, not even with Andy. No one else in her life had been able to ignite her with so little effort as Gilmarten Duchenay.

Hailey handed him the cake bowl, declaring virtuously that she was on a diet. Then she giggled disarmingly. "Actually I'll have to taste the cake when it comes out," she admitted. "I don't know how I'm going to keep from looking like a balloon when I begin catering in earnest." She looked enviously at Selina's slim figure. "How do you keep so slender when you're around delicious things all day?"

Selina shrugged, moving away from the gentle persistent pressure of Gil's thigh against hers. "After a while the novelty wears off," she told Hailey. "I got to the point when we were learning pastry, where if I'd seen one more bowl of whipped cream, I would have been sick. Sometimes after concocting a huge banquet of elegant dishes, all I want to eat is some fresh sourdough bread and a little good cheese.''

Gil laughed. "Confessions of a gourmet chef," he declared. Under cover of the table his hand found her thigh and began to trace feathery patterns on her leg. With all her heart Selina wished for the willpower to move away, but she could only sit, mesmerized by her own desire, while his hand continued to seduce her. She closed her eyes and took a deep breath, trying desperately to make her brain function. Somewhere in the room someone was speaking, but it was hard for the voice to penetrate the sensuous fog that surrounded her.

Slowly she came back to reality. The voice was Hailey's. ". . . okay if I use yours? It's closer than the one in the front of the house.''

"Sure. Okay," Selina muttered vaguely. Then she realized that Hailey was going to leave her alone in the kitchen with Gil, who had made it obvious he could reduce her to jelly in .05 seconds. "Wait!" she cried. "I'll go with you!"

She jumped off her stool and followed Hailey into her apartment, torn between relief at managing her escape and regret. She had no doubt that if she'd stayed, Gil would have subjected her to more of those blazing kisses that had occupied her dreams last night. *If only he were anyone else,* she thought, staring absently at her reflection in the bathroom mirror as Hailey chattered. *If he weren't my boss and so rich, I could just fall into his arms and never think twice about it.*

But she knew that wasn't true. Her hunger for stability in love would hamper her, no matter how ardent the lover. With Andy she'd realized on one level that he couldn't offer love that would never grow cold. With Gil, it seemed, love was out of the question entirely. She must call a halt to his gentle subversive seduction, no matter how badly her senses cried out for his caresses.

But when they returned to the kitchen, there was no need for her newly stiffened backbone. Gil wasn't there. He arrived back on the scene promptly as the timer went off, however, emerging into the kitchen from a small Gothic-shaped door in one shadowy corner that Selina had never noticed before. She straightened from removing a cake pan and stared at it in fascination.

"Where does that lead? Frankenstein's laboratory?"

He laughed easily. "You could say that, I suppose. It goes to the wine cellar. I've been checking the latest batch." He inhaled deeply. "That smells fabulous. When will it be ready to eat?"

Hailey slapped his hand away from the cake pan she set on a rack. "Not till it's cooled and frosted, so just abide in patience, Gilmartin Duchenay."

"Batch of what?" Selina broke in curiously. "Are you making wine down there?"

He glanced at her in amusement. "No. I brew beer—very fine beer," he added as Hailey snorted in derision. "My beer is famed throughout the greater St. Louis area as being very—"

"Frothy," Hailey broke in. With a laugh she dodged Gil's playful punch. "Actually it's not bad,"

Hailey admitted, "if you like beer." She wrinkled her nose distastefully. "It all tastes like dishwater to me."

"In that case, I suppose you won't want to help bottle it Friday night?" Gil's hand hovered over the bowl of frosting Hailey was beating. He stuck his finger in and licked the frosting off it with evident relish, deaf to her protests.

"Gil! It's so unsanitary!" Hailey shot a scandalized look at Selina.

"The chefs at school were always doing it," Selina said, laughing. She nipped up a fingerful of the frosting, too. "Superb," she exclaimed, affecting an exaggerated French accent and rolling her eyes in ecstacy. "Zis frosting is—how you say—*magnifique*, mamsell."

"Can we bottle in here, Selina?" Gil draped his arm around her shoulders in a gesture that probably looked casual to Hailey but sent an immediate electric message to all of Selina's nerve endings. She concentrated so hard on keeping her knees from sagging weakly under her that she forgot to answer. Gil gave her shoulders a gentle shake, and she leaned heavily on the work table.

"Sure. I guess so. What does it involve? I've never bottled beer before," she said, feeling the words bubble out of her mouth in an effort to distract Gil. He was circling her shoulder with rhythmic strokes of his strong fingers. She wanted to close her eyes and fall into his arms. Summoning her common sense, she straightened and moved out from under his arm, around the table, and sank gratefully onto her high-legged stool.

Gil pulled out another stool and sat across from her, his eyes lighted with amusement. "It means siphoning the beer out of its fermentation container and into lots of bottles," he said. "As you can imagine, it gets messy sometimes."

"And it's hard work," Hailey put in. She began frosting the cake with careful strokes. "All the bottles have to be washed, and filled, and capped, and put into the cases and lugged back downstairs. That's why Gil always rounds up as many victims as he can to help him."

"Well, are you going to pitch in or not?" Gil examined his fingernails with a show of unconcern. "Ricardo's coming to lend a hand," he said, shooting a look at his stepcousin from under his brows.

Selina saw the faint blush creep up Hailey's cheekbones. "Oh, I wouldn't think of letting Selina try to cope alone," she said airily. With elaborate care she smoothed on the last swirl of frosting. Selina hid a smile. It seemed that Hailey was attracted to the insouciant Ricky Carson. She caught Gil's eye, and they exchanged warm knowing smiles. To keep the silence from having too much significance, Selina jumped up and took the empty frosting bowl over the sink.

"It sounds very interesting," she said truthfully. "I'll be eager to see if your beer can compare to Anchor Steam beer. That's what we drink in San Francisco," she added kindly.

Gil threw her an exasperated look. "I *know* that," he growled. "I've even been known to bring back a few cases of Anchor Steam after a business trip." He shook his head. "It doesn't travel well," he said sadly. "Lots of things that are perfectly good in California act spoiled when they get out of state."

Selina couldn't help but respond to the teasing smile that lurked in his amber eyes. "It's just that the rest of the country doesn't have the right climate," she began, then grinned. "Actually I can't say that even in jest. I'm really enjoying this hot steamy weather."

Gil stretched his legs out under the table. Perhaps it was accidental that his feet tangled with hers. She stared across at him, her eyes unguarded as they met his. Suddenly the kitchen seemed blurred, a kaleidoscopic background against which Gil's face stood out sharply. Every detail of his expression, the finely arched eyebrow, the clean lines of nose and lips, seemed suddenly, indelibly, engraved in her mind. The urge to kiss him, to have him hold and caress her, struggled with her overpowering impulse to run.

She realized she had jumped to her feet. Hailey stared at her, her plump face distressed. "Gil didn't mean to slam California, Selina," she murmured. "He just has a smart mouth sometimes." She threw her stepcousin a reproachful glance.

"Of course," Selina said, pressing her hand to her forehead. "I don't know—I have a little headache." Not looking at Gil, she went to the sink for a glass of water. She stood there for a moment, oblivious to both Hailey's concerned stare and Gil's scrutiny. For a flash of a second she had seen, like a vision, herself and Gil together in a passionate embrace. Gil's face had been tender, triumphant, unbelieving, exultant.

The vision had shaken her to the core. The thought of bringing that look to any man's face was extraordinarily heady.

Then the door was flung wide, and Betsy came in with her usual exuberant gait. "I smell chocolate!" she exclaimed. She saw the cake and approached it reverently. "Chocolate cake! I'll get the milk."

Selina recovered her composure as Magda followed Betsy into the room. They sat around the worktable, eating Hailey's chocolate-velvet cake and drinking milk, discussing the bottling scheduled for Friday evening. Betsy offered to run the bottles through the dishwasher if Gil brought in the cartons.

"I'm afraid it's all going to get in Selina's way," Magda said, pressing the back of her fork into the cake crumbs on her plate, a thoughtful frown creasing her brow. She smiled suddenly, glancing at Gil. "Remember what happened the last time you bottled beer?"

Gil nodded, a mischievous expression making him look not much older than Betsy. "That was funny, wasn't it? Let's see, it was—not Martha—"

"Charlene, I think." Magda smiled ruefully at Selina. "We really do seem to have gone through an amazing number of cooks. Probably a sinister sign. Charlene quit because she came home from her night off—"

"She dated a drummer in a rock band!" Betsy interjected, her voice filled with awe.

"—and found the kitchen floor awash with beer and broken glass because Gil had knocked over a case."

"She didn't like beer, either," Gil said solemnly, frowning at Hailey. "And look what happened to her. Probably married to some rock 'n' roll drummer who mistakes her for the snare drum when he has a nightmare."

Hailey tossed her head. "Beer is fattening," she stated. "I don't need one more fattening thing in my life. But I'll help bottle even so. I think it's fun."

"You don't need to help, Selina, if you'd rather be elsewhere," Magda assured her.

"I'd rather not come back to find what Charlene found," Selina said darkly. Betsy's face fell.

"You will help, won't you, Selina? It really is lots of fun."

"Sure," Selina promised. "If for no other reason than to keep my kitchen intact." Involuntarily her eyes sought Gil's, then moved quickly away, disturbed at the expression she saw there. Why did he always have to look so *hungry* around her?

Magda invited Hailey over for dinner, with an aside to Selina—"if that's all right with you, my dear? Don't fix anything elaborate—just something simple. I understand Ricky Carson's going to be here, too."

"Pizza!" Betsy exclaimed.

"It won't bother Charlotte if you come, will it?" Magda looked guiltily at the empty cake plate and then at Hailey. "Oh, dear, we ought to have saved some of your cake for her."

Hailey shuddered. "Not a chance," she declared. "Mother might smell a rat if I took her a piece of cake. And she positively purrs when I come over here, Aunt Magda." She glanced at Gil and batted her eyelashes flirtatiously. "She'll just think Gil can't bear to have me out of his sight," she said, affecting a mock-Southern drawl.

Everyone laughed, but Selina felt a cold clutch at her heart. What if it were true? What if the easy give-and-take between Gil and Hailey were to blossom into something deeper? *Feeling this way about anyone is risky,* she thought, panic-stricken again. This warm family unit seemed suddenly exclusive, incapable of being penetrated. Her smile faltered.

"What is it, Selina? Your headache back again?" There was no missing the solicitude in Gil's voice. Selina saw Magda glance sharply at him.

"Yes," she said untruthfully, needing the solitude of her room. "I think I'll turn in. I have a lot to do tomorrow." She stacked the plates and lifted them, but Gil took them out of her hands.

"We'll clean up here," he said masterfully. "You run along. Can't have you going off your form—Ricardo is looking forward to dinner Friday night." He gave her a gentle push toward the door of her sitting room.

"All right." Selina turned at the door to say goodnight. Hailey sang out a cheerful farewell while using her finger to pick up leftover crumbs from the cake plate. Magda gave Selina a noncommittal smile. *She knows,* Selina thought miserably. *It must be written all over my face.* Gil said nothing, just giving her a long heart-stopping look as he put plates in the dishwasher. His gaze tangible as a kiss, lingered on her mouth. Selina bolted into her sitting room to spend another night in restless desirous dreams.

FRIDAY MORNING she woke late, having spent the evening discussing the next big dinner party with Magda. A glance at the clock sent her scurrying for the shower. She wasn't obliged to cook breakfast for the family, but she liked to be available in case anyone had a sudden desire for waffles or blintzes. In her haste she fumbled with the zipper of her jeans, caught it in her T-shirt and finally made it into the kitchen at 8:20.

Pete, the gardener, was setting down a dusty cardboard carton next to several others as she came into the room. From a large stone crock near the sink, a rich yeasty aroma permeated the room. Selina went to take the cover off the crock, but Pete stopped her.

"Mr. Gil says you mustn't disturb the brew 'less it's necessary," he told her. He pushed at the cardboard carton with his toe, aligning it against the wall with the others. "Mighty tasty brew he whomps up, too." He smacked his lips in anticipation. "Always gives me a case to take up over the garage."

"Are you coming to help with the bottling, Pete?" Selina moved to the refrigerator for a glass of juice.

"Wrestling's on tonight." Pete sounded shocked at her ignorance. "But I'll help him lug them bottles back down tomorrow." He left with a backward admonition not to "drink up all that brew before it's bottled!"

Selina laughed dutifully and concocted a bowl of fruit and yogurt for her breakfast. The presence of neatly rinsed bowls and cups in the dishwasher indicated that everyone else had already eaten. Thinking about Betsy, she flipped through her notebook looking for the pizza-dough recipe. She made a list, got her account book and set out to do the day's marketing with a light step. In spite of all her reservations, she could feel rising anticipation at the prospect of being with Gil that evening.

By midafternoon the yeasty smell of the beer was drowned by the rich aroma of simmering tomato sauce. Magda sniffed appreciatively as she brought in a basket of vegetables.

"Does this mean you're really making pizza?" Selina nodded, looking up from the dough she kneaded on the worktable. "Betsy will be ecstatic."

"Is it all right?" Selina paused, pushing her hair out of the way with the back of one floury hand. She glanced approvingly at the lettuce and cherry tomatoes in Magda's basket. "With green salad and fresh fruit for dessert I thought it would be sufficiently festive."

Magda smiled. "It sounds wonderful," she said. She settled on one of the high stools and watched in silence for a moment as Selina worked. "How's Hailey's business coming?" Magda asked casually. It seemed everyone in the family except Mrs. Drumm knew about it. Selina didn't mean to speak her thought aloud, but somehow it came out. "It's hard to believe Mrs. Drumm doesn't know about Hailey's plans."

"Ah, yes, Charlotte." Magda folded her hands together and regarded them for a moment, frowning. "I never know whether to refer to her as my stepsister-in-law or as James's stepsister, or what,'' she commented. ''You might have noticed that everyone seems to—rather tiptoe around her.'' She met Selina's eyes, a rueful smile in her own. ''The truth is, Charlotte has a very uncertain temper and is subject to the most alarming kind of—well, 'tantrum' is really the only word that describes it. Like cowards we all do our best to avoid being on the receiving end of Charlotte's anger. I don't usually like to talk about this sort of thing, but you will be seeing her, and you should know why we don't just tell her what's going on.''

Selina laughed. ''She sounds quite lethal. But don't worry, Mrs. Duchenay, I won't spill the beans.''

''My dear,'' the other woman smiled, getting up from the table, ''don't you think you should call me Magda?''

Selina smiled back, feeling unaccountable tears prick behind her eyelids at Magda's warm expression. ''Thanks, Magda.'' She turned away to hide her emotion, making quite a business of washing the flour off her hands.

''Why don't we all just eat out here tonight. Would that be too much trouble?'' Magda's voice was briskly practical. ''Then we wouldn't have to traipse back and forth to the dining room.'' Selina agreed, and after a bit of discussion about the next dinner party Magda left. Finishing up the pizza dough, Selina smiled with satisfaction. It was heartwarming to feel that she'd put down a few roots of friendship at the Château. Knowing Magda liked her seemed to make everything easier.

RICKY CARSON was the first of the bottle-party guests to arrive. He breezed through the back door and stood expectantly as he sniffed the air. "Ah, the intriguing aromas! Let me see if I can tell what we're having." He sniffed again. "Something Italian, certainly. Linguine with clams? *Rigatoni milanese*?"

Laughing, Selina opened the oven door to give him a peek at the pizzas, their colorful surfaces already beginning to bubble. "Tonight," she said teasingly, "you eat with the peasants. Pizza is what we're having."

Betsy, who'd been hovering around the oven since Selina had popped the pizza in, told Ricky gravely, "These are very special pizzas. Only the finest ingredients went into them."

"Betsy should know," Selina nodded. "She did most of the toppings."

Hailey came in with Magda, and they helped clear the big worktable, loading the dishwasher and spreading a cloth. In the midst of the bustle Gil arrived, still in his business suit and carrying his attaché case. He hurried to change when Magda told him they were almost ready to eat, and soon all six of them were assembled on either side of the worktable, drinking the remaining bottles of Gil's last batch of beer and eagerly biting into the hot spicy crispness of Selina's pizza.

After dinner Betsy and Hailey loaded the dishwasher while Gil and Ricky, their faces intent, carefully lifted the large crock of beer onto the worktable and lined up the shining rows of bottles.

"I get to cap!" Betsy cried, brandishing a strange machine that looked to Selina like a large perpendicular stapler. She rooted in one of the cabinets until she found a bag of bottle caps and rattled them with childish pleasure. "When I was young," she confided to Selina. "I thought they were play money."

Gil began deploying his forces. "All right, Ricardo," he instructed. "You fill the bottles. Hailey can move them on to Betsy for capping. I'll manage the siphon." He glanced at Selina and handed her a big sponge, his eyes twinkling. "You be on standby for spills, okay?"

She saluted smartly, clasping her sponge to her chest. "Yes, sir!"

Laughing, Magda left them to it. Gil inserted one end of a long clear plastic tube into the vat of beer. He sucked lustily on the other end, and the tube filled with amber liquid. Ricky took the free end from him and began filling bottles with it. As they were filled, Hailey took them, wiped off the top and handed them to Betsy, who placed them under the capper, put a cap on top and pulled down on a handle, which squeezed the cap onto the bottle. Selina watched in fascination until Ricky overturned a bottle.

"Sponge!" he bellowed, going on to the next bottle. Hastily Selina wiped up as best she could around the constantly moving bodies. Betsy and Hailey worked as fast as they could, but Ricky filled the bottles more quickly than they could process them. The tempo intensified until Hailey knocked over a full bottle.

"Enough!" She took the sponge from Selina and tried to sop up all the spilled beer. "We've got to catch up here."

Gil pinched off the siphon and smiled at Selina. "Goes like a well-oiled machine, wouldn't you say?"

At his words the sense of lighthearted well-being that had filled her all evening spilled over into uncontrollable merriment. "Not exactly," she managed to say between fits of laughter.

The frenzied activity continued in high gear until everyone was exhausted from laughing so much, and Gil's crock became empty.

"Well, that's that." Wiping out the crock with paper towels, Gil breathed a sigh of relief. "Mind if I leave it here, Selina? I've got to mix up a new batch tomorrow."

Selina assured him the crock would be out of her way in a corner of the kitchen. She glanced at the clock and began to shoo Betsy out of the room. "Mercy! Look at the time, Betsy Duchenay. Your mother won't like you staying up so late in a beer hall."

"Same here." Hailey nodded regretfully. "I should be getting back. Mother will think Gil's compromised my virtue."

"Don't walk out to your car alone, Hailey," Gil said warningly. "Pete told me today there were some shady-looking characters hanging around." He glanced at Ricky. "Could you walk her to her car, Ricardo?"

"My pleasure," Ricky said promptly, sweeping a low bow toward Hailey. "Come, my dear. Little does

your cousin know, I was one of those shady characters.'' He twirled an imaginary mustache and leered
at Hailey.

"Oh, boy," she laughed. "I'm in luck." Selena
winked at her and turned back to push the stools in
at the table. The kitchen seemed suddenly quiet
with just the two of them. Nervously she moved
to the door, looking out at the blackness of the
night.

"No moon," Gil said softly behind her. He clicked
off the lights, making the landscape outside seem
more luminous. Selina opened the screen door and
stepped outside, sensing him following her.

"You can see stars better with no moon," she
whispered. Above them the sky arched, filled with
the glittering pinpoints of light. "There's Arcturus."
She pointed it out. "And Altair and Mars—"

"Name dropper." Gil was standing just behind
her. She could feel the warmth of his body. His
breath stirred her hair. He put his arm around her
waist and moved her forward. "There's a good place
for stargazing over there."

He led her past the swimming pool into the
meadow behind the house. A small hill covered with
smooth grass was the observatory. She sat down at a
little distance from him. Despite the clearness of the
night she felt wrapped in a haze of enchantment,
where every movement, every word, had been or-
dained since the beginning of time.

Settling his long length beside her, Gil propped
himself up on an elbow and pointed. "I know the Big
Bear and the Little Bear, and that's about it," he

said, his voice quiet in the warm night air. "Where is this addle brain you're talking about?"

She smiled. "Altair. Down on the horizon, in the constellation Aquila." She pointed it out, tracing the constellation with her finger. Gil put his head close to hers to see where she pointed.

"Ah. The very bright star," he breathed in her ear. "Are there other bright stars out tonight?"

His lips began nibbling at her earlobe, their velvety softness making her shiver with pleasure. She swallowed uncertainly.

"There's—Vega." She raised her arm to indicate the star, and his hand slipped under it, capturing her breast. He pushed gently to lay her down at his side, one arm behind her head. She looked up at him in the starry darkness, her eyes wide.

"Don't worry." His voice was low and hoarse with suppressed emotion. "I'm not going to do anything you don't want, Selina." He buried his face in her hair, and with wonder she felt him tremble as he drew a ragged breath. "Tell me some more about the stars."

Her voice was unsteady. "At—at this time of year the Corona Borealis is—very prominent," she began. His hand stroked gently down her throat to her breast. She sucked in air sharply and heard his answering groan of delight. He brought his mouth to hers, speaking in a husky whisper against her lips.

"So smooth—so soft." His hand wandered down to the bottom of her T-shirt, lifting it slowly as his palm slid over her skin. "Like satin—the sweetest...." The way his lips moved against hers as he murmured his endearments made Selina feel a little crazy. She began nibbling at his lower lip with her teeth, exulting in the instant response she drew from Gil. He pressed her closer to his body, one hand finding the front catch of her bra and releasing it to play over the smooth eager slopes of her breasts. His mouth left hers as he pushed her T-shirt up, trailing fiery kisses until he captured first one nipple, then the other, using langorous movements of his tongue and teeth to bring wanton moans from Selina's throat. She twined her fingers in his crisp dark hair, pressing his head to her, lost in the surge of primitive emotions he aroused.

One of his hands brushed slowly up the inside of her thigh, increasing the delicious tension in her body. She slipped her own hands under his shirt and over the flat muscular planes of his back, taking fierce delight in the way he shuddered and pulled her even closer. They lay together on the soft grass, his legs entwined with hers, his need urgent against her body. She knew if she could see his face, it would be tender, triumphant, exultant....

He felt her stiffen and stopped his caresses to hold her tightly. "What is it?" he murmured into her hair. "Did I hurt you?"

Cautiously Selina moved away, and he let her put a little space between them. "It's nothing," she managed to say.

"Just a little case of *déjà vu*?" Gil's voice was matter-of-fact.

She gazed at him, surprised, trying to read his expression in the starlight. "How—how did you know?"

"I know." In the darkness, voices seemed to take on added nuances. She shivered at the quiet implacability she heard in his voice. He hesitated a moment, then continued. "Monday in the kitchen—you had a precognitive experience, didn't you?"

She wanted to deny it. "I imagined something," she said carefully.

His arms around her tightened. "Oddly enough, I imagined the same thing." The intensity of his tone took the lightness out of the words. "The two of us, lying together—like this." Their legs were still entwined, and he arched her lower body against his, leaving her in no doubt of his need for her. "Your face,—oh, sweetheart, I want always to see that expression on your face—"

"I saw *your* expression," Selina blurted.

"I've no doubt it was revealing." She felt him press his face into her hair. His voice was muffled. "I need you so much."

Despite his arms holding her, Selina felt cold. It was too eerie. Gil seemed isolated, shielded by his special knowledge. She struggled to sit up, and with a sigh he released her.

"Do you know everything that's going to happen?" Her voice was low and tight.

He answered warily. "It doesn't work like that." He was silent for a moment. "It's like your vision. I get a picture, and I know it will come true. I don't know when or how."

"Did you put that—picture—in my mind?" Suddenly she was afraid. Fragments of superstitions drifted into her thoughts.

"Don't be absurd." The words were bitten off curtly. Gil sat up, too, running his hands through his hair. When he spoke again, he had his exasperation under control. "I only wish I could put ideas into your mind," he muttered. "I have no idea why we shared the same precognitive vision. I only know that the visions are true ones. Let's make it true, Selina!" His hand came up, lightly tracing the outline of her mouth. She shuddered and moved away.

"I'm not going to lie here and make love to you just to keep your record of perfect prophecies unbroken." She jumped to her feet. He stood, too, looking taller and somehow menacing in the dark. A thin crescent of moon began to show behind the hill, casting his shadow over Selina.

"I've told you before, you can't fight this." He sounded implacable. She took a few steps back toward the house. His arm rose in a sweeping gesture. "It's in the stars. You're the expert on the stars. Read them for yourself."

Once again he was striding away from her into the house. But this time Selina didn't call him back. She looked up at the Milky Way streaming across the night sky and wished desperately that she had the power to see anything at all to help her figure out what to do about her runaway emotions.

CHAPTER SEVEN

SELINA THUMPED HER ROLLING PIN hard on the croissant dough. "That's for you, Gilmartin Duchenay," she muttered viciously. She gave the dough a quarter turn and attacked it again. "Precognitive. Hah!" Glaring down at the dough, she picked up a sharp knife. "I'll show you precognitive!"

Her frustrating encounter with Gil had left her disinclined for sleep, so she'd spent a couple of hours working on croissant dough for Saturday's breakfast. But a short spell of unrestful exhausted dozing had been broken by the early-morning sunlight, and she had stomped into the kitchen to finish the croissants, feeling a fit of redheaded temper coming on as she brooded over Gil's exasperating habit of starting to make love to her and then letting her scruples stop him.

With ruthless precision she began slashing the dough into squares. A knock at the back door made her put down her knife reluctantly. Although it was before 8:00 A.M., she supposed some of the food deliveries for that night's dinner party were arriving. Or perhaps it was Pete, the gardener, coming for a cup of coffee.

But when she opened the door, it wasn't Pete.

Andy Corbett stood there, his fair hair slightly rumpled, his expression a compound of impudent amusement and uncertainty.

Selina gaped at him for a moment, then closed her eyes hopefully. Maybe it was a hallucination brought on by late hours and lack of sleep. She opened her eyes again. Andy was still there, peering at her with friendly concern.

"You all right, Selina?" He smiled, the charming smile she remembered. "Can I come in?"

Weakly Selina stood aside and let him through the door. He looked around the spacious kitchen, taking in the modern appliances and cheerful atmosphere.

"Nice place," he said approvingly. "Lots of money here evidently. Don't let me interrupt you." He glanced at the croissant dough on the worktable. Selina picked up her knife and began cutting automatically, trying to assimiliate the fact that Andy, who should have been in San Francisco, was at this moment pouring himself a cup of coffee in her kitchen in St. Louis.

She rolled up triangles of dough and placed them carefully on a baking sheet while she tried to formulate the right questions. Andy anticipated her.

"You want to know what I'm doing here, right?"

"The thought had crossed my mind." Selina placed the baking sheet in the refrigerator and turned to face him. "What you're doing here, why and other related subjects."

He smiled winningly. "I came to see you, of course." Glancing at her unresponsive face, he took a thoughtful sip of coffee. "You didn't tell me you were leaving town, Selina," he said gently.

"You didn't ask."

"Now, now. Mustn't be flippant." A sorrowful look appeared on his face. "It was quite a shock to me to find out you'd left—and without telling me where." He answered her unspoken question smugly. "Marybeth finally gave me the address on the placement papers. Really, Selina, it would have been much simpler if you'd just answered my phone calls. Look at all the complications you've caused."

Selina's system began to recover from shock. Andy was a convenient object to vent her bad temper on.

"The only complication," she said with angry relish, "is you! I don't know why you bothered to come here, but I can assure you it won't do you a bit of good."

Andy refused to be provoked. "Having a temper tantrum, are we?"

"Not over *you*," she retorted bluntly. "You aren't even worth raising my voice about."

He narrowed his eyes, looking at her intently. "But someone else is, hmm? Fast work, Selina. You've only been here a couple of weeks."

She was momentarily taken aback by his unexpected acuity. She turned on the oven, lingering for a moment to adjust the oven thermometer, hoping to disguise the flush she could feel flooding her face. "Nonsense," she snapped. "Say what you came to say and go away."

Andy helped himself to more coffee. "Wouldn't want to be hasty," he said. She could hear the piqued vanity in his voice and writhed inside. She had really blown it. Andy would never leave until he'd ferreted out who she'd met to replace him. And his unwanted presence was the straw that broke the camel's back as far as she was concerned.

"I mean it, Andy," she snapped. "I have work to do. I want you out of here in five minutes, so start talking."

Andy ignored her words. "I brought a suitcase," he said in the self-satisfied tone that had always, she now realized, secretly irritated her. "Is there a spare room in this mausoleum, or shall I just bunk with you?"

"We usually like to book our spare rooms in advance." The voice was Gil's. Selina stifled a helpless moan. An encounter she would have given anything to prevent was going to take place. Gil stood by the swinging door into the kitchen. His face was expressionless, but Selina could tell, as she faced him, that he was angry. She swallowed nervously.

"Gil," she began, and then, remembering Andy's alert ears, she corrected herself. "Mr. Duchenay, this is Andy Corbett. He was in my class at the Culinary Academy."

Andy looked from Gil to Selina, taking in the tension that sparked between them. "Yes indeedy," he said, coming around the table to take Selina's hand. "We were in the same class, working side by side, night and day, right, honey?" He glanced down at her possessively, an unpleasant smile on his face. "In fact, I thought we were going to keep working shoulder to shoulder, but Selina had to have her fling."

She pulled away angrily, her eyes blazing. "You make me so mad, Andrew Corbett," she hissed, momentarily forgetting Gil. "Why don't you believe what I say and bug off? Once and for all, I will not work with you. I will not live with you. I don't even want to share the same air with you. So leave!"

Andy moved toward her again, but Gil stepped between them. "I think," he told Andy gently, "Selina's been very clear. Did you have anything further to say?"

Andy ignored him. When he spoke to Selina, his voice was soft, cajoling. "I've got the kitchen all set up and inspected, darling." He sent his most charming smile toward her as she stood defiantly, her back against the refrigerator. "Some of the wealthiest people in San Francisco want to use us for caterers. You have to come back. We'll work together just as we planned."

"No, Andy. No!"

He moved closer, concentrating on her, using the wheedling voice that probably got him anything he wanted from Marybeth, Selina reflected. She looked at his carefully styled hair, his eyes that were a little too close together, the amiable mouth, the faintly receding chin, and wondered how she could have ever found him attractive. Put together, the components of his face looked fine. Examined separately, they left something to be desired. Suddenly her anger drained away, replaced by reluctant pity. He was so confident that he had only to call, and she'd come running.

"Darling," he said softly, "I guess I didn't tell you

I wanted to get married, but believe me that's what I meant. I thought you understood. We make such a fine team.''

"It's no use, Andy.'' She opened the refrigerator and took out the baking sheet covered with croissants. "Excuse me,'' she said politely to Gil, who stood in front of the stove, his face a watchful mask. "I have to put these in the oven.'' She set the timer and turned back to face Andy. "I'm not available,'' she told him wearily. "It was—interesting to see you again. Now please go.''

He regarded her with baffled fury, one hand unconsciously clenching. "But you have to come,'' he cried. "I've made commitments! We're catering a cocktail party Wednesday!''

"Well, you'll just have to handle it by yourself,'' Selina snapped. "I have commitments, too.''

"I'll bet you do.'' He glared at Gil, who stared back stonily, arms folded across his chest. "This rich guy's bought you, huh? Got himself a cute little chef to serve him croissants in bed—and something else, too, I'll bet.'' The sneer in his voice made Selina wince. Suddenly the whole situation seemed too sordid. A recollection of her own abandoned response to Gil the night before brought a guilty blush to her face. Andy had never been able to make her respond like that. She'd never even realized such sensations were possible.

Reading something of her thoughts in her face, Andy laughed derisively. "What a cozy arrangement,'' he jeered. "No wonder you don't want to come back to San Francisco and work for a living!''

Gil moved then, one arm flashing out to grab Andy around the neck and haul him off his feet. Selina stared, petrified by astonishment. *People only do that in the movies*, she thought, unable to voice a protest at the brawl that was shaping up in her kitchen.

"Perhaps you'd like to reconsider some of your statements," Gil said, his voice a lazy drawl. "Miss Montgomery works long hours here..." he paused, his gaze sharpening as Andy snorted. "In the kitchen," Gil continued implacably. "I think you'd better apologize before you leave."

Andy pushed petulantly at the hand that gripped his collar. "Come off it, Duchenay," he said, his voice peevish. "Don't try this Hollywood macho stuff with me. A man in your position doesn't want to be slapped with an assault charge."

"Don't be too sure of that," Gil said, still in that soft dangerous voice. Selina shivered. "After all, a man in my position can afford to buy his way out of these things. And there's a lot of satisfaction to be got from physical violence."

Andy's face blanched. Selina felt her anger boiling up again, twice as hot now that it had two targets. She picked up a cast-iron skillet and held it threateningly. "You're both being ridiculous," she stormed. "But if you can be ridiculous, so can I. Let go of Andy, Gil, and Andy, get out of here. Otherwise I'll flatten you both with this skillet. I have a dinner party to cook for tonight, and no time to spend wrangling with a couple of overgrown adolescents!"

Gil and Andy turned glowering faces to her, and

she brandished the skillet. "I mean it now," she growled. "Just get out of here, both of you. I want my kitchen to myself."

The back door opened with a crash. Charlotte Drumm stood in the doorway, her perfectly sculpted hair a little awry, her clothes looking like she dressed in haste. "There you are," she cried, pointing at Selina and giving vent to a loud angry sob. "Jezebel! Slut!" she advanced into the room, her lips working, her hands unsteady. Gil and Andy, both taken by surprise, turned to face her. Gil slowly released Andy. Mrs. Drumm noticed them and turned an accusing finger in their direction, still hurling insults at Selina. "You have no compunction about seducing my nephew. This poor man is probably one of your victims, too! You will be punished, let me tell you!" she hissed venemously. Selina recoiled at the waft of alcohol on her breath.

"Now, aunt," Gil began cautiously. "You know this isn't good for you. Dr. Martin said—"

"I never neglect my duty! And it's my duty to save you from this—this immoral, promiscuous—"

It was too much. First Andy, then Mrs. Drumm, accusing her of behavior she'd not even had a chance to enjoy. "I will not stand here and listen—" Selina began.

Gil turned to her, frowning. "Please, Selina. You don't have to shout."

"I am not shouting!" Selina hollered. "I want everyone out of this kitchen. Out, now!"

Magda pushed open the swinging door. She wore a long velour housecoat, and her eyes were still sleepy.

"Selina? Is something wrong?" Her sweeping glance encountered Andy, looking huffy and curious, Gil and Selina squaring off with the cast-iron skillet on the floor between them, and Charlotte Drumm sobbing gustily by the worktable. Just then the timer went off. Selina whipped the oven door open and used a pot holder to pull out the croissants. She slammed them onto the table.

"Breakfast is served," she ground out. She stalked into her suite and shut the door behind her with cold finality.

IT WAS A GRAND GESTURE, but she couldn't spend the day skulking in her sitting room while preparations for the dinner party languished. She was still standing in the middle of the room, biting indecisively on a fingernail, when Magda tapped at the door and peeked around it.

"They're gone," she murmured in a conspiratorial whisper. "You can come out now."

Selina walked back into the kitchen without looking at her employer. She wasn't sure what impression Magda might have as a result of the scene she'd encountered. When Selina saw that Andy was gone, she heaved a relieved sigh.

"Your friend is being driven to the airport by Pete," Magda offered, pouring two cups of coffee and carrying them over to the worktable. "And Charlotte is in the front room, where Gil is playing the solicitous nephew. I'll have to go back to her right away, but I wanted to apologize to you first. Gil told me she had one of her—tantrums."

"She was drunk," Selina said bluntly, unable after the scene staged by Charlotte Drumm to acquiesce in comforting euphemisms.

Magda frowned, then sighed with resignation. "You're right, Selina," she said. "We've always tried to pretend that Charlotte's problem was just a matter of an uncertain temper." She smiled briefly, but there was no amusement in her smile. "Which it is. But it's exacerbated by her tendency to...drink rather heavily when she's feeling pressured. Then she creates a scene, and usually we all scurry around to alleviate her problem and make her feel better."

She hesitated, and Selina nodded wisely, adding, "For some reason I'm her problem, or she thinks I am. So are you going to solve it for her? Get rid of me, I mean?"

Magda raised her eyebrows, a faint smile on her lips. "I don't blame you for feeling belligerent, my dear. And Charlotte certainly picked her moment with a fine flair for the dramatic. But no, we certainly don't want to let you go. I'm willing to appease Charlotte with any reasonable request, and even some unreasonable ones, but there's absolutely no reason why I should pay the least attention to her in this instance. Gil is, I hope, explaining that to her now—tactfully, to spare us from having to send for the doctor. Unless, after this morning, you have developed such a distaste for us that you'd prefer to leave, which I must say wouldn't surprise me."

Selina's resentment had to melt away under Magda's soothing words. "I lost my temper this morning, too," she mumbled. "Andy—I didn't expect him to show up, and it made me a little—touchy.''

Magda hid a smile. ''Nevertheless, the croissants were excellent. That's only one of the many reasons why I hope you'll overlook this whole wretched episode and stay with us, Selina.'' She got to her feet. ''Of course, you'd have twenty job offers if news of this gets out. Anyone who's been to one of your dinner parties would be ecstatic over the opportunity to hire you away. But I want very much for you to stay, my dear.''

Selina looked up, a rueful smile on her face. ''Actually I never thought of quitting. I just hoped you wouldn't decide to fire me because Andy came around creating a scene.''

On her way to the swinging door, Magda cast a mischievous glance over her shoulder. ''Well, that depends. How many more enraged former boyfriends are going to show up at the crack of dawn?''

Selina laughed, too, but it was a hollow sound. Gil was the only other man in her life who fit that particular category. And after this morning she had to wonder about the likelihood of even that.

She set about her preparations for the dinner party with less than her usual enthusiasm. When Gil came in later for a wine conference, she was short with him, motivated not only by her professional concerns for the dinner, but by residual embarrassment over the scene with Andy. She felt that none of them had behaved very reasonably—certainly not Gil, whose rather theatrical response to Andy's insinuations had made her feel more like an old ham bone between two dogs than a *femme fatale* being fought over. But then, she had overreacted, too, she thought, remembering her grandstanding with the cast-iron skillet. Her lips quirked in a smile, seeing for the first time the funny side of it.

Gil, who was maintaining a polite facade, shot her a pained glance. "What's so funny about Chardonnay?"

Selina's smile widened. "I was just thinking how melodramatic we looked this morning." An irrepressible sputter of laughter burst from her lips. "Me with my skillet, and you about to punch Andy's lights out. How classic."

Gil laughed ruefully. "You're right. It's a wonder Aunt Charlotte didn't just faint on the spot—to add to the ambience."

Selina's laughter died. "She might have passed out, but I doubt she would have fainted," she remarked tartly, then wished she hadn't. Gil's face grew stern.

"My aunt has problems you know nothing about, Selina. It's not for you to judge her. I think you're overreacting to the situation."

"Well, I like that!" The note of reproof in his voice stung. She'd done nothing to deserve Mrs. Drumm's insults, and yet Gil could stand there and scold her for not lying down and letting his aunt trample on her. Selina jumped up, suddenly furious. The residue of the morning's humiliating encounter, coupled with a new sensation, the need for Gil's approval, combined in a flammable mixture. "Your aunt," she said, trying without much success to keep her voice level, "burst into my kitchen, gratuitously insulted me, didn't bother to offer an apology, and you sit there and smugly inform me that *I'm* the one overreacting. Why don't you just set her mind at rest and tell your precious aunt there's nothing between us and never will be?"

Gil's face turned white. "Is that what you want? Is that the way you really feel?"

Her heart shouted, *No, I want you, Gilmartin Duchenay!* But if she listened to her heart, she would be making a big mistake. "Yes," she whispered. "That's the way it is."

His mouth compressed into a thin white line, bringing harsh planes to his face. His eyes blazed with a dark consuming fury, and instinctively Selina stepped back. Without a word Gil turned on his heel and strode to the swinging door. He spoke over his shoulder, not looking at Selina.

"Thank you for the lesson, Chef Montgomery." His voice was biting. "You certainly taught me that I'm not always right about my predictions for the future. I just never thought I could go this far wrong."

Then he was gone. Dazed, Selina sank onto her stool. She put her trembling hands to her cheeks and found that tears were running down them. "This time, he's gone for good," she whispered brokenly. "I should be glad he won't be complicating my life anymore." But her wounded heart paid no attention to such false reasoning. For a long moment she sat there, feeling like a refugee in the tumbled rubble of her world. Finally she got up and splashed water on her face. Looking through the window over the sink, she saw Betsy come toward the back door, staggering from the garden with a gigantic basket of flowers and vegetables. Selina moaned and dashed for the door of her sitting room. Despite the dinner party she had to be alone, even if for just a few minutes. That way she would be able to pick up the pieces of her heart before someone else trampled on them.

THE DINNER PARTY that evening was as close to disaster as it could get. By the time the waiters and kitchen help left, Selina was as limp as overcooked asparagus. She poured a generous splash of the brandy normally used for cooking and slumped dejectedly at the worktable. She didn't even have the energy to seek the solace of her own room.

Hailey's entrance took her by surprise. "I didn't know you were invited to the dinner tonight," Selina said, gesturing across the table. "Pull up a stool and sit awhile."

"Gil called and invited me this afternoon," Hailey said, her glance straightforward. "Of course, mother was pleased."

"Of course." Selina tried to keep her voice neutral.

"Selina, exactly what happened here this morning? Mother was gone when I got up, and she didn't get back for hours. And Gil looks so—" She broke off, examining Selina's face closely. "You do, too," she said bluntly. "That wasn't the best dinner I've had from your kitchen. Have you two quarreled or something? And what did mother have to do with it?"

Selina was tempted to pour out the whole story of the morning's episode, but she sensed that Magda and Gil would rather Hailey did not know of her mother's behavior. "Gil and I had a fight," she admitted. "You must have noticed that he's been—that there was something—"

"A blind person would have noticed." Hailey patted Selina's hand sympathetically. "But you'll make up. You two are perfect for each other. You might have been fated to meet!"

Selina winced. "Please, Hailey. There's no future to any relationship between Gil and me. It just wouldn't work out. His family—" She broke off abruptly.

Hailey nodded with resignation. "Since I'm sure the rest of the family feels about you as I do, mother must be the fly in the ointment. Did she come over and make a big stink? Is that what nobody will tell me about?"

"Hailey, I—"

"Never mind. I can guess." The younger girl squared her shoulders. "I apologize for her, Selina. The truth is, my mother is a binge drinker."

This time it was Selina who patted Hailey's hand. "You don't have to say anything, Hailey. Really."

"No, I want to explain." Hailey's face looked strained, but her voice was steady. Selina felt sudden respect for the usually ebullient girl's ability to face facts.

"Mother is sometimes—a bit unbalanced in her mental outlook." Hailey threaded her fingers together on the table and looked down at them. "She's got a real thing about being big in society—wanting me to be the perfect debutante, wanting Gil to squire me around so some of the Duchenay glamour will rub off on me. Well, I've been quite a disappointment to her in that respect.''

Selina murmured a soft denial. Hailey shook her head soberly. ''I know I am. It turns out that mother borrowed a lot of money for my debut. I did have a small trust fund from my grandmother that was supposed to be earmarked for my debut, but it wasn't enough for mother. She was convinced I would marry splendidly, and the loan could be paid back then. When I found that out, it was one of the reasons why I finally decided to start my bakery instead of just dreaming about it. I can begin paying the loan back in another month if business continues to increase the way it has been.''

''That's great!'' Selina roused herself from her personal misery long enough to rejoice for her friend. It was a real triumph that Hailey had been able to earn success so quickly.

Hailey flushed modestly, though her smile was full of pleasure. ''I owe a lot to you,'' she said, dismissing her own hard work with a wave of her hand. ''I couldn't have done it without all your help. But anyway, the sad part is that no matter how profitable my bakery is, mother will be simply horrified when she finds out, as I suppose she must someday. That's what I mean about her being unrealistic. And deep down I think she recognizes that her view of the world just doesn't compute anymore. That's why she occasionally has these outbursts. She doesn't drink to excess any other time—just when reality begins to get too heavy for her.''

"I understand," Selina said in a low voice. She did understand, but she still resented Mrs. Drumm's attitude. No matter how good the reason for it, bad behavior was still bad behavior.

Hailey leaned forward, looking at her earnestly. "I don't know if you do, really. My mother also has a heart condition. The doctor's told her repeatedly not to let go of herself like this, but she can't help it. That's why we try not to oppose her when she has one of her fits. And she's pretty shaky for a couple of days afterward. We all treat her with kid gloves. I'm not sure that's so good for her, but, well—she's my mother, Selina. In spite of her faults I don't want her to have a heart attack."

Tears welled up in Hailey's eyes, and Selina came around the table to enfold her in a hug. "I can't pretend to like your mother," she said honestly, "but it won't have any effect on my friendship with you, Hailey."

A look of doubt crossed Hailey's face. "Uh—well, I don't know about that, Selina. It seems that Gil is taking me to a couple of parties next week. Mother must have wrung it out of him this morning. You won't mind, will you?"

Selina did mind. She knew Hailey would never be underhanded, but it was possible that Gil might fall in love with his cousin if they were thrown together for any length of time. *What's that to me,* she thought fiercely and repeated it out loud for Hailey's benefit. "I have nothing to say about anything Gil does," she added bleakly. "He can go out with hundreds of women for all I care—and probably will!"

"Don't say that, Selina!" Hailey wailed. "I feel so bad about you two fighting! You know I don't care if Gil takes me to parties or not. In fact—"

"You'd rather have Ricky Carson do it," Selina said when Hailey stopped short of completing her sentence. "A blind person could have seen that." She kept her voice light and teasing. Hailey sighed in relief.

"If you can joke, it can't be as bad as you think." Hailey got up from the table, stretched and yawned. "Lord, all this tension makes me sleepy. I've got two dozen chocolate cakes to get out Monday, plus sixteen carrot cakes and that new recipe to perfect. Can I come over Monday night and go over it with you?"

"Sure," Selina said absently. She was overwhelmed by fatigue. *Sleep*, she thought, *if I can sleep I'll be fine*. She barely heard Hailey's farewell. With heavy exhausted movements she raised the brandy glass to her mouth and emptied the spirit down her throat. It went down smoothly, without causing her to cough and sputter, and gave her the strength to get to her bedroom, where she retreated from her wrecked life in the torpor of sleep.

What made Marge burn the toast and miss her favorite soap opera?

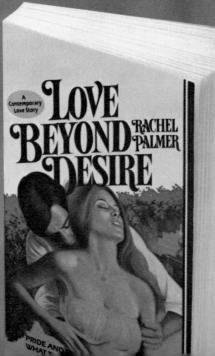

A Contemporary Love Story

LOVE BEYOND DESIRE

RACHEL PALMER

...At his touch, her body felt a familiar wild stirring, but she struggled to resist it. This is not love, she thought bitterly.

PRIDE AND
WHAT T

A SUPERROMANCE™
the great new romantic novel she never wanted to end. And it can be yours
FREE!

She never wanted it to end. And neither will you. From the moment you begin… *Love Beyond Desire*, your **FREE** introduction to the newest series of bestseller romance novels, SUPERROMANCES.

You'll be enthralled by this powerful love story… from the moment Robin meets the dark, handsome Carlos and finds herself involved in the jealousies, bitterness and secret passions of the Lopez family. Where her own forbidden love threatens to shatter her life.

Your FREE *Love Beyond Desire* is only the beginning. A subscription to SUPERROMANCES lets you look forward to a long love affair. Month after month, you'll receive four love stories of heroic dimension. Novels that will involve you in spellbinding intrigue, forbidden love and fiery passions.

You'll begin this series of sensuous, exciting contemporary novels… written by some of the top romance novelists of the day… with four each month.

And this big value… each novel, almost 400 pages of compelling reading… is yours for only $2.50 a book. Hours of entertainment for so little. Far less than a first-run movie or Pay-TV. Newly published novels, with beautifully illustrated covers, filled with page after page of delicious escape into a world of romantic love… delivered right to your home.

A compelling love story of mystery and intrigue... conflicts and jealousies... and a forbidden love that threatens to shatter the lives of all involved with the aristocratic Lopez family.

Mail this card today for your FREE gifts.

TAKE THIS BOOK AND TOTE BAG FREE!

Mail to: **SUPERROMANCE**
2504 W. Southern Avenue, Tempe, Az 85282

YES, please send me FREE and without any obligation, my SUPERROMANCE novel, *Love Beyond Desire.* If you do not hear from me after I have examined my FREE book, please send me the 4 new SUPERROMANCE books every month as soon as they come off the press. I understand that I will be billed only $2.50 per book (total $10.00). There are no shipping and handling or any other hidden charges. There is no minimum number of books that I have to purchase. In fact, I may cancel this arrangement at any time. *Love Beyond Desire* and the tote bag are mine to keep as FREE gifts even if I do not buy any additional books.

134-CIS-KAF7

Name	(Please Print)
Address	Apt. No.
City	
State	Zip

Signature   (If under 18, parent or guardian must sign.)

This offer is limited to one order per household and not valid to present subscribers. We reserve the right to exercise discretion in granting membership. If price changes are necessary you will be notified. Offer expires March 30, 1984.

PRINTED IN U.S.A.   **SUPERROMANCE**

EXTRA BONUS
MAIL YOUR ORDER
TODAY AND GET A
FREE TOTE BAG
FROM SUPERROMANCE.

↳ Mail this card today for your FREE gifts.

CHAPTER EIGHT

HAILEY'S CAR WAS ALREADY PARKED in front of the garage when Selina drove up Monday evening. Hailey stood in the driveway talking to Magda and Pete, who waved and loped over to put the Audi away.

Selina joined the other women, and all three of them stood for a moment watching the sun begin to stain the clouds rose and mauve. For the first time in days Selina spent a few moments in quiet contemplation. She let the beauty of the tranquil evening seep into her frazzled soul, while her frustrations seemed to dwindle to manageable size.

After a long moment Magda spoke, not taking her eyes from the gently rounded hills, surmounted by a few majestic oak trees and the deepening blue infinity of the sky. "I love this view," she said, her voice emphasizing the stillness around them. "It's even nicer from the top of that hill." She turned and smiled at the two young women, her expression one of reminiscence. "It's a good thing I knew I was in love with James before he brought me here. One look at this beauty—" her sweeping arm included the fields, the little stream, the huge bowl of sky— "and I might have married him just to spend the rest of my life here.'' She added, almost to herself, ''I was lucky to have both James and this for so long.''

Selina felt a sudden gush of affection for this woman she'd known for such a short time. It wasn't the grandeur of the Château or its swimming pool and fancy cars that Magda loved. When she looked at her home, she saw the surrounding hills and woods, the long slopes of meadow she'd tended so faithfully, careful that whatever she did added to the natural beauty.

Hailey slipped an arm around her stepaunt's shoulders. ''You sound as if you expect to be evicted any minute,'' she teased gently.

''Not exactly.'' Magda's eyes wore the penetrating expression Selina had observed a few times before, but she spoke in her usual vague manner. ''I've often thought it would be fun to build a little house over there, on the far side of the rose garden. Betsy and I could live quite comfortably there.''

''With another little house for Betsy's menagerie, and yet another little house for your garden tools....'' Hailey giggled. ''If you're looking for a new place to live, Auntie, I think you should let Hal MacMillan pick it out. He seems to be spending a lot of time with you.''

Selina heard this with surprise. She'd known that Mr. MacMillan was in town, since he'd attended the last two dinner parties and sent word back with the hired waiters afterward commending her performance. But she hadn't realized that he'd been seeing Magda specifically.

Magda replied with equanimity. ''Hal shares my

fondness for horticulture. We've been visiting some of the showplaces in the neighborhood. Tomorrow we're going to Shaw's Garden.''

"What fun," Hailey said, losing interest. But Selina was intrigued.

"I think I've heard of that place," she said. "Isn't there a climate-controlled dome there?''

Faintly surprised, Magda nodded. "The Climatron. And they have a beautiful Japanese garden.'' She regarded Selina thoughtfully. "You should come, too. It's about time you saw a few of the sights. Tell you what. Let's make a day of it. Betsy's been pestering me to go up in the Arch. We could go to the Jefferson Memorial in the morning, have lunch and then take in Shaw's Garden. Would you like to?''

"It sounds like fun," Selina said hesitantly, "but I don't want to horn in on your date.''

"Heavens, it's not a date." Magda insisted and turned toward the garage. "Betsy's already going, so you're not intruding at all. I must see Pete about blossom-end rot in the tomatoes.''

Hailey and Selina walked toward the kitchen door. Somehow Magda's invitation had relieved some of the tension Selina had felt since the Saturday before. Tonight she could enjoy the warm evening breezes, scented with honeysuckle. She looked around delightedly as fireflies began to blink on and off in the deepening dusk. But Hailey slapped irritably at her arm.

"Damned mosquitoes! I wish we lived in San Francisco. Gil said they don't have bugs there.''

"True," Selina agreed. "But that means we don't have fireflies. I'd gladly put up with mosquitoes if we could have fireflies."

"Lightning bugs." Hailey turned with Selina to look at the elusive glows before entering the kitchen. "It hasn't been that many years since I used to help Betsy catch them in jars and take them into the basement as lanterns." She saw Selina's expression and hastened to add, "We always let them go later, of course. Gil wouldn't let us keep them."

She spoke over her shoulder as she entered the kitchen, holding the door open for Selina so she didn't see Gil himself, sitting at the worktable and wolfing down one of his sandwich creations.

He swallowed a mighty bite and lifted a sardonic eyebrow in Hailey's direction. Selina he studiously ignored. "If I wouldn't let you keep something, you can bet you shouldn't have had it. What was it?"

"Lightning bugs." Hailey pulled out her notebook and plopped it on the table. "I could use a cool drink. All right if I get one, Selina?"

Selina nodded. "As long as you're pouring, I'll take some juice." She went to the cabinet to get glasses, wishing that Gil weren't in the kitchen, wishing that her body hadn't responded so instantly to the sight of him. When she turned with the glasses in her hand, Gil's dark brooding eyes were fixed on her. She wrenched her own gaze away to find Hailey eyeing them both speculatively.

"The glasses, please." Selina handed them over and fished a little wildly for something to say.

"They remind me of stars." As soon as the words

were out, she wanted to bite them back. Her eyes flew to Gil's face, and she knew he, too, was thinking of the passionate stargazing they had done on the small hill behind the swimming pool.

"What?" Hailey's face expressed her bewilderment. "Who reminds you of stars?"

"Fireflies—lightning bugs. They're like—accessible stars." Selina shrugged impatiently at Hailey's blank incomprehension. "Forget it. My thinking's a little muddled lately." Again she stopped short, feeling the words were an admission of some sort to Gil. She stole a glance at him and saw that he was regarding her steadily. Within the hooded depths of his gaze a flame began to flicker. She felt it ignite something in her own eyes, and a new sensation swept over her, a fierce desire to know all the mysteries that made up Gilmartin Duchenay. The intensity of the feeling frightened her. She turned away, trying to break the spell.

"Ahem!" Hailey said loudly, her eyes bright with curiosity. "Maybe we should take a look at this recipe some other time, Selina."

"No, no!" Selina didn't want to be alone with Gil. She hurried over to Hailey's notebook. "What is it you want to work on tonight?"

"Is this a regular seminar?" Gil picked up his sandwich and began eating again. For some reason his mood seemed lighter as he crunched into the unsteady layers with gusto.

"Sort of." Hailey opened her notebook. "Supposedly Selina's only helping me transpose my recipes into larger amounts. But I always learn a lot about procedures, too, so seminar is probably the right word for it.''

Gil finished his sandwich and stretched lazily. "Maybe I'll start attending the classes," he teased. "According to Chef Montgomery, I have no appreciation for food."

"Too true," Hailey shot back smartly, but Selina hardly heard. Her emotions soared at the tender intimacy in Gil's voice. The next second she had herself under control. Her pride would not allow her to give Gil the satisfaction of knowing that his feelings mattered to her.

Determinedly she threw herself into the calculations for Hailey's recipe. Gil sat silently, his face revealing nothing. After the recipe was modified to Selina's satisfaction, Hailey mixed up the cake and put it in the oven.

"This is the part I like," Gil said, using a rubber spatula to get all the leftover batter out of the mixing bowl. "Of course, it's nice when the cake comes out, too," he said kindly.

There was a small silence while Hailey wrinkled her forehead over her notes. Then Gil spoke, his words coming unexpectedly so that Selina jumped.

"Does it matter how many cakes you make at one time? Can you mass-produce this recipe?"

It took her a few moments to collect her wits enough to answer. "Probably not in huge quantities. There are few cakes you can really make in large batches."

"But you could mix up lots of small batches, right? You could have premeasured ingredients, make ten at a time."

He seemed oddly intent. Selina threw up her hands. "I suppose you could premix the dry ingredients. But for the best-tasting cakes everything has to be mixed just the right way. You've seen how particular Hailey is when she puts her ingredients together. I'm afraid Purity's computers would have a hard time understanding all that's involved in making cakes as good as Hailey's."

She hadn't meant to let that sarcastic note creep into her voice, but somehow it had. Gil eyed her balefully.

"Think you're smart, don't you? For your information, I didn't have computers in mind." He drummed his fingers on the table, suddenly immersed in thought. Hailey and Selina had resumed a low-voiced conversation before he spoke again.

"Tell me," he directed the question to Selina, his tone impersonal. "Do restaurant kitchens normally use modern production methods? I mean—" and his face grew teasing again "—do they all have this fetish for doing everything by hand that you have? Going out and grinding the flour before they make bread, that sort of thing?"

"It is not a fetish," Selina said with dignity. "I do insist on freshness, but not to that degree. Although if I ran a bread bakery, it might be worth thinking about."

"Answer my question, please." Gil's tone was light, but he caught hold of her hand and held it compelling. She fought to keep her voice level, though the pressure of his hand sent passionate signals to her overly receptive nerve endings.

"Of course, restaurants try to do things in the

most cost-efficient manner. But good chefs also recognize that you must deal with only the best of what's currently available. A really creative person will come up with the best menu no matter what season it is. That means labor-intensive work since fresh vegetable and excellent sauces require skilled people to deal with them.''

He still held her hand, but he seemed distracted. "Say you had a team...." he muttered. His eyes lost their absent look. He rose swiftly from his stool. "Thanks, ladies. I'll sit in again sometime." He strode toward the swinging door, not even waiting to taste Hailey's cake.

THROUGHOUT THE NEXT DAY'S EXCURSION Selina found her thoughts returning to Gil's odd behavior the night before. Magda mentioned that he had flown to Cincinnati that morning.

"Purity has a production company there," she added casually, moving the Audi through the traffic with practiced ease. "Gil's got some hot new technique he wants them to try out. I tell him he's gone overboard on computers, but I suppose he's just trying to stay on the wave of the future."

Then Magda began a gentle flow of information and reminiscence about St. Louis, but Selina barely listened, not knowing if she felt relieved that Gil was out of the way for a while or disappointed that they would be apart.

Magda exited the highway and negotiated a series of narrow streets. Ahead of them, glimpsed between buildings, Selina could see the glint of sunlight on water. Soon they were driving beside the Mississippi.

It was different from the rivers she knew, which were inclined to be narrow, fast and mostly shallow. This was a wide sluggish-looking mass of water, brown instead of clear, carrying barges and tugboats effortlessly, inexorably. It seemed to radiate a sense of barely leashed power. Selina was fascinated by it, only dragging her eyes away when Betsy pulled insistently on her arm.

"There's the Arch!" Ahead, soaring up into the sky, the Gateway Arch caught the sunlight on its sleek steel-clad sides. Selina felt a quiver of acrophobia at the thought of going up to the top. Magda found a parking place and eased the car into it.

"We'll walk from here," she announced. "Just like all the rest of the sightseers."

They walked along the sidewalk briskly, dodging photo-snapping groups. To their right the pavement sloped toward the river itself, which lapped with deceptive gentleness several feet below the muddy line that indicated the last flood's high-water mark. Ahead were steps leading down to the water. Anchored along the river was a whole parade of boats. There was a fast-food franchise housed in a boat designed to resemble a side-wheeler, and ahead of it, shaming it, was a proud blue-and-cream beauty of a stern-wheeler, the *Robert E. Lee*. When Selina commented on the obvious fakery of the hamburger boat, Magda told her that the other boat was also just a reproduction, although it was a much better one. "There are two restaurants on the *Robert E. Lee*," she remarked. "Both of them are supposed to be quite good. I wish I'd told Hal we would meet him there for lunch. It didn't occur to me in time.''

She pointed out the *Goldenrod*. ''That is a more authentic riverboat. It's a showboat—you can have dinner there and see an old-time melodrama.''

Selina was intrigued, although slightly disappointed at the prosaic appearance of the *Goldenrod*. The showboat had no tall gilt-topped smokestacks, no fancy painted pilothouse. Built as a floating theater, it was flat and functional looking, painted bright white and sporting matching white lights for nighttime.

She jumped as a blaring loudspeaker sounded, and a noisy little tour boat, decked out with imitation paddle-wheeler trim, chugged into place near the *Goldenrod*. People streamed off it, while others waited to board. ''Where does that go?''

Betsy dismissed it with a shrug. ''The *Huck Finn*. It goes a few miles up the river and comes back down again.'' Her eyes grew dreamy. ''I wish we could go on a real steamboat. Gil did once.''

Selina nodded. ''The *Delta Queen*. I've always wanted to take one of those cruises they advertise—''

''Not the *Queen*,'' Betsy interrupted. ''Some friends of mother's own this steamboat, and once Gil got invited on a trip all the way to Cincinnati.''

''The Rossfields own her,'' Magda corroborated. ''I think the name is the *Margaret B. Townshend*. They bought the boat years ago from some lumber company in Minneapolis. The lumber barons used to have their own boats for little junkets up and down the river. This boat was in pretty bad shape, but

Irene's husband made a hobby out of restoring it. I took an overnight trip with them a few years ago; it's quite comfortable for a stern-wheeler.''

"Imagine owning your own riverboat!" Selina shook her head ruefully. "I know people who own yachts and sailboats, but a stern-wheeler!''

The Gateway Arch experience was interesting, though a bit hard on Selina, who had no stomach for heights. When they finally emerged, she took a deep breath. "Ah, earth! Why do people ever want to leave it?''

Betsy scoffed at her fervid words. "I love it up there." Her face grew dreamy. "I think I'll be an astronaut when I grow up. Just think of looking out the window and seeing the earth from the stars.''

Selina smiled at her. "I prefer seeing the stars from the earth." An idea struck her. "Maybe you'd like to go with me to the planetarium some time. I went there one evening and found the program very interesting.''

Betsy thanked her graciously for the invitation. Magda cranked the car windows down instead of turning on the air conditioning, and the musty fishy smell of the river permeated the interior. Selina let the wind of the car's movement cool her flushed face. "The air is so—heavy here!''

"It is moist," Magda agreed. She glanced at the clouds that plied the sky. "We may get a storm tonight. It's so muggy. I hope it holds off till we're through at Shaw's Garden.''

The restaurant where they were to meet Mr. Mac-Millan was in an old, restored portion of St. Louis close to downtown, which was called Laclede's Landing. The narrow cobblestoned streets were thronged with people, making driving difficult. Magda pulled into a parking lot, and they walked a couple of blocks, past old brick buildings, formerly warehouses and tenements, that now held boutiques and antique stores, restaurants and supper clubs. Hal stood outside one of the restaurants, scanning the crowd till he saw Magda. His face lighted up.

"Now this is what I call fun," he exclaimed, tucking her arm under his and beaming genially at Selina and Betsy. "And for you, Miss Selina, I'm sure it will be a treat not to have to cook your own meal for a change."

"I'm looking forward to it," Selina said gaily. It would be hard not to enjoy yourself around Hal MacMillan, she reflected. Even Betsy, who at first seemed a bit wary, relaxed and was soon giggling delightedly at his jovial sallies. Magda lost her vague, faraway air and came to sparkling life, parrying Hal's compliments and keeping the conversation running smoothly.

After the hot glare of the city Shaw's Garden was cool and welcoming. Betsy dragged her mother and Hal MacMillan off to tour the Climatron, but Selina wanted nothing more than to sit quietly beside the beautiful lake in the Japanese garden. Agreeing to meet back at the entrance later, the party separated.

Selina found a secluded bench and sat facing the water, watching the wind ruffle it gently. Tall plumy grasses waved to and fro, and swans glided with silent grace. Her mind slowly emptied of tension and worry, and she allowed her thoughts to drift like fallen leaves on the water's surface.

And soon she realized they were drifting toward Gil. Instead of fighting it, as she had been for the past few days, she recognized the depth of her feeling for him, allowing it to surface gently, floating like gossamer through her tangled emotions. She had been foolish beyond belief, but it was done now. She was in love with Gil.

He didn't want her love. He wanted, or had wanted, her passion, to fill some predestined need. With her angry words last Saturday she might have destroyed that need, although once or twice since then she'd seen evidence of desire in his eyes. But physical need wasn't love. What should she do about that?

Once again she fixed her mind on the water, allowing her emotions to become still. She had reacted too often from the panic-stricken fear that Gil might be able to entangle her heart and cause her pain. Now that it had happened, there was no point in running away until she had had time to think about what she could do. So she relaxed on the bench in the warm flicker of dappled tree shadow, letting the sound of the gently flowing water wear away her doubts and fears.

Finally she rose and walked away refreshed. She paced slowly in the shade of the huge trees, past beds of flowers and even the crypt that housed Mr. Shaw's temporal remains. The sharp scent of lavender drew her to the herb garden, where raised beds carried Braille labels, and strollers were encouraged to pick leaves and enjoy their pungent aromas.

By the time she met the others at the entrance gate, Selina felt more serene than she had since Gilmartin Duchenay had entered her life. Somewhere in the green depths of the garden, she had realized that love is not something to run from. She loved him, and if she had anything to say about it, he would soon love her. She didn't know how to achieve this, and she hadn't let herself look beyond winning this love, but she felt a fierce determination to make him hers.

During the drive back to the Château, however, some of her certainty began to drain away. What if Gil did come to love her? What future could they possibly have? She felt shameless enough to throw herself into his arms and demand fulfillment, but an affair couldn't satisfy her for long. And if by some miracle they married, what then? She would never be able to give up her work. It filled a creative need she could not deny. But if she continued working—opened a restaurant or began catering—she would be working nights while Gil worked days. Her shoulders slumped in defeat as she realized that there was no future for her feelings about Gil.

But I can't not love him, she thought sadly. *It's too late for that. He's always in my mind. Life is too bleak without him. What will I do?*

Although Magda mentioned going out for dinner, Selina offered to whip up a quick meal when they got back home. Hal MacMillan accepted with alacrity. "The hotel I'm staying at has the worst kitchen staff I've ever encountered," he confided, his arm around Magda's shoulders as they walked through the back door of the Château. "If I decide to buy it, that's the first thing I'll change." He cocked an eyebrow at his hostess wickedly. "Do you mind if I try to hire Selina away as a new head chef?"

Magda frowned in mock reproof. "Don't even breathe it! I don't know what I'd do without Selina. Why don't you let Purity supply your kitchen instead? Give my poor boy some business instead of threatening to seduce my chef away."

Hal smiled but refused to commit himself. He was surprisingly helpful in the kitchen, tying on an apron and busying himself with the vegetables while Selina pulled another package of Rita's chicken breasts out of the freezer. Magda sat at the worktable and watched, laughing off Hal's suggestion that she help him with the vegetables. "My best role in the kitchen is to provide an admiring audience," she told him. "Betsy is the Duchenay with culinary expertise."

They all sat around the worktable, eating stir-fried chicken and vegetables and conversing amiably. When the telephone rang, Selina knew that it would be Gil, but she didn't move to answer it. Betsy bounded over and lifted the receiver.

"Gil!" she shrieked into the telephone. "We've had the most wonderful day! We went up in the Arch and saw everything, and the paddle-wheelers and Shaw's Garden. Gil, why can't we go on a riverboat?"

Selina could hear crisp staccato tones from the telephone as Gil tried to break his sister's flow of words. Betsy listened for a moment, becoming more subdued. "Sure, he's here. We've just finished dinner—Chinese stuff, but it was really good." She laid the receiver on a little table beneath the wall phone and spoke to Hal MacMillan. "He wants to talk to you. He called your hotel, and they said—"

But Hal had already picked up the phone and begun a low-voiced conversation with Gil. Magda helped herself to a little more rice and asked Betsy, "Is he still in Cincinnati?"

"Hmm?" Betsy was picking the mushrooms out of her chicken. "I guess so. He didn't say. Mother, why *can't* we go on a riverboat? We could go fishing—"

Magda laughed and began stacking plates. "At least you don't want us to get you a place on the space shuttle. Come on, help me with the dishes. Selina looks exhausted."

Selina blinked and came out of her unhappy thoughts. "I am a little tired," she admitted, since her face evidently showed her feelings so strongly. "But I'm perfectly capable of doing the dishes by myself."

"Nonsense." Magda opened the dishwasher and began loading plates. "It takes very little time, and it's something even I can do. You run along and relax for a while."

Hal hung up the phone and came forward, smiling genially. Selina longed to ask how Gil was. Instead she fled into the privacy of her suite before she could make the mistake of letting her love for the son and heir of the house show.

CHAPTER NINE

He was gone for two long weeks.

Selina spent the time battling with her emotions, striving to understand the unsettled longing that permeated her feelings toward Gil. One minute she was sure she loved him; the next she was afraid it was only the bewitching magic of his sensual touch that enthralled her. But it was certain that without him she could not feel whole.

In an effort to submerge her problems, she attacked the frequent dinner parties with an almost savage intensity, determined to produce a series of masterpieces. She succeeded, but the effort of honing her concentration so fiercely began to tell.

Two days before Gil was due to return, Selina sat with Magda in the living room planning the next dinner party. Gil would be home for it, and that fact alone made Selina's concentration waver. Though she listened with apparent interest to Magda's musings over what vegetables to use from the garden, Selina was lost in imagining Gil's return. It took her a few moment to notice that Magda had stopped talking and was regarding her quizzically.

"Sorry," she mumbled, blushing as if Magda

could read her thoughts. "Guess my mind was wandering."

"You know," Magda said slowly, "I think you've been overexerting yourself on the last few dinners." She continued talking over Selina's protests. "We've had some magnificent dishes, beautifully prepared and presented. But it's all been so rich! Why don't we do something different this time—something lighter. Not less beautifully prepared, but maybe less—fussy?"

Selina's objections faded as she mulled over Magda's words. "You know, you're right," she said slowly. "You've put your finger on something that's really been bothering me. I sensed something was going wrong, but I figured I wasn't putting out enough effort. I was trying harder and harder, getting more and more lavish, and it was all wrong." She lifted honest gray eyes to Magda's. "I guess I was just so anxious to show off my great culinary skills I stopped thinking about what would be best for the people eating the food."

Together they planned a light airy summer meal that would refresh the palate without weighing down the stomach. Magda smiled as she read the completed menu. "This will probably help Hal," she remarked. "He's been putting on a little around the middle lately. I tell him he needs more exercise—a garden to work in or something."

"Or something," Selina agreed soberly. "Of course, there are lots of forms of exercise...." She bent her head over the note pad. Magda stifled a laugh.

"I guess we're through here." She rose from the sofa, stretching. "Betsy and I have to go out this afternoon—one of James's aunts is passing through town, staying at the Breckenridge, and she always likes us to stop in and have an early dinner with her." She glanced out the window, where the air fairly sizzled with heat. "It's going to be a job just getting Betsy out of the pool. Trying to get her into a dress— oh, brother!"

Selina laughed sympathetically. She lingered in the gracious room after Magda left, idly examining the paintings in their extravagant gilt frames. Although the pristine white molding that framed the walls, the pictures with their overwhelming baroque images of princes and battles, gave the room an eighteenth-century air, the furniture was not the spindly cream-and-gilt variety associated with the period. Discreetly comfortable sofas and armchairs, slipcovered in muted gray and rose, invited easy lounging. The dark gleaming expanse of inlaid parquet floor was covered with an enormous well-worn and well-tended Aubusson rug. Selina paused in front of a glass-fronted cabinet containing a colorful collection of Art Nouveau glass, her eyes traveling vacantly over the graceful surfaces. Somehow it was hard to associate all this elegance with Gil, with the laughing man who brewed beer and coached little league softball for an inner-city team.

A car sounded in the driveway, and she moved to the window to watch Magda and Betsy drive away. Betsy was scowling, slumped in the seat so that her smart polished-cotton dress wrinkled around her.

The Mercedes disappeared down the driveway. Suddenly the big old house seemed to echo with emptiness.

On an impulse Selina left the living room, mounting the graceful curve of the balustraded staircase. Mrs. Murphy had given her a cursory tour of the house, including the guest rooms, which were to the right at the head of the stairs. But Selina turned left toward the family's quarters. She didn't mean to snoop, she told herself righteously. She just wanted to get rid of this feeling of being a stranger in a strange land.

She paused at an open door and knew immediately that it was Magda's room. It was large and airy but sparsely furnished. Instead of curtains at the window, there were tiers of glass shelves holding a living bouquet of blooming houseplants. The sunlight streamed in, highlighting a Cézanne that hung above the wide mahogany headboard. Selina studied the classic lines of the bed, the matching chiffonier, the lovely rug that echoed the colors of the flowers, and smiled to herself. Magda's room, like the woman herself, contained interesting contrasts between simplicity and luxury.

Betsy's room appeared to be schizophrenic. A feminine frilly canopied four-poster bed vied with a wildly overfilled bulletin board of animal pictures. More framed prints covered the walls, and the low built-in bookcases contained every horse book ever printed. A jumble of tennis racquets, soccer balls, a softball glove and a damp swimsuit huddled in one corner. The room was redolent with the scent of some musky cologne that Betsy had probably splashed on surreptitiously, and that Magda was probably even now lecturing her about.

After Betsy's room came several vacant ones. Gil's room, Selina knew from a casual remark of Mrs. Murphy's, was in one of the turrets that formed the corners of the Château. Selina walked slowly down the hall and pushed the door open.

The setting was dramatic enough. Four windows in the rounded sides of the room let in sunlight, their panes unfettered by the austere simplicity of striped Roman shades. A large low bed wore a tailored cover of the same striped fabric. Selina walked over to one window and looked out, taking in the panoramic view of the Château's grounds, the green hills and groves of Ladue receding in the distance, and the bright thread of the Mississippi winding through the background. Bookcases and drawers had been built in beneath the windows, the tops cushioned to provide seats. Selina sank down, her back to the windows, and contemplated the painting above Gil's bed. In contrast to the eighteenth-century masterpieces throughout the rest of the house, this picture was contemporary, a stark assemblage of shadowed planes that resolved itself into a face the longer she stared at it. Dark, brooding, with unfathomable eyes. With a shock of recognition Selina realized that it was a portrait of Gil. Not of the face he presented to the world, but the elusive gypsy side of him that could be hidden but never tamed. No wonder he kept this portrait here in the privacy of his room. She got quickly to her

feet, feeling like an intruder. There was a loneliness
and longing in those eyes, a vulnerability that she
would never have associated with Gil, but which,
now that she'd seen the portrait, seemed like something she had always known. She left the room,
closing the door protectively behind her.

She wandered back downstairs into her own
room, pausing in the kitchen for a handful of
crackers and cheese. Magda and Betsy were dining
out, and she was at loose ends, with no dinner to fix
for company, and nothing to distract her from her
chaotic thoughts. She stared out her French windows onto her patio, noticing the darkening of the
sky in the northwest as giant clouds began to build
up, their undersides purple with the threat of rain.
When she opened the door, sticky heat seemed to
ooze into the room, bringing with it a sense of op-
pression.

The atmosphere intensified her own restlessness.
She went into her bedroom and changed into running
shorts and shoes, hoping to work off her frustrations
in jogging around the acres of tree-dotted meadow
that surrounded the Château.

She ran slowly along the path from the house to
the garage, moving through the sultry air as if shaking off a restraining hand. *It's almost like running
and taking a sauna at the same time,* she thought,
laboring on with leaden legs and out-of-condition
lungs. Past the rose garden, where the scent of the
roses hung heavily; past the kitchen garden, where
there was no wind to rustle the tall cornstalks. By the
time she reached the wide sloping meadow behind the

house, she had got her second wind. Her legs moved of their own volition; the breeze she made cooled her damp forehead and molded her T-shirt against her body.

A sudden crack of thunder startled her as she neared the top of the field. She glanced over her shoulder at the storm clouds and saw that they were darker, lower, more ominous. As she watched, a thread of brightness seared the livid air, and a few seconds later the thunder boomed again.

Standing on the top of the hill, Selina looked at the rolling fields and beautiful gardens spread out below her. It seemed she could see for miles the lush Missouri countryside. Trees and grass assumed a brighter, acid green against the gray black formations of clouds. Straining her eyes, she imagined the dim towers of the city in the distance. A gust of wind buffeted her, and suddenly it was raining, huge globs of raindrops that drenched her in no time.

She had rarely seen thunder and lightning; even the rain in the Bay Area was inclined to be meek and well mannered. Selina gloried in this downpour, spreading her arms wide, turning her face up to the elements. She ran, swooping dizzily like a newly freed bird, laughing when she stumbled and fell. There was a stump nearby, and she climbed onto it, wanting to be one with the air, unbound from the earth.

Another fork of lightning darted toward the ground, closer this time. The thunder sounded almost immediately. The air seemed to surge with energy. She threw her arms out again in ecstacy.

Then, as she turned on her perch, she saw Gil running up the field toward her. The shock of his unexpected appearance was like lightning to her heart. For a moment she teetered, paralyzed, on the stump. Then, embarrassed to be caught acting like a child, she jumped down.

Gil's mouth was open in a shout, but she could hear only the storm, the loud rushing sound of rain as the clouds emptied their burden directly overhead. The strange excitement that possessed her mingled with the surprise of Gil's abrupt arrival to leave her breathless for the moment. She waited for him to reach her, anticipation overwhelming every other sensation.

But he didn't slow down as he approached. Instead he hooked an arm around her waist and swept her back toward the house, hardly slackening his speed. She ran with him, clamped to his side.

"What—what are you—"

"You little idiot," he panted breathlessly. Part of her noted his breathless state with savage satisfaction; her own lungs were pumping desperately. She stumbled, and he jerked her upright again as they ran. When they reached level ground, he slowed a little, still pulling her along without let up.

At the pool house he stopped. He opened the door and pushed Selina ahead of him into the little building. Hands on hips, he confronted her as she collapsed on a chaise longue.

"How could you stand there on a lightning-blasted stump in the middle of a thunderstorm? Don't you have any sense?"

Selina looked at him in bewilderment, her own anger fading as she saw that his sharpness was caused by concern.

"I don't know what you're talking about. How was I to know the stump had been struck by lightning—and what does it matter, anyway?"

Gil sighed in exasperation. "I suppose you haven't seen many real thunderstorms before, you poor Californian."

"No, I haven't. It's wonderful!" Selina's eyes flashed as another crack of thunder sounded outside.

"Lesson number one in how to survive the Midwest." Gil's voice had lost its angry edge. "Lightning strikes things that stick up alone in empty fields. Like trees, or stumps, or people."

This time Selina shuddered as the thunder pealed. "You mean—"

"Exactly. Kindly stay away from high places in a thunderstorm."

Again came the roll of thunder. She looked around fearfully at the pool house. Now it seemed too frail a shelter against the forces of nature.

Gil folded his arms across his chest as he stood against the door and watched her with a sardonic smile. "Relax. All the outbuildings are grounded— no danger in here."

She shivered nonetheless and realized vaguely that rivulets of rainwater were running down her hair. She was as wet as if she had been in a shower, a fact that Gil's eyes did not overlook. He was staring at the prominent outline of her nipples against the wet fabric of her T-shirt. Her lacy nylon bra provided no concealment.

She said the first words that came into her head. "What are you doing back so early? We didn't expect you till day after tomorrow."

He raised his eyes to her face, trapping her in that amber gaze that seemed to flow over her like warm honey. "I finished my business early." She nodded dumbly, unable to speak, while the tension increased and crackled around them. "You're cold aren't you?" he asked.

He turned away for a moment, breaking the tension, and she gulped, breathing deeply. She noticed that his jeans and polo shirt were as wet as her own, clinging to the broad muscles of his shoulders and outlining the lean taut planes of his buttocks and legs. After rummaging in the cupboard, he turned back holding a large beach towel. He moved toward her, a disturbing light in his eyes, giving her a momentary panicky sensation of being stalked.

"What are you going to do?" she managed to say while struggling to get out of the soft embracing confines of the chaise longue. Gil sat on the edge of the chair and pulled off his shirt in one swift motion, tossing it behind him. He used the towel on his chest, watching Selina, with that disquieting expression of the hunter. She tore her eyes away from his eagle gaze only to be mesmerized by the motions of the towel as he dried himself. The smooth interplay of muscles fascinated her. She stared at his chest, at the tanned skin with its network of dark hair that disappeared into the waistband of his jeans. Suddenly she longed to run her hand along his skin, to undo the snap of his jeans and follow the path of hair. When she looked at him again, he was smiling faintly.

"Like what you see?" His voice was husky. The repressed emotion in it sent tremors through her. He hung the towel loosely around his neck as he held her eyes. "Because I like what I see. I like it very much."

She whispered an assent, trying to still the trembling in her limbs that had nothing to do with being cold. "Oh, Gil. I want you so much." Something flamed in the amber depths of his eyes, and then they were in each other's arms, their lips meeting feverishly. She wrapped her arms around his neck, clutching a handful of the crisp dark hair to anchor herself, letting the fierce passionate kiss explode inside her, setting off a chain reaction through her body. She held him hungrily, giving him the sweetness of her mouth and seeking his in return.

He pulled up her damp T-shirt and slipped it over her head, letting it fall on the floor beside the chaise. His hands unfastened her bra and removed it, too, then moved slowly, questingly, over the soft peaks of her breasts, finding the nipples, bringing them to even greater prominence with his gentle caress. She arched unconsciously as his hand left her breast. "Don't stop," she whispered achingly. "Please don't stop, Gil."

He was fumbling in the pocket of the shirt he'd taken off. "I won't," he promised huskily. "But I brought you a present, and I want to give it to you now." He handed her a tiny silk pouch, embroidered with some jeweler's name, his eyes flaming with desire as they roamed ravenously over her face and torso. "Put it on," he commanded.

She opened the pouch and upended it over her palm. A delicate gold chain spilled out. From it dangled a tiny charm, a golden crescent moon with a silver star caught in the cusp. She fastened the chain around her neck, her fingers clumsy with the intricate catch. Gil drew in his breath in satisfaction. The tiny moon and star nestled in the hollow between her breasts. He traced the line of the chain with one finger while dropping gentle kisses on her nipples. Finally he murmured, "I've been waiting a week to see that chain around your neck. Now you wear the gypsy's brand, Selina. Will you want to take it off?"

Their eyes met. His fierce pride masked the loneliness and vulnerability she had glimpsed in his portrait. "Never," she whispered.

He breathed deeply. "I'm so hungry for you, my darling. But we mustn't hurry things." He gathered her feet into his lap, pulling off her shoes and socks, drying her damp skin with his towel. She watched in anticipation as his hands stroked slowly up her legs, pausing with uncanny knowledge wherever a deeper caress would evoke a deeper response. With agonizing deliberation he eased off her shorts and slipped his hands under the elastic of her lacy briefs, accompanying their journey down her legs with teasing, exciting kisses and gentle nips of his teeth. She strained to reach his belt buckle, managing to unfasten his jeans, pushing at them impatiently until he slid them off his lean body and lay beside her on the chaise longue, naked and glorious.

Their bodies met, flesh against flesh, twining with mounting excitement. Selina pushed the hard tips of her nipples against his chest, enjoying the sensations caused by contact with the rough curly hair. Gil groaned, and she felt the way his breathing quickened when her hands made demanding forays down the flat smooth plane of his stomach, reveling in his hard strength. He nibbled warmly at her ear as his hand trailed up the inside of her thigh, his fingers finding her innermost warmth. They exchanged slow langorous kisses while their fingers teased each other with sensuous emphasis.

Finally Selina could take no more of the love play. She closed her hand compellingly and moaned into his ear. "Gil—please, Gil!"

He drew a ragged breath. "Sweetheart." His voice trembled unsteadily. "I want you so—please, let me—"

"Oh, yes," she whispered, not recognizing her own voice. She moved against him, trying to enclose his length with her body.

"When you do that—oh, Selina—" He raised himself above her, his eyes burning into hers with an expression so fierce and tender she had to close her own eyes for a moment. With exquisite care he slid into her, holding her tightly against him, a look of unutterable sweetness suffusing his face. "Oh, darling...." His vulnerability in the midst of his strength opened her like a flower for him. She felt tears prick her eyelids, and then she was lost in the increasing intensity of the rhythm they set between them, rocketing up and up until at last she soared over the stars, returning in a slow drift to earth and reality.

Gil stroked the damp hair off her forehead and dropped butterfly kisses on her eyes. She let her palm trail with langorous possession across his back, kneading the smooth muscles with delicate movements of her fingers. He cupped one of her breasts firmly, closing his eyes in satisfaction as he gathered her closer. "I don't think I'll be able to let you go," he murmured. "I want to make love to you every minute for the next fifty years, although—" he moved a cramped arm "—in a more comfortable place."

Selina barely heard his words. She was still lost in the aftermath of love. He looked down into her dreamy face and gave her a gentle shake. "I've got an idea. Let's go take a shower."

She blinked up at him. "Huh? A shower? Do you have some sort of water fetish or something?"

He lifted her off the chaise longue, holding her away and admiring the slender roundness of her body for a moment. "After exercise you take a shower, right? Any reason why we shouldn't take it together?" As he spoke, he picked up her T-shirt and tugged it gently over her head. She shivered as the cold wet fabric touched her naked flesh. Gil placed his hands over her tautened nipples, the warmth welcome on her cold skin. "You ever thought of entering a wet-T-shirt contest?" He tossed her her shorts and pulled on his own blue jeans.

"Never." Selina raised a hand to her hair, hoping it didn't look as wildly disarrayed as it felt.

"Good. Don't ever do it. I want to be the only man who sees you like that." He leered wolfishly, fastening his belt buckle. "For your own protection, you understand. Come on, let's go."

She grabbed quickly for her underwear before he pulled her out of the pool house. The storm was over, the clouds rolling back to reveal a newly washed sky, already dyed with the beginning colors of sunset.

Somehow the beauty of the fresh-washed evening caused a melancholy ache to begin in Selina's heart. She glanced at Gil as he strode beside her. He looked relaxed, confident, assured. Obviously he wasn't plagued by doubts about what had just happened. But even his cheerful grin as he caught her eyes on him couldn't chase away her growing sense of something being wrong.

"Your place or mine?" He put his arm around her shoulders and held her against him as he opened the back door. There was contentment in his touch; unconsciously she nestled closer.

"My place is yours," she said seriously, realizing at once that was part of the problem.

Gil didn't seem to notice her suddenly grave expression, but when they were through the kitchen door, he wrapped his arms around her and brushed her forehead with his lips. "You've got that wrong, sweetheart," he murmured, planting tiny stirring kisses all over her face. "My place is yours. All yours."

His kisses woke her fierce desire for him that was always close to the surface. She guided him toward the door of her suite. Whether it was wrong or not didn't seem to matter while he was close. She would think about it later, after he'd gone.

Gil closed the sitting-room door behind him. As their eyes met, Selina felt her doubts and fears melting in a flood of sweet emotion. So much tenderness, so much desire, was plainly visible on Gil's face. For some reason she had become important to him, and that would be enough for now. She silenced the voice inside her that cried for love, for commitment. Perhaps both would come later, perhaps not. In the meantime she would take what he offered and explore it thoroughly.

When Gil's hands went to her T-shirt again, she forestalled him. "Let me," she breathed. Her words resounded in the tension-filled air of the little room. Slowly she pulled off the clinging T-shirt, noticing the sensations caused by the wet fabric as it slid over her swollen nipples, over the smooth skin of her shoulders. Bared to the waist, she faced Gil proudly, trembling slightly.

His eyes hooded with passion, he reached for her, but she pushed his hands away. "Now you," she said. Standing in front of him, she lifted her arms and let her hands trail down the muscular length of his torso. She closed her eyes while her fingertips learned the feel of him. When she encountered his belt, she fumbled with the fastening, slipping her hands inside to explore the muscular planes of his buttocks.

Gil moved then, no longer standing like a statue under her ministrations. In one motion he was rid of his jeans; in another she was minus her damp running shorts. He held her naked body against his, and she felt fire kindling along their lengths wherever their bodies touched. Desire rose in her so strongly that she shuddered, arching more closely to the maleness of him, fastening her lips on his and drinking the molten sweetness of their kiss greedily, like a child with no thought beyond the pleasure of the moment.

This time when they made love, it was more explosive, wrapping them together in a ceaseless sensuous oblivion. Dimly Selina realized that they were sprawled across her bed. She lay looking vacantly at the ceiling as her mind gradually came to full awareness of what she'd done.

I don't want to think about it now, she told herself fiercely. She turned and burrowed into Gil's side, clasping him with an urgency that could have been misconstrued. But with his usual prescience, he cradled her warmly.

"Having doubts, sweetheart? Just trust me. Everything will be fine."

Eventually they did take their shower, and eventually Gil left, casually wearing a towel, his clothes draped over his shoulder. Not a moment too soon, either; the Mercedes drew up in front of the garage as Selina emerged from her room, wearing clean jeans and feeling ravenous. Gil was already in the kitchen, hungrily munching on one of his Dagwood sandwiches.

"I should fix you some dinner," she cried, once

again assailed by the unpleasant feeling that things were out of joint.

Gil gestured toward the opposite side of the work-table. Another sandwich oozed untidily from its surrounding French roll. It had been raggedly cut across the middle, causing even greater loss of lettuce, tomato and assorted fillings. Beside it stood a glass of milk.

"I made one for you," he said after swallowing mightily. "Don't want you to get the idea that I'm not handy in the kitchen."

Selina sat across from him and took a tentative bite of the sandwich. It was surprisingly tasty. She took a large bite and washed it down with a thirsty gulp of milk. "Thanks," she said when her mouth was free. "I was just feeling starved. . . ."

"Exercise will do that to you," he agreed smoothly as the back door opened to admit Magda and Betsy. Selina felt a betraying blush creep into her cheeks and bent her head over her plate.

"What a storm!" Magda headed for the coffee maker and poured herself a steaming cup. "We would have been here an hour ago, but Aunt Ola didn't want us to go out in the lightning." She looked at Gil vaguely, then focused on him. "Gil, darling. I didn't even realize you were home! How nice that you got back early!"

Betsy came in, saw Gil and headed straight for him, giving him an exuberant hug. "Gil, you're back! Super! Did you see the neat thunderstorm?" She looked up at his damp hair. "I guess you did. Looks like you got caught in it." Gil exchanged a playful glance with Selina, but before either of them could say anything, Betsy was rushing on. "Gil, we passed the horse farm on our way home, and they still have that colt. Can we go see it now, huh? Please, Gil?"

Selina finished her sandwich quietly as the family chatter went on around her. She fought the feeling of being an outsider, excluded from the warm circle of family love.

When a propitious moment arose, she said good-evening and slipped into her sitting room. Gil, to her secret relief, said nothing in front of his family to reveal his new intimacy with her. But his eyes followed her as she moved toward her door, and she couldn't help glancing back at him before shutting it. The special warmth she saw in his smile was accompanied by something else, a considering, brooding look she couldn't interpret.

Alone in her room, she sat before the empty fireplace, staring vacantly at the row of brightly painted pottery angels that decorated the mantel. Closing her eyes, she imagined once more the ecstasy of being in Gil's arms, being completely his.

Her previous interest in Andy Corbett seemed long ago now. Her feelings for Gil ran so much deeper that to compare her love for him with her infatuation with Andy was to compare the distance to the farthest bright star in the sky with a trip to the corner drugstore. Now she could admit that she had never loved Andy, because it was obvious to her that she was deeply, madly, irrevocably in love with Gilmartin Duchenay.

But when she considered the future, she was

plunged into despair. If they continued as lovers, her situation would be untenable. She couldn't live in his house, cook his meals, take a salary from him and be his mistress at the same time. It would be too involved, would make her feel too much as if she were being kept by him. And if they were not to be lovers—what then? The thought was too painful to contemplate. The only solution she could see was to resign as chef. She would find another position, and they could continue seeing each other.

There was an unexpected pang at the thought of leaving the Château. She had grown to love the beauty of the surroundings, the gracious elegance of the building. *The trouble with you,* she scolded herself, *is that you want to have your cake and eat it, too.* She wanted Gil; she had the Château; she wanted to continue meeting challenges as a chef. But there was no scenario that fit her desires.

Marriage? She thought with desperate yearning of the delight of being Mrs. Gilmartin Duchenay. But just saying the name over to herself brought her to her senses. Wouldn't Mrs. Gilmartin Duchenay be expected to be a creature of society, able to move at ease through the most august gathering, beautiful and poised? Though reasonably attractive, Selina felt she was a far cry from that elegant passionless ideal. She was short, with stubby red curls and a distressingly down-to-earth manner. And she had no desire to make society her career. *I love my work. I have important career plans. Mrs. Gilmartin Duchenay's career revolves around her husband, her social life. That's not for me.*

Convinced that quitting her job was the only solution, she went to bed, to spend a restless night pounding her pillow and dreaming short agonizingly sweet dreams of being in Gil's arms again.

CHAPTER TEN

IT WAS DISCONCERTING the following day to find that everyone around her expected life to go on as usual. Perhaps if they'd known the momentous events of Sunday afternoon, they could have understood her dilemma. In the midst of ordering supplies for the next-evening's dinner party, Selina found herself reminded by the presence of the moon-and-star charm that she and Gil were lovers. Just the thought made it difficult to concentrate on how many pounds of mushrooms she needed, or when the lemons should be delivered.

Despite her absence of mind she'd completed her telephone ordering by the time Magda came in for morning coffee.

"I thought you were supposed to be off until tomorrow afternoon," she said around a yawn as Selina hung up the telephone.

Selina shrugged. "With a dinner party tomorrow night I thought I should get a jump on the ordering. I don't want to be stuck with everyone's leftovers."

Magda stirred her coffee, her expression apologetic. "I didn't realize that would be a problem when I planned a party for Tuesday night. It was the only night Mr. Hartner had free. Sorry, Selina. I'll give you another day toward the end of the week to compensate."

"You don't need to do that," Selina protested. She found a container of yogurt in the refrigerator and spooned it over her sliced peaches.

"My dear," Magda said, giving Selina's breakfast a dubious glance, "I would do more than that to keep the chef who's rapidly making my dinner parties the most popular events in St. Louis. I never have to dig up a substitute these days. No one's turned down an invitation from me since you started cooking."

Selina looked down at her bowl, all appetite suddenly gone. What would Magda do if she blurted out, "Your son and I made love, and I want to have an affair with him so I'm quitting as your chef"? Magda's warmth and friendliness toward her since she'd started working at the Château would make it very difficult when she handed in her resignation.

The kitchen telephone rang, and she jumped to answer it, relieved by the diversion. It was Gil's voice, resonant with sensual promise. "Good morning, gypsy's lady. Sleep well?"

"No, as a matter of fact, I didn't," she retorted, then remembered Magda sitting behind her. "What—what can I do for you?"

"I'll answer that in detail—very pleasurable detail—when I get home tonight. In the meantime, you can come downtown and have lunch with me. We've got things to discuss."

She had been counting the hours till evening when she would see him again. "All right," she said, trying for Magda's benefit to keep her voice neutral, not revealing the breathless anticipation that suddenly gripped her. "Where?"

She scribbled his instructions for finding the restaurant on her note pad and returned to her breakfast, appetite restored. Gil would help make it right for everyone. Magda's face was incurious, but Selina told her, anyway. "That was Gil. He wants me to meet him for lunch."

"What fun." Magda smiled placidly and got up to rinse out her coffee cup. "Now that's more like what you should be doing on your day off."

Selina stared bemusedly at the kitchen door as it swung shut behind Magda. It was hard to tell if her employer approved of a romance between the chef and her son, or if she was too sure such a romance was out of the question to worry about it. Selina shook her head, charged through the rest of the items on her action list in record time and went to her bedroom to ransack the closet.

She had few clothes in the dressing-up-for-lunch category, preferring to work in jeans and T-shirts. But she had bought one dress from the bargain rack at I. Magnin, a simply cut aqua halter dress in fine Swiss cotton. Its deep V-neck was a perfect setting for Gil's necklace. She pulled her hair back from her face with tortoiseshell combs, dabbed at her mouth with the one lipstick she owned and slipped into low-heeled sandals. When she viewed the final results in her full-length mirror, she was pleased. The woman she saw reflected looked fine—slender, rounded figure crowned by bright hair like a halo where the sun caught it. There was an added glow from being in love that owed nothing to the sun.

It was stifling in the Audi, and she couldn't get the air conditioning to work. Finally she cranked the window wide, preferring the hot blast of wind in her face to the breathless heat generated with the windows closed. She turned the radio up and hummed a cheerful tuneless accompaniment to the tender love song that was playing.

I'm in love, Selina thought with a sudden surge of elation. Being in love was wonderful, was right. The steady rush of sultry air, the vivid green banks of bushes and trees along the highway, the high blue arch of sky with its fast-moving clouds, all made her feel that she could drive off the road and up into the air with the exhilaration of love.

By the time she found the little Italian restaurant Gil had specified, her hair was disheveled and her dress creased and limp. She searched her handbag vainly for a hairbrush and finally settled for taming her hair as best she could with the tortoiseshell combs. She shook out her skirt and glanced uncertainly at her reflection as she passed a store window. She was no longer the immaculate figure that had left her bedroom, but the heat hadn't dimmed the happiness in her eyes.

Gil waited in the tiny entrance of the restaurant. His eyes ran over her appreciatively. "You're a dream," he murmured in her ear, holding her gently by the arms. "Except for your mouth. What happened?"

She stole a guilty glance in the mirror over the cash

register. The lipstick had left a rim around the edges of her lips and vanished completely from the rest. She scrubbed at her mouth with a tissue. "I just put on some lipstick—"

"Let me." Gil took the tissue away from her and bent his head, nibbling gently around the circumference of her lips. She stood still under the tender movement, torn between enjoying the delicious sensations he created and fear that people were looking at them.

Gil lifted his head and looked down at her with satisfaction. "There. Rosy lips the natural way. You don't need lipstick, Selina. You're beautiful just the way you are."

The restaurant was small, dark and intimate; the tables crowded together, but full of couples who paid little attention to anyone else. Gil didn't touch her while the waiter took their order, but his eyes were as warm as a kiss. "I could barely work this morning for thinking of you," he told her huskily after the waiter left.

"Me, too," she whispered, abashed by the fire in his gaze. "What—what did you want to talk about?"

"You, me, us. I've never felt this way before."

Selina nodded. "I feel the same. Only—"

He put a hand up to smooth the crease between her brows. "What worries you, sweetheart? I know there's something. Tell me all about it."

"It's—just too awkward," she blurted out. "Living in your house, being the chef and having an affair with you, too. That's why I . . . ."

He had gone very still. As she hesitated, he

prompted her, his voice suddenly cold. "Why you what?"

"Why I think it would be best if I got a different job. In a restaurant or somewhere. Then we could go on seeing each other in less—less conspicuous circumstances."

The waiter came back with their wine, and Gil sat silently while he poured, impatiently waving the cork away. Selina could feel his warmth had been withdrawn. She hunched her shoulders nervously, clasping her arms against the air-conditioned chill of the room.

Gil spoke, his voice grown remote. "I don't find the circumstances at all conspicuous. Perhaps you'd care to explain what exactly you mean. I thought—" He paused, his eyes plunging deep into hers. She forced herself to endure the scrutiny but couldn't help breaking into nervous chatter.

"Maybe you don't find it awkward. After all, it's your house; it's your money that pays my salary. It makes me feel too—kept."

"You work hard for your money," Gil said. Although his voice had lost some of its steely quality, his piercing gaze was fastened on the wine he swirled in his glass.

"I need my independence," she said tightly. His attitude bespoke rigid control, but she didn't understand what caused it. Somehow the conversation had gone terribly wrong. She pushed down the part of her that wanted to declare her love for him. If he didn't say he loved her back, it would be unbearable.

"As I recall," he said, biting off the words, "you

assured me you meant to work as my chef until it was time to move on to advanced schooling, like the Cordon Bleu. I doubt you've got the capital together to do that, so I don't intend to let you go to work for someone else. Is that clear?''

It was obvious that she was important to him as a chef alone, not as a lover. She blinked back tears and held her head high. ''You've made it very clear just what you expect from me, Mr. Duchenay. It's too bad that what you want me to do and what I want to do don't coincide. If you'd like me to submit a formal letter of resignation—''

He muttered a curse beneath his breath and grabbed her wrist, yanking her to her feet. Towing her behind him, he strode from the restaurant, thrusting a bill into the hand of the startled waiter with a curt ''We've changed our minds.'' Selina had time only to register the waiter's slightly reproachful look at her before they were standing on the sidewalk.

Gil clamped her hand under his arm and hustled her down the sidewalk. His face was grim and wrathful. She gaped up at him, amazed at the change. Where was easygoing Gil? ''Just a minute,'' she panted, almost loosing her footing trying to keep up with him. ''What do you—I don't have to put up with this!''

He paid no attention, but he did come to a halt before a nondescript car parked by the curb. He unlocked it and opened the door. ''Get in.''

''Now listen, Gilmartin Duchenay!'' Selina put her hands on her hips and glared up at him.

"Get in the car." His voice was implacable and stirred up the contrariness in Selina's nature. She turned to stalk away. His hand shot out and grasped her arm. The next thing she knew she was in the car, and Gil was sliding behind the steering wheel. He put the keys in the ignition but didn't turn it on. His hands gripped the wheel until the knuckles shone white beneath the skin. Although bewildered and confused by revolving emotions, Selina still refused to be intimidated by his anger and sat stiffly a good distance away from him.

Finally with an anguished groan he pulled her into his arms, his hands stroking her hair, her back. "Selina—" his voice was ragged. "Don't do this to me—to both of us. I go crazy when I think you're trying to leave me. Just don't—do it, that's all." She could feel his trembling beneath her hands. With a last attempt at salvaging her self-respect Selina looked up, searching his face.

"Then you don't just want me as a chef?"

His laugh was delighted. He pulled her closer. "Lady, haven't you figured out the answer to that? I want you in every possible way."

Hearing these words was all she needed, and Selina nestled closely against his shoulder. "I'm sorry about lunch," she mumbled.

"Forget it." He caught her hand and brought it to his lips. "Just don't put me through another half hour like that one. I might not survive." His teeth nipped gently at the soft mound of flesh beneath her thumb, sending shivers of delight through her. When he kissed the bare skin of her shoulder and neck, she let her head fall back, inviting his lips to follow the line of his chain to the hollow of her breasts. His hand stroked slowly with a feather-light touch down the side of her breast as his lips found hers. She parted her lips for the seductive exploration of his tongue, wrapping her arms eagerly around him, losing herself in the veil of desire he created.

"So you won't leave, right, sweetheart?"

It took a moment for his words to penetrate. When she realized what he'd said, Selina sat straight up, almost bumping her head on his chin.

"Gil," she began cautiously. "I thought you understood. I can't stay if we're—if you—I can't have an affair with you while I'm working under your roof."

Once again he subjected her to the bone-shattering scrutiny. "Why not?" he said finally.

She moved out of his arms. "I explained all that. I have to feel—I have to be independent. Have my own territory. Not accept everything in my life from you."

Impatiently he turned away to start the car, "Don't give me that Jane Eyre stuff," he growled, pulling out into traffic.

"Then don't act like what's-his-name," she retorted. "After all, I'm admitting that part of me wants to have an affair with you."

He gave her a strange look. "Thank you very much. An affair is not exactly what I had in mind."

Fear clutched her heart. He didn't love her. "I don't—was last night supposed to be a one-night stand?"

He shook his head in disbelief. "I can't make you see—" Taking a deep breath, he added more gently, "We're both confused by the state of our emotions. I know you'd like everything neatly measured just like a recipe. Unfortunately I can't do that." He was silent for a moment, then changed the subject. "Meanwhile we didn't discuss what I wanted to talk to you about. And no more of this nonsense about quitting your job. I have a real coup in mind, and I need to be able to depend on you, Selina."

"I don't know where we stand," Selina persisted. Gil turned the car onto the highway, heading toward downtown. "Where are we going? Gilmartin Duchenay, don't you realize I drove the Audi to lunch? And I'm starving!"

Gil laughed unreservedly. "First of all, we don't stand. We lie down whenever possible. Secondly we're going to my office, where I will send out for some sandwiches from the deli. When we're through discussing my business, I'll drive you back to your car. So no more back talk from you, Chef Montgomery!"

Selina sat quietly as he maneuvered the car through city traffic, turning their conversation in her mind, realizing she would get nowhere with Gil at the moment. He parked in a downtown garage, helped her out of the car and took her arm again, striding briskly toward the garage entrance. They moved through the crowded sidewalks, while Selina looked around with interest.

Downtown St. Louis was a study in contrasts: modern high-rise office buildings cheek by jowl with massive ornamented stone fronts of the 1880s, mostly in need of cleaning and repair. Gil guided her into the lobby of a magnificent example of late nineteenth-century urban architecture, a building whose facade was enriched with dignified swags and bouquets of masonry. The lobby inside was a wide gracious expanse of marble. Behind ornate wrought-iron doors the elevators were surprisingly large and sleek.

"My father had the whole building renovated and brought up to code ten years ago." Gil said, displaying again his extraordinary ability to read her thoughts. "New elevators, new bathrooms, new carpeting for the halls—he even had the lighting fixtures researched so we could get copies of the original gas ones—although, of course, we use electricity these days."

Selina glanced into one of the offices as they walked down a fourth-floor hallway. The room was full of computer terminals and noisy with the clatter of electronic printers.

Gil turned right at a bisecting corridor. Here the carpet underfoot was even thicker; the walls were hung with daguerreotypes in antique frames. Through an arched doorway was a beautifully appointed reception room. Gil nodded genially to the pleasant-looking woman seated at a large desk, her fingers flying over her word-processor's keyboard. A small picture beside the terminal depicted a chubby-faced little girl in pigtails, holding an even chubbier baby brother.

Selina slowed involuntarily to look at a wall-size blowup of an old photograph showing an upright

bearded old gentleman in frock coat and tall hat,
stoically regarding an elaborate wedding cake nearly
as tall as he was. "My grandfather," Gil said, hurry-
ing her along another corridor, this time carpeted
with beautifully tended old Persian runners. "He ran
a catering business. Got us started in food preparation. His father owned a chain of fruit-and-vegetable
stands. Here we are."

He pushed open a door made of some dark wood,
polished until it gleamed like the bright brass doorknob. Selina looked around, glad of a chance to
catch her breath.

The room was large, with a high ceiling and airy
proportions. The shirred swags that curtained the tall
windows were made like Roman shades so they could
be drawn up to reveal a view of the Gateway Arch
and the Mississippi River in the distance. He must
like his windows uncluttered, she thought, remembering the windows in his bedroom. In front of the
windows was an impressive mahogany desk, almost
as wide as a double bed. To one side were a Victorian
love seat and two chairs, upholstered in tasteful green
silk brocade, grouped around a marble-topped table.
Gil gestured Selina toward the sofa while he spoke
into the telephone.

"Helen, could you have the deli send up a couple
of sandwiches?" He cocked an inquiring eyebrow at
Selina. "Meatball subs okay with you? And two cof-
fees. And some potato salad, come to think of it.
Thanks."

Selina expected him to sit next to her on the love
seat, but he took one of the side chairs instead. He

pulled a notebook out of his pocket and shrugged the jacket off. "Now," he said briskly. "You've gathered from Betsy's ever fertile gossip that I'm being pressured by my board to come up with a new market. If I don't show some good projections at the next meeting, which is in New Orleans in three weeks, I will be up the well-known creek."

Selina interrupted. "Can they do that? It's your company, isn't it? That was your grandfather on the wall out there."

Gil smiled wryly at her indignant face. "Purity is a publicly held corporation. Although mother and I control a good deal of the stock, we're not invulnerable to takeover threats. I'm taking steps to make us more secure in that respect, but in the meantime my best protection is to do my job the best possible way. Actually I was already softening up some new customers when Fred Warner—he's the trouble-maker on the board—started making noise. I want to bring some luxury-hotel owners into our fold. We cater airlines—" he ignored Selina's involuntary chuckle "—and hospitals, and we've sold our components to some of the mid-range nationwide restaurant chains. But the luxury trade doesn't go for precooked portion-controlled frozen entrées or even the reconstituted stuff. I need to get some of the restaurant owners in a vulnerable position and find out what they want."

The receptionist, whom Selina guessed to be Helen, tapped on the door and came in with a paper bag and two full coffee cups balanced on a tray. Gil thanked her and began unwrapping the sandwiches.

He handed one to Selina and bit into his with gusto. "Have some potato salad," he said indistinctly. "I have some paper plates somewhere." He rummaged around in a closet for a moment, coming back with two paper plates.

Selina spooned the potato salad onto her plate, taking a cautious bite with her plastic fork. It was good. She tried the meatball sandwich and found it messy but tasty. "So what is your idea of a vulnerable position? Locking these people up in the wine cellar or something?"

Gil laughed. "I wouldn't lock Hal MacMillan in the cellar for any amount of money. It'd be dry when I let him out."

The coffee was good, too. "Hal is one of the hotel owners you want to work on? I wouldn't have thought he'd hold out on you."

"He's fond of a good business deal, but he likes good food too much to go for profit at the expense of taste." Gil didn't sound particularly approving of Hal's point of view. "But I have something in mind I know will soften him up, and Hartner, and Olen. I want to invite them on a cruise down the Mississippi on a steamboat, and I want you to treat them to eight days of the best food they ever ate. By the time they get to New Orleans, I should be able to sign them on the dotted line."

Selina swallowed a bite of meatball before it was properly chewed. She gulped the coffee, scalding her mouth. "I—I don't know what to say," she gasped.

"Think about it if you want to," he urged. "I'll give you a few minutes." He grinned at her, and she felt her indignation melt away. "It's really Betsy's idea, you know. She put it in my mind a couple of weeks ago, and I talked to the Rossfields before I left for Cincinnati. They own a stern-wheeler, the *Margaret B. Townshend*, which they rent to charter groups sometimes. However, they don't usually rent it for a trip to New Orleans because of insurance hassles. So they've agreed to let me use it if I pay expenses and let them go along. I dangled your talents in front of them, I'm afraid, and they took the bait in a flash. Like most of mother's friends around here, they've heard about your cooking."

"That was unscrupulous, Gil. What if I refuse to go?"

"You can't refuse." He moved to sit beside her on the love seat, taking her hands in his. "It's not just that I need you to say yes. You won't be able to resist the challenge. Mrs. Rossfield was worried that the state of the cook house on the boat would discourage you, but I knew you'd really enjoy the opportunity to prove that a great chef doesn't need all the latest equipment to turn out memorable meals."

Selina bit her lip as she heard one of her own grandiose statements, uttered one Monday evening while she and Hailey waited for an experimental batch of blueberry muffins to cook. "You are a grade-A wretch, Gilmartin Duchenay," she scolded. "What's the matter with the kitchen—cook house, I suppose you say? Wood stoves? Open fires?"

Gil waved her inquiry away. "Not that bad. We'll go up and take a look at the boat before we invite everyone to come. The worst problem is probably refrigeration. I don't imagine there's more than one or two refrigerators, and it will be difficult to replenish for such a large group during the trip.''

"Large group? How large? How many does this stern-wheeler sleep, anyway?"

He scribbled a few figures on his pad. "She'll sleep thirty or so in cabins. But I'm only inviting the Rossfields, Hal, the Hartners, the Olens, Mother, Betsy, you and me, plus the Rossfields' two sons, who are used to acting as stewards. There are three VIP cabins, and twenty more that are little better than closets. But it'll be fun."

Selina's eyes began to sparkle. The Mississippi, paddle-wheelers, hot summer days, banjo music drifting across the water—she could almost see herself in an antebellum crinoline and parasol. Gil would make a wonderful riverboat gambler, she thought wistfully. "A costume party! For the last night of the trip. We'll be near New Orleans, so Creole cooking would be in order. . . ."

Gil threw his arm around her shoulders. "Does that mean you're going to go?"

"Not necessarily. . ." she began cautiously. But he kissed her thoroughly and enthusiastically, refusing to listen. "Great! Let's plan on driving up to St. Charles tomorrow. The Rossfields berth the *Margaret B. Townshend* at a yacht club there." He looked at her plate. "You want the rest of your potato salad?" She shook her head, and he cleaned her plate in two bites. "Come on, let's get going. I've got a lot to do this afternoon. I'll give you a ride back to your car and get started."

All the way back to the Audi he chatted enthusiastically about his previous trip down the river, the
reasons why he was going to work on these three particular hotel owners first, his gratitude to Selina for
helping him out. She tried to insert a few words
about not having made up her mind about the trip
yet, about needing to look for another job, he
brushed them aside. "We'll talk about it later," he
said. "No point in planning too far ahead." For a
moment she caught a glimpse of something wary in
his eyes, but it was gone before she could be sure of
it, and he was pulling up next to the Audi. "See you
tonight, sweetheart. We'll have a lot of contingencies
to go over."

She watched him drive away and got into the Audi,
a forlorn slump to her shoulders. Nothing about this
lunch had been what she expected. Did Gil's urgency
to keep her working for him stem from passion or his
need for a good chef? She was no closer to knowing
that now than she had been this morning.

Come hell or high water, she told herself solemnly.
*I'm getting out of the Château after the riverboat
trip. If I'm still sane, that is.* She unrolled the windows to let the sticky heat out, but for the drive back
to Ladue she didn't turn the radio on.

CHAPTER ELEVEN

SELINA SAID NOTHING to Magda or Betsy about Gil's steamboat scheme as they shared an early supper of leftovers. He wasn't home yet, and she felt it would be mean to steal his thunder, although she was longing to ask Magda, who might have paid more attention than Gil to the kitchen areas, if she knew from her trip on the *Margaret B. Townshend* what the cook house was like.

Gil still wasn't home by the time Hailey arrived for their usual Monday evening session. This week they were working on cinnamon rolls. While she kneaded the satiny dough, Hailey confided her own worries.

"Mother suspects," she told Selina. "When she asked me where I went every day, I told her I'd joined a health club. She went through my purse one morning before I was up and didn't find any health-club membership cards. I told her they keep their list on a computer, and that stumped her for the time being. But I feel as if she's closing in on me."

"Doesn't it bother you to lie to her like that?" Selina was sorry she'd asked the moment the words left her mouth, but she found Hailey's facile ability to make up stories a bit disturbing.

Hailey shrugged. "It would if she wasn't such a

dragon. It's so silly, Selina. Here I am, becoming a successful small businesswoman—''

''Smaller than before,'' Selina interjected, with a laughing glance at Hailey's svelte figure.

''I think so, too,'' Hailey said eagerly, looking down at herself. ''I'll probably never be as slim as you, but at least I no longer qualify for blimp status. I think that's the only thing that has mother thinking twice.'' An exasperated sigh escaped her. ''She's so pleased with my new figure she wanted to borrow some more money for a new wardrobe!''

Hailey began rolling out the dough, her lips compressed in a worried frown. With silent sympathy Selina handed her the pot of melted butter. ''Anyway, I told her I could get my own clothes, but I couldn't explain where the money was going to come from. I hope she doesn't do anything foolish.''

''So you're really doing well, then.''

''Business has been super!'' Hailey's face lighted up with enthusiasm. ''I'm making so much money that the bookkeeping has become a real chore. I'm thinking of hiring a bookkeeper or something. People really go for the chocolate cake and the carrot cake. And if I can just get these cinnamon rolls to stay moist for more than a few hours, I think they'll be a big winner. Trouble is, they seem to get stale so fast. The restaurants don't like that, naturally. But I don't intend to use preservatives because I don't like the idea. Do you have any other solutions?''

While the cinnamon rolls raised, they discussed various possibilities. Hailey was just sliding the baking sheet into the oven when Gil came in the back door. He slung his attaché case into a corner and draped his jacket over a chair. "Wonderful," he exclaimed, looking greedily at the second sheet of rolls as Hailey put them in the oven. "I forgot it was Selina's seminar night. How long before they're done?"

Selina brought out the leftovers again, which he devoured eagerly. "I've never seen anyone eat like you," she mused, watching him dispose of an apple in three bites. "What do you do with it all?"

"I work it off—in various ways." He leered at her suggestively. "Perhaps you'd like a demonstration."

"Down, boy." She backed behind the table, glancing apprehensively at Hailey, who watched the by- play with a knowing smile. Abruptly Gil gave up the chase and disappeared through the wine-cellar door. "Collect mother and Betsy," he yelled over his shoulder. "We need to have a pow-wow."

Selina looked helplessly at Hailey, who walked over to the intercom phone and dialed the living room. "Aunt Magda," she said into it, "Gil's here and wants everyone to assemble in the kitchen." She sent a wicked glance toward Selina. "No, we haven't the *foggiest* idea why."

Gil came up from the wine cellar just as Magda and Betsy entered the kitchen. He cradled a bottle in each arm. "Champagne," he announced. "And a quart of my best homebrew. Which would you prefer to drink, Selina?"

Without hesitation she chose the champagne. "Your homebrew I can get anytime. Champagne this good is a real treat. Why the celebration?"

He said softly, "Can't you guess?" She dropped her eyes and shook her head. Magda was getting an ice bucket out of the china closet, and Gil turned to fill it with ice. He thrust the bottle in and gestured to everyone to sit around the table. "I have something to announce."

Betsy squirmed with suppressed excitement. "I bet I know," she burst out. "I bet it's about you and—"

Magda quelled her with a sharp glance. "Please put us out of our misery. What's the announcement?"

He turned the champagne bottle in its bucket of ice. "I've arranged to use the *Margaret B. Townshend* for ten days, starting in a week. We're going down the Mississippi to New Orleans on a gourmet riverboat cruise."

Betsy whooped with delight, all further speculation gone. Magda murmured a surprised comment, her eyes flying swiftly to Selina's face. Hailey watched her, too, her eyes both puzzled and sympathetic. It was obvious they'd expected Gil to make some sort of announcement concerning Selina and himself. Did they expect he would become engaged to the chef? Selina shook her head in frustration. To add to her confusion, Gil seemed to have forgotten that she hadn't yet agreed to stay for the riverboat cruise.

"It's very brave of Selina," Magda said, fetching some champagne glasses. Selina sat at the table, overwhelmed by a tidal wave of lethargy. Dimly she realized that she, too, had expected a different announcement from Gil. Where did this leave her, anyway?

"Have you seen the facilities on the boat?" Magda inquired. "I know you're a good improviser, but—"

Selina roused herself. "No," she snapped, "I have not seen the facilities. I haven't even said for sure I'd go on the cruise, let alone—" She stopped, not wanting to reveal her plans for quitting and have everyone worm the reason out of her. Gil's wicked glance showed that he knew exactly why she hesitated.

"Selina hasn't seen the galley yet, or cook house, as they call it," he said easily, "but I know she's up to it. She's got a week to prepare, and a very competent *sous-chef*." He bowed to Betsy, who grinned delightedly back.

"It sounds wonderful," Hailey said wistfully. "If only I didn't have a business to run. . . ."

"We could trade," Selina suggested half in earnest. "I'll do your baking; you go on the trip for me."

Magda laughed, but Gil drew his eyebrows together forbiddingly. "If we only wanted to eat pastry. . ." he began and was interrupted by the timer. Not the least insulted, Hailey laughed.

"Saved by the bell." She pulled on her oven mitts and took the baking sheets out of the oven. She began making glaze while Gil watched absentmindedly.

"Nevertheless, Gil," Magda said firmly, "you mustn't pressure Selina to agree to the trip until she's seen the accommodations. I gather this is more than a pleasure cruise?"

"I'm also inviting the Hartners, the Olens and Hal MacMillan," he said curtly. "After being on a riverboat with them for over a week, I should be able to find some way to sell them on Purity.''

Magda looked thoughtful. Gil pulled the champagne out of the bucket and popped the cork, a towel draped over his arm. ''Meanwhile, let's drink to going down the lazy river. No matter what happens, we'll have a great adventure together.'' His eyes met Selina's with a meaningful message. ''I know we're all going to enjoy it.''

She accepted a glass from him, still troubled but unable to summon the courage to announce her desire to quit when everyone was drinking champagne and feeling festive. Suddenly she realized Gil had known his premature speech would make it extremely hard for her to back out. She glared at him, and he winked, his expression annoyingly complacent.

Under cover of Betsy's eager questions to Magda about her previous jaunt on the *Margaret B. Townshend*, Selina edged closer to Gil. ''Pretty underhanded,'' she hissed, with a defiant gulp of champagne. ''It would serve you right if I said I was quitting immediately.''

''But you won't do that,'' he murmured back, capturing her empty hand and holding it in his lap. His thumb began making lazy circles in her palm. She bit her lip at the sudden spike of desire that shot through her. ''After all, if you quit in a huff, we might not resume our affair. And if we don't have an affair, why should you quit at all?''

Unable to appreciate his flippant remark Selina searched his eyes, not realizing how much of her love she revealed to him at the same time. With a muttered oath he crushed her hand passionately and thrust it away. "Don't look at me like that," he whispered roughly. "I might have to drag you off into your bedroom right now and show you how wrong you are to doubt me." He took a deep breath and picked up the champagne bottle. "Let me fill your glass." His voice sounded normal, but Selina saw Magda shoot a quick glance at him.

Betsy's attention was attracted by the effervescent sound of champagne bubbling into a tulip glass. "I don't see why I can't have champagne," she complained, looking with distaste at the glass of ginger ale in front of her. "Willa Graham's mother lets her have some when they have a party."

Gil offered her a sip from his glass and laughed when she wrinkled her nose at the taste. "I like ginger ale better," she said flatly.

"Your palate must not be mature enough to appreciate this fine wine," Gil said. He didn't look at Selina, but she couldn't help recognizing the echo of their first meeting on the airplane. How long ago it seemed, though it was only a matter of weeks. When she'd boarded the airplane, she hadn't known Gilmartin Duchenay existed. Now it seemed he was at the very core of her life. She strove to shake off the darkness of her mood with another draft of champagne.

Gil turned his teasing smile toward Selina. "Perhaps Chef Montgomery will gratify us with a display of her own wine-tasting abilities."

Selina obligingly swirled the wine in her mouth and swallowed, trying to enter into the gaiety of the moment. "Ah, yes," she said, mustering a deep thoughtful expression and a faint French accent. "Truly a fine champagne. There is only one cellar in the world that could produce such a bouquet, such dryness, such a nose. It has body, and yet it seems to float in the mouth. It's assertive—one might almost say impudent—"

Laughing, Gil interrupted her. "Yes, one almost might! Is that how they taste wine in California?"

"Some people."

Betsy abruptly lost interest in wine. "Can we eat these now?" she asked Hailey politely, indicating the plate of cinnamon rolls.

Hailey nodded. "I've put some aside to see how they last overnight. We can eat the rest of them." Selina noticed that she broke one in two, only nibbling at it while Betsy and Gil wolfed down several.

"Maybe we should bring Hailey along," Gil said, starting on his third roll. "You want to be pastry chef for the trip? I'll make up your losses of revenue and kick in some salary besides."

Hailey was sorely tempted. "I don't want to alienate my customers," she began.

"Lots of bakeries close for a week or two in the late summer," Selina mentioned.

"I'll think about it," Hailey told Gil, finishing her champagne and gathering up her equipment. "It certainly sounds interesting."

She left through the back door, and Magda shooed Betsy away, too. Selina rinsed the glasses and plates they had used and stacked them in the dishwasher, uneasily aware of Gil's eyes on her. He put away the champagne bucket, threw the bottle into the trash and came up behind her as she stood at the sink. "Are you still mad at me?"

She was too busy responding to his nearness to be mad. "No," she whispered honestly. "Just confused." She turned to face him, resting her palms on his chest. "Terribly confused."

He looked down at her, his gaze growing hot with desire. "Selina," he began, his voice thick.

She put her hand over his mouth. "Don't say anything," she begged. "Don't. Just—love me, please."

"I will," he promised, bending his head. She kissed him eagerly, fiercely, searching in the passion he created for an answer that would not hurt her. There was no permanence in passion, she knew. But she didn't want to face the thought that there was no love in it, either.

When they were naked in her bed, she would not let him move slowly toward their union. Her urgent need to lose herself in the oblivious aftermath of desire thrust him along, too. Their ascent was primitive and tumultuous, and when at last he shouted her name in a voice hoarse with passion, she realized her goal. Still clasping him with her body, she drifted into sleep.

But when she woke in the chill dead hours after midnight, she was alone. Her skin felt cold and tight, and she got up to wrap herself in a light flannel robe. She spent unknown hours on the padded chaise longue of her terrace, staring fixedly at the stars. When the crescent moon finally disappeared in the western horizon, she went inside to fall into an uneasy sleep.

BECAUSE OF TUESDAY'S DINNER PARTY it was Wednesday morning before Selina finally saw the *Margaret B. Townshend*. Magda and Betsy came along on the drive to St. Charles. Selina sat quietly in the back seat. She had exchanged only commonplaces with Gil since their frantic lovemaking. Now, with the agonizing self-doubt of love, she scrutinized her behavior. Had she seemed too demanding? Had she shown her desperation for his love? Perhaps he was disgusted with her behavior. She barely saw the rolling hills and flat lush cornfields that seemed incongruous so close to a major metropolis.

As they drove through St. Charles toward the river and the yacht club, Selina roused herself to talk to Magda. "You've been on the boat before, haven't you? Do you remember what the kitchen was like?"

Magda laughed ruefully. "It was only an overnight trip—up to the Ohio and back again. As I dimly recall it, we had to forage for breakfast in a pantry off the ladies' cabin, and we tied up at some town for dinner. Irene made sandwiches for lunch. That's why I'm a little worried about the facilities."

Gil turned the car into a gravel parking lot. Beyond the gleaming white yacht-club buildings, moorings had been constructed. The *Margaret B. Townshend* was tied up there, looking out of place amid a flock of sailboats. She was brightly painted, her gingerbread trim blindingly white, with her name picked out in bright red-and-gilt lettering on the paddle box above her scarlet wheel. Her twin smokestacks rose proudly into the blue sky, and her pilothouse stuck up jauntily from the top deck. Betsy jumped out of the car, gazing raptly toward the steamboat.

"Now this is really something," she breathed, starting toward the gangplank. There was a woman standing in the shadows of the bottom deck.

"Irene Rossfield promised to meet us here," Magda said as they followed Betsy. "Be sure to be frank if the galley won't meet your needs, my dear." She didn't say it, but Selina knew that she meant it was better to cancel the trip than to have it fail because the facilities were inadequate.

They walked up the gangplank and were met at the top by Irene Rossfield. She was tall, older than Magda, but with that ageless look wealthy people can often achieve. Her perfectly tailored pants and top showed a figure rigorously disciplined.

She greeted Magda affectionately and smiled at Selina. "So this is your famous chef. I've been hearing lots about you, my dear." She turned to Magda, a twinkle in her eye. "As I told that son of yours, we'll waive the charter fee if we're invited to go along."

Magda tucked her arm inside Irene's as they moved along the deck. "Gil told me," she said. "It'll be fun, I think. But before we can make any decisions, Selina must see the kitchen—cook house, or whatever you call it. I don't even know where the main one is. Do you use it at all, Irene?"

Mrs. Rossfield led the way past a low shedlike enclosure. Through an open door Selina could glimpse

boilers and pulleys and other ancient components of
the engines. "Actually," Mrs. Rossfield said, "we
don't use the cook house that much. When we renovated the cabins, we turned the former serving pantry
into a sort of kitchenette, and we do most of our
cooking there. But the cook house is down here."

She led the way around the engine room. There was
another enclosed area on the far side. Mrs. Rossfield
pushed on the door, and after sticking for a minute, it
opened reluctantly. Selina looked inside with trepida-
tion. It was dark and crowded with a discouraging collection of disconnected refrigerators, stainless-steel
tables and sinks, a huge old stove hulking in one corner and a tangled huddle of dish drainers.

Mrs. Rossfield laughed at Selina's expression.
"It's pretty awful, isn't it?"

"Why are the appliances unplugged? Don't they
work?" Selina opened the oven door and was
pleasantly surprised to find it clean inside.

"Everything works. But since we usually only
charter for day trips, there's no elaborate cooking
done. It's been a while since this stuff was used." She
gave the room a disparaging glance. "However, it
can be cleaned up if you need it. Now let's look at the
pantry upstairs."

They mounted the broad staircase that led to the
next deck. Mrs. Rossfield told Selina that it was
called the boiler deck, although the boiler was on the
main deck, next to the cook house. The outside rim
of the deck was circled by a white-painted wooden
balustrade. Ahead of them were double doors. Mrs.
Rossfield pushed them open.

"This is the gentlemen's cabin." She led them down a long room, covered with a faded Brussels carpet. The walls were a combination of wainscoting and paneling painted white, with framed pictures hung at intervals. Stateroom doors opened off each side of the room, and graceful chandeliers hung from the ceiling. There was the smell of old wood and dusty fabric in the air. The total effect was one of slightly shabby, old-fashioned elegance.

At the end of the room was a short hallway. On the right were two doors, one bearing the silhouette of a Southern belle in hoopskirts, the other a dapper Southern gentleman in cutaway and top hat. "The bathrooms," Mrs. Rossfield said. She pushed open a swinging door opposite. "And this is the pantry."

It was a far cry from the dismal room below. Although it was smaller, the space was efficiently used. Sunshine poured through a window overlooking the promenade. The walls were lined with cupboards. A small refrigerator and stove were separated by gleaming white counters.

Magda looked around, a frown creasing her forehead. "It's much nicer, but rather small." She glanced apologetically toward Mrs. Rossfield. "I don't mean to criticize, Irene. I know it's perfectly adequate for what you need. But Selina—"

"Now let's not jump to conclusions," Selina interrupted. "I need to look at this place and the cook house before I can tell if the whole plan is feasible or not." She took a notebook out of her pocket and glanced speculatively around the pantry. "You do have electricity, I take it?"

Irene pointed to a strip of outlets above one counter. "Don't you want to see the rest of the boat?"

"Certainly—later," Selina murmured, beginning to open cupboard doors. Magda and Mrs. Rossfield looked at each other helplessly. A few minutes later, Selina noticed that they'd left. But she was too intent on gauging the capacity of the small freezer and measuring counter space to pay much attention.

After noting her observations, she left, meaning to take another look at the old cook house. But she couldn't resist checking out the rest of the boiler deck while she was there.

As she stood in the doorway of the pantry, the men's cabin was to her right. To the left she could see sunlight blazing in where the hall ended. She turned that way.

A smaller version of the gentlemen's cabin lay before her. The carpet here had a more delicate pattern, and a large window had been cut in the rear of the room. Staterooms also opened off this room—three on each side, she counted as she went toward the window. It looked out the stern of the boat, over the big paddle wheel. Looking down at the debris collecting in the cage formed where the blades of the paddle wheel met the water, she suddenly realized that this frail boat would be out there on the treacherous Mississippi River, motivated only by an out-of-date mechanism that had seen its heyday more than one hundred years before.

A step sounded behind her, and she turned to see Gil entering the room. "Should have known I'd find you in the ladies' cabin."

"Ladies' cabin? Oh, like the gentlemen's cabin." Gil's expression lightened the apprehension that had weighed her for the past two days.

"A place where the ladies could be uncontaminated by the menfolk. Or more probably," he twirled an imaginary mustache, "a place to shoo them off to so the men could tell risqué jokes. The staterooms are the same for the men and women, though." He opened one of the doors and revealed a pleasant but austere room. It was tiny, with double bunks built in one side and a washstand in the opposite corner. The closet was improvised from a flowered calico curtain that hung down from a shelf.

Gil's smile was mocking. "Not exactly a honeymoon suite," he said, closing the door. "The Rossfields built four VIP staterooms on the texas deck when they renovated. Don't suppose I can persuade you to share one with me." His question was more of a statement. Selina automatically shook her head. "I didn't think so. Well, one thing's for sure. We're not going to have much time alone together on this cruise."

He transfixed her with his piercing eagle's gaze. She moved toward him as if she were in a trance, feeling his arms fold around her. His polo shirt was smooth under her cheek. His hands moved soothingly up and down her spine, finding the tense knots of muscles and freeing them.

"Something's wrong, isn't it?" he crooned. "You want to tell me why you're afraid?"

She stiffened. "How—what makes you think I'm afraid?"

She could feel his smile. "I know," he said simply. "I could tell when we made love Monday night. What I don't know is what to do about it."

She nestled her cheek more closely to his chest, clasping his broad back as if he were her sole support. "I don't know, either," she said almost inaudibly. "I don't know—what the matter is."

There was stillness for a moment. "That's a lie," he said calmly. She drew in an outraged breath, but his arms clamped her to him. "But I won't press you. In fact, the enforced celibacy on this trip is probably a good idea. Gives us a chance to get to know each other better. Gives you a chance to trust me enough to tell me what's bothering you."

She pushed his arms away. "One thing that bothers me is that you don't listen to me. I've told you before, I want to know where we stand. Where I stand. I mean it, Gil. I won't play Jane Eyre to your Rochester. I need my own life!"

His face darkened, and she felt a moment's intense fear. Suddenly it didn't seem to matter as much that she be independent of him. She'd rather remain his chef than risk losing him forever. But pride stiffened her resolve. He placed her under too great an obligation. She felt cheapened paying it back with her body. And he'd given her no indication that he wanted her love.

With an effort Gil produced a smile. "Don't quit," he said softly. "We'll work something out. I do understand what you're saying, Selina. I just don't want you to leave me."

She was helpless against the appeal in his eyes. She

wanted to shout at him, "There's a way to make sure I won't leave. Just tell me you love me! Just let me love you!" But if she had to ask for his love, it was no good. She nodded dumbly. "All right," she whispered in acquiescence. "I won't quit for a while."

"And if it bothers you that we have an affair while you're working under my roof, I guess we could always put it off for a while," Gil said with the air of one making a large concession.

"Is that supposed to make me happy?" Selina stared at him in disbelief. "I think I'm in the well-known no-win situation."

Gil moved closer and gathered her into his arms again. "I don't promise not to excite you madly," he said into her ear, nibbling around its tender circumference. "I just won't take you to bed, no matter how much you might want me to."

Selina mustered an expression of disbelief to mask the growing desire he created when he moved his hand to cup her breast, his thumb teasing her nipple. "Maybe the shoe will be on the other foot," she said, licking her lips and staring into his eyes. She could not stop her body from melting against him as his lips came down on hers. Only the sound of footsteps in the gentlemen's cabin pried them apart. It was Magda and Mrs. Rossfield, come to carry Gil off for an inspection of the VIP cabins. Selina took her notebook in hand and forced a deep breath of air into her lungs as she reached the promenade of the boiler deck. She had work to do. The more absorbing it was, the easier it would be to forget Gil's proposed solution to their problem.

She approached the dark gloomy cook house with determination. The refrigerators hummed reassuringly when she plugged them in, and they were clean inside. The stove was an old hot-top, converted to run on propane. One look at its massive brooding surface, and she knew it would be unbearably hot when it was fired up. She tried opening one of the windows, but they were stuck shut. Grimly she noted that fact on her pad.

There was no dishwasher, and not much freezer space in the antiquated refrigerators. But if everything were cleaned up, and the worktables moved around, it would do—barely.

She moved out in the sunshine to complete her list of action items. Magda found her there. "What's the verdict, Selina?"

Selina showed Magda her list. "If these things are done, I can make up menus that will adapt to the surroundings. There's no microwave, but perhaps we can bring ours. There's not enough freezer space, either, but we'll think of something. Will it be possible to get fresh produce every other day or so?"

Magda nodded. "We can tie up at towns along the river to do the marketing. Everyone likes going ashore for a little while, no matter how nice the boat is."

"Well, the meals should be quite good, although not perhaps up to any exacting standard. I've found some big old barbecue grills, so we could bring along a lot of mesquite charcoal and do a lot of grilling— that would capture the spirit of the trip." Selina consulted her notebook. "I'll still need to do some in-depth planning, but I can be ready in time."

They added up the number of probable passengers, their heads together over Selina's notebook. With the hotel owners and the Rossfields in the VIP suites; Magda, Betsy and Selina in the ladies'-cabin berths; Gil and the Rossfields' two teenage sons in the gentlemen's cabin; everyone was accommodated. Magda explained that the crew had their own quarters and their own kitchen and dining room, preferring to look after their meals themselves.

The Rossfield boys would act as stewards for the passenger dining room, Magda said, something they'd often done before. Selina was thinking about possible menus as they collected Betsy from the pilot-house and climbed into the car. Everyone was quiet on the drive back. Now that she was committed to it, Selina felt a little overwhelmed with the magnitude of the task she'd assumed. It would not be easy to produce meals good enough to soften up the hotel owners when all she had were that gloomy cook house and the little pantry above. But she would manage. She would have to.

CHAPTER TWELVE

SELINA USED ONE HAND to wipe the perspiration out of her eyes while pointing in the direction of the main galley with the other one. "Take it through there," she told the young Rossfield boy—either Mike or Eric, she hadn't yet figured out which tall blond boy was which. The sun bored through the humid air like a laser, making her wish she'd worn a hat. She held her damp T-shirt off her back for a minute, enjoying the brief sensation of coolness it caused.

She could hear Betsy's excited cries from the deck above. Magda, Hal and the senior Rossfields were sitting in air-conditioned comfort at the yacht club, waiting for Gil to arrive from the airport with the Hartners and the Olens. Hailey was busy stowing away food and equipment in the lower galley.

Selina smiled grimly. If it hadn't been for Charlotte Drumm's hysterical interference, Hailey wouldn't have agreed to come to the riverboat trip. But Aunt Charlotte had burst into the kitchen at the Château a week ago during one of the Monday-night seminars. Selina had been explaining to Gil and Hailey simple rules of produce selection in preparation for the trip—Gil's idea, in case she became pressed for time during the excursion. They were listening to her instructions intently when the back screen door burst open, and Charlotte Drumm appeared.

It was too much like the earlier humiliating scene with Andy. Selina decided that this time she wouldn't stand tamely by; if Aunt Charlotte wanted to call names, she would find two could play that game.

But Aunt Charlotte had leveled her guns at her daughter. "So, Hailey!" Her usually well-modulated voice had been close to shrill. "You've been deceiving your own mother. What next!"

Hailey had exchanged a resigned look with Gil. "Sit down, mother," she said, her impatience thinly disguised. "Tell me what I've done now."

Mrs. Drumm had subsided onto one of the tall stools around the worktable. She touched a delicate embroidered handkerchief to her perfectly made-up eyes. Selina detected no odor of alcohol on her breath this time and was relieved. "I might have known," Mrs. Drumm sobbed, her handkerchief remaining pristine. "You'll bring social disgrace on us all. Running a—a *bakery*!" Her voice made it clear that a bakery was only one step up from a trash heap. "Really, Hailey, like any common person. You have a heritage to keep up. You do agree with me, don't you, Gilmartin?" She swiveled and laid a skinny hand on Gil's arm.

The suddenness of the appeal took him by surprise. "Of course I don't agree," he told her firmly. "If Hailey's bakery is a disgrace, what can you think of Purity? We do business on a much larger scale than she does."

Mrs. Drumm dismissed his remark with a wave of her hand. "Dear Gilmartin," she murmured, giving him a reproachful look. "It's entirely different, of course. After all, such a well-established business—a man like you in charge—totally different from Hailey's little nasty hole in the wall."

Hailey began to seethe. "You've poked around in my bakery?"

"You are my daughter, my dear. However much that may pain me at the moment. But this time at least I expect you to consider my feelings. You will quit this ridiculous business at once. I'm sure Gilmartin, as head of the family, sees this my way."

Hailey interrupted before Gil could speak. "Mother," she said firmly, "this ridiculous business you despise so much has been making a very nice income for me in the two months I've been operating. I have no intention of giving it up. I never wanted to be your little debutante, and now I'm going to take charge of my own affairs. If you don't like it, I can move out."

There had been tears and recriminations from Aunt Charlotte, but Hailey had stood firm. To ward off the hysterical fit that threatened, Gil had suggested a compromise. Hailey would take a short vacation from her work and serve as pastry chef on the *Margaret B. Townshend*. If at the end of the trip she still wanted to run her bakery, Aunt Charlotte would accept her decision.

Grumbling that no one had any consideration for her, Aunt Charlotte had grudgingly agreed. Hailey, once she'd been assured that her customers would still buy from her after she returned, was thrilled to be included in the trip down the Mississippi. Now Selina could hear her cheerful voice calling from the cook house. "Anything else to go here?"

One more large box was coming up the gangplank, propelled by Mike—or Eric—Rossfield. It contained the china and serving utensils Mrs. Murphy had packed to supplement the boat's small stock. "That goes to the pantry," she told the boy and called back to Hailey, "All done in there."

Hailey appeared on the lower deck, fanning her face with a stainless-steel pot lid. "The heat!" she said expressively. "I didn't think anything could be worse than my kitchen in Maplewood, but I guess I was wrong."

Selina nodded in agreement. "Will it be cooler on the river, do you think?"

"Maybe." Hailey shaded her eyes with her hand and looked up the road that led away from the yacht club. "I think I see the limo coming. Is all our stuff loaded up?"

"Everything but our own luggage. Guess we might as well take that upstairs."

Hailey giggled as they headed toward the Audi. "You make it sound so domestic—upstairs, indeed! I think you're supposed to call it 'above.'"

Selina shrugged. "My expertise is in cooking, not nautical jargon. But I noticed the older Rossfield boy was eager to give you lessons. Which one is he—Mike or Eric?"

"The oldest one is Eric." Hailey's laughter bubbled up again. "And he's only eighteen, Selina. He probably thinks of me as a boring old friend of his parents.''

Selina let it drop, although she was pretty sure that Eric was well on the way to a crush on Hailey. Her newly slender figure made him look at her in a way she probably didn't recognize yet. But it was her own sunny personality that was really attractive. Selina sighed. Since her encounter with Gil the day they'd inspected the steamboat, they hadn't been alone together. Gil, she understood from Magda's inconsequential conversation, was clearing up his work so he would be free to enjoy his trip on the *Margaret B. Townshend*. And she had been busy researching food-preparation techniques, trying to come up with the optimal combination of freshness and convenience.

She had done her research thoroughly and felt tolerably well prepared, but she would have to be on her toes during the entire trip. It didn't look as if there'd be much time for relaxation, let alone time for romantic interludes. And where on this boat full of people would you have a romantic interlude? Unconsciously she sighed as she carried her duffel and garment bags up the gangplank. Work, no matter how much she enjoyed it, was no match for love. It was beginning to look as though she couldn't have both.

The arriving vehicle was not Gil with the out-of-town hoteliers, but a delivery van from the wineshop. Gil had refused to plunder his own cellars for the trip. Selina saw that the wine was stored where it would receive the least vibration.

When she came back on deck, the limo had arrived. Gil was helping out a stout woman dressed suffocatingly in black, followed by a wispy woman in fluttering sea green jersey. The limo driver carried their bags, and the men followed, wiping their faces with handkerchiefs as the full weight of the moisture-laden air hit them. Magda appeared from the yacht-club lounge, shepherding Hal MacMillan and the Rossfields. Selina had met Bill Rossfield earlier and liked his hearty unpretentious manner. The *Margaret B. Townshend* was evidently his pride and joy. It was obvious from the loving way he regarded the engines that he'd spent lots of time making sure they'd run smoothly.

Gil gestured her forward as the group of hotel owners approached the gangplank. "This is our chef for the voyage, Selina Montgomery," he said, the formality of his voice belied by his warm expression. "She's promised us some real treats during the trip."

The man he'd introduced as Mr. Hartner, a paunchy florid person in his mid-fifties, grunted disbelievingly. "Hope it's better than what Purity puts out, Duchenay. Tried some in my Florentine Room once. Nobody ate it."

Gil preserved his amiable countenance, but Selina could see that it cost him some effort. "Miss Montgomery doesn't believe in mass-producing food. I'm sure you'll be pleased with her cooking."

Mrs. Hartner was a stolid square woman who would have looked older than her husband except that her hair was an improbable shade of blonde. Mr. Olen was thin with nervous mannerisms, and Mrs.

Olen was equally thin and fluttery. They were eager to get to their stateroom since Mrs. Olen had a migraine. "She always gets one when we travel," Mr. Olen announced importantly. "Come, Chloe, my dear." Magda attended them solicitously up the broad staircase.

Another car had arrived at the yacht-club parking lot, and Selina glanced at it casually. It was unusual to see a man in a correct navy blue business suit, with a bulging briefcase under his arm, at a yacht club where everyone seemed to wear the latest in sports clothes. She speculated idly that he must have been a lunchtime sailor, snatching a few minutes with his sailboat from a busy day. Then he took a small overnight case out of his trunk and started toward the steamboat. "Do you know that man," she said to Gil in a low voice. "He seems to be coming this way."

Gil looked and did a double take. "Oh, no!" he groaned. "It's Fred Warner! What in the world is he doing here?"

He strode down the gangplank toward the advancing Mr. Warner. Selina watched curiously as they met a short distance from the boat. She couldn't see Gil's face, but Warner's was definitely unfriendly, suspicious, accusatory. After a short colloquy Gil led the way back to the boat, Warner following grimly.

"Mr. Warner has decided to join us for the trip," Gil said, biting off his words. "He's a member of Purity's board of directors and thinks that this will be a novel way to get to the annual meeting in New Orleans." Hal MacMillan, the Hartners and Selina stared at Gil blankly, then swiveled their gaze to Fred Warner.

The new arrival said rather belligerently, "Figured this was a company trip. Thought I might as well get in on it. I assume you have a spare room?" This last question was directed toward Gil.

"It's not precisely a company trip," Gil said gently. In response to some inner prompting, Selina picked up one of the Hartners' bags and urged them toward the staircase. It was obvious that Gil was unhappy about Warner's arrival. If they were going to quarrel, it was better they did it alone.

She led the Hartners up to the texas deck, one floor above the boiler deck where she would be sleeping. The texas deck was smaller, broken up into two sections. One-half of it had been converted into four tiny but luxurious apartments, each with its own small bathroom. There was a sunny deck with chairs just below the ladder that led up to the pilothouse. Beyond that were the crew's quarters and mess, politely fenced off with white railings.

Selina thought the little VIP staterooms were charming, but the Hartners were evidently in a mood to be censorious. "Only a double bed?" Mrs. Hartner sank massively onto the structure in question. It groaned protestingly. Her husband came back from a quick tour of the bathroom. "No tub," he said gloomily.

There was a luggage stand near the door. Selina hefted the suitcase she carried onto it and backed away. "I'm sure you'll enjoy your trip," she murmured, escaping as fast as politeness would allow.

She trotted down the steep companionway to the
boiler deck, then down the broad staircase to the bottom deck. Gil and Fred Warner still stood silently
near the gangplank. Gil spoke to her as if she were a
stranger.

"Chef Montgomery, will it upset your arrange-
ments too much to feed an unexpected mouth? Mr.
Warner is most anxious to come along on our little
pleasure cruise." The savage sarcasm in his voice surprised her. She looked uncertainly from one stony
contenance to another.

"Sure—I mean, there's always enough for one extra." Because Gil obviously was not going to play the
genial host, she added, "Welcome aboard, Mr.
Warner."

Fred Warner bestowed a tight smile on her.
"Thank you, Miss, er, Chef Montgomery. Now if
you'll excuse me, I'll find my way to my berth."

He turned away abruptly and stalked over to the
staircase. Selina started after him to show him the
way but then saw Irene Rossfield meet him on the
stairs, tuck her hand under his arm and guide him
into the gentlemen's cabin. Selina turned back to Gil.

"Why are you so rude to him?" And why so distant to me, she wanted to ask, but didn't.

"I don't want him here." Gil's voice was bitter.
"He just wants to shoot me down at the board meeting, and he's afraid I have something up my sleeve
that will make me impregnable. Well, I do. And having him on the trip will interfere. I thought if I was
blunt enough about it, he might change his mind
about crashing the party."

"No dice, huh?" Selina leaned on the railing beside him. "Guess you'll just have to make the best of it."

"And so will you." He bent his intense gaze toward her, starting her heart in a slow uneven thump. "Now that Warner's coming along, we'll have to pretend there's nothing at all between us."

Selina's brow furrowed in bewilderment. "I don't understand. Pretend what? And if it comes to that, what's between us? You might enlighten me about that."

Gil gripped her shoulders, his breath escaping impatiently between his teeth. "You know what's between us," he growled. "Have you forgotten you wear the gypsy's mark?" He twitched the gold chain around her neck, pulling it until the tiny moon and star charm came into view. "You'll have to trust me. And take this to think about till we get rid of Warner in New Orleans." He bent his head and captured her lips in a fierce hard kiss. Then he released her shoulders with a hard squeeze. "You're my woman. No matter what happens, don't forget that."

The intensity of his voice held her speechless. She gaped up at him, unable to understand what Fred Warner could have to do with their relationship. Gil took a couple of deep breaths and relaxed, leaning against one of the tall gingerbread-trimmed posts that supported the upper-deck promenade. Selina blinked and slowly regained her awareness of the world around them. She inhaled, smelling the green fishy odor of the river, a compound of rotting weeds and primeval slime. The wind rustled the leaves of the oak trees that studded the yacht-club's lawn. A faint constant roar from the nearby highway reminded her of the sound of the sea heard from a distance. Nearer, a car drove noisily up to the yacht club. She looked absently toward the parking lot and saw that it was a taxi. A woman wearing a flowered hat got out as the cabbie opened the door. She stood beside the cab while the driver went around to the trunk and opened it. With a sensation of sinking into a deep pit, Selina watched him hoist a large well-strapped traveling bag out of the trunk and turn toward the dock with it.

"Don't look now, Gil," she said, her voice strangled by the irrational laughter that threatened her. "I think we have another uninvited guest arriving."

Gil poked his head around the post. "Good God!" he groaned. "It's Aunt Charlotte."

Selina backed toward the shadows of the engine room. "I believe I have something to see to in the kitchen. I'll just—"

Gil's hand shot out and closed around her wrist. "If you leave me here to face that woman alone, I'll never forgive you."

Aunt Charlotte advanced across the strip of lawn that separated the dock from the yacht club, with the taxi driver toiling along behind, lugging her bag. Feet slapped noisily on the staircase, and Betsy hurtled up to them, her face excited.

"Gil! Selina! Do you see—Aunt Charlotte's coming!"

Gil nodded resignedly. "Go find mother. Maybe she'll be able to cope."

Mrs. Drumm reached the gangplank as Betsy vanished back up the stairs. "Well, Gilmartin. I trust you intend to help me aboard?"

Gil leaned out and stretched a helping hand. "Certainly, auntie. You'll forgive me, but I didn't realize you were coming. Did mother, um, invite you?"

Mrs. Drumm advanced up the gangplank, gripping Gil's hand, and was assisted at the last minute by a shove from the sweating taxi driver. "Get a move on, lady," he said impatiently. "I ain't got all day." He heaved her bag up to the deck and turned to leave.

"Just a minute," Gil said. "You may be required."

The taxi driver turned, clearly exasperated. "Mister, I don't make no money standing here waiting for you to make up your mind."

"You may go," Aunt Charlotte said with a regal inclination of her head. Muttering under his breath, the man went. "Really, Gilmartin. I have not come all this way to be sent back again like a naughty child. If you had had the decency to invite me on what was plainly a family cruise, I would not have been reduced to this stratagem."

Her speech was as authoritative as ever, but Selina discerned that Mrs. Drumm, underneath her air of massive assurance, was really ill at ease. She felt an unwilling rush of sympathy.

Magda hurried up, a concerned expression on her face. "Charlotte! I don't understand—"

"I cannot find it in myself to let my daughter make this trip unchaperoned," Mrs. Drumm said. She took off her hat and fanned herself with it. Her face seemed suddenly paler. "The heat," she said faintly. "Isn't there somewhere cooler to continue this discussion?"

"I'm afraid we don't have much air conditioning, auntie." Gil's sardonic expression would have daunted a lesser woman. "This is a trip back to an earlier era. Perhaps your constitution isn't up to it."

Magda broke in, sending her son a slightly reproachful glance. "It's true, my dear, that the only accommodations left are rather primitive. And it will be hot. The discomfort is one reason why we didn't invite you to come."

Mrs. Drumm sank into a convenient deck chair. "If you can take it, Magda," she said, a hint of resentment in her voice, "so can I. However, I understood that there were air-conditioned staterooms aboard."

Selina quailed inwardly at the thought of trying to deprive either lugubrious Mrs. Hartner or hypochondriacal Mrs. Olen of their air-conditioned bedroom. Gil spoke firmly.

"This is primarily a business trip, auntie. The people who are occupying the air-conditioned rooms are people necessary to the success of Purity. I cannot ask them to sleep in more uncomfortable rooms just because you've taken it into your head to come along. If you want to come with us, you'll have to rough it."

"Gil!" Magda spoke sternly. Then she turned to Aunt Charlotte. "I'm afraid he's right, although I don't care for his tone of voice. Why don't you take a look at the room next to mine? If you don't fancy it, we'll call you a taxi and have you driven back home.''

She bent to put a comforting arm around her stepsister-in-law, and Selina suddenly realized that Charlotte was very little taller than her own five-foot-three. Her imperious manner made her seem much more imposing than she was. Now she laid one skinny hand on Magda's arm. ''You know, Magda—I really need to come along. Surely you must agree?'' Magda could not resist the pleading in her voice.

Hailey hurried toward them. ''Mother! Whatever are you doing here?'' She knelt in front of her mother's chair, and Selina saw with an inward squirm of embarrassment that Mrs. Drumm was going to cry. She turned away, wishing she could retreat to the kitchen without having to pass everybody. She stared vaguely at a little sports car that had pulled up in the parking lot. A slim light-haired young man vaulted out of the car, reached into the luggage compartment and pulled out a duffel bag. Selina tapped Gil on the shoulder.

''Is this another one?'' she asked in an undertone. Again Gil followed her pointing finger, staring with numb resignation at Ricky Carson as his friend waved cheerily and bounded up the gangplank.

''Well, here I am,'' he announced. ''Better late than never. Guess you thought I wasn't going to make it.''

''What are you doing here, R.C.?'' Gil's voice was threatening. Ricky grinned and punched him lightly on the arm.

''Didn't Hailey tell you, old man? I'm here because I never miss a free trip down the river. She said you wouldn't mind.''

Magda turned away to hide a smile, and Selina choked back a giggle. Compared to their other uninvited passengers, Ricky Carson was confidently assured that he would be welcome wherever he went.

''If I'd wanted you along cluttering up the landscape,'' Gil growled, ''I would have invited you.'' He moved closer to Selina. Ricky noticed and shook his head deprecatingly.

''Hey, man, what kind of person do you think I am? All I want is a simple family outing—right, Mrs. Drumm?'' He smiled winningly at Aunt Charlotte, who regarded him with distaste.

''I wasn't aware that you were a member of this family, Richard.'' Her voice was heavy with censure.

''You never can tell, ma'am. May I take your bag up? Gil will show us where we bunk, I'm sure.'' He laughed. ''Of course, it won't be together—my loss, dear lady.''

Gil's lips twitched at Aunt Charlotte's mingled expression of suspicion and gratified vanity. ''All right, Ricardo. You can stay on the condition you make yourself useful—for a change.''

Ricky smote his chest with his free hand. ''I will clean out the heads! I will swab the deck! I will peel potatoes—gladly!'' He winked at Selina.

Gil pushed him toward the staircase. ''March. You're too late for potato peeling. I've already bagged that job.''

They went up the stairs, bickering companionably. Magda helped Aunt Charlotte out of her chair. ''Let me show you your stateroom, Charlotte. I hope the trip won't prove too fatiguing for you.''

Charlotte tottered bravely away. ''Not at all, my dear. I feel it's a mother's duty. . . .''

As they vanished in Gil's wake, Selina slid down until she was sitting on the deck. As soon as she was sure Mrs. Drumm was out of earshot, she broke into gales of laughter. Hailey, who had been trying to efface herself while Ricky was around, looked at her for a moment, then frowned.

''How can you laugh! Mother coming along, of all things, just when Ricky—''

''Her face,'' Selina sputtered. ''When Ricky said they wouldn't be sleeping together—it almost makes up for everything else! I can't wait to see what happens next.'' She dissolved into helpless laughter. Hailey smiled reluctantly.

''I guess it is funny, but you'll laugh out of the other side of your face once mother gets started. She'll have us both under constant surveillance. And I was counting on this trip to—well, it's going to be very awkward.''

Magda rejoined them, a harried look on her face. ''Your mother's lying down,'' she told Hailey. ''I hope she doesn't feel the heat too badly. Of course, the gentlemen's cabin is air-conditioned, and she can spend the days there. But I don't know how she'll make it through the nights.''

Hailey sighed. ''I'm sorry she decided to crash the cruise, Aunt Magda. It wasn't my idea at all.''

''But Ricky Carson was, I suppose.'' Magda smiled knowingly at Hailey's blush.

"I'm sorry for that, too. I guess I did sort of invite him along. I mean—"

"Never mind, my dear. He'll be a lot of fun, if he can keep himself from playing those practical jokes he's so fond of on Gil's hotel executives. I'll rely on you to keep him in line."

Hailey threw her arms around Magda in a spontaneous hug. "Thanks," she mumbled. "I'd better go see how mother is."

Magda watched her for a moment as she ran up the stairs, then turned back to Selina. "Three extra passengers," she said starkly. "Can you handle that many, my dear?"

Selina smiled reassuringly. "It may be awkward, but for the most part I can stretch things quite satisfactorily. I brought extra of everything just because I knew Mr. McMillan would be on the cruise."

Magda chuckled. "I'll drop a hint in his ear not to ask for seconds. It'll be good for his waistline." She added with a faintly proprietary air that Selina found endearing, "He's given up his nice air-conditioned room to Fred Warner—says it'll be more fun to bunk in one of the staterooms off the gentleman's cabin with Gil and Ricky and the Rossfield boys. Irene offered to give up their suite to Charlotte, but I wouldn't hear of it. For once Charlotte will have to take the consequences of her behavior. In fact, I was thinking of suggesting to her that she work her passage some way, but I couldn't think of anything she could do."

They were strolling toward the cook house. It was cooler in the shade. Selina opened the door for

Magda. Hailey had brought a large floor fan from her bakery, and the air inside the galley was less stuffy than before. They had been at work since early that morning, arranging the work space, stowing their supplies and checking all the appliances. Magda looked around in approval.

"This looks very different. If it weren't so airless, you might be very comfortable here. Can't you open the windows?"

Selina shook her head. "I asked about that earlier, and the boys said that they'd fix it as soon as they could. I get the feeling that open windows won't make much difference in here. But we'll manage. I'll just get up early and do the hot stuff then."

After listening to Selina's plans for the rest of the day, Magda left to see that everyone was aboard. They would be starting soon. With a feeling of last-minute nerves Selina checked her supplies. There would be opportunity to buy anything she'd forgotten, but not until they tied up in Cairo the next day. She didn't want the first meals to bomb. She glanced at her watch; it was time to go into high gear for lunch.

Hailey joined her, and together they prepared the trays for the buffet. Selina and Magda had decided that by serving the meals buffet fashion whenever possible, they would avoid many of the problems associated with amateur waiters and too elaborate menus. Selina was arranging slices of cold meat when she was startled by a loud blast from the steamboat's whistle. Another blast sent them running on deck.

The Rossfield boys were busy at the mooring ropes that held the *Margaret B. Townshend* to the dock. People had come out of the yacht club and were standing by the door, drinks in hand, waving farewell. The boys cast off, jumping aboard nimbly as the boat began to move. Again came the blast of the whistle. From the bottom deck Selina couldn't see the pilothouse, but she knew the pilot would be at the big wooden wheel, swinging the boat out into the current. Bill Rossfield emerged from the engine room, wiping his hands on a greasy rag. He beamed at the two women.

"We're off!" he said unnecessarily, cocking an ear to listen to the humming of the engines. The deck vibrated beneath their feet, and Selina could hear the rhythmic splashing of the stern wheel turning. Giving in to an impulse, she seized Hailey's hand and pulled her up the staircase to the boiler deck. They raced around the promenade to the stern, where they could overlook the wheel.

It turned majestically beneath them, churning up the water into a white froth that left a graceful sweep of wake. The sight was somehow exhilarating. Selina's feet capered in a snatch of square dance, and Hailey impulsively do-si-doed with her. Over the roar of the water they barely heard a rapping at the window of the cabin behind them. When they turned, Aunt Charlotte was alternately frowning at Hailey and glaring at Selina. Selina smiled happily back, then shouted at Hailey. "Guess we'd better get back to lunch." They made their way back, casting delighted glances at the bank of the river moving slowly by. Betsy joined them as they leaned over the rail for a moment before descending the staircase.

"I'll help with dinner, but just now can I not be shoes chef?" she said beseechingly. "Captain Morris said he'd let me blow the whistle next time."

Exchanging an amused glance with Hailey, Selina nodded. It was obvious that Betsy wouldn't be too much help on the trip until the novelty wore off, if it ever did.

Gil emerged from the gentlemen's-cabin door and came to stand beside them at the railing. His face was grim, and Selina felt her own exhilaration fade. "Well, we're off," he said heavily. "I only hope it works." He glanced behind him, and through the glass panels of the double doors Selina could see that the other passengers had assembled in the air-conditioned comfort of the cabin. Mrs. Hartner's face wore an expression of peevish dissatisfaction; Mrs. Olen was reclining limply on a sofa, tended by her solicitous husband. Mr. Hartner was standing at the improvised bar with Fred Warner, replenishing his glass and listening stolidly to Hal McMillan. Magda tried vainly to entertain Mrs. Hartner, and the Rossfields were sitting together, the only relaxed people in the cabin. Ricky was nowhere to be seen.

Selina smiled confidently up at Gil. "Don't worry. You'll see—Magda will get them interested in something, and we'll feed them so well they'll have to be happy."

"I hope so," Gil said. He looked down at her, and his face split into a grin. "Dammit, I know so!"

CHAPTER THIRTEEN

THEY STEAMED past the St. Louis waterfront while Selina was changing out of her shorts and T-shirt in preparation for lunch. Magda had made it clear that the cooks were to eat with everyone else. Selina and Hailey had fixed the buffet dishes, brought them up to the pantry and left them there for the Rossfield boys to set out while the women changed.

Her cubicle was on the right side of the boat, so Selina got to see the Gateway Arch loom into view and be left slowly astern as the *Margaret B. Townshend* made her way through the busy waters of the St. Louis docks. Selina paused after splashing cool water on her face and leaned out of her porthole, delighted with the novelty of their progress. Passing boats hooted at them, people on shore waved excitedly, traffic stopped on bridges while they went beneath. It was thrilling to be the focus of so much attention. Gil had mentioned that the only overnight steamboats on the river these days were the *Delta Queen* and the *Mississippi Queen*, unless, like the Rossfields, you happened to be lucky enough to own your own paddle-wheeler. For a few minutes Selina daydreamed about what it might have been like in the heyday of the steamboats. There was a small library in the pilothouse. She resolved to visit it when she had some leisure time and see what she could learn about the boats and the river.

She was slipping her white piqué sun dress over her head when she heard a gentle tap at her door. Zipping the dress hurriedly, she opened the door; Hailey pushed past her and shut the door quickly behind her.

"I don't really know what to do," she began unhappily. "I splurged after Ricky said he might come along. I spent some of my profits on new clothes. And I didn't bring any of the old stuff with me, except grubbies for working in. Do you think mother will give me much trouble about this?"

Selina whistled in approval. Hailey was wearing a low-cut short-sleeved T-shirt that emphasized her full breasts, and fetching wide-legged shorts of candy pink fabric. The weight she'd lost working in her hot bakery had slimmed her plump figure, but she retained a cuddly rounded outline sure to captivate most men.

But it wasn't necessarily guaranteed to captivate her mother, especially when compared to the school-girlish, slightly dowdy clothes she'd chosen for Hailey before. "I don't know what she'll say," Selina replied slowly. "But you're a grown woman now, and you earned the money yourself. You have the right to wear what you want."

They went into the gentlemen's cabin to check the buffet. Mike and Eric had set up the meal according to Selina's diagram, and everything looked beautiful. Someone—Magda, probably—had found time to ar-

range a centerpiece of fruit and wild flowers. The
tables were covered in snowy linen; elegant china
plates were stacked at the service table, along with ice
buckets bearing the champagne Gil had thought ap-
propriate for their first meal of the trip. Glassware
gleamed, silver shone, and the whole room wore a
gently festive air.

"I'll see to the rolls," Hailey said, vanishing into
the pantry. The passengers milled around near the
door, eyeing the buffet table. Selina smiled and
gestured toward the food; that was enough for Mr.
Hartner and Hal MacMillan. Hailey brought out a
basket of hot rolls, Gil started pouring champagne,
and people began moving through the buffet line.
Selina hung back with Hailey until everyone else was
sitting down. As she filled her own plate, she noticed
automatically which dishes had seemed most popular; later she would record it in her notebook. Mrs.
Drumm was staring with hostility at Hailey's provocative outfit, but Magda, who sat with her, would
probably manage to keep her from making a scene.

Her plate full, Selina hesitated for a moment,
glancing around the room. The Hartners sat with Gil
and Fred Warner at one table, and the Olens were
eating with Magda and Mrs. Drumm. The Rossfields
were laughing over something Hal MacMillan had
said, and Betsy listened, awestruck, to the superior
conversation of Mike and Eric. Everyone seemed
content with their lunch partners. On a sudden impulse Selina took her plate out to the veranda, perch-
ing on the top step of the wide staircase that led down
to the bottom deck. Hailey followed her. They had

no sooner begun eating than Ricky Carson came out, his plate heaped with an unsteady pile of food. "Mind if I join you?" With a quick glance at Hailey's blushing face, Selina nodded a cordial assent. "It's a little full of tycoons in there for my liking," Ricky added as he settled on the step below them. He bit into a roll before noticing Hailey's tanned legs as she stretched them toward the sun. His gaze traveled up till it finally reached her face. When she felt his eyes on her, Hailey turned, her glance startled and shy. "Well, well, well," Ricky said softly. "Have we been introduced? I just can't believe this is Gil's little cousin Hailey."

Selina ate quietly, wishing she were somewhere else. Ricky seemed to have discovered, finally, that Hailey was an attractive woman worthy of his attention. But their new absorption in each other gave her the feeling of being alone and left out. She turned her face, scanning the shore. The steamy air was much hotter than the air-conditioned gentlemen's cabin, but the river unfolded before her, changing from one minute to the next as they rounded its bends. The gentle wind of their progress was cooling, and the warehouses that had lined the banks were giving way to trees and parks on high sandstone bluffs. She waved back to a worker on a huge slab of barges, roped together and going down the river under the urging of three important-sounding tugboats. From the front of the *Margaret B. Townshend* the sound of the paddle wheel was a muted roar, punctuated occasionally by the whistle's deafening scream. The boat vibrated steadily in a reassuring rhythm of movement. She sighed wistfully. It would all be perfect if only Gil were sharing it with her.

She glanced back into the gentlemen's cabin. People were beginning to go back to the buffet. Hailey had provided dessert—one of her beautiful chocolate cakes. Selina could see the end of the buffet and a couple of the small tables from her perch on the steps. Mrs. Hartner was putting two pieces of cake on her plate. Gil's table was visible. He leaned back in his chair, listening to Fred Warner with an impassive face. She watched him wistfully for a moment, and his gaze flicked out the door and locked onto hers. Though he didn't move, didn't change his expression, she felt transfixed, unable to look away. His eyes carried a steady burning message that outflamed the sun; helplessly she felt herself begin to kindle like tinder under a magnifying glass. Then he was bending courteously toward Mr. Hartner, and she was released from the bondage of his scrutiny.

"Selina?" Hailey was regarding her with concern. "You're white as a sheet. Are you feeling all right?"

She blinked and forced herself to laugh. "Of course. Perhaps I'm feeling the heat a little. I think I'll go inside and make sure the coffee is holding out." She got to her feet. Behind Hailey's back, Ricky winked at her gratefully, thinking, no doubt, that she was leaving them to a tête-à-tête.

It was impossible to keep from passing Gil's chair, but he paid her no more attention than if she'd been Eric Rossfield. She checked the level of the coffee

maker and returned her plate to the pantry. Mike and
Eric had somehow rigged up a dumbwaiter in a dis-
used ventilation shaft, which they had blithely
assured her would be just the thing to transport
dishes down to the main galley for washing and back
up for storage. They were in charge of cleanup, so
there was nothing to stop her from going to her berth
and resting for a while—nothing but the stifling heat
that surged out when she entered the ladies' cabin.
She opened the window in the rear wall and stood
there for a moment, watching the paddle wheel froth
up the water, watching the outskirts of a small town
disappear behind a bend in the river. She wanted to
think about Gil's perplexing behavior, but it hurt too
much when she realized he was merely treating her as
hired help. He had told her to trust him, and she
fingered the slender gold chain as she tried to bolster
her self-esteem. *Gil has lots of business worries on his
mind,* she reminded herself. *You know he cares for
you. He's shown it in a number of ways.* But her
treacherous heart merely insisted that he'd never told
her so.

She went into her tiny cubicle and opened the porthole wide. Thinking about the difficulty of getting
laundry done on board the boat, she slipped out of
the piqué dress and hung it up, replacing it with
shorts and a T-shirt. There was time for a short rest
before she had to start working on dinner. Perhaps
after dinner she would make an opportunity to speak
with Gil and find out why, after behaving as if he
didn't care who knew they were lovers, he suddenly
seemed to be concealing that information.

DINNER WAS GRILLED FRESH-CAUGHT CATFISH, accompanied by a warm green-bean-and-beet salad, preceded by tender sautéed quail with mushrooms. The food melded together into a harmonious whole and achieved the same effect with the oddly assorted passengers. The mood was mellow as everyone enjoyed Hailey's delicious peach tart. Even Fred Warner seemed to have forgotten his grudge against the Duchenays and talked amiably to Charlotte. Eric Rossfield had a harmonica, and Ricky Carson found a battered old banjo in the pilothouse, which he played with unexpected panache. The passengers all adjourned to the veranda before the gentlemen's cabin and enjoyed an impromptu sing-along.

Selina could hear them from the main galley, where she was kneading bread sponge for the next day. Hailey's sweet soprano drifted into the evening air. "'Yes, I'll forsake my house and land,'" she sang plaintively, the banjo a yearning accompaniment, "'to follow the Gypsy Davey.'" The haunting refrain caught at Selina's emotions, but she determined to ignore it as best she could. She finished writing up her notes, bone tired but proud of the fact that everything had gone off without a hitch despite a few frantic moments adjusting to her less than professional equipment. She shut the galley door behind her and moved to the forward railing of the lower deck, feeling disinclined to trudge up the staircase and make a grand entrance before the rest of the group.

The *Margaret B. Townshend* was making for the Missouri side. Ahead she could see a dock and a ferry slip, and realized they were going to tie up for the night. The paddle wheel stilled for the first time that day. The absence of sound was somehow shocking after she had grown accustomed to its roar. Voices called from shore, and she heard one of the crew members bellow in reply. Mike and Eric assisted the crew in securing the boat for the night. As they finished their tasks, deliberate footsteps descended the stairs, and the portly figure of the captain appeared. Selina watched him from the shadows as he left the boat, walking up the dirt road toward the ferry office.

The wooden floorboards of the deck over her creaked and groaned as people began moving toward their rooms. Above the trees on the shore the sunset colors were quickly fading, overcome by the deepening dusk. Frogs croaked around the boat, and a bird replied sleepily. A gentle breeze rustled the leaves of the trees, bringing the sweet scent of honeysuckle from the shore.

She leaned on the railing, filled with nostalgic yearning for life as it once was, before railroads and jet planes took the leisure out of traveling. The welcome coolness of the balmy air lulled her senses. She lifted her face to the disk of the rising moon, letting its mysterious force flow through her. When Gil materialized behind her, she knew it, though he made no sound.

"Gypsy's lady." His voice was a rough whisper. He pulled her back into the shadows of the lower deck and turned her until her face was tilted up to his. She stared at him wordlessly, hoping to read in his expression some intimation of his thoughts. But the moonlight, though it threw a silver bar across her face, left his obscured.

His hand came up to trace her features, lingering on the full outline of her lips. The touch awoke an overwhelming desire that washed through her and left her weak, trembling in its wake. The longing for him was so intense that she closed her eyes, afraid he would see how badly she needed and wanted him. He snatched her to him, groaning her name, and fastened his lips to hers, meeting her urgent response with an even greater demand that carried her past all former doubts and reservations. She clutched his back as his hands molded her feverishly to him, pressing their bodies together as if they could never be close enough. His mouth, open against hers, panted fervid words of love that she drank in greedily. She thrust her hips against him, hungry to feel again the ecstasy he'd shown her, made her crave.

"Selina," he whispered, his hands pressing her head into his chest so she could feel the way his heart hammered. "I want to make love to you so desperately. I want—"

She sought blindly for his lips, hearing only the need that thickened his voice, not the words. "Love me, Gil. I need you tonight. Please, Gil—"

He laughed raggedly. "Selina, sweetheart. There isn't a private spot on this boat. We can't make love here."

She nipped gently at his earlobe and slipped her hands under his shirt to rake her fingers delicately across his back. "Let's go ashore, then."

He was still for a moment. "You want to risk getting poison ivy?"

"Could poison ivy be any worse than this?" She moved urgently against him, and he sucked in his breath.

"Wait here for a moment." He vanished into the shadows. She hugged herself nervously, feeling chilled despite the warmth of the air. The captain came back down the road, his pipe glowing red in the darkness. His footsteps ascended weightily to the texas deck. A door shut in the distance. Then Gil was by her side again, a thick blanket over his arm.

"This is crazy," he breathed as they stole down the gangplank. He guided her to the dusty verge of the gravel road, where their feet would make no sound. Halfway between the ferry office and the dock a path branched off, leading up through a tunnellike tangle of saplings and underbrush. Gil used a pencil flashlight to light their way, keeping one arm tightly around Selina. "We must be nuts," he growled in her ear. "We're acting like a couple of teenagers!"

"I feel like a teenager." It was true. Her body was feather light, invincible. She felt drunk with love and adventure.

The path bent to the right around a huge outcropping of stone and climbed steeply, leveling off as the trees and undergrowth thinned around them. They emerged on top of one of the limestone bluffs that lined the riverbank. This one was flat, soft underfoot with grass and moss, and surrounded on three sides by trees and boulders. Selina surveyed the sky with bemused interest.

"You can really see some stars from here," she whispered. "The sky is positively crowded with them." In spite of the moon's radiance, stars clustered thickly over their heads.

Gil inspected a section of the ground with his flashlight, then spread the blanket carefully. "Have a seat," he said hospitably. He pulled her down against him, holding her close for a long moment. They were about ten feet from the edge of the bluff. Selina could hear the river, a deep steady rushing like the sound of sleep claiming a tired mind. "Where's the boat?" She kept her voice soft, unwilling to allow a human voice to impinge on the night's sound track.

Gil pulled her closer to the edge of the bluff so they could see up the river. The *Margaret B. Townshend* was a dark blur on the gleaming water a quarter of a mile back, her riding lights bobbing up and down as the river shifted under her. In the moonlight the gilt crowns on her smokestacks shone faintly.

"It's like being carried back in time." He spoke the words directly into her ear, sending an uncanny shiver down her back. The wide implacable river, trees rising darkly on either bank; the pagan disk of the moon riding across the star-studded sky; the stern-wheeler tied up for the night, with no other human interference save the ferry office for miles around; she almost expected to see Mark Twain come striding up the path and onto the bluff behind them. Then Gil gripped her arm, pointing downstream. Around a bend in the river came a huge stern-wheeler, gliding like a ghost through the moon path.

Except for the din of her paddle wheel, which grew louder as she passed them, she might have been a specter of Selina's imagination. Lights gleamed at intervals along her four decks. On the transom above the paddle wheel, as she moved majestically by, Selina could read the words "Delta Queen." Then she was gone around a bend. Her wash lifted the *Margaret B. Townshend* and rocked her gently.

Selina let out her breath, though she hadn't been aware of holding it. "Doesn't the *Queen* tie up for the night?"

Gil whispered, too. "She does at some point during the night. We're supposed to tie up at dusk, but I guess the big boats have a different charter."

The *Delta Queen*'s passage moved the night into the realm of fantasy. Selina felt her spirits bubble and overflow like champagne released from its bottle. Gil's mouth found hers, making her explode into unquenchable flames. He guided her back to the blanket, laying her gently down while he rained soft kisses over her face and throat. He sat back on his heels for a moment, watching her. "You are so beautiful," he said, his voice thickened by emotion. "Let me—" He began unfastening her shirt, undoing the front catch of her bra, removing her clothes gently to the accompaniment of murmured exclamations of delight as she moaned and arched her body upward, inviting more and more of the maddening caresses. Finally she lay naked, ivory skin gleaming in the moonlight, arms imploring him to come to her. He stood for a moment, shedding his clothes rapidly.

"You're like a goddess," he rasped, pulling his shirt over his head. She couldn't help thinking that he was more beautiful than any god as he stood in the silvered light, his supple body suffused with masculine grace. He knelt beside her, his hands gliding in feathery touches over her shoulders, around her breasts and over the nipples, making her gasp with desire. She pulled him down to her, letting her own hands wander over the smooth compact muscles, learning again the feel of the places that brought groans of pleasure from his throat. With slow primitive motions they joined their bodies, surging in mutual delight, consummating their passion beneath the radiant mystery of the moon.

She lay dreamily in his arms, her skin damp with the exertion of love. He moved one hand slowly through her hair, parting the tangles with his fingers. "Your hair reflects the moonlight magnificently," he whispered. "Stars in your crown."

She wriggled with happiness. "This is really something! I wonder why anyone makes love indoors."

As if in answer, a high-pitched whine began at her ear. Gil slapped at his back and swore. "Mosquitoes. Time to decamp, I think."

They scrambled back into their clothes, and Selina bent to fold the blanket. Gil pulled her back up into his arms. "Selina," he said, his voice abrupt. "As long as I've got you where no one can interrupt, let me tell you something." He searched her face intently, turning it to the moonlight. "I *know* the outcome," he muttered, his eyes taking on an unfathomable opacity. For a long moment they stood thus. Selina shivered, scanning Gil's face uneasily. Though they were together, Gil seemed to be somewhere far away. The cold remoteness of his gaze was like a closed gate to which she had no key.

Then a door slammed at the ferry slip, and a car started up noisily. Gil blinked and dropped his hands from her shoulders. "Better not," he said briefly. He took the blanket from Selina and pulled her to him with a strong arm around her waist. "Just remember that you've got to trust me," he said ferociously. "No matter what I say, no matter how it looks."

"But can't you tell me what it's all about? I won't give any secrets away."

He guided her toward the break in the trees where the path began. "If I told you—well, there might not be any secret. No, my sweet chef, you'll just have to take my actions on trust. In fact, I meant to tell you when I found you on deck tonight that it would be wise if we didn't meet alone during the trip. But I can't be near you without wanting you."

"Me, neither," she said in a small voice.

He drew in a deep breath. "Well, we'll just have to avoid each other. It would spoil my plans if Warner—if people—knew my feelings for you."

What are your feelings for me, she wanted to cry. *Spoil what plans?* But Gil had put his finger to his lips as they neared the ferry road. Silently they crept back onto the boat and up the creaking stairs. At the door to the gentlemen's cabin he stopped. "You go first,'' he breathed. He kissed her, his lips hard, possessive, demanding, as if he realized her doubts and could suppress them with the force of his passion. But though she would not question him, she could not understand his reluctance to share his thoughts with her. She left him, slipping softly through the swinging doors, pausing, hoping for one look, one last kiss that would make everything right. But he had turned away to stand by the railing, and she could read nothing in the rigid lines of his back.

She tiptoed through the gentlemen's cabin, where the air-conditioned air seemed close and stale after the breezy freshness outside. The ladies' bathroom was empty. She didn't turn on the light, preferring the faint light that filtered in from an outside floodlight to the harsh glare of the ceiling fixture. They had been told to use water sparingly, so she took a sponge bath instead of the shower she longed for. Her tiny cabin, when she reached it, seemed like a sanctuary. She slid into cotton pajamas and crawled wearily into her berth. Now the wild fierce beauty of their lovemaking on the bluff was overshadowed by their furtive return to the boat. She clutched a pillow to fill her empty arms and let the sobs burst from her aching throat to be swallowed up in the pillow's impassive depths. How was it that love could be so exquisite one minute and so miserable the next? ''I hate it,'' she wept. ''I don't want to be in love anymore. He doesn't love me, or he wouldn't put me through such hell.''

But she knew her love could not be wept away like a passing grief. She could fight it, she could deny it;

but it would be there, waiting, ready to ignite the moment Gil chose to unleash his incendiary power over her. Long before she could finish weeping over that fact, she was asleep.

CHAPTER FOURTEEN

SQUINTING AGAINST THE MORNING SUNLIGHT that streamed in the cookhouse door, Selina gave the big cast-iron skillet she held an expert shake. Link sausages spat and hissed but rolled over obediently. At the next burner Hailey, between huge yawns, scrambled eggs in another skillet. Of the three occupants of the main galley, only Betsy was bright eyed and talkative.

"Captain Morris says that going down the Mississippi's not easy nowadays, even if they do dredge the channel," she informed them while she cut out biscuits. "He says we could hit a snag anytime if he wasn't the best dad-blamed riverboat pilot alive."

"More like the only riverboat pilot alive," Hailey mumbled. Betsy paid no attention.

"Captain Morris was an apprentice of Samuel Clemens," she said importantly. "You know, Mark Twain. The first time he ever piloted a riverboat it was because old Sam Clemens was drunk and fell asleep in the pilothouse, and Captain Morris had to take over. He says—"

"Are those biscuits about ready?" Selina interrupted, exchanging a glance with Hailey. "I don't know that you should take everything Captain Morris says as the absolute truth.''

"He's a very truthful man. He told me so himself." Selina pointed commandingly at the paper towels, and Betsy handed them to her. "We're passing a town," she cried out, looking out the door. "Do you need me anymore?"

Selina shook her head, smiling, and Betsy scampered out into the sunshine. "How wonderful to have so much enthusiasm at this ungodly hour," Hailey said around another yawn.

"I thought bakers always got up at the crack of dawn," Selina teased, scooping sausages out of the frying pan and blotting them with the paper towels. She arranged them swiftly into a chafing-dish liner and loaded the whole apparatus into the dumbwaiter.

Hailey scraped her scrambled eggs into another liner. "This baker doesn't. Do we have some coffee made down here?"

"Chef's private reserve." Selina poured two cups from the drip-coffee maker on the back of the stove. She sipped hers as she laid flat little circles of biscuit dough in glass pie plates. "You don't have to get up and help with breakfast, you know. You signed on as pastry chef."

"I wouldn't mind," Hailey said, stifling another yawn, "except I got to bed kind of late last night. Ricky and I sat out on the texas deck and talked for hours."

Selina averted her eyes, loading the biscuits and scrambled eggs onto the dumbwaiter. Had Hailey and Ricky noticed other comings and goings? Probably not, she reasoned, since they'd been at the rear of the boat and absorbed in each other. "You go on up to the pantry," she said with an assumption of briskness, "and I'll send this stuff up. Then I won't need you anymore if you want to get some more sleep."

She halted at the pulley as soon as Hailey shouted down the shaft. Then she raced upstairs to set up the chafing dishes and finish breakfast preparation.

The hoteliers seemed in better spirits this morning, although Mrs. Olen mentioned wistfully how pleasant it was on cruises to be served early coffee in one's stateroom. Selina ignored the comment. Her own spirits hadn't been improved by a night spent crying into her pillow. She found her wretched temper building throughout the meal. How could other people talk, and laugh, and admire the changing view as if everything were perfect? Tight-lipped, she accepted compliments on breakfast without encouraging conversation.

She'd had Eric push one of the tables in the gentlemen's cabin into a corner, with the idea that it would be easier to have a staff table than to have to mingle with the hoteliers. She sat there now, sipping her coffee glumly while she tried not to watch Gil charming Mrs. Hartner. He'd put Ricky to work on Mrs. Olen, who seemed to find the young man's impudent humor and blatant flattery amusing. How did Hailey feel about that, Selina wondered. It certainly wouldn't occur to Gil that his young cousin might prefer to have Ricky dancing attendance on her than on the wife of a man who might prove useful. Hal

MacMillan and Magda were seated together, deep in conversation. As she watched, Hal took Magda's hand in his own for a moment, his expression serious, tender. Selina looked hastily away. She didn't mean to spy, and she didn't really want to see anyone else's romance running smoothly when her own was so inexplicably complicated. Her feeling of unhappy isolation increased her anger toward Gil. How could he put her in such a position? It was obvious he cared more about his company, his business deals, than about her feelings. She was just a little something to amuse himself with on the side.

She was distracted from these bitter thoughts when Fred Warner sat down at her table. Evidently he didn't realize, or didn't care, that it was for the staff. She kept herself from glowering at him with an effort.

"So how long have you been a chef?" He plunged into conversation intently, his eyes fixed on her face in a surprisingly penetrating stare.

"Long enough," she retorted, forcing a smile on her face. "I've attended the California Culinary Academy for the past couple of years."

He fished a cigar out of his breast pocket and unwrapped it, still keeping that disconcerting stare on her. "A real professional, eh?" He contrived to make it sound somehow like an insult. As an afterthought he waved the cigar at her before lighting it. "This bother you?"

"Yes," she snapped. "And probably everyone else in here. I'd prefer you didn't smoke when you sit at this table."

To her surprise he took it mildly enough. "Quite a little libber, aren't you? But I suppose you're right. M'wife didn't like it, either, rest her soul." With regret he put the cigar back in his pocket and leaned forward, one pudgy fist on the table. "Tell you what I wanted to talk to you about, Miss Montgomery. What's young Duchenay up to?"

The suddenness of his question deprived Selina of speech. She blinked at him in confusion. "Up to? I don't understand." For a moment she thought he must have seen something that made him suspect a relationship between Gil and herself. Then common sense took over. This man made it plain that he was interested only in what affected Purity. He wouldn't be so blunt about a suspected affair between the chief executive officer and his personal chef.

His next words confirmed her opinion. "So you don't know? Pity. I thought if anyone did, you would, since you're handling the food end of things. He's got some little scheme up his sleeve, and I'd really like to know what it is." His hand went to the pocket of his casual polyester jacket, and Selina saw the corner of a hundred-dollar bill. For a moment she stared at him, puzzled. Then she realized that he was trying to bribe her to spy on Gil.

She should have been angry, but it was suddenly blindingly funny. She started laughing helplessly, trying to smother the sound in her napkin and only partially succeeding. Through the tears that streamed from her eyes she could see the passengers glancing over curiously and Fred Warner's impassive face. With an effort she got herself under control.

"You're talking to the wrong person if you want information about Gilmartin Duchenay," she gasped, wiping her face with the napkin and taking a gulp of ice water. "I'm the last person he'd tell anything to."

As she spoke, the desolate certainty contained in her words dispelled any traces of mirth. Fred Warner looked at her closely and appeared satisfied that she was being honest. For a moment, in fact, he relaxed into a semblance of normal human concern.

"Lots of your grand families are that way," he said, giving her hand a quick clumsy pat. "I can see they don't treat you like anything but a servant, and I think it's a crying shame. You're a wizard in the kitchen, miss. You deserve better than being treated like a second-class citizen by Mr. High-and-Mighty Duchenay."

Selina gaped at him and he reddened. "Nothing personal," he added, his voice stiff. "But you can be glad you're not one of those fancy society debutantes. Breaks their hearts right and left, from what I hear. At least you don't have to deal with that."

"Just a minute," Selina began. "I don't think you quite understand, Mr. Warner—" She broke off as Gil appeared, his face wearing the mask of the genial host.

"Didn't know you were a ladies' man, Warner. You appear to be entertaining Chef Montgomery very well."

She winced at the faintly possessive note in his voice. Fred Warner would obviously attribute it to a feudal attitude toward the hired help. She opened her mouth, but Warner spoke before her.

"Just telling this little lady what a fine cook she is. She should have a wider scope for her talents. Maybe I could persuade her to open a restaurant so we could all enjoy her expertise."

Selina had the feeling that the past few minutes were straight out of one of those deep art films, where every conversation has at least three meanings. Gil was obviously interpreting Warner's remarks in that way. His brows drew together thunderously. Before he could say something that would reveal their relationship, Selina jumped up.

"Time to get back to work," she exclaimed in a voice full of false jauntiness. "Mr. Duchenay, I need to see you about ordering those supplies from the provision boat. Would it be convenient now?"

Mr. Warner shook his head sadly at the evidence of so much obsequiousness. Gil stared at her, his eyes narrowing dangerously. "All right," he said with ominous quietness. "Where?"

"Well, my list is down in the cook house." Mustering up a bright smile for Warner, Selina led the way from the gentlemen's cabin, Gil stalking silently beside her. Many of the passengers were carrying their coffee out to drink in the warm morning sunshine. No one seemed to notice or remark on their progress down the stairs toward the bottom deck.

Gil shut the door forcefully when they were both inside. "All right," he exploded. "What are you playing at? What were you and Warner talking about so cozily?"

Selina faced him indignantly. "Why don't you use your psychic powers and find out?"

He moved toward her, his body exuding a dangerous control. "Before I listen to what my psychic powers really tell me to do," he growled, "perhaps you'd like to explain." Selina was too angry to reply, afraid if she opened her mouth she'd simply gibber with rage. He exhaled impatiently. "Perhaps," he said, biting off his words, "I didn't make myself sufficiently clear last night. That man is my enemy! What did you tell him? Did you tell him about us?"

Selina could no longer control her temper. "That's rich! What would I tell him about us? 'Oh, yes, Gilmartin Duchenay and I are having a squalid little affair, which you mustn't talk about because it's secret'? How the hell could I tell anyone about something that doesn't exist? Since you obviously don't trust me, why don't you just go and ask Fred Warner about his conversation with me? Tell him I'm sorry I turned down the money!"

She stopped, aghast, realizing that she'd been carried away by her anger. Gil's face was white, his lips tightly compressed. After a moment he spoke.

"Is that what you really think? You find our relationship squalid?" He took a deep breath, visibly trying to get control of himself. Selina could find nothing to say. He turned away, clenching his fist around the edge of a worktable until the skin strained white over the bones. "You're a fine one to talk about trust," he said bitterly over his shoulder. "You don't seem to trust me when I ask you to, and yet you expect me to trust you. Don't you understand the hell I'm going through? Having to play the polite host, the astute businessman, when all I can think about is you?"

She stared at him, wide-eyed. "Gil—"

He whipped around, moving fast, seizing her and crushing her to his chest. "I think about your body last night in the moonlight, your skin so white, like cream...." One hand came up to capture her chin, forcing her head up to meet his eyes. "I think about the way you taste when I kiss you, and I want to kiss you everywhere—" He whispered the words, his mouth coming closer to hers. His eyes were blazing, devouring. She shut her own eyes helplessly as his lips began to plunder her mouth, moving with ruthless determination to conquer any small resistance she could put up. His hand moved from her jaw down her throat and seized on the soft fullness of her breast. He groaned triumphantly as the nipple peaked under his thumb. Unable to withstand the sensuous assault, she writhed against him, feeling her body go up in flames once again. "Gil," she whispered achingly against his lips, "oh, please—"

"Selina," he said hoarsely. "Why do you torture me?" He thrust her away, his chest heaving. "I believe you're a witch," he muttered, running a hand through his hair, pushing back the lock that always fell forward.

"You've got that wrong," Her voice was shaky, too. "You're the one with supernatural powers. I just happened to get in the way of them."

"You can't really believe that." His eyes probed deep into hers until she turned away, uneasy at the scrutiny. What he saw there seemed to reassure him. He sat on one of the tall stools and pulled her over to stand between his legs. "I think I've found the way to control you and your redheaded temper," he said, a teasing note in his voice. "Now I'm going to ask you some questions, and if you start spitting at me like a little wildcat, I'll just begin taking off your clothes. Understand?"

"A reward for losing my temper? Mighty tempting." Selina grinned at him, then drew in her breath as he began a negligent massage of her breasts, his hands cupping their warm contours, his thumbs moving with maddening lightness over her nipples.

"Now," he said, watching her desire-slackened face with satisfaction. "What did Fred Warner want?"

"Huh?" Selina wet her lips with her tongue, hoping her knees didn't buckle under her as the heavy langour of the passion he was creating spread through her limbs. "He just—sat down at my table and—look here, Gil, I can't—"

His hands moved down her waist to pull her hips closer to him. "What did he say?"

Two can play this game, Selina thought. She pressed herself closer and felt the immediate response in his loins. "He commiserated with me for having to work with a snob like you."

"Did he really?" Gil nibbled judiciously at her earlobe, sliding his hands inside the waistband of her jeans and down the smooth globes of her buttocks. "What was that about the money?"

Selina was busy with her hands, too. She slipped them inside his shirt and up his chest, gently palming the male nipples. At the same time she began a rhythmic movement of her hips, smiling wickedly as his breathing became ragged. "He didn't exactly offer me money. He just implied that I might be fed up with my treatment as a servant, and he was paying for information about what you were up to."

Abruptly Gil abandoned their game. He buried his face in her hair, holding her closely and breathing deeply. "Oh, sweetheart," he groaned. "I don't think I can last until New Orleans. I need you—you know how much—"

The words echoed strangely in Selina's head. She stood for a moment as if petrified, feeling the warmth drain from her face. Gil sensed the change in her. He tipped her head up to his. "What is it?" he questioned urgently. "Be mad, fight me, but don't withdraw like that. Tell me what's wrong."

"I don't know how much you need me. I don't know—anything!" The words burst from her before she thought about saying them. "That's what I can't live with! I've got to do *something* about it!"

She stepped away from him, twisting her hands together in agitation. "You could try asking me," Gil said quietly. His face wore the shuttered look she dreaded. "I might have a good idea or two."

"I don't see how you could," Selina said bleakly. She turned away and smoothed her hair with her hands. "It's too hopeless," she sighed. "I went over it in my mind last night until I thought I was going nuts. What does the future hold for us? Marriage is out of the question—"

"It is?" Gil's voice was neutral. She faced him wearily.

"You know it is. Your work is conducted during

business hours. You socialize and entertain at night. My work is evening oriented. Even a restaurant, as Fred Warner so aptly suggested, wouldn't work out. It would just be getting busy when you got off work. What kind of life is that? We'd never see each other. I saw marriages break up over that issue at school.''

Gil seemed as if he were about to say something, but she rushed on without letting him speak. "You see how difficult it is to be married to a chef. And without my work, I'd be—'' Words failed her. She stared at him helplessly. "Well, you know. Think about having to give up your work for a social round!''

Gil nodded. When he spoke, his voice was gentle. "Believe me, I understand, Selina.

She fought back the tears that threatened to overcome her. "Then maybe you can tell me just what we're heading for. See if you can read it in my palm, Gypsy Davey!''

She thrust her hand close to his face, and he took it gravely. He pored over it for a moment, then raised his eyes to meet hers. "I see—pain,'' he said unwillingly. "Separation. But eventually—happiness.''

She laughed unbelievingly. "Separation—just as I thought. We'd better call it quits, Gil. The longer it goes on, the worse it will be in the end. Do you agree?''

He stared at her for a moment, then seized her roughly. "The hell with it,'' he growled.

She twisted out of his grasp. "I have plans, Gil. You just don't fit into them. And if I change them

for you, and then—'' She felt anger and frustration
building up inside her. ''All we have is an affair, with
no commitment from either of us. I don't want to
sneak around like this. So let's just—'' Despite her
attempts to control herself, she found herself too
overcome by emotion to continue speaking. ''Please,
just—'' She sat down wearily at the table, her shoulders bowed, letting the cool smooth surface of the
scrubbed wood offer support for her heavy limbs.
She gestured dismissively toward Gil. ''Just go!'' she
asserted. ''Please!''

He put one arm around her shoulders. She could
feel the comforting warmth of his breath on her
cheek. ''Selina,'' he began, his voice strained.
''Don't do this to yourself.''

With an effort she met his gaze squarely. She knew
he was truly concerned, but it didn't help. ''I'm all
right, Gil,'' she mumbled. ''Just leave me alone,
please.''

She heard the rustle as he straightened. The
warmth of his breath and arm were withdrawn. His
footsteps echoed hollowly on the wooden floor. They
stopped. He spoke from the door.

''I'll go since you wish it. But I'm telling you,
Selina, this isn't the end. I can't let you go for
good.''

The door shut behind him. For a long moment
she sat on her stool, taking deep even breaths. Her
cheeks felt flushed, her eyes were stinging. Dully
she wondered what had been accomplished. ''It's
over,'' she said aloud. ''No matter what he says, it's
over.''

THEY WERE TO TIE UP at Cairo, Illinois late that afternoon. It seemed impossible that they'd only been on the boat two days, or that they could have driven to Cairo from St. Louis in a few hours. The leisurely progress of the boat, the winding, constantly changing aspect of the Mississippi, combined to alter internal clocks. They'd been heading north, then west, all morning; to get to Cairo, they left the Mississippi and turned up the Ohio for a little way, crossing to land on the north bank just above the point where the finger of land Cairo occupied thrust itself between the two rivers.

Selina set up the lunch buffet and then left Hailey in charge, retiring to her cabin with a fictional headache, which the stifling heat soon turned into reality. The kitchen was to be closed for dinner; she welcomed the prospect of a few hours away from the boat.

Hailey elected to stay on board and have leftovers for dinner. Selina was not surprised, when she climbed onto one of the vans that were to take them to the downtown area, to see that Ricky was also absent. This caused a brief scene when Charlotte Drumm discovered it after the buses had driven away from the river. Selina turned her face to the window, feeling numb and alienated.

There was a farmer's market in progress in downtown Cairo. When Selina jumped out of the van, Gil was suddenly beside her. "Going shopping?" She stared at him mutely and moved away, vaguely surprised when he followed.

Fred Warner ambled up. "Think you know enough to get us something fit to eat, Duchenay?

This stuff isn't already cooked and frozen, you know.''

Gil smiled silkily. "Perhaps you'd like to take my place, Warner. I'm sure Selina could teach even you how to tell a cabbage from an onion." He handed Warner his basket and sketched a mock bow to Selina. "A good chief executive knows when to let the board take over. Enjoy yourselves, now."

Warner watched meditatively as Gil strolled over to the hoteliers, taking Mrs. Hartner on one arm and Mrs. Olen on the other, while their husbands fell back to smoke. "I wish I knew what that young punk is up to," he muttered.

Selina experienced a novel mixture of relief and chagrin at being so casually disposed of by Gil. "Well," she said, assuming a briskness she didn't feel. "We'd better get started if we want to finish at a decent hour. Unless you'd rather not bother, Mr. Warner?"

"No, no," he said, falling into step beside her gallantly. "If you need somebody to give you a hand with the marketing, I'll be glad to do it, seeing as how I kind of crashed this party."

They strolled along the crowded aisles, looking for the freshest produce. Selina explained what to look for as they selected tomatoes and melons. Then she stood back to let Fred Warner put into practice what she had advised him about picking out cantaloupes.

"Let's see." He hefted one consideringly. "I look at the netting first and feel it to make sure there are no bruises." Gravely he turned the melon in his pudgy hands. "Supposed to press on the stem end—"

"Gently," Selina interposed. "It should be soft because it's ripe, not because you squashed it."

"I got you." His bushy eyebrows drew together. "There's something else—oh, yeah, I'm supposed to smell it, too." He lifted the melon to his nose, sniffing deeply.

"Looks like you're really getting into it, Warner." Gil reappeared, this time with Magda and Betsy. Magda smiled warmly at Fred Warner.

"Don't listen to him, Mr. Warner." She took the melon from him and gave it a quick scrutiny. "A perfect choice. You're really a natural."

Warner shook his head deprecatingly. "Miss—I mean, Chef—Montgomery is a good teacher. It's interesting to know there's more to grocery shopping than buying TV dinners."

They moved along in a group, chatting amiably. Warner refused to give up his task, but gradually it was Magda he turned to for tips. Selina was busy arranging with the vendors of the best produce to send up their purchases to the boat, where Hailey would store them immediately. She wanted to buy enough to last until Memphis, when they would be stopping again, and where she would have to visit the butcher, as well as the vegetable sellers.

After a fried-chicken dinner at a local inn, Gil mentioned Dixieland jazz. Mrs. Olen visibly repressed a shudder. "I would rather go back to the boat and lie down for a while. But don't feel you must all come back on my account."

Mr. Olen looked wistful at the mention of Dixieland jazz. Selina spoke up. "I'll be glad to go back with you, Mrs. Olen. I've got a bit of headache, too. Perhaps I could escort you back, and your husband could stay on for the jazz.''

"If you wish to stay, Vernon," Mrs. Olen said faintly, "please don't concern yourself about me. I shall be quite all right.''

To everyone's surprise Mr. Olen stayed behind. Magda sent Betsy back, much to Betsy's disgust. Mrs. Drumm seized the opportunity to return. Selina hoped that Hailey and Ricky were prepared for her mother's vengeful descent.

Gil didn't look at her as she climbed into the van, but Selina knew he was furious. No doubt he'd planned some way to get around her as he always did. She leaned her head wearily against the cool glass of the window. It was hard to resist his magnetism. But it was harder to imagine how, loving Gil as she did, she could cope when he ceased to need her. She was torn by doubts and indecision, overwhelmed by the desire to hold him and love him.

Time to go to bed, she told herself firmly, watching the tender light of sunset wash over the river as they reached the boat dock. *Time to go to bed alone.* Stretching in front of her was a long succession of nights she would spend alone. Time to get used to it.

CHAPTER FIFTEEN

BETSY FELL ASLEEP in the van on the return trip, and Mrs. Drumm flounced sulkily into the seat farthest from everyone else. That left Selina captive to Mrs. Olen, who spent the journey back to the boat landing indulging in a monologue about her various ailments. By the time they reached the boat, Selina was heartily tired of the sound of that wispy quavering voice. Betsy yawned her way up the gangplank and vanished into the ladies' cabin. Selina didn't see what happened to Mrs. Drumm. She was too busy with Mrs. Olen, who evidently couldn't walk more than three steps without assistance. Grinding her teeth, Selina escorted Mrs. Olen to her stateroom.

"Might I have a little hot milk?" Mrs. Olen asked plaintively. "After all that fried food I need something to settle my stomach. Will you see to it for me, please?"

Selina took a deep breath to keep from snapping that she was not a parlor maid. "Certainly," she hissed politely.

She found Ricky and Hailey in the main galley. Hailey was showing Ricky how to shape loaves of bread. Selina paused for a moment in the doorway to watch, an unwilling smile curving her lips. She recognized Hailey's manner as an unconscious parody of her own teaching style.

"You have to flatten it out well," Hailey said, a faint dictatorial note in her voice. "Otherwise there'll be air bubbles after it's baked. Now roll it up—that's right—"

Someone knocked into Selina from behind, and she let out a pained exclamation, causing Hailey to look up. "Back already," she said, smiling. The smile changed to a frown when she saw the person behind Selina. "Hello, mother."

Mrs. Drumm pushed past Selina angrily and entered the kitchen with defiant fascination, as if it were the most sordid of love nests. Her usual flower-veiled hat was askew, and the white gloves she had worn for the excursion to Cairo had long since been soiled. She clutched her bag and fixed Hailey with her sternest glare.

"Why, may I ask, did you deceive me? I expected you to come with everyone else on the trip. It looked very strange that you stayed behind with this—this—" Unable to find a word depraved enough, she switched her glare to Ricky. He smiled easily.

"Stowaway?" he suggested. "Banjo player? Amateur bread baker? Wealthy young bachelor?"

"Don't be flip." Aunt Charlotte had been on the point of gibbering, but Ricky's last words caused her to refine her glare from gimlet to considering. Apparently unaware of her scrutiny, Ricky turned back to Hailey.

"I think I'm getting the hang of it," he confided. "Like this—" He lifted a cloth that covered several mounds of bread dough and selected one. With careful motions he flattened it, rolled it up, pinched the ends and placed it in one of the nearby loaf pans. "How was that?"

Hailey started to speak, but her mother interrupted her. "You should never roll the dough," she said authoritatively. "You fold it, like so." She stripped off her gloves and picked up another round of dough, flattening and folding it with expert moves. The others watched, dumbfounded, as she deposited it into a loaf pan. "There."

"Why, mother." Hailey's eyes were round with surprise. "I never knew you could make bread."

"My grandmother believed every woman should know how to make a good loaf of bread," Aunt Charlotte said, dusting off her hands. "She read Louisa May Alcott," she added irrelevantly.

"You're a wonder, Mrs. D." Ricky laughed as he scrambled to his feet and bowed gracefully. "Perhaps you'd like to help us dispose of our afternoon's labor?" He gestured toward the remaining lumps of dough.

"Have you been making bread all afternoon?" Selina asked the question, though she knew if she waited four seconds more, it would have been on Mrs. Drumm's lips.

"Well," Hailey said with her customary giggle, "Ricky wanted some cinnamon rolls. So I came down to mix them up. He said he wanted to learn how to do it, so after we finished the cinnamon rolls, we started on some bread." She gave Ricky an admiring glance. "He learns very quickly. I'm thinking of offering him a job."

This time Mrs. Drumm did start to gibber. Ricky

produced Selina's apron and presented it to her with
a flourish. "Dear lady," he said smoothly, "if you
would deign to help, we could get the bread finished
in time to bake in the cool of the evening. An expert
like yourself would be a real asset."

Hailey didn't look as if she agreed, but Aunt
Charlotte was mollified. "Just this once," she said,
taking the apron with a show of reluctance. Ricky led
Mrs. Drumm over to the table and assumed an awestruck expression as she began to form loaves. "Why
don't you take Selina up to her cabin and let me just
bask in your mother's know-how for a moment."

Hailey glanced at him, an undecided frown on her
face. "I have to make some hot milk for Mrs. Olen,"
Selina interposed with a sigh. She got out a saucepan
and put the milk to heat on the stove.

"I'll take it up to her," Hailey offered, searching
for a cup and saucer. "Drat, all the dishes are in the
pantry. Why don't I just carry it up and heat it in the
microwave?"

"Good idea." Selina headed for the door, and
Hailey followed, sending a doubtful look over her
shoulder toward Ricky. He blew her an airy kiss and
turned back to her mother.

Selina started to follow Hailey into the pantry, but
Hailey shooed her into her own cabin. "I'll take care
of Mrs. Olen," she said, pouring the milk into a cup
and setting it in the microwave. "You go lie down for
a while, or something. You look exhausted."

"Thanks," Selina said dryly. Hailey shrugged.

"The truth hurts." She took the milk out and
started toward the stairs to the texas deck. "When

I come back, you'd better be relaxing in your room."

The little cabin was suffocating. Selina opened the tiny window to allow the cool evening breeze in. She was leaning on the window, letting the fragrant air bathe her hot face, when Hailey entered. Selina turned and sent a quizzical glance in Hailey's direction. "Did you really spend the afternoon making bread?"

Hailey collapsed on the lower bunk, her face puzzled. "Yes! I was expecting—well, I don't know what I was expecting, but it certainly didn't happen. Ricky wanted to make cinnamon rolls, and all the time we were working, he kept asking me about my bakery, and what I planned to do with it in the future. He didn't even kiss me once!" She turned anguished eyes upon Selina. "I thought he was beginning to see me as a woman, not as Gil's roly-poly little cousin. I guess I was wrong."

Selina shook her head slowly. "I don't think so." There had been a warm admiration in Ricky's eyes when he looked at Hailey that was quite different from the usual bold appraisal he directed toward women. "Maybe he—respects you too much to try anything."

"I don't want to be respected," Hailey wailed. "I want—I think I want to have an affair with him! I want passion, like you and Gil have—" Aghast, she put her hand to her mouth.

Selina's mouth felt dry. She turned away and busied herself washing her hands at the tiny sink. "How do you know what Gil and I have?" she asked quietly.

"I shouldn't have said that," Hailey mumbled. "I'm just guessing, really. I've seen the way you look at each other, and I just assumed—I mean, it seemed obvious—"

"That we were having an affair?" Selina kept her voice level.

"Well—something of that nature." Hailey cleared her throat uneasily. "Actually we thought you would be getting married. That's why—"

"*We* thought?" Selina spun quickly. "Who's 'we'?"

"I—well, Aunt Magda, Betsy and I." Hailey darted a miserable glance at Selina's white face. "We were just—talking, and Aunt Magda said something—anyway, it seemed—"

"Obvious?" Selina laughed bitterly. "Too bad it's not obvious to me. Or to Gil, if it comes to that."

"You're not—I mean, we thought maybe in New Orleans...." Hailey's voice trailed off. Selina hardly noticed. She squirmed internally at the thought that her emotions had been so transparent. "What did Magda think about it?" she asked suddenly.

Hailey's expression brightened. "She thought you'd be perfect for Gil, and I must say I agree." She hesitated a moment, then asked diffidently, "Has he asked you?"

Selina didn't answer, and Hailey rushed into an apologetic speech. "I'm sorry, I shouldn't have asked that. I know you're going to be happy, though. Any man would be a chump not to fall in love with you. In fact—" she paused with a shy laugh "—maybe I shouldn't tell you this, but I thought at first that

Ricky had a crush on you, and that's why he came on this trip.''

With an effort Selina shook off her dark thoughts. They would keep. In the meantime she could change the subject. "When he got one good look at you," she said, smiling weakly, "he knew why he'd come. If you ask me, just the fact that he's treating you with more respect than he normally does proves that he thinks of you in a different way."

Hailey blushed rosily. "That had occurred to me, too," she said innocently. "I don't want to just— throw myself at him. But he is so handsome and charming—I've been in love with him since I was fifteen." She smiled dreamily and moved toward the door. "I'd better go down and see to the bread. Isn't it the strangest thing about mother? You could have knocked me over with a feather when she picked up that dough."

"Amazing," Selina agreed hollowly. She wanted nothing more than to have a few minutes of solitude. With an effort she replied to Hailey's inconsequential chatter as the other girl lingered in the doorway. Hailey paused, directing an earnest look at Selina.

"I hope I didn't say anything to upset you earlier." She twisted the doorknob nervously. "Gil really cares for you—I know he does. I know you'll be happy together. Believe me!" She leaned forward and gave Selina an impulsive peck on the cheek. "I've always felt as if Gil was my brother. I'm glad you're going to be my sister someday."

After she was gone, Selina sank limply onto her bunk, staring at the wall above the washstand blankly. There seemed to be a conspiracy to throw her into Gil's arms. God knew she wanted to be there! Hopeless longing swept over her when she thought of him. But it was madness to think of him too long. She wrenched her mind away and fixed it on her solitary future. Where would she go when she left the Château?

Mentally she counted up her savings. She'd banked much of her salary since starting to work for the Duchenays, but two months' pay, no matter how munificent, didn't go far. However, it would buy her a plane ticket to France. Once there, she could find work in a restaurant, perhaps under one of the great chefs. She sighed bleakly, returning to reality. With no recommendations she would be lucky even to get a job dishwashing for someone like Paul Bocuse or Jean Troisgros.

Moving aimlessly, she went to the window and leaned out again, grateful for the coolness of the outside air. Her brain felt overheated from the effort of spinning its wheels for the past half hour. Her gaze roamed idly over the boat landing to the discouraging-looking shed bristling with padlocks on its dilapidated door, to the phone booth standing beside it—the phone booth! Feverishly she dived for her purse and counted her change. After all, she wasn't exactly alone in the world. She could scrape up some recommendations. She went down the stairs and over the gangplank, glad that the deepening summer twilight would obscure her from curious eyes. Surely Molly would be home this late on a Monday evening. She lifted the receiver. "Operator? I'd like to place a call to San

Francisco. Yes, California!" Molly would be able to help.

Seven dollars and thirty-five cents later she hung up the telephone. Molly had told her, with real regret, that there was nothing promising in San Francisco. "Costs are up," she bemoaned, "and nobody wants to pay a living wage." But she had promised to get letters of recommendation from the chefs at school, several of whom had been apprentices of some of Europe's most influential chefs. With those letters Selina stood a much better chance of getting a *sous-chef* position in a premier French kitchen. Training with one or two big names would mean even more than attendance at the Cordon Bleu.

She should have been ecstatic. "Most people," she lectured herself sternly, "would not regard the necessity of working in France as any hardship." But the thought of leaving Gil thousands of miles behind was desolating. Though she knew their parting was inevitable, contemplating it was too painful.

Shutting the door of the phone booth, she thrust all thought of what would happen after New Orleans into the back of her mind. Molly would send the letters to the hotel where they were to stay for a few days before flying back to St. Louis. When the letters arrived, Selina resolved, she would think about her future. She stood by the phone booth for a moment, regarding the *Margaret B. Townshend* with affection. The stern-wheeler bobbed gently on her mooring ropes, her graceful outlines filagreed with the lights that bloomed in the thickening dusk like fireflies. A golden oblong was outlined briefly as the cook-house door opened and shut. The clear sound of Hailey's laughter mingled with Ricky's deeper tones and the slightly peevish voice of Mrs. Drumm. Dimly she could make out Hailey's white shorts moving up the grand staircase. Another flash of light as the door of the gentlemen's cabin opened. The darkness descended more thickly.

There was an old bench outside the shed, splintery with years of carved initials. She smoothed the skirt of the aqua cotton dress under her and perched for a moment, tilting her head up to view the stars. The moon was on the wane, its silver disk partly devoured. The thick cluster of the Milky Way flowed overhead. She picked out the zigzag of Cassiopeia, and the bright necklace that was the Corona Borealis. She gazed raptly, losing herself in the depth and infinity of space, feeling its unfathomable vastness put her own problems into perspective. No matter what happened to her, to Gil, even to the earth they inhabited, the stars would still be there, serenely fixed in their endless dance.

The rumble of an approaching vehicle roused her from her reverie. She rubbed her neck, which had grown stiff, and jumped to her feet. She had no desire to be found lurking around the boat landing by the returning passengers. Retreating up the gangplank, she reached her cabin just as the van pulled up. Without turning on her light, she watched from the window while the van disgorged its contents. Mr. Olen hurried up the gangplank, no doubt intent on checking on his wife to see if she had survived a few hours without him. Fred Warner pulled out a cigar and strolled up and down the gravel front of the boat landing, smoking contentedly. Magda and Hal went up the gangplank arm in arm, laughing in low voices. The Hartners followed, for once smiling happily— Selina could catch the gleam of Mrs. Hartner's false teeth in the moonlight. The Rossfields exchanged a few words with Gil and watched their sons check the mooring ropes to see that they were secure for the night. They, too, strolled up the gangplank, the boys trading playful punches as they followed behind.

That left Gil. He was exchanging a few words with the driver of the van. He stepped back, and the van reversed and roared up the road toward town. Gil stood for a moment, his head thrown back, searching the velvet sky. Then he lowered his head, and his eyes fixed directly on her window across the distance that intervened. Selina drew back instinctively. He couldn't see her in the dark that far away! But his eyes narrowed perceptively, and she knew he could. For countless moments they stared at each other. Selina thought her love and longing would make her cry out, so strong was her desire to fly into his arms. Insensibly she stole nearer the window, drawn by a magnetic attraction she couldn't resist. Gil's face was no longer impassive. She could clearly see his vulnerability as he raised his fingers to his lips. His eyes burning into hers, he let his fingers drift slowly toward her, the kiss almost perceptible on them. Then his hand dropped to his side, and he turned away, striding up the gangplank without a further look.

She put her own hand up to her cheek, feeling as if

the kiss had floated on the breeze from his lips to her face. Lost in wonderment, she turned toward the door, half expecting it to open and reveal him standing, waiting. But as the long minutes passed, she slowly realized that Gil wouldn't come to her now. If she wanted him back, she would have to go to him.

With an effort she stripped off her clothes and crawled into the bunk. She reached a weary hand toward the alarm clock, setting it for 5:30 A.M. Morning came early when there was breakfast to prepare for so many people. She was worn out with emotions, unable to think of anything but rest and sleep. Her heart could wait. She knew the pieces would still be there in the morning.

CAPTAIN MORRIS adjusted the Cardinals baseball cap on his sparse gray hair, spat with great accuracy into the brass cuspidor beside him and tilted back in his old wicker-bottom chair until the legs shrieked with protest. "Yep," he said, sending a sideways glance toward Selina, who slumped on a bench by the pilothouse door, "we could still hit a snag anytime, no matter how much they dredge. River's high right now, what with all that rain we got in July. Reckon it's a lucky thing for you I signed on as pilot."

Betsy, perched on the bench beside Selina, leaned forward eagerly. "How do you know when you've hit a snag?" Her eyes were bright with excitement.

"First there's a ruckus if it tears a hole in the bottom," Captain Morris said obligingly, tamping more foul-smelling tobacco into his pipe. "She lurches one way or tother, depending on whar she got ripped.

Then she goes down, fast or slow, depending on the size of the hole.'' He lighted the pipe and puffed a cloud of evil-smelling smoke into the little room. "But you ain't going to experience none of that, because you got Cap'n A.J. Morris aboard.'' He set his chair legs back on the floor and stood up to get a better grip on the wood-and-brass wheel that dominated the room. "Got to git around this island,'' he mumbled, peering through the window. He looked sternly at Betsy. "You goin' to sound that bell for me?''

Betsy jumped up with alacrity, ringing the bell that signaled the engine room. Then she gave two enthusiastic blasts on the whistle. Selina jumped and shook her head to dispel the momentary deafness caused by the whistle.

"Which side are we going down, Cap'n Morris?'' Betsy copied the captain's stance as well as she could, not having a wheel to lean negligently against.

"You tell me,'' the captain replied, frowning at her. Betsy peered out the window, anxiously important. "Left,'' she said. "I mean, inside.''

Captain Morris scowled fearfully, which seemed to be his way of expressing approval. "I could make this little lady into a pilot if you give me fifty years,'' he said, swinging the wheel around and guiding the boat into the narrower arm of a fork in the river. Selina watched the island, which was little more than a large sandbar covered with scrub vegetation, as it passed slowly by. She could see the channel markers ahead, where they rejoined the rest of the Mississippi. The river was hypnotizing, its inexorable strength and depth concealed for the most part beneath its smooth brown surface. Watching it gave her something of the same feeling that stargazing did—that of observing implacable forces beyond the control of man. But in the river's case, that wasn't true. Men had channeled, and dredged, and sandbagged and constructed levees until the river was chained, forced into the path they wanted it to go. "Too bad," she murmured aloud.

"What's that?" Captain Morris cocked an eyebrow at her. "Beginning to think the cat got your tongue, gal. What'd you say?"

"I said it's too bad that the river is so—tame now. I don't suppose you agree, but I think it's a shame we've imprisoned it so thoroughly."

Captain Morris gave her a surprisingly shrewd glance from under his bushy brows. "Don't know as we've tamed her that well. Come flood time, she's all over the place, breaking out here, overflowing there." He shook his head. "Know what you mean, though. People like everything cut-and-dried. The river, she don't care about states' boundaries or crops or cities or houses. She wants to go where she wants to go. Someday we won't be able to keep her captive any longer. She'll either bust loose or die." He cleared his throat and spit again. "Daggone it, here comes another one of them pesky barges."

"But Captain Morris," Betsy said, sounding shocked. "You've piloted the tugboats that move the barges—you told me so yourself."

"I've drunk water before, but that don't mean I like it," he retorted, signaling the approaching mass that was acres of barges roped together and impelled along by several tugboats. The tugboat pilots signaled back, waving in a friendly fashion. Captain Morris returned their salutes laconically. "A man gets work where he can on the river. Me, I prefer drinking good whiskey and piloting paddle-wheelers." He patted the *Margaret B. Townshend*'s wheel affectionately. "This here's my beauty," he said without the acerbic note that characterized most of his speech. "There ain't many more of these ladies left. Now there's the *Julia Belle Swain*, but she don't do overnights. There's the *Belle of Louisville* and the *Natchez*, and of course, the *Queens*. But this little lady is the only private pleasure boat that goes all the way anymore." He cleared his throat again, winking fiercely as he stared over the wheel.

Selina found her own troubles diminishing for the first time that morning. She glanced around the little pilothouse, perched on top of the texas deck, commanding a view of the countryside and the river that was unequaled. All four sides were windows from the waist up, white-painted wainscoting from the waist down. The big wood-and-brass wheel gleamed from its platform forward. Benches were built in beside the door in the aft wall. There was a rickety table bearing a clutter of charts, scrawled notes, an ashtray. The only other furnishings were the cane-bottomed chair and the cuspidor. She squinted at the calendar that hung crookedly from a nail in the door. It was from a feed store in Herculaneum, Missouri, and sported a drawing of a scantily clad dairymaid and some overweight cows. Looking closer, she saw that it dated from 1957.

She twisted around on her bench to look out the window at where they'd been. On the texas deck the Hartners and the Olens basked in the sun on lawn chairs outside their staterooms. Hanging over the railing of the deck, Eric and Mike were flying kites out above the paddle wheel. Disappearing slowly behind them, the island they'd just passed looked somehow remote, primitive, untouched by civilization.

The high sandstone bluffs had been replaced by wide fertile fields, green in the August sunlight with tall geometrically planted corn. Roads bounded the fields, straight as if drawn by a ruler. Absently she watched the tiny cloud of dust that followed a car until it disappeared in the distance. "Who is she," she asked abruptly. "Margaret B. Townshend, I mean."

Captain Morris blinked at the abruptness of her question. "One of the lumber-baron's wives or daughters, I reckon," he said. "Mostly these boats are named for someone in the family that owns them." He stretched and pulled out a pocket watch. "My watch below," he said, looking toward the stairs that led to the crew's quarters on the texas deck. "Where is that gal?"

"Captain Morris's niece is the other pilot," Betsy informed Selina. "And his nephew is the engineer, and his other nephew is the deckhand."

Selina blinked. "I didn't know there was another pilot," she said. "And I thought Mr. Rossfield was the engineer. He's always down there in the engine room."

Captain Morris chuckled indulgently. "Mr. Rossfield fancies his engines," he said, knocking out the pipe's dottle in the overflowing ashtray. "But he ain't a licensed engineer and don't want to be. My nephew Frank is in charge down there. As for Sylvie, my niece, she's a right smart little pilot, though she's got a ways to go before she can overcrow her old uncle." This was said with a ferocious grimace at the young woman who hurried into the pilothouse, finishing the last of a peanut-butter sandwich. Selina did a double take. She wouldn't describe Sylvie as little, since she must stand close to six feet tall in her sneakered feet. She had long brown hair confined by a clip and wore a baseball hat emblazoned with a patch that said "Flying Fish." In her faded dungarees and T-shirt she looked more like a player on an intramural college team than a riverboat pilot.

She flashed a wide friendly smile at Betsy and Selina, then listened intently to her uncle. "Tugboater awhile back told me there was a brush snag just above island 78," he said, relinquishing the wheel. "Mind you keep your eye on the river instead of gabblemongering around with these visitors."

"Yes, *sir*," Sylvie said smartly. With a final grimace for Betsy and Selina, Captain Morris ambled out.

Selina realized after a few minutes that he had been joking when he told Sylvie not to be a gabblemonger. The tall young pilot made a friendly response to every question, but she initiated no conversation and seemed devoid of the stock of tall river tales that her uncle could trot out so easily. Glancing at her watch

Selina saw that it was time for her to start working on dinner. "Sylvie," she asked suddenly, "does the crew exist on peanut-butter sandwiches? Mrs. Rossfield said you were provided for, but—"

Sylvie glanced at her briefly as she put the wheel over to make a crossing. "My mother came along to cook. She likes to go down the river, and the Rossfields said it would be all right. But thanks for thinking about us." Her eyes twinkled suddenly. "I don't know what Uncle Alvin would say about food that wasn't meat and potatoes, but it would be interesting to hear."

After this long speech Sylvie had evidently expended her alotted words. She fell silent, and Betsy couldn't coax any more tidbits of information from her about the river or the science of piloting. Selina rose to return to the kitchen, and Betsy reluctantly went with her.

"So when do we get to Memphis?" From the door Betsy fired her parting salvo.

"Depends," Sylvia said noncommittally. They waited a moment, but she didn't elaborate. Finally Selina pulled Betsy outside and shut the door.

They started down the steps leading to the texas deck. "Is she always so closemouthed?" Selina lifted her face to the fitful breeze, grateful for any coolness under the sweltering sky.

Betsy shrugged. "Usually. Yesterday I got her fired up talking about bluegrass music, but she generally doesn't say much." She began jumping down the steps, holding onto the railing. "I like Captain Morris best because he tells such interesting

stories. Ooph!'' The stairs made a right-angled turn,
and Betsy, jumping down them too fast, had can-
noned straight into Gil, who was coming up.

"So this is where you were," he said, setting Betsy
on her feet but looking only at Selina. "We wondered why you weren't at lunch.''

She couldn't reply. She'd set up the buffet with
Hailey, but she couldn't face acting the part of
gracious chef. So she'd begun roaming aimlessly
around the deserted decks while everyone else was
eating. Betsy had found her leaning over the railing
of the texas deck, watching the paddle wheel beating
water into froth, and dragged her up to visit the pilothouse. Now she seized Gil's arm, her words tumbling
out eagerly.

"Gil, Captain Morris says he could make a real
pilot of me after fifty years. Gil, could we get our
own paddle-wheeler? Captain Morris likes them so
much, and then we could hire him to work for us all
the time, and he wouldn't have to work on the tugboats—"

"We'll talk about it later," Gil said absently,
pushing her gently down the steps. "Right now I
need to consult with Selina. Run along, scamp.''

With slumping shoulders Betsy rounded the angle
of the steps. Selina watched her sympathetically. She
frowned at Gil. "You know, she absolutely idolizes
you, and I don't know why. You barely give her the
time of day. Why don't you spend a little more time
with her?''

Standing a couple of steps below her, he squinted
up, and she realized that for the moment she was

taller than he. She discovered that she liked the sensation of dominating him. "I can't spend time with
Betsy," he said softly, "when I spend all my time
thinking about you." She made no reply, staring
down into his mesmeric eyes, her thoughts chasing
around frenetically in her mind. "Selina," he
breathed, reaching up to place his hands on her
shoulders. The movement was gentle, explorative, as
if he expected her to shrug him off. And she should,
she realized dimly. But somehow when he was close
to her, the air turned so thick with trembling anticipation that she felt immobilized. She forced
words from her throat.

"Gil—I told you—"

"I know what you said," he murmured soothingly. "But you didn't really mean it, did you? Tell me
you want me as much as I want you. I know it's so,
but I need you to tell me."

His hands slid off her shoulders, moving down to
rest just below the rounded swell of her breasts. With
infinite care he cupped them gently, brushing his
thumbs lightly across the stirring nipples, bringing an
involuntary gasp to her lips. She watched dumbly as
his head moved forward, seemingly in slow motion,
and his warm breath approached the aching flesh he
held so softly. His eyes closed as he pressed his head
into her breasts, and her heart turned over at the expression of tender yearning she saw on his face. "Oh,
Gil," she whispered, feeling her knees weaken beneath his unexpected behavior.

There was a scrabbling sound from around the corner of the stairs, and a soft thump. Gil straightened

up, grim faced, and ran down a couple of steps, reaching a long arm around the bend and dragging Betsy back into sight. Red-faced and defiant, she broke into speech. "I was only—"

Gil gave her a shake and turned her loose. "Spying, eh? Just what did you hear?"

Betsy sent a shamefaced pleading look toward Selina. "I just wanted to know what sweet-talking sounds like. Aunt Charlotte said Selina was sweet-talking you, but it sounded to me like you were—"

"It's all right, Betsy," Selina said quickly. "But you mustn't listen to other people's conversations. Eavesdropping is very rude."

"Okay. I'm sorry," Betsy whispered, mortified tears springing to her eyes. She disappeared around the corner, and Selina seized her chance to follow.

"Wait a minute," Gil said, trying to grab her arm as she slid past him. "We have to discuss—"

"Not now," she mumbled, moving fast. "have to start dinner. Lots to do." She reached the texas deck and paused for a moment. Gil stared after her, his face showing a mixture of frustration and anger.

"Damn!" He sent his fist crashing into the wall that enclosed the staircase. Unwilling to assuage his feelings, she fled.

CHAPTER SIXTEEN

SELINA ENJOYED COOKING while steaming majestically down the Mississippi. Especially when she could cook outside on the open deck. Basking in the sun, inhaling the aromatic odors of roasting tenderloin that was being grilled over mesquite charcoal, she realized suddenly that she'd become so preoccupied with her own problems that she'd almost let the excitement of the trip get away from her. She waved gaily to a passing towboat, herding its covey of barges down the river, before she had to dash back into the cook house and attend to the vegetables.

Finally everything was ready. Selina was standing behind the buffet table carving filets steadily for each plate when she realized that one plate stayed in front of her even though it already contained a choice serving of meat. She glanced up and saw Gil. He smiled at her, and her heart turned over, a phrase she'd often read in books but had never before experienced in real life. She took hold of herself. "Well?" She tried to make her voice calmly matter-of-fact.

"May I fill a plate for you?" Gil, she realized indignantly, wasn't following her lead. If anything, his voice was even warmer than it had been, for instance, that night they'd deserted the boat.... She felt the blood rising in her cheeks and beat it down furiously.

"No thanks. I'll wait until everyone's served."

"All right." Amiably he moved on. She had expected some sort of protest, some insistence. His easy acceptance of her excuse made her feel as if the ground was dissolving unexpectedly under her feet. She gaped after him and saw him greet Irene Rossfield easily and sit down beside her. Shutting her mouth with a snap, Selina turned back to the line in front of her. She served the Hartners and the Olens mechanically, but Fred Warner's complimentary words woke her up.

"Now this is really something I like," he said enthusiastically as she placed a tender juicy filet on his plate and added a roasting ear of corn, still wrapped in its browned husk. "I tell you, Miss Selina, you're the first woman I've ever met could cook just as good weekday fare as she could Sunday dinner." He took generous servings of everything else and seated himself at Gil's table, his face once again assuming its suspicious squint.

Selina smiled with pleasure. For some reason she was grateful for Fred Warner's diversions. Despite Gil's insistence that Warner was out to get him, she couldn't really believe that. *He's an epicure in embryo,* she mused with a smile. He had mentioned TV dinners; probably his digestion had been affected by the poor food he'd eaten since his wife died. With a little attention he could be converted quite easily to the cause of good food, a cause she was always ready to champion.

One by one the passengers finished their meals.

They were cruising past the Memphis bluffs now, and
most of them moved out onto the veranda to see
Captain Morris bring the boat into the channel that
served Memphis as a harbor. Selina forked up the
last bites of carrot cake, enjoying the sensation the
Margaret B. Townshend caused among the more prosaic commercial shipping concerns that proliferated
along the wharves. The tall towers of the city
gleamed invitingly, and she stifled a sudden yearning
to be more than a passenger, entitled to enjoy a
leisurely tour of the city without having to think
about restocking her larder. They were to tie up in
Memphis overnight, not leaving till after breakfast
the next day. Their next excursion stop would be one
of the restored plantation mansions below Baton
Rouge, so she would have to get enough provisions to
last for a while, since she wanted to personally ensure
that the quality was as good as possible.

Wistfully she listened to scraps of conversation as
everyone planned their entertainment for the afternoon and evening. Gil had arranged a dinner at one
of the noted barbecue houses for those who wanted
to rejoin the party. But the Hartners and Olens had
decided to strike out on their own at a hotel dining
room owned by mutual friends.

"You'll be joining us for dinner, surely?" Magda
turned back to Selina. "If you have more shopping
than that, we should certainly help you with it."

"I'll be done by then," Selina stammered, afraid
that the "help" would take the form of Gilmartin
Duchenay, who had a paralyzing effect on her ability
to perform efficiently. She got directions to the res-

taurant and went down to the kitchen to finish her list and dismiss Mike and Eric from further kitchen help for the rest of the day. They raced out with joyful whoops. Selina was still checking her list a few moments later when Gil and Fred Warner entered the cook house.

"Warner and I have a bet on," Gil began without a preamble. He was once again the cool watchful businessman, with no trace of the caressing warmth that was so disconcerting—and so captivating. "He thinks that with a few basic instructions in the art of cooking, he could do better than Purity's computers. I say it takes more than twenty-four hours to make a silk purse out of sow's ear—if you'll pardon the expression, Warner."

Fred Warner laughed sarcastically. "You think those computers are nearly as powerful as the Almighty," he gibed. "But I'm willing to bet you that this little lady here can teach me enough to make me a better cook than they are in just twenty-four hours. Are you willing to take me on, Miss Chef?"

Selina blinked bewildered gray eyes. "I'm not sure I understand," she said cautiously. "You want me to teach you how to cook in twenty-four hours?"

Gil nodded, tight-lipped. Selina could sense, looking at him, that the outcome of this preposterous wager was somehow immensely important, but she couldn't for the life of her figure out how he wanted her to respond. "A sort of overnight sensation," he said smoothly. "Think you can pull it off, Selina? After all, Purity's computers have been programmed by experts."

His final thinly disguised challenge resolved Selina's mind. "Anything your computers can do, I can do better," she said rashly, tilting her nose into the air. She looked doubtfully at Fred Warner. "And yes, I could give you the basics in a short time, provided you're motivated to learn. But it takes practice to make perfect. All the theory in the world won't alter the fact that you're a novice when it comes to putting your knowledge to work."

He gestured impatiently. "I'm willing to risk that. Just take me in hand. We'll have to hammer out the ground rules, but surely Miss Selina here will be allowed to advise me in lieu of that practice?" He turned to Gil, who nodded reluctantly.

"I suppose that's fair. You get until 3:00 P.M. tomorrow to learn all Selina can teach you. Then you cook the dinner without any help other than advice from her. If the other passengers find your food acceptable—as good as or better than standard airplane fare—you win the bet. Otherwise, I do."

"Now wait a minute." Selina looked from one determined face to the other. "What exactly are the stakes here? I'm not sure I want to participate if it's too high-pressure."

"I'm playing just for the pleasure of making him eat crow," Warner drawled. "He's so all-fired convinced that those computers of his have all the answers. I prefer to believe in the ability of the human brain."

"I have nothing against the human brain," Gil said quietly. "After all, computers are the servants; we are the masters. I just want you to realize,

Warner, that people are fallible, especially in areas like food preparation. A computer can learn what you want it to know overnight; a person simply cannot. That's all there is to it."

"This person can," Fred Warner asserted stoutly. "Anyone can if the stakes are big enough. So just what are the stakes, Duchenay?"

Gil was silent for a moment. "Whoever wins gets to retail his triumph at the board meeting," he said softly. "That will provide us both with motivation, Mr. Warner. I know I would enjoy telling everyone just how wrong you are about the computerized process. And I'm sure you'd like a nice triumph over me to relate with great attention to detail. Does that satisfy you?"

Warner chuckled and turned to Selina, rubbing gleeful hands together. "I'll enjoy rubbing your nose in it, Duchenay. Now, Miss Selina, let's get started. What do I need to know first?"

THE REST OF THE AFTERNOON was a blur to Selina. Far from wandering the markets alone and lonely as she had pictured herself doing, she had the attendance of two men, since Gil wouldn't be deterred from following every move Fred Warner made. He commanded taxis to drive them to the suppliers Selina had selected from a list Irene Rossfield had given her. At first bewildered by the gradually growing pile of produce and animal carcasses that filled his cab, the cabbie finally entered into the spirit of things, enthusiastically offering his opinion of where to get the freshest fruits and vegetables.

Typical of newly fledged gourmets, Fred Warner
wanted to serve something elaborate and intimidat-
ing for his first dinner. But Selina persuaded him not
to. "Things are going to be tough enough," she said
feelingly, "without me having to watch you attempt
something like sweetbreads in puff paste." They finally reached a compromise on *fondue de poulet à la
crème*, which sounded very grand but was only a
dressed-up chicken fricassee. Selina went down the
list of ingredients in her head, making out the shopping list, watched attentively by both men. At the
butcher's she expounded on the way to judge chickens for freshness and for flavor amply aided by a
philosophic butcher who added tips drawn from his
own observations.

In the produce market Warner showed he'd remembered his previous lesson by the way he chose
peaches and turned his nose up at the asparagus.
Later, back on the boat, Selina had them unpack and
store the purchases properly. Then they rushed to the
restaurant for dinner. Fred Warner lost no opportunity to ask questions on anything that occurred to
him. Selina went through several paper napkins
sketching the kinds of utensils that would be used for
various cooking methods. The others at the table
listened with interest, with even Mrs. Drumm fore-
bearing to sniff in disapproval more than twice.

Lingering over dessert, Warner fired off several
more questions, then rose abruptly. "Well, I don't
reckon I can retain one more bit of information. Perhaps it's a mite more complicated than I thought it
would be." He shot an oblique look at Gil, who sat

impassively. "But it's a challenge, for sure, and Fred Warner's never backed away from that. I'll see you bright and early in the cook house, Miss Selina. I think I'd better make an early night of it."

Magda, Betsy, Hal and Mrs. Drumm also elected to go back to the boat after dinner. But Hailey and Ricky were going to take in a few of the blues clubs abounding in Memphis and invited Gil and Selina along. After a moment's hesitation Selina accepted. She wouldn't be alone with Gil, so there was no reason to forgo the treat, she argued with herself.

She fought down the excitement that flooded her as Gil moved into the taxi next to her, the long length of his thigh pressing warmly against hers. Now that Fred Warner was gone, his manner was relaxed, even expansive. The first club they visited had a band with an enthusiastic horn section and a minuscule dance floor. Ricky promptly invited Hailey to dance, and they left the secluded table to Selina and Gil.

She propped her chin on her fist and watched him undetected for a few moments. There were lines of tension in his face that seemed fresh, but the tautness was one of purpose, of striving toward a particular goal. When he turned his head and caught her looking at him, his face creased with a lazy smile. "How much does it take to buy your thoughts these days when a penny's not worth much?" His voice was friendly, with none of the seductive overtones she'd half expected. She found herself smiling spontaneously in return.

"You may have them free of charge," she said "I was just thinking...."

"Well?" He raised the glass of dark frothy beer to his lips and tasted it judiciously. "A little heavy on the hops," he pronounced. "What were you thinking?"

"You're pleased about this bet with Fred Warner," she said slowly. "At first I thought you didn't want it, but I guess that was just to egg him on. What are you scheming, Gilmartin Duchenay? I don't know if I want to be a party to it."

"You've got nothing to worry about." He sipped his beer again and glanced at her reassuringly. "Just do the best you can with the old son of a gun and let the chips fall where they may." She was silent, her inner doubts evidently finding their way to her face. "I can't tell you what I'm up to," he began impatiently. Then his voice softened. "Really, Selina, it's nothing bad. Don't worry about it. If all goes well, things will be all right—more than all right." He leaned back, a satisfied smile on his face, and listened intently as the tenor saxophone broke into a long melodious riff.

Selina relaxed into her chair, giving herself up to the insistent rhythm of the music. He was right. There was no need for her to worry about it. If two grown men wanted to make silly bets with each other, it didn't really affect her. She took a lusty swallow of her own beer and let her fingers tap the beat on the Formica tabletop.

Gil leaned toward her to be heard over the loud applause that followed the number. "I didn't know you liked blues," he said directly into her ear. She moved away a little, pretending that she hadn't felt the frisson of pleasure that his warm breath in her ear had caused.

"There's lots you don't know about me," she retorted.

"So fill me in. What makes Selina tick? What makes her give the push to a perfectly adequate guy who wants—"

She cut him off with one abrupt gesture. "I don't want to go into all that, Gil. I've explained my reasons for bringing our relationship to a close. If you want to rehash the past, I'll have to discover that it's getting a little late—time to go back to the boat—" Glancing at her watch, she half rose from her chair. Gil pushed her back, smiling ruefully.

"All right, you've made your point. Absolutely no talking about anything controversial tonight, and that includes our feelings toward each other. But that doesn't mean we can't talk about other things. Like, how did you come to like the blues?"

"I got the blues with my baby down by San Francisco Bay," Selina said guilelessly.

Gil looked at her, trying to keep from smiling. "I see," he said finally. They burst into simultaneous laughter.

After that the mood was more relaxed. Gil asked her about growing up in San Francisco, and she found herself telling him about her childhood, the tragedy of losing both her parents at once, the years of dutiful affectionless care by Aunt Thelma and Uncle Mark. Her usual reticence was swept away, and she easily poured out a flood of memories, egged on by his attentive face. When she flagged, he asked questions to set her going again. The music swirled and pulsed around them, and she didn't realize how long she'd been talking until Hailey and Ricky, breathless from dancing, dropped into their seats.

"Aren't you two ever going to dance?" Hailey glanced at them curiously. "Every time we looked over here, you were deep in conversation."

"Did you solve the problems of the world?" Ricky signaled the harried waitress for more beer.

"Not exactly," Gil said, smiling at Selina. "Ours was a more—domestic—conversation. Care to dance?" He held out a compelling hand, and Selina arrived on the dance floor in his arms before she realized she'd assented. The saxophone moaned achingly, and Gil swept her close against him. The physical contact with his long lean body went to her head with much more effect than the beer she'd drunk. She stumbled awkwardly as he moved to the music.

"Sorry," she mumbled into his shirt. "I'm afraid I don't know how to dance very well." *That's putting it mildly,* she thought. She tried to pull away, but he tightened his grip.

"Who wants to dance," he whispered into her ear. "I just wanted a legitimate reason to hold you close." He kept her wrapped warmly in a snug embrace, moving with slow deliberate steps that exerted their own hypnotic influence. Gradually she relaxed, confident that he wasn't going to try anything tricky. The heavy pulsating beat of the rhythm section, topped by the soaring aching song of the saxophone, seduced her, starting a sensuous fire in her loins that Gil's suggestive movements did nothing to put out. She found herself winding her arms around his neck, listening to his whispered honeyed words with a sense of enchantment. She paid no attention to the warning voice within that tried to tell her she might just as well be playing with dynamite. When Gil's lips began feathering light kisses along her jaw, she turned her head blindly into his seeking embrace. Their lips met and clung, sending a sudden shock of heat coursing through her. Abruptly she realized Gil's need as his hands in the small of her back pressed her to him. She withdrew tentatively, raising an apologetic face to his. To her surprise he made no attempt to follow through his temporary advantage. The music ended, and he released her with a rueful smile.

"Too good to last," he said lightly. Wonderingly she examined his face and saw the strain written there.

"I'm sorry, Gil," she said in a low voice. "I shouldn't have let you—I guess I sort of led you on."

"Honey," he said fervently, guiding her back to their table, "you didn't lead me anywhere I wasn't willing to follow. Just let me know when you feel like a repeat."

She shook her head mutely as they sat down. Any fear that Hailey and Ricky would have noticed their intimate dancing was banished. The other couple didn't even realize they were back for a moment. Their heads were close together, with Ricky sketching something on a napkin. Hailey sent a blissful smile toward Selina. "Ricky's showing me how to remodel my kitchen."

"How exciting." Selina's voice was dry, but they didn't notice. Hailey folded the cocktail napkin reverently and stowed it in her handbag.

"We're thinking of getting back," Ricky said to Gil. "Want to share a cab, or are you staying for a while?" He smiled fondly at Hailey. "My girl needs her sleep if she's going to get up and bake at the crack of dawn."

Hailey giggled delightedly. Their romance seemed to be going smoothly, Selina thought and felt even bluer than the song that was playing. Suddenly she was exhausted. "We'd better be going, too," she said abruptly.

Gil raised one eyebrow but made no comment. He didn't attempt to snuggle up in the cab, either, though Hailey and Ricky were practically sitting in each other's laps. He was polite, courteous and attentive, the perfect escort, Selina acknowledged sourly. But he wasn't at all like a lover. She might have imagined that explosive moment on the dance floor for all the effect it had on his subsequent conduct. But she knew it had happened. The effects still lingered in her own body, making her tense with frustration. How could he sit so decorously beside her and talk blandly of cotton warehouses and flood control? She longed to shake him, to press herself against him and make him lose control the way she did. Aghast, she realized what she was thinking. Her treacherous body was betraying her, intent on its own gratification, with no thought for the inevitable consequences of giving in to these desires. Licking her lips, she stole a glance at Gil. In the faint light from the streetlights and dashboard she could see him watching her, his lips curved in a knowing smile. She swallowed and attempted a casual remark, but her voice floundered and died away.

He leaned closer. "Just remember," he breathed in her ear so softly no one else could have heard. "I can read your mind. I know what you were thinking about just now."

She tried to scoff. "I'm surprised, Gypsy Davey. Why are you interested in my thoughts about the blintzes I'm making for breakfast?"

He shook his head sorrowfully. "Don't tell lies, Selina. You were thinking about what you'd like to do to me. And I just want you to know, I'm always available when you decide to do it."

She pressed herself as far into the armrest of the cab as she could. "You couldn't be more wrong," she said distantly and refused to rise to his further whispered teasing remarks. She would conquer the hopeless feelings she had for this man if it was the last thing she did. And it probably will be, she reflected bleakly. She must remember there was no future in it. And she was the kind of person who must always have a future and be firmly in control of it. *I'm going to France,* she thought fiercely. *I have my work.*

But she began to wonder in earnest if that would be enough anymore.

CHAPTER SEVENTEEN

FRED WARNER looked dubiously at the pile of raw naked chickens that confronted him on the cutting board. "I thought they came in pieces," he said tentatively.

"Nope." Selina threw the word over her shoulder as she maneuvered around him with a huge bowl of *salade niçoise*. "You're lucky they're not still alive." She winked at Hailey and pretended not to see the imploring look Warner cast at her. He had shown up at the kitchen right after the breakfast buffet, looking spry and eager. Already in the throes of getting the lunch buffet together, Selina had greeted him hurriedly with a clean white apron and a mound of apples to cut for the *tarte des demoiselles Tatin*. "Dessert first?" he'd asked with raised eyebrows. Selina hadn't had the time to do more than point to the apples, then to the big knife. Half an hour later, when she'd finished shredding cabbage for the cole-slaw, she noticed he was still cutting apples, laboriously coring and peeling, slicing with mathematical precision.

It had been almost lunchtime before he finished his task, and he wilted a little as he regarded the chickens. "Cooking seems to be all cutting up," he said petulantly, watching Selina and Hailey assemble the salads and rolls for their trip up in the dumbwaiter.

"Too true," Selina said, wiping perspiration off her forehead with a clean section of her apron. Warner's apron was already stained with damp marks and a big blotch where he'd accidentally got in her way while she was skinning tomatoes. The cook house was hot and steamy, receiving little benefit from the breeze that moved fitfully through the door. Selina opened the refrigerator to get out the butter and stood for a moment drinking in its cool exhalation. Out the low age-darkened screens of the windows she could see the green banks of southern Arkansas moving slowly past.

Warner brightened as he watched the dumbwaiter disappear up the shaft. "I guess I'll have to stop for lunch," he announced. "I'll get to these chickens later."

Selina eyed him sternly. "After lunch you have exactly five hours to get your act together," she said. "Unless you want me to end up doing the whole thing, you'd better think speed."

He looked abashed, then affronted. "You're supposed to help me," he pointed out. "It's in the terms of the bet."

"I'm supposed to direct you," she corrected gently. "I'll tell you how to do it, never fear. But you have to realize you're starting out with a handicap. Obviously you're totally unused to working in the kitchen."

"Well," he began defensively, "since my wife died, I've been feeding myself."

"*I* know." Selina ushered him briskly out the cook-house door and headed for the gentlemen's cabin. "Soup out of a can and TV dinners. Not much better than the Purity computers."

"Do I hear my computers being taken in vain?" Gil appeared in the doorway of the gentlemen's cabin, looking fresh and cool. Fred Warner had forgotten to take off his stained apron, and his face glistened with moisture. He hesitated for one second, then marched up the steps with a sangfroid Selina admired greatly.

"Well, Duchenay, while you lounged around all morning, I've been preparing quite a treat for your dinner. It's going nicely, right, Selina?"

Touched by his spunk, Selina nodded in agreement. "The man's a natural chef," she said. "Give me a week with this guy and Paul Bocuse would have to watch out."

Warner looked puzzled but let it pass. Selina breezed past Gil, who made no move to detain her. With a hypersensitive awareness of his unpredictable moods she realized that he was very pleased with himself.

Inside the gentlemen's cabin one of the tables had been cleared of linen. Hal MacMillan, Mr. Olen and Mr. Hartner were sitting around it like men who've just finished talking about business. The air was blue with cigarette smoke, in spite of the fact that the air-conditioners in the transoms above the doors were running at full blast. Selina fanned the door vigorously for a moment. "How do you expect people to eat in here?" she said in a furious undertone to Gil.

"If you wanted to have a poker game, couldn't you have had it somewhere else?"

"We'll go to the ladies' cabin next time," he said promptly. Her glare bounced off him as though he were encased in plate glass. Mike and Eric came running up the steps.

"You ready for us now, Selina?" Mike looked at her anxiously. "Gil said we could lay the tables late today. Was that all right?"

She smiled wanly. "Sure. Next time clear it with me first, okay? We're having salads today, so we can use the small plates. And see what you can do about this smoke, all right?"

She joined Hailey in the pantry to arrange the food, her mind seething with conjecture. Gil had obviously been as pleased as punch to have Fred Warner out of the way all morning so he could talk to the hoteliers privately. Was that why he'd engineered this bet about the food? She chewed her lip thoughtfully while she smoothed the mound of imported tuna in the huge platter of *salade niçoise*. It annoyed her for some reason that Gil got everything so easily. She resolved that if it were in her power, he'd lose his bet with Fred Warner.

THAT AFTERNOON she drove everyone unmercifully, determined the dinner would be perfect. Fred Warner slaved over his chickens, cursing under his breath. "Couldn't the butcher have cut them up?" His voice was plaintive.

"No." Selina spoke didactically, rooting in a dark storage cupboard for the sack of onions. "The less that's done to food before it comes into the kitchen, the better. Besides, every chef needs to learn how to use knives." She flipped an onion into the air, centered it on her cutting board and began slashing away at it with her big chef's knife. In seconds it lay tamed and neatly sliced. "Like so," she added smugly.

Warner sighed and went back to his laborious dismembering. When the chicken was finally simmering in its big pot, she turned his attention to the vegetables. "You need to prepare the asparagus for a vinaigrette," she said briskly, "and get your carrots ready, too." She showed him his timetable they'd conferred over that morning. "Remember what I said about getting everything to come out at the same time? That's the really tricky part, not this."

He groaned but doggedly worked on. After a great deal of hard work and surprisingly little help from Selina, Fred Warner's masterpiece was ready. He stepped back for a critical overview. "Looks very professional," he said delightedly. "If this don't beat the pants off anything you get on an airplane, may I be stuffed and roasted!"

Hailey was already upstairs supervising the serving of the appetizer. Warner would not trust his masterpiece to the dumbwaiter. He carried it up the stairs, stained apron and all, marching into the gentlemen's cabin and exhibiting it proudly to the spontaneous applause of the other passengers. While Fred Warner stood by, beaming, the line of hungry people quickly demolished his pride and joy. He was kept busy answering questions.

"It's *fondue de poulet à la crème*," he said, pronouncing the French words carefully. "Nope, made it all myself." He wiped his face on a corner of his apron, unconsciously leaving a smear of flour across his cheek. "Talk about doing things by the sweat of your brow—I'll say chefs end up almost better cooked than the food! If you don't think I did it, you should see the way I can cut up a chicken now. Of course, Miss Selina here told me what to do, but I did it myself, didn't I?"

He appealed to Selina, who answered promptly. "You certainly did. And a very good job, too."

Hailey filled a plate for her mother, who tasted the food warily. "Why, this is nothing more than fricasseed chicken," she announced. Fred Warner's face fell, and he looked at Selina anxiously.

"That's correct," Selina said patiently. "The chicken is fricasseed, or cooked in a broth that is enriched with the addition of cream and eggs. Like many dishes that originated in other countries, it's become very popular as a regional dish here."

Mrs. Drumm sniffed, clearly not satisfied by this explanation. She pointed to the apple tart, which sat grandly on its plate next to the coffeepot. "And I suppose next you'll tell me that isn't an apple upside-down cake."

"You're right." Selina couldn't keep the crispness from her voice. "It's called *tarte des demoiselles Tatin* after the ladies who invented it in the Loire." She turned away, disliking the sharp predatory face of Hailey's mother, disliking herself for overacting to the woman. Fred Warner sat down at Mrs. Drumm's table and began telling her about his day in the kitchen. When Selina had filled her own plate and started toward the staff table, she was astounded to see Mrs. Drumm actually laughing at something Fred Warner had said.

Hailey, who followed her to the staff table, was also astounded at the change in her mother. "Look at that," she breathed, watching her mother's subjugation with an avid gaze. "I don't think I've seen mother so pleasant for quite a while." She sent a speculative look toward Selina. "Didn't I hear him say something about being a widower this morning?"

"I don't know anything about it," Selina said hastily, not wishing to encourage Hailey's penchant for matchmaking. "What's the matter with everyone on this boat? Is it the ark or something? You'd think we had an obligation to go two by two."

"And so we do," Hailey said firmly. She frowned at Selina. "Why didn't you stay on the deck with us last night for a few minutes? The way you ran for your bedroom, you'd have thought someone was after you with a hatchet."

"I was tired," Selina said weakly. She saw Gil standing up with his wineglass raised high and quickly shushed Hailey's next remark, glad of a chance to change the subject.

"Fellow travelers," Gil said, smiling sardonically at Fred Warner, "you may or may not know that tonight's dinner was the result of a bet between Mr. Warner and myself. I won't go into details, but since you are the judges, I must ask you to respond to a question or two. First, in your opinion, is this food better than a typical mass-produced meal, such as Purity puts out?"

"Yes!" replied a chorus of voices. "I should say so," Mrs. Drumm squeaked indignantly.

"In that case I suppose Warner wins. He gets to scourge me in front of my board of directors. But I'd like to ask him a question first."

Fred Warner leaned back in his seat. He had removed his grimy apron, but his face was still flushed from the cook-house heat in spite of the current air conditioning. "Shoot," he said genially.

"You've now had firsthand experience preparing a meal for fewer than twenty people. How well could you prepare a meal for twenty thousand?"

Warner shook his head slowly. "Now that you mention it, that would be pretty hard to do. Damn near impossible for one person."

"And yet with the help of Purity's computers, which you despise so much, one person can program any amount of food, to feed far more mouths than you've managed tonight. It's true, we've sacrificed some quality. But we've achieved a great deal of uniformity, and the food, although not gourmet, is palatable." He fixed a stern eye on Selina, and she flushed hotly, thinking of her words to him on the airplane when they'd first met. "I'm not saying we should rest on our laurels," Gil went on. "But if you're a fair person, Warner, as I'm sure you are, you'll admit that Purity's achievement rivals yours of tonight."

After a moment Fred Warner spoke. "You have a point, Duchenay, much as it pains me to admit it."

He took another bite of chicken, smiling blissfully. "But it's a crying shame this kind of food can't be fixed your way. Imagine getting this in a TV dinner!"

Selina noticed the three hoteliers exchanging secretive glances. She looked thoughtfully at Gil as she sampled the chicken. He didn't look as if he'd lost the bet. On the contrary, although he wasn't making any overt displays of triumph, it was obvious to her that he was very pleased with the outcome of his wager.

She stretched her legs under the table, suddenly feeling very tired. Since the cruise had begun, she'd been up early every day, late to bed every evening. She pushed away the reason why she hadn't been sleeping too well. It was ironic, considering that even Mrs. Olen, that perennial hypochondriac, had remarked how restful it was to fall asleep to the gently rocking motion of the boat, that Selina couldn't fall asleep until her mind was worn out with chasing the futility of a relationship with Gil around for hours.

The result of too much work and too little sleep was catching up with her. Her eyes felt heavy, gritty; it was an effort to get up and take her plate into the pantry. Mike and Eric, with Betsy's help, were cleaning up the dishes. After watching them for a moment, Selina realized she might as well have some dessert. She got some of the apple tart and decided against coffee. Skirting the chatting groups of passengers in the gentlemen's cabin, she made her way to one of the deck chairs that lined the veranda encircling the boiler deck.

The night air was warm and balmy, with fragrant

scents floating from shore, and stars hovering brilliantly in the sky. A faint brightness on the eastern horizon signaled the advent of the waning moon. She propped her feet on the railing, took a bite of tart and munched contentedly. In the darkness she could see only an indistinct blur of trees on the riverbank as the boat moved along, close to the Louisiana side. Here and there beyond the batture, the land that bordered the river and was not enclosed in protective levees, she could see small clusters of lights denoting towns. Ahead on the bank a lonely electric light hung from a tall pole, illuminating a stretch of shingle and a rickety dock. The note of the paddle wheel changed as the *Margaret* approached her resting place for the night. Then the wheel stopped, and in the sudden silence Selina could hear a whippoorwill calling plaintively.

She found herself vaguely listening to the muted sounds of human activity aboard the riverboat. The VIP passengers were beginning to make their way up the narrow zigzag staircase to their suites. No one saw her as she sat around the corner. She felt as if she'd donned the mantle of invisibility common in fairy tales. She could hear their laughing comments about Fred Warner's dinner, could hear Hailey asking, "Where's Selina?" But she was powerless to respond. One property of the cloak of invisibility seemed to be that it made her immovable, too. Gradually the noises faded away except for the distant sound of water running in the bathroom.

She tried to watch the stars again, but the light at the dock interfered, brightening her field of vision until she could discern only the stars of greatest magnitude. With an effort she roused herself from the lethargy that possessed her, intending to go to the other side of the boat and watch stars without that light in her eyes. But as she crossed the veranda in front of the gentlemen's cabin, a tall figure detached itself from the shadows and stood in her way. It was Gil.

A slash of light from the dock highlighted the angles of his face. It occurred to Selina that he looked as emotionally exhausted as she felt. The dark brooding gypsy eyebrows shadowed his eyes, but she could see the lines of fatigue etched across his features. He said nothing, just watched her with those unfathomable eyes.

She couldn't speak. The air between them vibrated with voiceless messages. As clearly as if he'd spoken, she knew the depth of his feelings. And her own love, which she'd tried so desperately to deny, raised its insistent head. She felt it blossom in the core of her body and spread in glowing waves through all her veins. *I love you, Gil,* she thought, feeling that her love was tangible, that it could reach him through the intervening space.

He straightened as if electrified, and she saw for the first time the expression in his eyes. The fierce tender pleading she saw there was strong enough to make her reel. Without realizing that she'd moved, she was in his arms, swept so closely to him that the surge of his heartbeat might have been happening in her own breast. Their mouths met urgently, melting passionately together until she felt fused to him.

When at last he dragged his mouth away, she followed it with her own, protesting until he captured her earlobe in his teeth, nipping with gentle enticement and groaning her name in a raspy whisper that sent shivers of desire through her. She ached for him to caress her; she pressed herself even closer, longing to twine herself around him until nothing could separate them.

He smoothed her hair with his hand; she could feel it trembling. "I want you so much," he whispered, imprisoning her hands as she sought to draw him back to her. "But this is not the place, my darling."

"Gil—" Her voice implored him. She turned her face up to him in the stark white light, knowing her love and need were clearly evident. He drew in his breath and crushed her fiercely to him for the space of a heartbeat. Then, with one arm around her shoulders, he led her to the shadowed side of the boat. Pulling two deck chairs together, he pushed her almost roughly into one.

"Sit there and stop trying to seduce me, woman." She loved the husky purr of his voice. It gave her the heady knowledge that she had power over this strong mysterious man. Once and for all she gave up the notion that she could turn her back on what they had together. She wanted him; she loved him. If it was in her power, she would make him want her just as much. The problems of the future were still there, but with love perhaps they would prove less insurmountable than she had feared.

Gil sat next to her and took her hands in his. Faintly in the starlight she could see the amber glitter of his eyes. "I never mean to lose control," he said, his voice slightly unsteady. "But then I look into your eyes, and I have to—" He dropped his head to her hands, kissing them. They were still for a moment, Selina gazing in wonder at his bowed shoulders, the glossy hair soft to the touch where it spilled into her hands. She cradled his face gently, responding with a surge of love as his lips touched her fingertips. He lifted his head, turning one of her palms to the starlight. "Shall I tell you what I see in your hand, love?"

Too emotional to speak, she nodded mutely. He lifted her palm to his mouth, nipping with sensuous restraint at the swelling mount of flesh beneath her thumb. The voluptuous feeling of his velvety lips moving over her palm sharpened the ache of unfulfillment in her loins. Unconsciously she arched toward him, her breasts feeling swollen with desire, pleading for his touch. He brought his hands up to cup them gently, his eyes searching the softness of her face with ceaseless wonder. She closed her own eyes at the exquisite sensation of his slow caresses, feeling as if she would melt. She craved the total union that brought such sensations spiraling to the highest possible threshold of ecstasy.

Abruptly Gil's hands left her. She opened her eyes to see him throw himself back in his deck chair, running his fingers through his hair in frustration. "Damn!" His voice was shaking. "I told myself I just wanted to talk to you. But all I seem to be able to think about is making love to you until neither of us can move!"

Selina blinked, clearing her throat because her mouth had suddenly gone dry. "Well," she said cautiously, "what's wrong with that?"

His laugh was more of a groan. "Sweet Selina." He sat sideways on his chair and took her shoulders in a hard grip, giving her a gentle shake, then releasing her quickly. "There is absolutely no privacy on a steamboat. That's the only thing that's wrong with the *Margaret*. I wouldn't be surprised if someone could overhear our conversation right now."

"Neither would I." Ricky Carson's voice startled both of them. It came from the window behind them. They whirled around simultaneously, catching the white gleam of Ricky's jaunty grin behind the dark oblong of screen that kept the mosquitoes out of the cabins. "Sorry to intrude," he said, his voice laughingly apologetic. "But if you must canoodle right outside my room, you have to expect me to listen. It's too hot to close the window."

Selina felt hysterical laughter bubbling up inside her. Gil shook his head helplessly. "Ricardo," he began. "If you so much as—"

"Hey, what do you take me for?" Ricky sounded injured. "As far as I'm concerned, I was disturbed by a couple of owls, hooting outside my window. As soon as I knew they were only owls, I went back to bed. Nighty-night."

Gil hauled Selina to her feet and guided her back to the doors of the gentlemen's cabin. "Honey," he said, interpreting her shaking shoulders as a sign of distress. "I'm sorry, sweetheart. I should never have let you in for that." A tiny snort escaped her, and he turned her face to the light with concern. "Selina, love, please don't—"

She collapsed against him, giggling helplessly. "I can't help it," she gasped. "Talk about throwing cold water—" She pointed at Gil, trying to stifle her laughter with her fist. "Your face," she choked when she could speak again. "Your face, when he said—"

Gil smiled reluctantly. "Your face was pretty interesting, too," he drawled. Weak from laughing so much, she clung to him. He hugged her gently, then pushed her toward the door of the gentlemen's cabin. "No point in trying to talk here, obviously." His voice was wry. "We'll have to slip away from everyone in Natchez tomorrow. Have dinner with me ashore?"

"Sure, I guess." Selina stood, hesitant. "What about—"

"I told everyone tonight that tomorrow was a free evening. Nothing scheduled, no meal served here." Suddenly he sounded impatient. "Surely we can meet somewhere without the whole boat knowing what we're doing." He bent forward and seared her lips with a brief hard kiss. "Sweet dreams."

Dazed with the lingering vestiges of desire, Selina found herself in her cabin without knowing how she'd got there. She brushed her teeth and got ready for bed in the same somnambulistic state, asleep almost before she crawled into her narrow berth. And that night her dreams were sweet.

CHAPTER EIGHTEEN

SELINA SAT IN THE AIRY SILENCE of the pilothouse, watching absently as Baton Rouge disappeared behind them. She had finished the last dinner she would cook on board the *Margaret B. Townshend* but had slipped away while everyone else was still eating. She felt the need for quiet and solitude, and with Sylvie manning the wheel, the pilothouse was a good source of both.

The sun was beginning its descent, lengthening their shadow on the water. Behind and in front of the boat the Mississippi had cut a broad meander from the flat alluvial soil. On either side of the river, refineries smoked eerily, sending up their plumes of flame.

Tonight they would dock in New Orleans, and the trip would be over. She sighed. The eight days they had taken to come from St. Louis seemed like eight weeks, so easily had the river stolen her sense of time. During the past two days she'd tried hard to get her emotions back into order. But Gil's inexplicable behavior made it difficult to keep from bouncing up and down like a yo-yo.

Their plans to meet in Natchez had backfired. Fred Warner had insisted on dogging Gil's every footstep, ably seconded by Mrs. Drumm, who was positively peppy at the prospect of keeping tabs on Fred and Gil in one fell swoop. She'd been so preoccupied preventing a tête-à-tête between Selina and Gil that she hadn't seemed to notice that Hailey spent all her spare time with Ricky Carson. Selina felt ashamed at the stab of discontent that went through her when she thought of Hailey's new radiance. She ought to be glad that others' romances were going so well. But like a dog in the manger she felt aggrieved. It wasn't fair for Magda to glow like a lantern when Hal was around, for Hailey and Ricky to be so prettily absorbed in each other, even for Mrs. Drumm and Fred Warner to be exchanging lumbering compliments. Amid all this cruise-inspired *amour*, where was her own happy ending?

Nowhere, she reflected glumly. Although Gil whispered the promise of delights to come, although she felt herself go up in flames at his merest touch, she was uncomfortably aware that he hadn't said anything about marriage. *It always happens on board ship,* she thought, conveniently ignoring how much had happened on the dry ground of Ladue. *It's almost a cliché, shipboard romance. At the end of the trip you say, "Thanks for the memories," and go your separate ways.*

She pulled up her feet and wrapped her arms around her legs, resting her chin on her knees and staring ahead at Sylvie's tall lanky figure silhouetted against the front window of the pilothouse. As if she could feel Selina's eyes, Sylvie spoke, without turning away from the big wheel she spun so easily.

"Makes me feel like a fly on an elephant," she said, nodding toward the huge tanker that bore down on them from downriver.

"Heading for Baton Rouge?" Selina tried to sound decently interested in the river but felt that her voice failed miserably to convey any sense of wonder at the busy shipping traffic they'd encountered since leaving Natchez.

"Yep." Sylvie negotiated a deep bend in the river, waving cheerfully at a train engineer as the train sped past them on the right bank. The train hooted its whistle, and obligingly she pulled the shrill steamboat whistle, making conversation impossible till everyone's ears had recovered from the blast. "You know," she said when the echoes had died away, "I never cease to wonder at the Mississippi River. I've worked the Ohio and the Illinois, but the Mississippi is the one I keep coming back to."

Selina moved to the padded bench at right angles to the wheel. She hadn't heard so many words out of Sylvie during the entire trip. "Why is that?"

Sylvie took her time replying. "I reckon it's because this river's so contrary," she said finally. "All rivers have a lot of variety to 'em. But the old Mississippi really knows how to confuse you. Some places she's so shallow you'll gut your boat on her if you don't know the crossings. Other places no one's ever found out how deep she is." She thought for a moment, then added, "A lot like some people—changing her mind, switching around, but always there, always the same underneath."

Selina looked at Sylvie's profile suspiciously. "Is

this little homily supposed to have something to do with me?''

Sylvie chuckled. "You've been sitting back there nigh on twenty minutes, sighing and moaning to beat the band. I figured it's either work or love. And both of them go by the same rules as the river. You can't predict what will happen next. You just got to take it as it comes and meet every bend with the best attention you can muster up.''

Selina mulled over this unexpected advice for a moment. Before she could ask for clarification, Betsy burst through the door, still wiping away the traces of *sorbet* on her face. "I want to see us come into New Orleans," she announced, pushing Selina over on the bench so she could plop down. "Golly, look at all those big ships!''

"Goin' to be a while," Sylvie said, taking the *Margaret* deftly past another huge tanker. The crew of the tanker, which flew some foreign flag, crowded the side to stare down at the saucy little paddle-wheeler, waving their caps and shouting unintelligble comments. Sylvie lifted her hand in brief reply, but Betsy was less restrained. She flew to the open window and leaned out, semaphoring as broadly as the smile on her face. When the tanker was left astern, she drew her head reluctantly back inside the pilot-house.

"Is it this way all the way to New Orleans?'' Her eyes were round with excitement. "What nationality was that ship? Do you know, Sylvie?''

"Lithuanian." The pilothouse door opened to admit Captain Morris, who saved his niece the trouble of replying. "We'll be seeing lots of them furriners, missy." He tapped his pipe on the ashtray and jerked a thumb toward the door. "I'll take her in. You've been up here long enough."

Sylvie shrugged and relinquished the wheel. Feeling unable to cope with Captain Morris's stories or Betsy's round-eyed credulity, Selina followed Sylvie out the door. Once outside the pilothouse, Sylvie paused and glanced back inside. The deepening dusk showed the tiny pinpoints of light that were the compass light and Captain Morris's new pipeful of tobacco. "Old show-off," Sylvie said affectionately. "Wants to make sure none of his cronies sees him letting me bring the boat in."

Selina lingered on the texas deck after Sylvie had disappeared into the crew's quarters. In the fading light the flares from the refineries and the brilliant clusters of lights that surrounded them gave the riverbanks a spuriously festive air. The tall levees that enclosed the river shut off their view of any part of the shore that didn't rise above the walls. She wrinkled her nose distastefully at the pervasive smell of sulfur. Because of that smell she'd made a strongly garlic-flavored jambalaya, using just-caught shrimps bought from a young boy in a fishing boat who'd passed them that morning on his way to sell his catch. He'd also supplied her with the tender sweet little crayfish so prized in the bayous, and she'd composed a crayfish bisque that melted in the mouth. Since Fred Warner's fling at cooking many of the passengers had taken to dropping in at the cook house, and Hal MacMillan had tied on an apron today and helped enthusiastically with the jambalaya, not getting in her way any more than he could help. Even so, Selina had been hard pressed not to snap at him occasionally when her own exacerbated temper had made some passing mistake of his seem more important than it was.

She faced the distressing realization that her temper had been increasingly bad since the debacle at Natchez. After that, Gil had seemed to avoid her. She scolded herself for minding so much, but it was impossible to regain her former sense of detachment. She wanted Gil with her whole heart and was miserably certain that it was her independence, her very pride in her profession, that would keep her from getting him.

For the hundredth time she asked herself what it was Gil wanted from her. The past two nights she had found a single beautiful fresh flower on her pillow, and she assumed it had come from him. But there was no accompanying note—nothing on paper—to give him away. Why did he seem to blow so hot and cold? Why was he so tender, so seductive, melting her so completely at one moment, then pretending there was nothing between them the next?

Well, the trip was almost over. The romantic culmination she'd imagined before embarking hadn't happened. In fact, it was quite the reverse. Now she was even more in love with Gil and dreadfully afraid that he would prove as untrustworthy as Andy. Of course, she hadn't been in love with Andy, so his venality hadn't really hurt her. During this timeless, exquisite, harrowing eight days on the river she'd found out how much hurt is really possible when one is in love.

Slow footsteps approached along the deck leading to the VIP staterooms, and she froze behind the concealing wall of the staircase that led to the pilothouse. Magda's voice drifted to her ears. ''. . . should tell her before he springs it on her unexpectedly,'' she said, her voice for once shorn of its usual vague quality. ''But he thinks he knows best. I told him it might backfire—''

Selina had no desire to play the part of eavesdropper. She moved into sight, trying to school her face not to display the depression that threatened to overwhelm her. Magda stopped speaking abruptly, giving Selina the uncomfortable idea that she had been the topic of their conversation.

''Hello, my dear.'' Magda's voice was warm and friendly. ''We wondered what happened to you. Hal proposed a lovely toast to the chef who's kept us all so happy, but you missed it.''

''Sorry,'' Selina mumbled. ''I just wanted a little—room to breathe.''

Hal sucked in a draft of the sulfur-scented air. ''Out here?'' His face was incredulous. ''It's not this bad in the gentlemen's cabin. Will it smell like this all the way to New Orleans?''

Magda answered his appeal with one of her rich chuckles. ''No, we'll leave the refineries behind soon.'' She looked at Selina with warm concern. ''I'm just going to help Mrs. O₁en get packed. Do you feel all right, Selina? You look kind of peaked.''

Selina managed a hollow smile. ''Maybe a little too

much heat in the cook house this afternoon,'' she acknowledged. ''I'm sorry the cruise is ending, but I can't say I'm sorry to see the last of that hot-top. It could heat the entire Arctic.''

Magda laid one cool hand on Selina's forehead. ''You need a good rest,'' she said, frowning slightly. ''While we're in New Orleans, I want you to concentrate on taking it easy and forget about the kitchen for a while. Is that a deal?''

Selina nodded, unable to speak for fear the tears that crowded her eyes would cause her voice to wobble. She edged past the couple, noticing that Hal's arm was firmly, tightly around Magda's waist, and that her arm was draped across his shoulders. Not wishing to spend any more time in the vicinity of a happy couple, she fled to the gentlemen's cabin, intending to go to her tiny berth and pack up. They would be leaving the boat tonight to spend a few days in New Orleans, and she hadn't even begun to think about how to handle the kitchen equipment, let alone her personal luggage.

Her quest for solitude was thwarted, however. The gentlemen's cabin was crowded with convivial passengers, who'd evidently been paying homage to the really excellent Bordeaux that Gil had poured for dinner. Ricky raised his glass when he caught sight of her hesitating on the threshold. ''Here she is,'' he cried. ''Here's to good food, good wine, good company and good-looking chefs!''

''Hear, hear!'' Mr. Hartner seconded him loudly, waving his glass so vigorously that some of the wine sloshed out and left a crimson stain on the pale cream background of the rug. His wife frowned and pulled imperiously at his arm.

"You've had quite enough," she said, her voice minatory. "Time to go get packed up. Excuse us, please." They made their way to the door, Mr. Hartner a bit unsteady on his feet. Mrs. Olen seized the opportunity to tow her husband away, too. The Rossfields got to their feet reluctantly.

"It really is time to pack," Irene Rossfield said, setting her wineglass on the buffet table. "We'll have to continue this party in New Orleans."

After they left, there was a small silence in the gentlemen's cabin. Mrs. Drumm broke it, carefully pouring the last of a bottle of wine into her glass. "Disgraceful," she said, hiccuping slightly. "That Mr. Hartner was positively incoxitated—I mean, intoxicated—he was positively drunk."

Hailey sent her mother a worried glance. "We've all had time to get pretty happy," she said cautiously. "Have you finished packing yet, mother? Perhaps we should go see to your luggage."

"Nonsense." Mrs. Drumm drained her glass and looked at Selina. "I could use some coffee if our famous chef is still working."

"I'll make it," Hailey said quickly before Selina could reply. "We could all stand some coffee, I think."

"I'd like a glass of wine if it hasn't all been drunk," Selina said defiantly, copying Mrs. Drumm's hostile tone. She found a half-full bottle and a clean glass and poured some out, taking a moment to admire the ruby richness before she sipped.

Hailey reappeared from the pantry with coffee cups on a tray and glanced anxiously at Selina as she served her mother. Selina interpreted the look as a plea not to stir things up, but she felt angry and reckless, and inclined to give as good as she got. If Mrs. Drumm didn't initiate hostilities, all would be well. But she was damned if she'd sit back and take any more abuse from the woman.

Luckily Hailey's mother, after staring with distaste at the sight of Selina now drinking her wine, transferred her gaze to Ricky Carson. He'd been watching everyone with his bright-eyed interested look. "Perhaps this is the time to bring up our news, Hailey," he said, finishing his wine. "Although Gil and Magda aren't around, we really should tell your mother right away."

"Gil's around." At the sound of his voice Selina glanced quickly at the doorway. Gil stood there, his hair windblown, his hands thrust deep into the pockets of his well-cut trousers. He was watching Selina with a look of quiet intensity that she found unnerving. But she lifted her chin defiantly and tossed back the rest of her wine, determined not to let him see how strongly he affected her.

"Great," Ricky said with a show of enthusiasm. He crossed to Hailey and wound an arm around her. She looked flushed, happy and apprehensive all at once. "Hailey has made me very happy by consenting to marry me."

Mrs. Drumm leaped stiffly to her feet, her well-manicured hand pointing in horror at the couple before her. "You—but—" Hailey moved to her, trying to soothe her, but was repulsed. "How can you marry this—this *playboy?*" Mrs. Drumm's voice was full of loathing. "He doesn't even work! Not like dear Gilmartin—it's all your fault!" She turned on Gil, who was still watching Selina with heavy-lidded intentness. He took no notice of her attack.

Not seeming at all disconcerted, Ricky smiled gently at his prospective mother-in-law. "It's true I don't work now." She swiveled her head to glare at him, and he added simply, "I don't have to. And indeed, some mornings it takes me so long to climb over all my piles of money, I barely make it out the front door before dark."

Hailey elbowed him discreetly; her mother looked at her with sadness. "You see," Mrs. Drumm said, her voice now a mournful wail, "he's never serious. Are you taking this—this clown's word for it that he's rich?"

Ricky interrupted Hailey as she was about to speak. "Oh, I'm rich all right," he said negligently. "But you're wrong that I never work. I haven't in the past, it's true. But Hailey's promised to give me a trial in her bakery." He pulled her to him and smiled affectionately down into her rosy dimpled face. "I've spent a lot of time looking for what I wanted in a woman, without even knowing what it was," he said, his voice low and sincere. "But now I've realized that Hailey's got it. I feel very lucky that she's willing to share it with me."

Even Mrs. Drumm was quiet for a moment as Hailey raised her hand lovingly to Ricky's face. Then Selina jumped up and hugged Hailey, unconscious of the tears streaming down her face, while Gil thumped Ricky energetically on the back. In the happy turmoil no one had time to reply to Mrs. Drumm's peevish voice. "Just what is it that she's got? Is it the bakery? I'll never understand that boy if I live to be a hundred years old."

"I always knew your stomach would trap you some day," Gil said, enveloping Hailey and Ricky in a bear hug. "You take good care of my little cousin, or I'll have your lips sewn together so you can't eat."

"Don't worry." There was something in Ricky's boyish face that had been lacking until now. Selina looked in wonder at the expression of love and responsibility he directed toward Hailey. "She's really wonderful," he said enthusiastically. "Most of the women in our set would have jumped at the chance to live in idle luxury with me. Hailey offers me a job! And man, does she have plans for that bakery of hers. She'll go far, I can tell you."

Magda ushered Betsy into the room. She looked at Ricky and Hailey, at Mrs. Drumm's woebegone face, and asked, "Have we missed something important?"

Mrs. Drumm rushed to pour her grievance into Magda's sympathetic ear. Betsy seized her opportunity to wriggle away and came over to Selina. "What's up?" she asked, lively curiosity in her voice. "Whatever it is, it beats packing."

Selina told her the news and was immediately cheered by Betsy's reaction. "Oh, goody," she said. "Now Aunt Charlotte will stop chasing Gil around for Hailey, and he can—" She stopped short and glanced guiltily at Selina. "I mean, will there be champagne? Shouldn't we have some champagne for this?"

Gil overheard her and pulled one of her curls gently. "What difference would that make to you, scamp? You don't like it, remember?"

Betsy looked at him solemnly. "I was talking to Willa Graham about it, and she said you had to cultivate your palate, which means you have to drink it a lot and then you get to like it. So I need to start cultivating."

Gil shouted with laughter, and suddenly the atmosphere in the room was festive, celebratory. Hal McMillan came in, adding his booming voice to the party air. Feeling suddenly hungry, Selina went into the pantry to see if there was any of the *sorbet* left. She didn't bother to turn on the overhead light, knowing she could find it easily in the tiny freezer if it was there. She had dished up a big bowlful, admiring the bright raspberry color, and was eating it with furtive enjoyment when she heard Magda and Mrs. Drumm speaking outside the door, which she'd left ajar.

"But who was his father? Who was his grandfather?" Mrs. Drumm's voice was a petulant whine. "He's just some rich little upstart nobody. How can you be so complacent watching your only niece thrown away like this?"

Magda's voice held a note of impatience. "You're sounding irrational, Charlotte." Hear, hear, Selina said mentally. "Ricky has been a playboy in the past. But he seems very sincere in his feeling for Hailey, and I think she'll keep him busy enough to keep him out of trouble. As for his antecedents, certainly his grandfather was a plumber—a very rich plumber, as it turns out. Gil's great-grandfather was a vegetable vendor—poor for most of his life. And his grandfather was a caterer, much like your daughter. How does that make us better than Ricky?"

"You know what I mean." Charlotte's voice was sulky. "Gil is family, he understands me—"

"I'm afraid I do know what you mean." Magda sighed. "We've all made a mistake in letting you blackmail us with your heart condition, I suppose. You're afraid Ricky won't be as easily controlled. I hope for your sake he's not."

Mrs. Drumm unleashed a howl of outrage. Selina didn't notice her *sorbet* melting. She was torn between dismay at being an eavesdropper and delight at hearing Mrs. Drumm's comeuppance so competently delivered by Magda. But the embarrassment of all parties if she should suddenly reveal herself kept her quiet in the pantry. She would never tell anyone about it, so she might as well hear it all, she reasoned.

"Stop behaving so badly, Charlotte." Magda's voice was now matter-of-fact. "If you make yourself ill, you'll only succeed in being flown home alone ahead of everyone else. Try to be realistic for once. Hailey's of age, so there's really nothing you can do. You have little to gain by alienating yourself from the two of them."

Mrs. Drumm was silent at last. Magda's voice receded toward the ladies' cabin as the two women moved away. Selina strained shamelessly to hear her words. "Why don't you lie down for a while and pull yourself together? Things could be a lot worse. Hailey could choose never to marry at all. Then how would you feel?"

"But that bakery—that impudent young man— and then Gil—your presumptuous cook—"

Magda's voice answered, low and soothing, as they moved beyond Selina's range of hearing. She rinsed out the melted *sorbet* and dried the bowl, pondering what she'd heard. It was hard to feel anything but contempt for Mrs. Drumm, but she tried to understand the other woman's point of view, complicated no doubt by an inferiority complex. She was putting the bowl away when Gil appeared at the door of the pantry.

"So this is where you've been hiding yourself." He didn't move toward her, but in the dying light from the window his eyes fairly smoldered. With an effort she turned her own gaze away and began washing up the wineglasses that stood by the sink.

"Great news about Ricky and Hailey, eh?" She could tell from the volume of his voice he now stood behind her. She could feel his warm breath stirring the tendrils of hair on the back of her neck. She fought down the urge to turn and melt into his arms. "You know what they say: 'Weddings beget weddings,' " he said softly.

She didn't trust her voice to speak. With infinite concentration she removed a speck from a glass.

"Do you want to get married?" The question was abrupt, stilted; she felt as though she were dropping fifty stories in a very fast elevator. That couldn't be Gil, cool collected Gil. Was he asking her to marry him or simply trying to find out her price? The wine-glass shattered as her nerveless hands dropped it into the sink.

"Well?" He turned her roughly to him, his face intent. "Aren't you even going to answer?"

Clearing her throat, she pushed tumbled curls out of her eyes and stared up at him. The strain of this off-again-on-again courtship was just too much for her reason. Soon she would begin to rant as badly as Mrs. Drumm. She groped for the security of rational thought and forced herself to respond evenly. "Would you mind telling me," she said with careful emphasis, "just why you want to marry me? Then perhaps I can answer the question."

His breath hissed impatiently between his teeth. He molded her body to his, thrusting against her until she could feel the urgency of his need in her every pore. The counter behind her supported the small of her back. "I'm tired of waiting," he said fiercely. "I'm tired of you doubting me. I said I wouldn't ask you till this business is all finished, but—" he glared down at her "—you make me lose what little wit I have! I want you, dammit! I'll never stop wanting you! Can you get that through your head?"

Dazed by the ferocity of his voice, she gaped up at him. "Yes," she whispered, "yes, I can get that through my head. If—if you really mean it—"

"What do I have to do?" His grip lessened a little, but he didn't let her go. "Disintegrate before your eyes? You stubborn, ill-tempered, wonderful—" He lifted her up until she balanced precariously on the counter, standing between her parted legs, still holding her in his relentless grip. Perched so, her face was more even with his, and she gazed in wonder at the traces of torment she saw. With a groan he wrapped her still closer, burying his head in the soft juncture of her throat. She could feel the thudding of his heart; she could feel him tremble. Insistently she forced his head up, staring into those eagle's eyes, so bright with conflagration that she had to close her own. When his lips burned against hers, she gave herself up to the passionate flood he evoked. Every small, infinitely tender movement of his mouth sent fresh waves of ecstasy surging through her. Their tongues met in delicate delicious combat. She was drowning, awash in voluptuous desire, and she never wanted to surface. When at last he tore his mouth away, she uttered a primitive cry of loss.

"My darling, my darling...." His words came brokenly through his heaving chest as he gasped for air. "I love you so much. Don't ever forget that, Selina. I couldn't bear—"

She laid a finger across his lips, puzzled at the pain in his voice. "Hush," she crooned, responding instinctively to his distress. "Hush now, my love."

They were quiet in the dark room for a few moments, holding each other. Contentment and happiness filled Selina, bringing tears of release to her eyes. At last she knew that he loved her. That fact made all the obstacles seem to melt away.

But Gil didn't seem to share her certainty. "It must be right," he muttered fiercely, tightening his grip on her. "But why...." His voice trailed off, and after a moment she tried to scrutinize his face in the gloom.

In the faint light from the partly opened door she could see his face was rigid, his eyes fixed on something beyond her.

"Gil? Gil, what is it?" Her voice didn't rouse him from his trance. Frantically she grasped his shoulders and shook him, trying to bring him back. At last he relaxed, and his eyes focused on her.

"The happy ending—yes." His tone was impersonal, almost mechanical. "But first there is sorrow, parting, doubt. Then the prize will be sweeter."

Selina felt a chill like a cold arrow striking her heart. She wound her arms around Gil, trying to bring back the warmth. He sighed deeply, his arms tightening around her.

"Oh, Gil—where were you? I . . . I was afraid!"

He stood very still for a moment. "I said—what? Sorrow, parting, doubt?" She nodded against his chest. "Damn!" His voice held explosive force. He helped her down from her perch and kept one arm around her. "I don't suppose you'd believe me if I said it meant nothing." She shook her head silently. "Right. Well, that—what I said—is in all probability going to happen. I'd like to pretend it's hogwash, but past evidence is pretty conclusive and I can't explain it, but I know we have to wait, Selina."

"You mean—the stuff about parting and all—"

"Will occur, though I can't give you dates and places." His voice seethed with suppressed anger. "I would have given anything to spare you this."

"Does it happen—often?" Her voice was small. Gil turned away, looking out the window at the glow of city lights visible beyond the levee's steep sides.

"Not too often," he replied curtly. "Only about important things. The last time was when my father got the flu—four years ago. We thought it was just a passing illness, but I had a—vision." He ground out the word. "It can be—unpleasant. Selina—"

" 'Sorrow, parting, doubt,' " she whispered. "Can you be sure about the happy ending?"

He grabbed her shoulders firmly. "I am sure," he murmured in a strained voice. "Oh, what's the use? I should never have come in here tonight. I felt danger in the air."

Somehow his words loomed like a dark shadow in between them, and she knew there would be no more talk of marriage tonight.

She twisted out of his grip, her mind a tumble of confused emotions. "I have to go finish packing," she said, trying to keep her voice from trembling. "It looks like we'll be landing soon." Their conversation had been punctuated with frequent hoots from the *Margaret*'s piercing whistle as she steered through the busy shipping traffic of a part river.

Gil passed an agitated hand over his face. "If I could only explain—only tell you...."

She waited. "Well?"

But when he caught her eyes, his own were disturbingly shuttered. "I'm sorry, Selina," he said. "A lot depends on my playing a lone hand right now. I'll be free to tell you everything after the board meeting."

She felt rebuffed. "I see." If Gil noticed the hurt in her voice, he gave no sign.

"Get your packing done," he said roughly. "I'll see you when we dock." He strode from the room, and she was left standing in the dark, wondering dazedly how she could feel so miserable. The man she loved had told her he loved her. He'd even mentioned marriage. But for some reason she didn't feel like celebrating.

CHAPTER NINETEEN

SELINA'S HOTEL ROOM in New Orleans provided quite
a contrast with her cubicle on board the *Margaret B.
Townshend*. The hotel was an elegantly restored
building in the French Quarter, with high ceilings and
elaborate moldings, beautiful Louis XIV reproduction furniture, lustrous brocaded draperies and bed-
spread. She disposed of her scanty wardrobe in the
bowfront bureau and sank limply onto a love seat,
one of a pair that were placed at right angles to the
tiny marble-manteled fireplace. She stared vacantly
at the gilt-framed mirror that hung above the fireplace. Light from a central electric chandelier gave
her hair a wild fiery glow while bleaching the color
from her skin; she seemed pale, washed-out, the few
freckles across her nose more prominent in the
whiteness of her face. Her eyes, she noted dully,
looked huge, dilated with fatigue and anxiety. At her
side a telephone rang. She looked at it for a moment
as if it were totally alien, before she could pick it up
and answer it.

Magda's voice came over the wire, vibrant, gay.
"We're going to meet in the lobby for an evening
tour of the Quarter. Will you be joining us?"

Selina's mouth moved automatically before her

mind realized what she would say. "No. No, I don't think so. I'm rather tired—I'm very tired."

Concern warmed Magda's voice. "Can I get you anything, my dear? I'm afraid that hot old cook house has been too much for you."

Your son has been too much for me, Selina thought. "No," she said into the receiver. "Thank you, but I'm fine. I just need some rest."

Magda hung up after repeated offers of help, and Selina sat for a moment staring at the phone, half expecting Gil to call and demand her presence. After five minutes of silence she got up and went to the window. It opened onto a tiny balcony that looked out over a narrow picturesque street. She was on the third story, not too high to decipher the lively action below her. Though it was after ten o'clock, throngs of noisy party goers surged along the sidewalk, spilling into the street, laughing and calling to each other. The air was warm and close, as if the city breathed gently against her skin. It even had a peculiar musky, ancient scent that seemed to exude from the very bricks of the buildings and stones of the street.

She took a deep breath. A little of the numbness that had enveloped her since Gil had left her in the pantry evaporated. But she didn't want to think about it, not now, so she turned and went inside, closing the windows with finality. She did not see Gil emerge from the hotel three stories down and step back to scan the facade, his eyes homing in on her window just as she switched off the light and burrowed wearily into her bed. But somehow, as she drifted into sleep, she heard his voice, whispering in her mind, "Trust me. Please trust me."

MAGDA AND HAILEY were sharing a table in the hotel dining room when Selina arrived downstairs for breakfast next morning. They were absorbed in their conversation but looked up when Selina would have gone past them to an unoccupied table.

"Please sit with us." Magda examined Selina in a way that reminded her of Gil's eagle gaze. "You look better this morning. Did you rest well?"

Selina felt better and said so. There was something in the air of New Orleans, a gratuitous spirit of joie de vivre that wouldn't allow melancholy feelings to dominate. As she was dressing, she had decided to accept that fact that Gil loved her, and that they could work out the rough spots in their relationship. It was harder to integrate his prediction of "sorrow, parting and doubt" into this feeling, but she pushed those thoughts into the background. It was time to be optimistic, she had decided, donning a gaily embroidered Indian cotton blouse and dirndl skirt to match. The blouse had short puffed sleeves and a drawstring neck, which she daringly allowed to fall open, exposing the tops of her creamy breasts. In case Gil was wavering, that ought to do the trick, she had thought with grim humor. So by the time she sat down with Magda and Hailey, she was in brisk control of herself.

"We're discussing my wedding," Hailey said, her face radiant. "I still can't believe that I'm so lucky." She leaned across the table and confided in a whisper, "I've had a crush on Ricky for so long, but he never saw me for myself till this riverboat trip. I can never thank you enough for having me along, Aunt Magda."

"Gracious, you worked your passage." Magda patted Hailey's hand. "I'm glad you're so happy, honey. But I don't think Charlotte's going to go for this idea of a simple wedding."

Hailey's face clouded over momentarily. "I know. Mother always wants to do things in the splashiest possible way. But I'll find some way to get around her."

Irene Rossfield came up just then, pulling out the spare chair and seating herself gracefully. Her severely elegant silk dress was as chic and perfect for New Orleans as her well-cut sports clothes had been on board the *Margaret*. "Good morning, all," she said lightly. "Much as I love the boat, it's certainly a pleasure to see a civilized closet again—not to mention a bathtub." She ordered grapefruit and coffee, explaining that Selina's food had been irresistible, but she was now obliged to diet "if I want to be able to fit my clothes." Bill Rossfield had gone down to the Poydras Street Wharf to check on Mike and Eric, who were sleeping on the boat and would return with it up the river instead of flying back with the others. "He said not to worry about your equipment, Selina," Irene volunteered, finishing her grapefruit. "The boys will crate it all up on the return trip and take it out to Ladue for you."

Her mind relieved of that responsibility, Selina felt herself relax more completely. Irene finished her coffee and stood just as Gil approached the table.

Although he greeted everyone amiably, his eyes lingered longest on Selina. He fished a couple of envelopes out of the pocket of his lightweight linen jacket. "Bonuses for the two ladies of the cook house," he said, bowing and presenting them to Hailey and Selina. "Just a token of Purity's esteem for valor under primitive conditions."

Selina took her envelope uncertainly. "I don't know—" she began dubiously. But Hailey, unencumbered by any delicate scruples, opened hers with enthusiasm.

"Oh, boy!" She jumped up and kissed Gil resoundingly. "What a perfect time for some extra cash. I think I'll shop for my wedding dress here!"

Irene smiled warmly. "Good idea, Hailey. New Orleans is the next best thing to being in Paris."

Selina opened her envelope under the table. A check for five hundred dollars fell out. Dumbfounded, she stared at Gil. "I can't take this," she gasped.

Magda closed her hand firmly around Selina's. "You earned a bonus for all the extra work you put in during this trip," she said quietly. "Spend it on something you'd never have bought otherwise. But you can't give it back because it's already been appropriated as a corporate expense."

"That's right." Gil nodded as he pulled a chair from a nearby table and straddled it between Magda and Selina. "And before I forget—the rest of the board members will be arriving today; late this afternoon, I believe. We've scheduled the meeting for tomorrow morning in the LaSalle Room here in the hotel. I want you to be there."

It took Selina a moment to realize that he was speaking to her. "Me? But why—"

"Don't ask me any questions until after the meeting. Then you can deluge me, and I promise to answer every one. But I can't tell you anything till the board meets." He stood up, looking down at her gravely. "Remember what I told you yesterday on the boat," he said, his voice low and intense. "It still holds."

Selina stared after him as he strode from the room. Here was another puzzle on top of the accumulated series of them she'd collected about Gilmartin Duchenay. "I think," she said faintly, "that if I don't find out what's going on here pretty soon, I'll just go quietly crazy."

Magda heard her and smiled sympathetically. "I know Gil's asking a lot of you, my dear. But he really does have reasons for what he's doing. Please don't distress yourself about it. Just put all this out of your mind and have a good time today. No point in worrying about the board meeting until it happens."

Selina bit back her confused questions when she realized that Magda was reassuring herself as much as her chef. Smiling weakly, she attempted to follow the older woman's advice, turning to Hailey, who listened intently as Irene Rossfield listed the best places for shopping. Hailey scrawled some of the shop names on a paper napkin and put a finger to her lips as her mother approached. "Don't tell her," she hissed. "I don't want her coming along and decking me out in puffed sleeves!"

Mrs. Drumm's lips wore an unaccustomed, coy smile as she stopped at the table. "Up early, my dear?" Her voice, too, had an added note of graciousness. "Sorry I wasn't able to take breakfast with you. What are *your* plans for the day?"

Hailey looked at her cautiously. "Oh, just some sight-seeing—you know. Did you have something planned, mother?"

The smug smile broadened on Mrs. Drumm's thin lips. "Well, yes, I did. Mr. Warner has been kind enough to offer to show me around. If you're sure you won't need me, dear child. . . ."

"No," Hailey replied, watching with a dazed expression as Fred Warner came up and took her mother's arm with a proprietary air. "You go right ahead and enjoy yourself, mother. Don't worry about me."

There was silence at the table as everyone watched Mrs. Drumm walk away on Fred Warner's arm. Her elegant perfectly groomed figure seemed incongruous next to his rotund shape, clothed in a mass-produced suit of the wrong color blue. "Well, shut my mouth," Hailey said at last, her voice wondering. "Did you ever see such an odd couple?"

Magda coughed and sent Hailey a reproving frown. "Your mother looked very well entertained," she said, only the faintest tremor in her voice revealing to Selina that she was having trouble controlling her own desire to laugh. "Oh, here's Betsy at last."

Selina stood up to make room for Betsy at the table. Her face still creased with sleep, Betsy let a huge yawn escape her as she studied the menu. Hailey jumped up and caught Selina's arm before she could leave.

"Will you come shopping with me?" Her bubbling gaiety was infectious. "This big check is just burning a hole in my pocket, and I need another female along to help me spend it."

SELINA AGREED and found herself later that morning sitting in a pink satin-covered chair in one of the discreetly elegant shops of St. Charles Avenue. The saleslady, seeming to recognize at a glance that Hailey was the one to concentrate on, was bringing out various frothy confections of silk and lace, Hailey having adamantly declared that she didn't want a wedding dress that would be no use to her after she was married. Selina soon found that all the dresses began to look the same to her and let her gaze wander around the tastefully appointed salon. A stand in one corner held several beautifully cut suits, and as she stared at them, it dawned on her that she had nothing to wear to the board meeting the next day. Aside from the two sun dresses, she had only the outfit she was wearing and her one dinner dress, neither of which conformed to the world of business. She went to examine the suits, and instantly a saleswoman was at her side, murmuring into her ear, "If madam wishes to try something on?"

In the end she spent the whole five hundred dollars on garments that might have been made just for her, so perfectly did they fit. A beautifully tailored jacket in gray silk shantung; a matching skirt with three exquisite pleats just off center in front; a pair of shoes that managed to look dignified and frivolous at the same time; a silk blouse in taupe and rose with extravagant little ruffles that peeped out from beneath the severe suit jacket like a demure promise; and lacy underthings, finer than anything she'd ever owned—"almost good enough," she told Hailey in a whispered aside, "to wear alone!" In a daze she handed over the crisp hundred-dollar bills (Magda had told them where to get their checks cashed) and received a ridiculously small handful of change. The saleswoman smoothed her purchases into sleek boxes and added a scarf woven of cobwebby silk and wool in jewel tones of rose and turquoise that had caught Selina's eye. "I didn't buy that," she hastened to say, knowing that she hadn't enough money left to pay for it, expensive trifle that it was.

"For lagniappe," the woman said, smiling. Confused, Selina let it go. Hailey pulled her aside to whisper, "They give it to you—a little something extra."

Hailey had decided on a dress that was a swirl of the finest cream-colored muslin, lightly frosted with hand embroidery and ribbon-and-lace insertion. It complimented her rosy complexion and glossy brown hair, and gave her a deceptively fragile, romantic air. With it went a transparent picture hat wreathed in gauzy illusion and tiny silk rosebuds. Illusion floated from the back of the hat as she moved, and she twirled in delight to see her reflection in the pier glass.

While Hailey browsed happily among the silky undergarments, Selina stood staring at the pile of boxes that was five hundred dollars, feeling herself wake slowly as if from a trance. She'd just spent enough money one one outfit to buy all the clothes she currently owned. *I've been around rich people too long,* she thought frantically. *I'm starting to think like them. If I don't get out pretty soon, I'll begin to envy their money.*

Hailey chattered gaily during the expensive lunch she treated Selina to at Brennan's, not seeming to notice that her companion was less than talkative. But in the cab back to the hotel she turned sideways in her seat and fixed Selina with a look of good-humored penetration. "What's the matter? You're so glum, no one could ever guess you'd just bought the most luscious creations of your life."

"I can't believe it," Selina murmured miserably. "I spent all that money on clothes I probably won't wear more than once. What use does a chef have for fancy suits? How could I have been so stupid?"

"Relax." Hailey patted her hand comfortingly. "In the first place, you don't have to wear things like that every day to need them. That sort of suit is classic. You can wear it the rest of your life. Good tailored ensembles never go out of style. In the second place, it was found money—you didn't expect it, did you?" She waited for Selina's low-voiced confirmation. "Right. You look smashing in your outfit, Selina. Think what a sense of confidence it will give you whenever you feel the need to be dressed just right."

Selina looked at her curiously. "I thought you objected to buying this sort of thing. Didn't you say that your mother—"

Hailey blushed. "I certainly think it's foolish to borrow money for clothes when you have no way to pay it back. But I confess I love fine fabrics and well-cut styles. When I was so tubby, nothing looked good on me. Now I can wear lots of things I couldn't before—it's almost intoxicating. I could get carried away easily, but I won't because I've had mother for a fine example of what not to do." She was silent for a moment and added speculatively, "Maybe she'll marry Fred Warner. He's really rich, you know, despite his appearance." She lowered her voice. "Otherwise I'm afraid she'll want to live with Ricky and me—she's already hinted as much. I don't think that would work at all!"

IT WAS MIDAFTERNOON before they got back to the hotel. Selina was glad of a chance to escape into her cool room from the humid heat. Hailey had told her that everything shut down in the afternoon while people rested, and she could well understand why after experiencing the weighty heat of midday. Her purchases had already arrived, and she stared at the boxes with guilty fascination. One by one she lifted out the beautiful garments, admitting that they shamed everything else she owned. She hung them up, fighting down the urge to get another taxi and take everything back. The telephone rang as she smoothed the silk blouse onto its hanger.

"Front desk," said a brisk voice when she answered. "You have some mail here, Miss Montgomery. Do you want me to send it up?"

"Of course." It took Selina a moment to figure

out who would be writing her here. Then she remembered her phone call to Molly Hutton. When the bellboy tapped at her door, she seized the envelope eagerly. Molly had written a breezy note enclosing letters of recommendation from three of the chefs at the Culinary Academy, including a personal one from Chef Robert to none other than Jean-Marie Legrand himself!

She sat limply on the love seat, the letter clutched in her hand. Legrand was the most revered chef in France, surpassing even Bocuse and the Troisgros brothers. The thought of working with him in even the humblest capacity was intoxicating. She read Robert's letter to Legrand, blushing at the almost fulsome praise he bestowed on her. With such a letter she would be sure to be taken on in the kitchen of Legrand's famous restaurant, La Petite Marmite, which was in one of the country villages near Paris. Her salary would no doubt be minimal, but she was certain she had saved enough to take her to France and supplement her income until she'd learned enough from Legrand to ensure her employability at any French restaurant in the United States. That meant there was only one question left to decide: Could she bear to leave Gilmartin Duchenay behind?

There was a knock on the door. Still holding the letter, she moved to answer it. Gil stood there, his face grave. "I need to talk to you," he said.

She stood aside, and he stalked into the room, glancing at the boxes that disgorged a welter of tissue paper. He swept some of the litter off the love seat and uncovered the envelope addressed to Selina in

Molly's best typing and bearing the return address of the Culinary Academy's placement office. For a moment he stared at it, then raised his face to hers. Aghast, she saw the stricken expression that branded him. "Gil!" she cried. "Don't—"

"You're leaving. Selina, I thought—" He broke off, and she could see him make a visible effort to mask his emotions. "Where are you going?" he said finally, his face rigid.

She ran across the room and grabbed his hands, the letter falling unheeded to the floor. "Gil," she said beseechingly, "don't look like that. I...I didn't know what to do so I called Molly, it's true. But I haven't—Gil, I'm too confused to know what's best!"

He picked up the letter from the floor. "May I?" She nodded dumbly, and he read it without speaking. When he looked at her again, there was a new expression in his eyes. "Just who is this Legrand person?"

She looked at him in disbelief. "Surely you've heard of Jean-Marie Legrand? He's only the most sought-after chef in all of France. Why, his restaurant is like Mecca for anyone who knows anything at all about French cooking."

His face tightened perceptibly. "Quite a temptation for you," he said softly. She got the impression that he was thinking furiously. "How can you turn this down merely to be a hired hand for us?"

"Gil," she said seriously. "You know there's more involved in my decision than that. Please, help me...."

He stood up, handing the letter back to her with

grave courtesy. "I can do nothing until after the
board meeting. Ultimately you must make up your
own mind." He laughed mirthlessly. "It's all too
possible," he said, walking to the door, "that after
tomorrow I may be looking for a new job, too. An
interesting complication, don't you think?"

He shut the door behind him with quiet finality.
She stared, unbelieving, for a full minute before she
realized that he wasn't coming back. By the time she
flew across the room and wrenched open the door, he
had vanished.

THE LASALLE ROOM was an imposing combination of
French antiques and gold brocade. Selina hesitated at
the door, trying to conceal her dismay as seven pairs
of unfamiliar eyes raked her curiously. She was glad
she had her new suit to bolster her confidence as she
walked across the room and took a chair against the
wall next to one of the tall French windows. Fred
Warner followed her into the room and took his
place at the table with the other board members.
Then Hal MacMillan walked in, saw her and came
over to sit beside her. "Stuffy things, these board
meetings," he whispered, leaning close so he
wouldn't be heard. "No wonder Magda gets out of
them whenever she can."

"What are you doing here?" Selina whispered
back, but before he could answer, Gil came in, striding to the head of the table and taking charge of the
meeting with a commanding glance around the table.

Old business was swiftly disposed of, and Selina
pricked up her ears as Gil began to speak of the *Mar-*

garet B. Townshend. "You may not know why I chose this rather unusual method of getting from St. Louis to New Orleans." He glanced around, his eyes finding and passing over Selina so impersonally that she shivered. "As you recall, at our last meeting Mr. Warner challenged me to come up with a new market for Purity. I propose to meet that challenge by telling you of a new division I'd like to create—Epicurean Dining. Subject to the approval of the board, I've already signed up three prestigious clients for this division, and there will be more when its success becomes known."

Fred Warner stood up, an incredulous expression on his face. "Do you mean to tell me—" he began. Gil waved an imperious hand.

"I still have the floor, Mr. Warner. I'll tell you everything if you'll give me a chance. You had the goodness to question the quality of food Purity serves up, and with some justification. For those who want palatable food on a budget, certainly Purity's regular meals fit the bill. But—" he held up his hand to stop Fred Warner from interrupting again "—there is a segment of the food-service industry that needs special attention—that wants to combine efficient, money-saving preparation with luxury, gourmet service. For that segment I've devised Epicurean Dining."

"Give it to them, Gil," Hal MacMillan muttered irrepressibly at Selina's side. She frowned at him and turned her attention back to Gil, who stood so straight and handsome at the head of the polished conference table. She still didn't know exactly what part she was supposed to play in this, but she began to realize the strain Gil must have been under these past few months.

Gil explained that he had been trying to think of a way to apply the money-saving portion-control operation to more esoteric meals when a chance conversation showed him a different route. "I realized that I was looking at the problem from the wrong end of the telescope. Kitchens in fine hotels like that of Mr. MacMillan's there—" he gestured toward Hal, who nodded genially "—were sinking into a sea of debt, with wasteful procedures in the kitchen, poorly trained staff and less than high-quality materials. Instead of offering them complete prefabricated meals like those served of necessity in airplanes and other places without adequate kitchen facilities, I would be better served offering them the opportunity to upgrade their staff and the foods they need by processing the more expensive raw materials through a central plant and training individual staffs in proper selection and preparation techniques to make the best of the local offerings."

Fred Warner bounced up again, with no intention of being suppressed. "You are a clever, twisty rascal, Duchenay," he roared, but Selina saw with surprise that his face expressed only admiration, not anger. "By God, you maneuvered me as prettily as I'd ever want to see." He turned to the other board members. "I just got off that riverboat," he said, "where I was privileged to eat the best cooking of my life, done by that little lady there." He pointed to Selina, and all the heads swiveled to scrutinize her, then swiveled back as Warner continued talking. "I got involved in a bet with this young rascal." He thumped Gil mightily on the back. "He bet me I couldn't learn enough in one day to dish up a gourmet feast that evening. Well, sir, I took the bait hook, line and sinker, and I don't mind telling you it was one of the hardest things I ever did, but in just one day Chef Montgomery taught me enough to produce a class-A dinner. I reckon Duchenay figures if a rank amateur can do that, a professional kitchen staff would pick up fancy training in no time."

There was a moment of silence, and then one of the board members cleared his throat and spoke. "I'm not sure just what you propose, Duchenay. Don't most restaurant kitchens already have a trained staff, however poorly organized? Just what advantage could we offer?"

Gil smiled easily. "I'll tell you, Squire. First, we can make bulk purchases of prime meats and fowl, quick-freeze and ship them to our clients. This provides a substantial savings since quantity purchases always get a hefty discount. We prepackage—as much as possible without sacrificing freshness—the individual components of a standard menu that can be easily adapted to any region's specialties. Second, we arrange a training program that covers basics such as pantry management and includes information on how to use the best fresh produce of the areas in creating exciting dishes. Regarding existing staff, I'd like to have Hal MacMillan say a few words. He owns several hotels across the country."

Hal stood up, smiling easily around the conference

table. "It's true," he began, "that in some of my restaurants I have a staff that is up to anything. But those are the ones that aren't losing money. I've found the operations that bring in the least revenue are the ones with the worst food. What I like about Gilmartin's plan is that it allows me to upgrade the quality of my kitchen staff in these borderline operations without letting people go, unless, of course, they are not open to receiving training. The steps he's suggested could be done independently by me, I suppose, but he's offering me a package deal that can be implemented in several of my operations without needing much attention from me. That's attractive. During the trip down here, a couple of other hoteliers and I kicked this around with Gil, and we all felt that Epicurean Dining could be the difference between a first-rate hotel dining room that turns a profit, and one in which no one wants to eat."

Gil thanked Hal for his information and turned back to the board members. They were whispering among themselves, but when he began to speak again, he had their undivided attention. "I have some charts and figures for you, projecting the number of premium hotels across the nation with marginal dining-room operations, the number of new hotels that would be interested in our services as a way of initially setting up their kitchens, and projected revenues. But before getting into that, I'd like to introduce you to Chef Selina Montgomery, a graduate of the California Culinary Academy in San Francisco and currently serving as my mother's personal chef. Most of you have eaten one of Selina's meals since she began working in our kitchen—I know she's been the object of several takeover bids from mother's friends and my business associates in the past month or so. I feel that with a little advanced training in restaurant management, perhaps serving under a master chef in France, Chef Montgomery would be the ideal choice to handle the creative side of Epicurean Dining for Purity. Her performance on the *Margaret B. Townshend*, with indifferent equipment and very little support staff, shows that she's capable of brilliant planning. In effect, she carried out the premise that I've expounded here by pre-selecting and pre-preparing many of the entrées she later served. I'm sure no one on board had any inkling that the meals had been partly cooked in the kitchen of the Château. Isn't that so, Mr. Warner?''

Fred Warner spoke decidedly. ''That little lady is a wizard in the kitchen, take my word for it. If she is available to work in this new division, I say we snap her up before someone else gets in first.''

Gil's face tightened as he turned to face Selina. She rose to her feet unconsciously, trying to read his expression, but his face was a mask. ''What do you say, gentlemen. Shall we offer Chef Montgomery the position of research-and-development chef in Epicurean Dining, contingent upon her successful completion of advanced training?''

Led by Fred Warner's resounding yes, the board members murmured their assent. ''If you think she's the right choice, Gil,'' the one he'd called Squire spoke, ''we'll certainly back you up on that.''

A momentary expression of triumph flickered in

Gil's eyes, to be replaced by as fleeting an expression of anxiety. Selina was totally bewildered by the fast turn of events. She could think of nothing to say. There was silence for a moment; then Gil spoke.

"You don't need to answer at once, Miss Montgomery." His voice was coldly formal, as if they were mere acquaintances. "I know you were unprepared for any such offer as this. Please take your time and think about it, but let us know if you're not interested because we'll have to begin looking for someone else."

She nodded dumbly. He added, "The meeting is adjourned until after lunch."

Chairs were pushed back from the gleaming table, and Selina found herself in the center of a group of well-dressed businessmen, with Fred Warner pumping her hand enthusiastically. "Well, Miss Selina," he said, beaming at her, "so this is what that young rascal had up his sleeve. I must say it's a pleasant surprise for me. Didn't know he had it in him to come up with such a novel plan. Or should I say *nouvelle*?" He chuckled comfortably and introduced the other board members, none of whose names she remembered five seconds later. As if in a dream, she smiled and chatted, counting the minutes until she could leave. Gil had vanished somewhere, she discovered upon craning her neck to see around all the discreet business suits that surrounded her. She felt the beginnings of a tension headache throb in her temples. With difficulty she excused herself and found her way to her suite.

There was a carafe of water on the little table by

the bed, and she poured a glass and drank it with thirsty gratitude, glad of the opportunity to indulge in so mundane an act. Her brain was numb; she couldn't seem to think about Gil's surprising announcement at all. Wandering aimlessly around the room, she found herself standing in front of the mantel, holding the letter of recommendation to Legrand. Slowly reality began to penetrate her mind. So even last night, when he had seemed so shaken, he was thinking of how to turn her intention to leave for France into an advantage for himself. Little flames of anger began to lick through her body, thawing her frozen core. What was his game, anyway? Had he ever wanted more than a chef for his precious Purity Corporation? Was she just a convenience to be kept on ice for the purposes of Epicurean Dining? There was a tap on the door, and she flung it open, certain that it would be Gil. He stood there, his jacket bunched to accommodate hands thrust into his pockets, and he regarded her warily. "I hate that name," she spat out angrily.

He blinked. "What?"

"Epicurean Dining. I think it stinks!"

He moved inside and shut the door, leaning against it as if uncertain of his reception. "Does that mean you don't want the position?"

"I don't know," she mumbled ungraciously. "What are you here for?"

"I came to tell you about the perks," he said, his mouth twisted into a wry smile. "And to explain—if you'll listen."

She faced him from the mantel. "Just what," she

hissed between her teeth, "makes you think I wouldn't listen?"

Still regarding her with that wary gaze, he moved to sit on one of the love seats. "Nothing much," he murmured. "You seem to be having one of those fits of redheaded temper, that's all. Mind telling me what's bothering you?"

"Bothering me?" She tried to keep her voice from turning into a shriek. "Why should anything be bothering me? Just because I'm stupid enough to fall in love with a man who sees me as another rung on the corporate ladder." She glared at him, even more enraged because his face continued to be impassive. "You know," she snarled, "there are lots better chefs than I am. Perhaps you should have seduced one of them!"

"Selina." His voice was even. "Please believe me when I say I would never have offered you the job if I didn't think you would make a success of it." His mouth twisted in self-deprecation, and now she saw that what she had taken for impassivity was just a shield for his feelings. But she was too wrought up to care.

"Why didn't you tell me earlier?" she cried. "Why make such a big mystery of it? You put me through hell on that boat, and for what? Just for business matters. Just for a job!"

His voice was tight. "I couldn't tell you earlier. Once I knew how much you meant to me—once I knew I wanted to marry you—I had to keep it secret from you that I also wanted you for this position. Purity has nepotism rules, although there's no ban on marriage between employees. If you had been known to be engaged to me, you would never have been considered.''

His explanation simply fueled her anger. "So you meant it when you asked me to marry you! I was beginning to wonder—not that it matters. Perhaps I don't want to marry you!''

He sprang up, his face coming alive with a reflection of her own rage. "Don't lie to me, Selina. You'll never get away with it." In one stride he reached her, pinning her against the wall, raking her defiant face with his amber eagle's eyes. He twitched the gold chain from beneath her collar until the tiny charm swung free. "Don't forget," he rasped. "You wear the gypsy's brand. Does that mean nothing?''

"I ask you!" she rejoined. His touch on her shoulders was a hot igniting flame, and she writhed to escape it. " 'Trust me,' you said. But did you pay me the same compliment? I can't bear the thought of you going behind my back, using me—" Her treacherous voice broke, and she was silent, not wanting tears to betray her weakness. But Gil knew. He always knew.

"You love me, Selina." His voice was urgent, demanding. "You must know how much I love you. I almost went crazy when you insisted that we couldn't get married because of external considerations. I decided then that since working as a chef was so important to you, I'd try to figure out something that wouldn't conflict with our time together. This job is nine-to-five, sweetheart. As far as I'm concerned, you can write your own ticket about training, time off, travel—I just want you with me."

She wrenched away, going to the table for a tissue to blow her nose. "And what if I don't like it," she said dangerously. "What if I want to quit, open my own restaurant, go back to San Francisco? What happens to all your careful plans then?"

He paled. "I'm sorry if I give you the impression that I want to arrange your life for you," he said after a moment, his usual acuity showing him where the problem was. "You're free to take it or leave it—makes no difference to me. I want to marry you if you work twenty-four hours a day, or if you want to live in a tent. I'm flexible."

She heard the implied criticism. "And I'm not, I suppose?" Emotionally depleted, she sank onto the love seat, refusing to look at him. "It all comes from you, don't you see?" she said tiredly. "If I could think clearly, I'd make you understand that I can't live with everything coming from you. Working for you all day, being your wife—"

"Loving me all night? Letting me love you? That sounds too difficult?" He shook his head wearily. "Lady, I don't understand." He came and knelt before her on the faded floral carpet. "I just want you so much. I just need to love you all the time. I thought you felt the same."

"I don't know what I feel." She was calm but angry. Nothing made any sense; nothing mattered, not even her love for Gil. "I'm going to France," she said abruptly, almost as startled at the words as he was.

He stood, his face expressionless. "I see. As a free agent, or as part of Purity?"

She raised her eyebrows mockingly. "Are we on opposite sides of the fence?"

He turned away, and she barely caught his muttered words. "I suppose we always have been." At the door he turned back, his eyes fixed on her intently. But he didn't speak, and at last she broke the silence.

"I'll take the job," she said, suddenly tired. "I'd be a fool not to if my career is as important as I've always said it was. In France I'll be your research-chef-in-training. But all other bets are off, Gil."

She meant to add that she needed time to think, but he was too quick. "I see," he said, and for a moment she caught a glimpse of his face, stark with anguish. Then he was gone. She tried to summon the words to call him back, tried to make her leaden legs reach the door in time. But he was gone, and there was no turning back.

CHAPTER TWENTY

SELINA PLUNGED HER HANDS into the bag of fresh black truffles, inhaling their pungent fragrance blissfully. She examined them with care, then nodded to the young boy who held the sack. *"Merveilleux,"* she said, smiling. *"Merci, monsieur."* He grinned and accepted the fistful of franc notes she held out, scampering off down the alley behind La Petite Marmite, Jean-Marie Legrand's establishment in a small village near Paris.

Despite the chilly November wind that sent a scrap of paper scudding down the alley, Selina lingered outside for a moment, clasping the fragrant sack of truffles against her and sniffing at the scent of bouillon that came from the partly opened kitchen door. Over the roofs of the adjacent buildings she could see the sun reddening toward sunset. Bare branches of plane trees moved nervously in the breeze. She shivered and took a last look at the early-rising evening star. Even that familiar object appeared exotic in French skies. Though she'd been working at La Petite Marmite almost four months, she still felt the same half thrilling, half scary sensations of being in a country far from her home.

She carried the sack of truffles back into the

steamy fragrant warmth of the kitchen and began sorting them, some to be used immediately and some to store, individually wrapped, in a box of rice that Jean-Marie kept in the cool flagstone pantry he called the *office*.

The kitchen was a baffling mixture of ancient and state-of-the-art culinary tools. Next to the back door was a huge stone fireplace, complete with spit, where one of the kitchen helpers was trussing a brace of ortolans for roasting. Behind her, as she worked at the long central scrubbed-wood table, Selina could hear the whir of the big mixer—Tinette, the pastry chef, was making *bombe* for dessert tonight. In one corner, cheek by jowl with the latest in convection ovens, skulked a huge range, like an outsize version of the hot-top she'd used in the cook house of the *Margaret B. Townshend*. She frowned as that memory surfaced and tried vainly to suppress it. But her mind seized on any excuse to think of Gil, and her hands slowed their movement as she gave herself up to recollection.

She had been a fool. She had known that as soon as she'd had time to cool down that fateful day in New Orleans. But her pride had been strong enough to keep her from going to Gil and telling him just how much she wanted to marry him. If he'd come to any of the subsequent committee meetings about Epicurean Dining, if he'd put himself in her path.... But he had evidently been avoiding her, and by the time she'd admitted to herself that it was up to her to make the first move, it had seemed too late. Things had moved fast; within a week she had flown back to

St. Louis to pack what she needed and was on a plane heading for Paris. There was little time for reflection at the restaurant, where Jean-Marie kept everyone in a constant state of turmoil. When Selina had finally allowed herself to go over the whole denouement with Gil, she had bitterly reproached herself for letting her reactions get out of hand. Gil had been trying to find a solution to obstacles she'd thrown in the way of their love. How could she have been so inflexible as to spurn his efforts when he had gone to such lengths? Sometimes she felt it would be fairer to resign her position as research chef for Purity. But with Jean-Marie's rather skeptical help she was learning much that would make a success of Epicurean Dining. Besides, she still cherished the hope that when she was working in St. Louis, no matter who her immediate superior was, she would likely be thrown together with Gil. Perhaps then she would have a chance to mend matters. For even after only a few weeks away from him, no matter how hectically filled with activity her time was, she knew she'd never be able to feel complete without him.

She could have written him. She'd been meaning to do so for more than a month now. But it seemed so awkward to write into a void. She'd heard nothing from him, although she'd received several letters from Betsy and a couple from Hailey. She smiled to herself, thinking of her last letter from Gil's ebullient cousin. Hailey had alternatively raved about married life and bemoaned the fact that her mother had come one-hundred-eighty degrees from despising her bakery. "She's started coming in regularly every day,"

Hailey wrote. "If it weren't for Ricky, I don't think I could stand it. Imagine, she was telling me how to make muffins the other day!" The rest of the letter was fulsome praise of Ricky, the perfect husband according to Hailey. The only passing mention of Gil was that he was working hard to set up the mechanics of Epicurean Dining. Hailey hadn't said anything overt about Selina's relationship with Gil, but the whole letter had been suggestive of "Go ye, and do likewise."

Sighing, Selina admitted how much she would give to be married to Gil, doing work she loved. When she had time to think about her personal life at all, she fashioned her plans around seeing him in another month when her training would be complete. Until then, her daily litany was the self-accusatory: "You have only yourself to blame."

Strangely, despite the chaotic state of her emotions, she was not unhappy. She was in France, where every little village and market town boasted some claim to gustatory excellence, where the Normandy cream was thick enough to use as a sauce alone, where eating well was taken as seriously as politics. Although she might have been tempted to dwell on her longing for Gil, she had little time to do more than tell herself what a fool she'd been two or three times a day.

An impatient tap on her shoulder brought her out of her reverie. "And will you be all evening about it, *mademoiselle*?" Jean-Marie's heavily accented English was easier for her to understand now than it had been when she arrived in August. He picked up one of the truffles, examining it closely, his seamed lively face breaking into a piquant smile. He was no longer young, though no one could or would tell his exact age. But his lean wiry body could work tirelessly in the kitchen for long hours, and his bright blue eyes sparkled with humor even when he was in the throes of one of his frequent tantrums. Selina found him entertaining and one of the best teachers she'd ever encountered.

"These are quite fine," he pronounced, looking over the truffles. "We will make use of them in stuffing the ortolans. You may prepare the mixture, *mademoiselle*. I myself have worked far too hard already today because of your lazy ways!"

Selina smiled guiltily. "Sorry, Jean-Marie. I've been a little absentminded today." She selected the ingredients she would need and began to compose the stuffing. Wielding her big knife industriously, she could feel Jean-Marie's eyes on her.

"Do you wish the *brunoise*?" He handed her the pot of diced vegetables, glancing at her keenly from those lively eyes. "It is not spring, *ma petite*," he added gently. "Love should not trouble you so."

She glanced at him, startled. "Who says it does?"

He chuckled and turned away. "I am not *aveugle*," he said over his shoulder. "An American in love is an amusing sight." He watched the *sous-chef* critically for a moment, then threw up his hands in sudden rage. "Ah, no, not like that," he cried in savage French. Although Selina's French had been limited to little more than kitchen vocabulary when she'd arrived, she had quickly learned to interpret those five words. For the most part, the people she'd met spoke English with much more fluency than her French, inspiring her to spend her occasional spare time learning the language.

She finished the stuffing and lost herself in the accelerating bustle of preparation that invades any restaurant kitchen toward dinnertime. Jean-Marie was everywhere, tasting ecstatically one minute, his voice shrill with rage the next. Tonight Selina was responsible for one of the entrées, the components of which she had prepared the week before and frozen in the one deep freeze boasted by the restaurant. Jean-Marie threatened her with dire consequences if any of his clients complained, but even he had to admit, tasting the finished result, that her ragout of duck was very little different than if it had been freshly prepared that afternoon. "Next time," he remarked, "we will see what you can do with something more complex—say *quenelles*."

Selina thought for a moment. "That might not be too bad. One could freeze them raw—or perhaps it would be better to poach them first—"

But Jean-Marie was off again, harrying an unfortunate Tinette about some fancied flaw in the macaroons. Selina busied herself presenting the ragout, adding it mentally to the menu she was making up for submission to the hotels that planned on subscribing to Purity's new service. With Jean-Marie's help she'd already worked out several appetizers, soups and entrées that could be packaged almost like kits and, with proper assembly in the destination kitchen, emerge as tempting as if made totally on the premises. Of course, there would always be dishes that defied such preparation, and she for one was glad of it.

It seemed like no time before the main rush was over, and she could lean against the table and wipe the perspiration from her face. One of the waiters approached her, his own face shiny with the exertions of the last couple of hours. *"Pardon, mademoiselle,"* he murmured apologetically. "Someone without wishes to speak to the chef who prepared the ragout."

She followed him hastily into the dining room, unwilling to have any complaints about the ragout reach Jean-Marie's ears. How he would gloat if someone detected her secret! The waiter paused just inside the door to the dining room and nodded discreetly. "There he is, *mademoiselle*. The tall man, dining alone."

Selina pushed her tall white hat to a rakish angle on her defiant curls and started toward the solitary diner. His back was toward her, broad-shouldered in an impeccable dinner jacket, his dark hair curling a little over the collar. Before she had gone four steps, Selina knew who it was. She forced herself to walk normally across the room, although she wanted to dance, to fly, to shout with joy. "Hello, Gil," she said, standing beside his table.

He looked up from his after-dinner cognac, his face grave, eyes serious. "Hello, Selina." His mesmerizing amber gaze held her speechless for a moment. Drowning in it, she couldn't tell if the overpowering wave of love and desire she felt for him was reciprocated. And the dining room of La Petite Marmite was no place to throw herself into his arms and find out.

"How—how did you know I cooked the ragout?" Her voice was shaky, and she took a deep breath to steady it.

"I knew." The intensity in his voice sent a delicate frisson of delight down her spine.

"You always did know," she whispered. Her mouth was suddenly dry; she licked her lips and swallowed nervously.

"Do you have to stand there like a comic-opera butler?" he asked irritably. His question struck her as immensely funny. She suppressed a snort of laughter.

"We observe the proprieties, *monsieur*," she replied in her best French accent. "Only *le patron* is permitted to sit with the customers."

"So you mock me, eh?" Jean-Marie appeared at her elbow, his mobile face creased into disapproval. He glanced from Selina to Gil and raised his eyebrows slightly. "It is an acquaintance of yours, *mademoiselle*?"

Selina introduced them, adding that Gil was the president of the corporation for which she would be working when she finished her training. Jean-Marie accepted Gil's offer of a liqueur graciously, allowing Selina with a lofty sweep of his hand to sit, also. She never could recall what they chatted about, so lost was she in speculation at the wonder of Gil's unexpected appearance.

Jean-Marie's gentle prod reclaimed her attention. "Pardon?"

"I said, *mademoiselle*, that I have no objection to your taking the rest of the evening off as Monsieur Duchenay requests." He winked conspiratorially at Gil, who was already rising from his chair. "But please do not be late tomorrow. As you recall, we attempt the *quenelles*!"

Selina led Gil through the kitchen so she could deposit her apron and hat. When she returned from the closet that served all the employees as a locker room, she found him watching with fascination the red-faced kitchen helper whose job it was to turn the spit before the roaring fire. "I thought that sort of thing went out in the Middle Ages," he said in awe as they walked down the alley behind the building.

Selina shrugged. "Jean-Marie likes the taste of spit-roasted birds best." In spite of the heavy wool sweater she'd pulled on, she shivered as Gil took her arm. "Where—where are we going?"

He looked down at her, his eyes impenetrable in the faint light of a waning moon. "I have a car. We could go into Paris if you'd like. It's not that late."

Her eyes sparkled. "Super! I haven't had much time to sample the nightlife because of working so hard." She tried to instill a little pathos into her voice and was rewarded with his rich chuckle. "But we'll have to go to my place first. I can't go to Paris looking like this."

Her voice faltered a little as they passed a street lamp, and she saw the expression in his eyes. But he only said, "You look fine to me. But your place, by all means."

She had rented a tiny room in an ancient building a

few minutes' walk from the restaurant. They didn't speak on the walk, though Selina felt as if the air between them was fairly shouting with everything they were leaving unsaid. He followed her up the stairs and into the room, frowning at its smallness and the shabby furniture. "Why do you live here? I thought we were paying you while you trained. Can't you find something decent?"

She shrugged again. "It's close to the restaurant, and it's clean. I don't spend much time here, so it doesn't matter to me. And the view's spectacular." She gestured toward the one window, with tall panes opening onto a tiny balcony from which the glow of the Paris skyline was dimly visible in the distance. She didn't tell him that the room reminded her of her New Orleans stay. "Did you want—" she hesitated diffidently. "I have to change...."

"Don't let me stop you." When he turned to face her, his wicked smile told her he knew there was only one room. "I wanted to check something out, anyway."

"What's that?" There was an ancient dressing screen in front of the tiny closet, and she moved behind it, angry with herself for feeling shy. She found a dress in the closet and pulled her T-shirt off with quick bravado. When she freed her head, Gil's face was looking over the top of the screen. She stood transfixed by the naked vulnerability, the desire she saw there. He lifted the screen and set it aside but made no motion to touch her. His eyes dropped to the thin gold chain with its moon-and-star nestled in the hollow between her breasts.

"I wanted to know if you still wore—this." With a careful finger, as if it might break, he reached to touch the tiny star. "Selina, love—"

The yearning expression deepened on his face, and Selina could no longer dam the torrent of her feelings. "Gil," she cried, "I want to marry you. I love you so much! Please say you still feel the same!"

A flicker of tremendous relief dawned in his eyes. "I can't say that," he said sadly, pulling her close. She felt an instant's alarm at his words, but the smooth velvet of his lips on hers assuaged her fears before he whispered, his mouth hovering erotically close to her ear, "I'm more in love with you than ever, you vixen. I haven't been worth a plugged nickel in the office lately because I spend all my time thinking about—" His hands behind her back found the clasp of her bra and removed it. "Please, sweetheart, can you. . . ? That's right," he breathed as her eager hands found the buttons of his elegant shirt, fumbling in her haste. Impatiently she tried to push his dinner jacket off his shoulders. "Be careful, now," he said, pulling back for a moment to shrug out of it and his shirt. "I've got the license in there."

"License?" His lips found her neck, moving with infinitely slow kisses down the slope to her breast. Drugged with desire, she found it difficult to speak.

"I thought perhaps we could be married in Paris this weekend. Do you think Monsieur Legrand would give you time off for a honeymoon?"

"Gil!" Selina tugged at the thick crisp hair so that she could see his face. "Do you mean it?"

He raised his head, and suddenly Selina knew he

meant it with a powerful certainty that sent a wave of elation through her. "You said you wanted to get married. I'm not refusing," he said intensely. "But before you can change your mind—" His lips found her nipples, kissing first one and then the other in gentle triumph. She let the sensations she'd craved flood through her.

"Gil," she whispered as he guided her toward her narrow bed. "Gil, doesn't this sort of thing traditionally come after the wedding?"

"Right now tradition doesn't concern me," he murmured huskily. "According to tradition you're not supposed to ask me to marry you."

Of course, she thought hazily, kissing him as though she could never have enough. They would have a lifetime to make their own traditions, stronger than the age-old spells of Romany. The sorrow, parting and doubt were behind them. From now on— happiness.

About the Author

Leigh Roberts has always had a special place in her heart for Missouri. Not only did she grow up in a small town there, but she eventually married a man from St. Louis.

Now Leigh and her husband make their home in Palo Alto, California with their two little boys. Leigh was pregnant while writing *MOONLIGHT SPLENDOR*. Her "cravings" included many of the delicious recipes found in her book. She prefers to call it "research."

This is Leigh Robert's first Superromance with Worldwide Library. Readers will be happy to know she's hard at work on her second. So stay tuned for more from Leigh Roberts!

A Harlequin

ROBERTA LEIGH

Collector's Edition

A specially designed collection of six exciting love stories by one of the world's favorite romance writers—Roberta Leigh, author of more than 60 bestselling novels!

1 **Love in Store**
2 **Night of Love**
3 **Flower of the Desert**

4 **The Savage Aristocrat**
5 **The Facts of Love**
6 **Too Young to Love**

Available now wherever paperback books are sold, or available through Harlequin Reader Service. Simply complete and mail the coupon below.

Yours FREE, with a home subscription to SUPERROMANCE™

Complete and mail
the coupon below today!

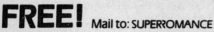

- -

FREE! Mail to: SUPERROMANCE

In the U.S.
2504 West Southern Avenue
Tempe, AZ 85282

In Canada
649 Ontario St.
Stratford, Ontario N5A 6W2

YES, please send me FREE and without any obligation, my **SUPERROMANCE** novel, LOVE BEYOND DESIRE. If you do not hear from me after I have examined my FREE book, please send me the 4 new **SUPERROMANCE** books every month as soon as they come off the press. I understand that I will be billed only $2.50 for each book (total $10.00). There are no shipping and handling or any other hidden charges. There is no minimum number of books that I have to purchase. In fact, I may cancel this arrangement at any time. LOVE BEYOND DESIRE is mine to keep as a FREE gift, even if I do not buy any additional books.

NAME _____ (Please Print)

ADDRESS _____ APT. NO. _____

CITY _____

STATE/PROV. _____ ZIP/POSTAL CODE _____

SIGNATURE (If under 18, parent or guardian must sign.)   **134-BPS-KAGD**
SUP-SUB-1

This offer is limited to one order per household and not valid to present subscribers. Prices subject to change without notice.
Offer expires March 31, 1984

HARLEQUIN
PREMIERE AUTHOR EDITIONS

6 top Harlequin authors – 6 of their best books

1. **JANET DAILEY** Giant of Mesabi
2. **CHARLOTTE LAMB** Dark Master
3. **ROBERTA LEIGH** Heart of the Lion
4. **ANNE MATHER** Legacy of the Past
5. **ANNE WEALE** Stowaway
6. **VIOLET WINSPEAR** The Burning Sands

**Harlequin is proud to offer these 6 exciting romance novels by
6 of our most popular authors. In brand-new beautifully
designed covers, each Harlequin Premiere Author Edition
is a bestselling love story—a contemporary, compelling and
passionate read to remember!**

Available wherever paperback books are sold, *or* through
Harlequin Reader Service. Simply complete and mail the coupon below.

- -